WILLIAM GOLDING

THREE NOVELS

INCLUDES

PINCHER MARTIN

FREE FALL

THE INHERITORS

MJF BOOKS
NEW YORK

Published by MJF Books
Fine Communications
Two Lincoln Square
60 West 66th Street
New York, NY 10023

Library of Congress Catalog Card Number 97-72754
ISBN 1-56731-220-9

Manufactured in the United States of America on acid-free paper

MJF Books and the MJF colophon are trademarks of Fine Creative Media, Inc.

10   9   8   7   6   5   4   3   2   1

THE INHERITORS

". . . We know very little of the appearance of the Neanderthal man, but this . . . seems to suggest an extreme hairiness, an ugliness, or a repulsive strangeness in his appearance over and above his low forehead, his beetle brows, his ape neck, and his inferior stature. . . . Says Sir Harry Johnston, in a survey of the rise of modern man in his *Views and Reviews:* 'The dim racial remembrance of such gorilla-like monsters, with cunning brains, shambling gait, hairy bodies, strong teeth, and possibly cannibalistic tendencies, may be the germ of the ogre in folklore. . .' "

H. G. Wells, *Outline of History*

FOR ANN

ONE

❧❧❧❧❧❧❧❧❧❧❧

Lok was running as fast as he could. His head was down and he carried his thorn bush horizontally for balance and smacked the drifts of vivid buds aside with his free hand. Liku rode him laughing, one hand clutched in the chestnut curls that lay on his neck and down his spine, the other holding the little Oa tucked under his chin. Lok's feet were clever. They saw. They threw him round the displayed roots of the beeches, leapt when a puddle of water lay across the trail. Liku beat his belly with her feet.

"Faster! Faster!"

His feet stabbed, he swerved and slowed. Now they could hear the river that lay parallel but hidden to their left. The beeches opened, the bush went away and they were in the little patch of flat mud where the log was.

"There, Liku."

The onyx marsh water was spread before them, widening into the river. The trail along by the river began again on the other side on ground that rose until it was lost in the trees. Lok, grinning happily, took two paces towards the water and stopped. The grin faded and his mouth opened till the lower lip hung down. Liku slid to his knee then dropped to the ground. She put the little Oa's head to her mouth and looked over her.

Lok laughed uncertainly.

"The log has gone away."

He shut his eyes and frowned at the picture of the log. It had lain in the water from this side to that, grey and rotting. When you trod the centre you could feel the water that washed beneath you, horrible water, as deep in places as a man's shoulder. The water was not awake like the river or the fall but asleep, spreading there to the river and waking up, stretching on the right into wildernesses of impassable swamp and thicket and bog. So sure was he of this log the people always used that he opened his eyes again, beginning to smile as if he were waking out of a dream; but the log was gone.

Fa came trotting along the trail. The new one was sleeping on her back. She did not fear that he would fall because she felt his hands gripping her hair at the neck and his feet holding the hair farther down her back but she trotted softly so that he should not wake. Lok heard her coming before she appeared under the beeches.

"Fa! The log has gone away!"

She came straight to the water's edge, looked, smelt, then turned accusingly to Lok. She did not need to speak. Lok began to jerk his head at her.

"No, no. I did not move the log to make the people laugh. It has gone."

He spread his arms wide to indicate the completeness of that absence, saw that she understood, and dropped them again.

Liku called him.

"Swing me."

She was reaching for a beech bough that came down out of the tree like a long neck, saw light and craned up with an armful of green and brown buds. Lok abandoned the log that was not there and swung her into the crook. He heaved sideways, he pulled, gaining a little backwards with each step as the bough creaked.

"Ho!"

He let the branch go and dropped on to his hams. The bough shot away and Liku shrieked delightedly.

"No! No!"

But Lok hauled again and again and the armful of leaves bore Liku shrieking and laughing and protesting along the edge of the water. Fa was looking from the water to Lok and back. She was frowning again.

Ha came along the trail, hurrying but not running, more thoughtful than Lok, the man for an emergency. When Fa began to call out to him he did not answer her immediately but looked at the empty water and then away to the left where he could see the river beyond the arch of beeches. Then he searched the forest with ear and nose for intruders and only when he was sure of safety did he put down his thorn bush and kneel by the water.

"Look!"

His pointing finger showed the gashes under water where the log had moved. The edges were still sharp and pieces of broken earth lay in the gashes, not yet disintegrated by the water that covered them. He traced the curving gashes away down into the water until they disappeared in that obscurity. Fa looked across to the place where the broken trail began again. There was earth churned up there where the other end of the log had lain. She asked a question of Ha and he answered her with his mouth.

"One day. Perhaps two days. Not three."

Liku was still shrieking with laughter.

13

Nil came in sight along the trail. She was moaning gently as was her habit when tired and hungry. But though the skin was slack on her heavy body her breasts were stretched and full and the white milk stood in the nipples. Whoever else went hungry it would not be the new one. She glanced at him as he clung to Fa's hair, saw that he was asleep, then went to Ha and touched him on the arm.

"Why did you leave me? You have more pictures in your head than Lok."

Ha pointed to the water.

"I came quickly to see the log."

"But the log has gone away."

The three of them stood and looked at each other. Then, as so often happened with the people, there were feelings between them. Fa and Nil shared a picture of Ha thinking. He had thought that he must make sure the log was still in position because if the water had taken the log or if the log had crawled off on business of its own then the people would have to trek a day's journey round the swamp and that meant danger or even more discomfort than usual.

Lok flung all his weight against the bough and would not let it get away. He hushed Liku and she climbed down and stood by him. The old woman was coming along the trail, they could hear her feet and her breathing. She appeared round the last of the trunks, she was grey and tiny, she was bowed and remote in the contemplation of the leaf-wrapped burden that she carried in two hands by her withered breasts. The people stood together and their silence greeted her. She said nothing but waited with a sort of humble patience for what might come. Only the burden sagged a little in her hands and was lifted up again so that the people remembered how heavy it was.

Lok was the first to speak. He addressed them generally, laughing, hearing only words from his mouth but wanting laughter. Nil began to moan again.

Now they could hear the last of the people coming along the trail. It was Mal, coming slowly and coughing every now and then. He came round the last tree-trunk, stopped in the beginning of the open space, leaned heavily on the torn end of his thorn bush and began to cough. As he bent over they could see where the white hair had fallen away in a track that led from behind his eyebrows over his head and down into the mat of hair that lay across his shoulders. The people said nothing while he coughed but waited, still as deer at gaze, while the mud rose in square lumps that elongated and turned over between their toes. A sharply sculptured cloud moved away from the sun and the trees sifted chilly sunlight over their naked bodies.

At last Mal finished his cough. He began to straighten himself by bearing down on the thorn bush and by making his hands walk over each other up the stick. He looked at the water then at each of the people in turn, and they waited.

"I have a picture."

He freed a hand and put it flat on his head as if confining the images that flickered there.

"Mal is not old but clinging to his mother's back. There is more water not only here but along the trail where we came. A man is wise. He makes men take a tree that has fallen and———"

15

His eyes deep in their hollows turned to the people imploring them to share a picture with him. He coughed again, softly. The old woman carefully lifted her burden.

At last Ha spoke.

"I do not see this picture."

The old man sighed and took his hand away from his head.

"Find a tree that has fallen."

Obediently the people spread out along the water side. The old woman paced to the branch on which Liku had swung and rested her cupped hands on it. Ha was the first to call them. They hurried to him and winced at the liquid mud that rose to their ankles. Liku found some berries blackened and left over from the time of fruit. Mal came and stood, frowning at the log. It was the trunk of a birch, no thicker than a man's thigh, a trunk that was half-sunken in mud and water. The bark was peeling away here and there and Lok began to pull the coloured fungi from it. Some of the fungi were good to eat and Lok gave these to Liku. Ha and Nil and Fa plucked unhandily at the trunk. Mal sighed again

"Wait. Ha there. Fa there. Nil too. Lok!"

The log came up easily. There were branches left which caught in bushes, dragged in the mud and got in their way as they carried it heavily back to the dark neck of water. The sun hid again.

When they came to the edge of the water the old man stood frowning at the tumbled earth on the other side.

"Let the log swim."

This was delicate and difficult. However they handled the sodden wood their feet had to touch the water. At last the log lay floating and Ha was leaning out and holding the end. The other end sank a little. Ha began to bear with one hand and pull with the other. The branched head of the trunk moved out slowly and came to rest against the mud of the other side. Lok babbled happily in admiration, his head thrown back, words coming out at random. Nobody minded Lok, but the old man was frowning and pressing both hands on his head. The other end of the trunk was under water for perhaps twice the length of a man and that was the slimmest part. Ha looked his question at the old man who pressed his head again and coughed. Ha sighed and deliberately put a foot into the water. When the people saw what he was doing they groaned in sympathy. Ha inserted himself warily, he grimaced and the people grimaced with him. He gasped for breath, forcing himself in until the water washed over his knees and his hands gripped the rotten bark of the trunk till it rucked. Now he bore down with one hand and lifted with the other. The trunk rolled, the boughs stirred brown and yellow mud that swirled up with a shoal of turning leaves, the head lurched and was resting on a further bank. Ha pushed with all his strength but the splayed branches were too much for him. There was still a gap where the trunk curved under water on the farther side. He came back to the dry land, watched gravely by the people. Mal was looking at him expectantly, his two hands now holding the thorn bush again. Ha went to the place where the trail came into the open. He picked up his thorn bush and crouched. For a moment he leaned forward then as he fell his feet caught up with him and he was flashing across the open space. He took four paces on the log, falling all the time till it seemed his head must strike his knees; then the log threshed up the water and Ha was flying through the air, feet drawn up and arms wide. He thumped on leaves and earth. He was over. He turned, seized the head of the trunk and hauled: and the trail was joined across the water.

The people cried out in relief and joy. The sun chose this moment to reappear so that the whole world seemed to share their pleasure. They applauded Ha, beating the flat of their hands against their thighs and Lok was sharing their triumph with Liku.

"Do you see, Liku? The trunk is across the water. Ha has many pictures!"

When they were quiet again Mal pointed his thorn bush at Fa.

"Fa and the new one."

Fa felt with her hand for the new one. The bunched hair by her neck covered him and they could see little but his hands and feet firmly gripped to individual curls. She went to the water's edge, stretched out her arms sideways and ran neatly across the trunk, jumped the last part and stood with Ha. The new one woke, peered out over her shoulder, shifted the grip of one foot and went to sleep again.

"Now Nil."

Nil frowned, drawing the skin together over her brows. She smoothed the curls back from them, she grimaced painfully and ran at the log. She held her hands high above her head and by the time she reached the middle she was crying out.

"Ai! Ai! Ai!"

The log began to bend and sink. Nil came to the thinnest part, leaped high, her full breasts bouncing and landed in water up to her knees. She screamed and lugged her feet out of the mud, seized Ha's outstretched hand and then was gasping and shuddering on the solid earth.

Mal walked to the old woman and spoke gently.

"Will she carry it across now?"

The old woman withdrew only in part from her inward contemplation. She paced down to the water's edge, still holding the two handfuls at breast height. There was little to her body but bone and skin and scanty white hair. When she walked swiftly across the trunk scarcely stirred in the water.

Mal bent down to Liku.

"Will you cross?"

Liku took the little Oa from her mouth and rubbed her mop of red curls against Lok's thigh.

"I will go with Lok."

This lit a kind of sunshine in Lok's head. He opened his mouth wide and laughed and talked at the people, though there was little connection between the quick pictures and the words that came out. He saw Fa laughing back at him and Ha smiling gravely.

Nil called out to them.

"Be careful, Liku. Hold tight."

Lok pulled a curl of Liku's hair.

"Up."

Liku took his hand, seized his knee with one foot and clambered to the curls of his back. The little Oa lay in her warm hand under his chin. She shouted at him.

"Now!"

Lok went right back to the trail under the beeches. He scowled at the water, rushed at it, then skidded to a stop. Across the water the people began to laugh. Lok rushed backwards and forwards, baulking each time at the near end of the log. He shouted.

"Look at Lok, the mighty jumper!"

Proudly he pranced forward, his pride diminished, he crouched and scuttled back. Liku was bouncing and shrieking.

"Jump! Jump!"

Her head was rolling helplessly against his. He came down to the water's edge as Nil, his hands high in the air.

"Ai! Ai!"

Even Mal was grinning at that. Liku's laughter had reached the silent, breathless stage and the water was falling from her eyes. Lok hid behind a beech tree and Nil held her breasts for laughter. Then suddenly Lok reappeared. He shot forward, head down. He flashed across the log with a tremendous shout. He leapt and landed on dry ground, bounced round and went on bouncing and jeering at the defeated water, till Liku began to hiccup by his neck and the people were holding on to each other.

At last they were silent and Mal came forward. He coughed a little and grimaced wryly at them.

"Now, Mal."

He held his thorn bush crossways for balance. He ran at the trunk, his old feet gripping and loosing. He began to cross, swaying the thorn bush about. He did not get up enough speed to cross in safety. They saw the anguish growing in his face, saw his bared teeth. Then his back foot pushed a piece of bark off the trunk and left a bare patch and he was not quick enough. The other foot slid and he fell forward. He bounced sideways and disappeared in a dirty flurry of water. Lok rushed up and down shouting as loud as he could.

"Mal is in the water!"

"Ai! Ai!"

Ha was wading in, grinning painfully at the strangeness of the cold touch. He got hold of the thorn bush, and Mal was on the other end. Now he had Mal by the wrist and they were falling about, seeming to wrestle with each other. Mal disengaged himself and began to crawl on all fours up the firmer ground. He got a beech tree between himself and the water and lay curled up and shuddering. The people gathered round in a tight little group. They crouched and rubbed their bodies against him, they wound their arms into a lattice of protection and comfort. The water streamed off him and left his hair in points. Liku wormed her way into the group and pressed her belly against his calves. Only the old woman still waited without moving. The group of people crouched round Mal and shared his shivers.

Liku spoke.

"I am hungry."

The people broke the knot round Mal and he stood up. He was still shivering. This shivering was not a surface movement of skin and hair but deep so that the very thorn bush shook with him.

"Come!"

He led the way along the trail. Here there was more space between the trees and many bushes in the spaces. They came presently to a clearing that a great tree had made before it died, a clearing close by the river and still dominated by the standing corpse of the tree. Ivy had taken over, its embedded stems making a varicose entanglement on the old trunk and ending where the trunk had branched in a huge nest of dark green leaves. Fungi had battened too, plates that stuck out and were full of rain-water, smaller jelly-like blobs of red and yellow so that the old tree was dissolving into dust and white pulp. Nil took food for Liku and Lok pried with his fingers for the white grubs. Mal waited for them. His body no longer shook all the time but jerked every now and then. After these jerks he would lean on his thorn bush as though he were sliding down it.

There was a new element present to the senses, a noise so steady and pervasive that the people did not need to remind each other what it was. Beyond the clearing the ground began to rise steeply, earthen, but dotted with smaller trees; and here the bones of the land showed, lumps of smooth grey rock. Beyond this slope was the gap through the mountains, and from the lip of this gap the river fell in a great waterfall twice the height of the tallest tree. Now they were silent the people attended to the distant drone of the water. They looked at each other and began to laugh and chatter. Lok explained to Liku.

"You will sleep to-night by the falling water. It has not gone away. Do you remember?"

"I have a picture of the water and the cave."

Lok patted the dead tree affectionately and Mal led them upward. Now in their joy they also began to pay attention to his weakness, though they were not yet aware how deep it was. Mal lifted his legs like a man pulling them out of mud and his feet were no longer clever. They chose places of their own unskilfully, but as though something were pulling them sideways so that he reeled on his stick. The people behind him followed each of his actions easily out of the fullness of their health. Focused on his struggle they became an affectionate and unconscious parody. As he leaned and reached for his breath they gaped too, they reeled, their feet were deliberately unclever. They wound up through a litter of grey boulders and knees of stone until the trees fell away and they were out in the open.

Here Mal stopped and coughed and they understood that now they must wait for him. Lok took Liku by the hand.

"See!"

The slope led up to the gap′ and the mountain rose before them. On the left the slope broke off and fell down a cliff to the river. There was an island in the river which extended up as though one part had been stood on end and leaned against the fall. The river fell over on both sides of the island, thinly on this side but most widely and tremendously on that; and where it fell no man could see for the spray and the drifting smoke. There were trees and thick bushes on the island but the end towards the fall was obscured as by a thick fog and the river on either side of it had only a qualified glitter.

Mal started off again. There were two ways up to the lip of the fall; one zigzagged away to their right and climbed among the rocks. Although that way would have been easier for Mal he ignored it as though he were anxious above all things to reach comfort quickly. He chose then the path to the left. Here were little bushes which held them up on the edge of the cliff, and while they were threading these Liku spoke to Lok again. The noise of the fall took the life out of her words and left nothing of them but a faint sketch.

"I am hungry."

Lok smacked himself on the chest. He shouted so that all the people heard.

"I have a picture of Lok finding a tree with ears that grow thickly——"

"Eat, Liku."

Ha stood by them with berries in his hand. He poured them out for Liku and she ate, burying her mouth in the food; and the little Oa lay uncomfortably under her arm. The food reminded Lok of his own hunger. Now they had left the dank winter cave by the sea and the bitter, unnatural tasting food of beach and salt marsh he had a sudden picture of good things, of honey and young shoots, of bulbs and grubs, of sweet and wicked meat. He picked up a stone and beat it on the barren rock by his head as presently he would beat on a likely tree.

Nil pulled a withered berry off the bush and put it in her mouth.

"See Lok beating a rock!"

When they laughed at him he clowned, pretending to listen to the rock and shouting.

"Wake up, grubs! Are you awake?"

But Mal was leading them onward.

The top of the cliff leaned back a little so that instead of climbing over the jagged top they could skirt the sheer part over the river where it ran out of the confusion at the foot of the falls. The trail gained height at each step, a dizzy way of slant and overhang, of gap and buttress where roughness to the foot was the only safety and the rock dived back under, leaving a void of air between them and the smoke and the island. Here the ravens floated below them like black scraps from a fire, the weed-tails wavered with only a faint glister over them to show where the water was: and the island, reared against the fall, interrupting the sill of dropping water, was separate as the moon. The cliff leaned out as if looking for its own feet in the water. The weed-tails were very long, longer than many men, and they moved backwards and forwards beneath the climbing people as regularly as the beat of a heart or the breaking of the sea.

Lok remembered how the ravens sounded. He flapped at them with his arms.

"Kwak!"

The new one stirred on Fa's back, shifting the grip of his hands and feet. Ha was going very slowly for his weight made him cautious. He crept along, hands and feet flexing and contracting on the slanting rock. Mal spoke again.

"Wait."

They read his lips as he turned to them and gathered in a group at his side. Here the trail expanded to a platform with room for them all. The old woman rested her hands on the slanting rock so that the weight was eased for her. Mal bent down and coughed till his shoulders were wrenched. Nil squatted by him, put one hand on his belly and the other on his shoulder.

Lok looked away over the river to forget his hunger. He flared his nostrils and immediately was rewarded with a whole mixture of smells, for the mist from the fall magnified any smell incredibly, as rain will deepen and distinguish the colours of a field of flowers. There were the smells of the people too, individual but each engaged to the smell of the muddy path where they had been.

This was so concretely the evidence of their summer quarters that he laughed for joy and turned to Fa, feeling that he would like to lie with her for all his hunger. The rain-water from the forest had dried off her and the curls that clustered round her neck and over the new one's head were glossy red. He reached out his hand to her breast so that she laughed too and patted her hair back from her ears.

"We shall find food," he said with all of his wide mouth, "and we shall make love."

Mentioning food made his hunger as real as the smells. He turned again outwards to where he smelt the old woman's burden. Then there was nothing but emptiness and the smoke of the fall coming towards him from the island. He was down, spread-eagled on the rock, toes and hands gripping the roughness like limpets. He could see the weed-tails, not moving but frozen in an instant of extreme perception, beneath his armpit. Liku was squawking on the platform and Fa was flat by the edge, holding him by the wrist, while the new one struggled and whimpered in her hair. The other people were coming back. Ha was visible from the loins up, careful but swift and now leaning down to his other wrist. He felt the sweat of terror in their palms. A foot or a hand at a time he moved up until he was squatting on the platform. He scrambled round and gibbered at the weed-tails that were moving again. Liku was howling. Nil bent down and took her head between her breasts and stroked the curls down her back soothingly. Fa pulled Lok so that he faced her.

"Why?"

Lok knelt for a moment, scratching in the hair under his mouth. Then he pointed into the damp spray that was drifting at them across the island.

"The old woman. She was out there. And it."

The ravens were rising under his hand as the air poured up the cliff. Fa took her hand away from him when his man's voice touched the matter of the old woman. But Lok's eyes stayed on her face.

"She was out there——"

Complete incomprehension silenced them both. Fa was frowning again. She was not a woman to lie with. Something of the old woman was invisibly present in the air round her head. Lok implored her.

"I turned to her and fell."

Fa closed her eyes and spoke austerely.

"I do not see this picture."

Nil was leading Liku after the others. Fa followed them as if Lok did not exist. He clambered after her sheepishly aware of his mistake; but as he went he murmured:

"I turned to her——"

The others had gathered in a group farther along the path. Fa shouted to them.

"We are coming!"

Ha shouted back:

"There is an ice woman."

Beyond and above Mal there was a gully in the cliff loaded with old snow that the sun had not reached. Weight and cold and then the pelting rain of late winter had compacted the snow into ice that hung perilously and water ran out between the melting edge and the warmer rock. Though they had never seen an ice woman still left in this gully when they came back from their winter cave by the sea, the thought did not occur to them that Mal had taken them into the mountains too early. Lok forgot his escape and the strange indefinable newness of the spray-smell and ran forward. He stood by Ha and shouted:

"Oa! Oa! Oa!"

Ha and the others shouted with him.

"Oa! Oa! Oa!"

Over the insistent drumming of the fall their voices were puny and without resonance, yet the ravens heard and faltered, then glided smoothly once more. Liku was shouting and waving the little Oa, though she did not know why. The new one woke again, passed a pink tongue over his lips like a kitten and peered out from the curls by Fa's ear. The ice woman hung above and beyond them. Though the deadly water still trickled from her belly, she would not move. Then the people were silent and passed swiftly till she was hidden by the rock. They came without speech to the rocks by the fall where the huge cliff looked down for its feet in the turbulence and smother of white water. Almost on a level with their eyes was the clear curve where the water turned down over the sill, water so clear that they could see into it. There were weeds, not moving with slow rhythm but shivering madly as though anxious to be gone. Near the fall the rocks were wet with spray and ferns hung out over space. The people hardly glanced at the fall but pressed on quickly.

Above the fall the river came through a gap in the range of mountains.

Now that the day was almost done the sun lay in the gap and dazzled from the water. Across the water the current slid by sheer mountain that was black and hidden from the sun; but this side of the gap was less uncompromising. There was a slanting shelf, a terrace that gradually became a cliff. Lok ignored the unvisited island and the mountain beyond it on the other side of the gap. He began to hurry after the people as he remembered how safe the terrace was. Nothing could come at them out of the water because the current would snatch it over the fall; and the cliff above the terrace was for foxes, goats, the people, hyenas and birds. Even the way down from the terrace to the forest was defended by an entry so narrow that one man with a thorn bush could hold it. As for this trail on the sheer cliff above the spray pillars and the confusion of waters, it was worn by nothing but the feet of the people.

When Lok edged round the corner at the end of the trail the forest was already dark behind him, and shadows were racing through the gap towards the terrace. The people relaxed noisily on the terrace but then Ha swung his thorn bush so that the prickly head lay on the ground before him. He bent his knees and sniffed the air. At once the people were silent, spreading in a semicircle before the overhang. Mal and Ha stole forward, thorn bushes at the ready, moved up a little slope of earth until they could look down into the overhang.

But the hyenas had gone. Though the scent clung to the scattered stones that had dropped from the roof and the scanty grass that grew in the soil of generations, it was a day old. The people saw Ha lift his thorn bush until it was no longer a weapon and relaxed their muscles.

They moved a few paces up the slope and stood before the overhang while the sunlight threw their shadows sideways. Mal quelled the cough that rose from his chest, turned to the old woman and waited. She knelt in the overhang and laid the ball of clay in the centre of it. She opened the clay, smoothing and patting it over the old patch that lay there already. She put her face to the clay and breathed on it. In the very depth of the overhang there were recesses on either side of a pillar of rock and these were filled with sticks and twigs and thicker branches. She went quickly to the piles and came again with twigs and leaves and a log that was fallen almost to powder. She arranged this over the opened clay and breathed till a trickle of smoke appeared and a single spark shot into the air. The branch cracked and a flame of amethyst and red coiled up and straightened so that the side of her face away from the sun was glowing and her eyes gleamed. She came again from the recesses and put on more wood so that the fire gave them a brilliant display of flame and sparks. She began to work the wet clay with her fingers, tidying the edges so that now the fire sat in the middle of a shallow dish. Then she stood up and spoke to them.

"The fire is awake again."

TWO

At that the people talked again excitedly. They hurried into the hollow. Mal crouched down between the fire and the recess and spread out his hands, while Fa and Nil brought more wood and placed it ready. Liku brought a branch and gave it to the old woman. Ha squatted against the rock and shuffled his back till it fitted. His right hand found a stone and picked it up. He showed it to the people.

"I have a picture of this stone. Mal used it to cut a branch. See! Here is the part that cuts."

Mal took the stone from Ha, felt the weight, frowned a moment, then smiled at them.

"This is the stone I used," he said. "See! Here I put my thumb and here my hand fits round the thickness."

He held up the stone, miming Mal cutting a branch.

"The stone is a good stone," said Lok. "It has not gone away. It has stayed by the fire until Mal came back to it."

He stood up and peered over the earth and stones down the slope. The river had not gone away either or the mountains. The overhang had waited for them. Quite suddenly he was swept up by a tide of happiness and exultation. Everything had waited for them: Oa had waited for them. Even now she was pushing up the spikes

31

of the bulbs, fattening the grubs, reeking the smells out of the earth, bulging the fat buds out of every crevice and bough. He danced on to the terrace by the river, his arms spread wide.

"Oa!"

Mal moved a little way from the fire and examined the back of the overhang. He peered at the surface and swept a few dried leaves and droppings from the earth at the base of the pillar. He squatted and shrugged his shoulders into place.

"And this is where Mal sits."

He touched the rock gently as Lok or Ha might touch Fa.

"We are home!"

Lok came in from the terrace. He looked at the old woman. Freed from the burden of the fire she seemed a little less remote, a little more like one of them. He could look her in the eye now and speak to her, perhaps even be answered. Besides, he felt the need to speak, to hide from the others the unease that the flames always called forth in him.

"Now the fire sits on the hearth. Do you feel warm Liku?"

Liku took the little Oa from her mouth.

"I am hungry."

"To-morrow we shall find food for all the people."

Liku held up the little Oa.

"She is hungry too."

"She shall go with you and eat."

He laughed round at the others.

"I have a picture——"

Then the people laughed too because this was Lok's picture, almost the only one he had, and they knew it as well as he did.

"—a picture of finding the little Oa."

Fantastically the old root was twisted and bulged and smoothed away by age into the likeness of a great-bellied woman.

"—I am standing among the trees. I feel. With this foot I feel——" He mimed for them. His weight was on his left foot and his right was searching in the ground. "—I feel. What do I feel? A bulb? A stick? A bone?" His right foot seized something and passed it to up his left hand. He looked. "It is the little Oa!" Triumphantly he sunned himself before them. "And now where Liku is there is the little Oa."

The people applauded him, grinning, half at Lok, half at the story. Secure in their applause, Lok settled himself by the fire and the people were silent, gazing into the flames.

The sun dropped into the river and light left the overhang. Now the fire was more than ever central, white ash, a spot of red and one flame wavering upwards The old woman moved softly, pushing in more wood so that the red spot ate and the flame grew strong. The people watched, their faces seeming to quiver in the unsteady light. Their freckled skins were ruddy and the deep caverns beneath their brows were each inhabited by replicas of the fire and all their fires danced together. As they persuaded themselves of the warmth they relaxed limbs and drew the reek into their nostrils gratefully. They flexed their toes and stretched their arms, even leaning away from the fire. One of the deep silences fell on them, that seemed so much more natural than speech, a timeless silence in which there were at first many minds in the overhang; and then perhaps no mind at all. So fully discounted was the roar of the water that the soft touch of the wind on the rocks became audible. Their ears as if endowed with separate life sorted the tangle of tiny sounds and accepted them, the sound of breathing, the sound of wet clay flaking and ashes falling in.

Then Mal spoke with unusual diffidence.

"It is, cold?"

Called back into their individual skulls they turned to him. He was no longer wet and his hair curled. He moved forward decisively and knelt so that his knees were on the clay, his arms as supports on either side and the full heat beating on his chest. Then the spring wind flicked at the fire and sent the thin column of smoke straight into his open mouth. He choked and coughed. He went on and on, the coughs seeming to come out of his chest without warning or consultation. They threw his body about and all the time he gaped for his breath. He fell over sideways and his body began to shake. They could see his tongue and the fright in his eyes.

The old woman spoke.

"This is the cold of the water where the log was."

She came and knelt by him and rubbed his chest with her hands and kneaded the muscles of his neck. She took his head on her knees and shielded him from the wind till his coughing was done and he lay still, shivering slightly. The new one woke up and scrambled down from Fa's back. He crawled among the stretched legs with his red thatch glistening in the light. He saw the fire, slipped

34

under Lok's raised knee, took hold of Mal's ankle and pulled himself upright. Two little fires lit in his eyes and he stayed, leaning forward, holding on to the shaking leg. The people divided their attention between him and Mal. Then a branch burst so that Lok jumped and sparks shot out into the darkness. The new one was on all fours before the sparks landed. He scuttled among the legs, climbed Nil's arm and hid himself in the hair of her back and neck. Then one of the little fires appeared by her left ear, an unwinking fire that watched warily. Nil moved her face sideways and rubbed her cheek gently up and down on the baby's head. The new one was enclosed again. His own thatch and his mother's curls made a cave for him. Her mop hung down and sheltered him. Presently the tiny point of fire by her ear went out.

Mal pulled himself up so that he sat leaning against the old woman. He looked at each of them in turn. Liku opened her mouth to speak but Fa hushed her quickly.

Now Mal spoke.

"There was the great Oa. She brought forth the earth from her belly. She gave suck. The earth brought forth woman and the woman brought forth the first man out of her belly."

They listened to him in silence. They waited for more, for all that Mal knew. There was the picture of the time when there had been many people, the story that they all liked so much of the time when it was summer all year round and the flowers and fruit hung on the same branch. There was also a long list of names that began at Mal and went back choosing always the oldest man of the people at that time: but now he said nothing more.

Lok sat between him and the wind.

"You are hungry, Mal. A man who is hungry is a cold man."

Ha lifted up his mouth.

"When the sun comes back we will get food. Stay by the fire, Mal, and we will bring you food and you will be strong and warm."

Then Fa came and leaned her body against Mal so that three of them shut him in against the fire. He spoke to them between coughs.

"I have a picture of what is to be done."

He bowed his head and looked into the ashes. The people waited. They could see how his life had stripped him. The long hairs on the brow were scanty and the curls that should have swept down over the slope of his skull had receded till there was a finger's-breadth of naked and wrinkled skin above his brows. Under them the great eye-hollows were deep and dark and the eyes in them dull and full of pain. Now he held up a hand and inspected the fingers closely.

"People must find food. People must find wood."

He held his left fingers with the other hand; he gripped them tightly as though the pressure would keep the ideas inside and under control.

"A finger for wood. A finger for food."

He jerked his head and started again.

"A finger for Ha. For Fa. For Nil. For Liku——"

He came to the end of his fingers and looked at the other hand, coughing softly. Ha stirred where he sat but said nothing. Then Mal relaxed his brow and gave up. He bowed down his head and clasped his hands in the grey hair at the back of his neck. They heard in his voice how tired he was.

36

"Ha shall get wood from the forest. Nil will go with him, and the new one." Ha stirred again and Fa moved her arm from the old man's shoulders, but Mal went on speaking.

"Lok will get food with Fa and Liku."

Ha spoke:

"Liku is too little to go on the mountain and out on the plain!"

Liku cried out:

"I will go with Lok!"

Mal muttered under his knees:

"I have spoken."

Now the thing was settled the people became restless. They knew in their bodies that something was wrong, yet the word had been said. When the word had been said it was as though the action was already alive in performance and they worried. Ha clicked a stone aimlessly against the rock of the overhang and Nil was moaning softly again. Only Lok, who had fewest pictures, remembered the blinding pictures of Oa and her bounty that had set him dancing on the terrace. He jumped up and faced the people and the night air shook his curls.

"I shall bring back food in my arms"—he gestured hugely—"so much food that I stagger—so!"

Fa grinned at him.

"There is not as much food as that in the world."

He squatted.

"Now I have a picture in my head. Lok is coming back to the fall. He runs along the side of the mountain. He carries a deer. A cat has killed the deer and sucked its blood, so there is no blame. So. Under this left arm.

37

And under this right one"—he held it out—"the quarters of a cow."

He staggered up and down in front of the overhang under the load of meat. The people laughed with him, then at him. Only Ha sat silent, smiling a little until the people noticed him and looked from him to Lok.

Lok blustered:

"That is a true picture!"

Ha said nothing with his mouth but continued to smile. Then as they watched him, he moved both ears round, slowly and solemnly aiming them at Lok so that they said as clearly as if he had spoken: I hear you! Lok opened his mouth and his hair rose. He began to gibber wordlessly at the cynical ears and the half-smile.

Fa interrupted them.

"Let be. Ha has many pictures and few words. Lok has a mouthful of words and no pictures."

At that Ha shouted with laughter and wagged his feet at Lok and Liku laughed without knowing why. Lok yearned suddenly for the mindless peace of their accord. He put his fit of temper on one side and crept back to the fire, pretending to be very miserable so that they pretended to comfort him. Then there was silence again and one mind or no mind in the overhang.

Quite without warning, all the people shared a picture inside their heads. This was a picture of Mal, seeming a little removed from them, illuminated, sharply defined in all his gaunt misery. They saw not only Mal's body but the slow pictures that were waxing and waning in his head. One above all was displacing the others, dawning through the cloudy arguments and doubts and conjec-

38

tures until they knew what it was he was thinking with such dull conviction.

"To-morrow or the day after, I shall die."

The people became separate again. Lok stretched out his hand and touched Mal. But Mal did not feel the touch in his pain and under the woman's sheltering hair. The old woman glanced at Fa.

"It is the cold of the water."

She bent and whispered in Mal's ear:

"To-morrow there will be food. Now sleep."

Ha stood up.

"There will be more wood too. Will you not give the fire more to eat?"

The old woman went to a recess and chose wood. She fitted these pieces cunningly together till wherever the flames rose they found dry wood to bite on. Soon the flames were beating at the air and the people moved back into the overhang. This enlarged the semicircle and Liku slipped into it. Hair crinkled in warning and the people smiled at each other in delight. Then they began to yawn widely. They arranged themselves round Mal, huddling in, holding him in a cradle of warm flesh with the fire in front of him. They shuffled and muttered. Mal coughed a little, then he too was asleep.

Lok squatted to one side and looked out over the dark waters. There had been no conscious decision but he was on watch. He yawned too and examined the pain in his belly. He thought of good food and dribbled a little and was about to speak but then he remembered that they were all asleep. He stood up instead and scratched the close curls under his lip. Fa was within reach and suddenly he desired her again; but this desire was easy to forget because most of his mind preferred to think about food instead. He remembered the hyenas and padded along the terrace until he could look down the slope to the forest. Miles of darkness and sooty blots stretched away to the grey bar that was the sea; nearer, the river shone dispersedly in swamps and meanders. He looked up at the sky and saw that it was clear except where layers of fleecy cloud lay above the sea. As he watched and the after-image of the fire faded he saw a star prick open. Then there were others, a scatter, fields of quivering lights from horizon to horizon. His eyes considered the stars without blinking, while his nose searched for the hyenas and told him that they were nowhere near. He clambered over the rocks and looked down at the fall. There was always light where the river fell into its basin. The smoky spray seemed to trap whatever light there was and to dispense it subtly. Yet this light illumined nothing but the spray so that the island was total darkness. Lok gazed without thought at the black trees and rocks that loomed through the dull whiteness. The island was like the whole leg of a seated giant, whose knee, tufted with trees and bushes, interrupted the glimmering sill of the waterfall and whose ungainly foot was splayed out down there, spread, lost likeness and joined the dark wilderness. The giant's thigh that should have supported a body like a mountain, lay in the sliding water of the gap and diminished till it ended in disjointed rocks that curved to within a few men's lengths of the terrace. Lok considered the giant's thigh as he might have considered the moon: something so remote that it had no connection with life as he knew it. To reach the island the people would have to leap that gap between the terrace and the rocks across water that was eager to snatch them over the fall. Only some creature more agile and frightened would dare that leap. So the island remained unvisited.

A picture came to him in his relaxation of the cave by the sea and he turned to look down river. He saw the meanders as pools that glistened dully in the darkness. Odd pictures came to him of the trail that led all the way from the sea to the terrace through the gloom below him. He looked and grew confused at the thought that the trail was really there where he was looking. This part of the country with its confusion of rocks that seemed to be arrested at the most tempestuous moment of swirling, and that river down there spilt among the forest were too complicated for his head to grasp, though his senses could find a devious path across them. He abandoned thought with relief. Instead he flared his nostrils, and searched for the hyenas but they were gone. He pattered down to the edge of the rock and made water into the river. Then he went back softly and squatted to one side of the fire. He yawned once, desired Fa again, scratched himself. There were eyes watching him from the cliffs, eyes even, on the island, but nothing would come nearer while the ashes of the fire still glowed. As though she were conscious of his thought the old woman woke, put on a little wood and began to rake the ashes together with a flat stone. Mal coughed dryly in his sleep so that the others stirred. The old woman settled again and Lok put his palms into the hollows of his eyes and rubbed them sleepily. Green spots from the pressure floated across the river. He blinked to the left where the waterfall thundered so monotonously that already he could no longer hear it. The wind moved on the water, hovered; and then came strongly up from the forest and through the gap. The sharp line of the horizon blurred and the forest lightened. There was a cloud rising over the waterfall, mist stealing up from the sculptured basin, the pounded river water being thrown back by the wind. The island dimmed, the wet mist stole towards the terrace, hung under the arch of the overhang and enveloped the people in drops that were too small to be felt and could only be seen in numbers. Lok's nose opened automatically and sampled the complex of odours that came with the mist.

He squatted, puzzled and quivering. He cupped his hands over his nostrils and examined the trapped air. Eyes shut, straining attention, he concentrated on the touch of the warming air, seemed for a moment on the very brink of revelation; then the scent dried away like water, dislimned like a far-off small thing when the tears of effort drown it. He let the air go and opened his eyes. The mist of the fall was drifting away with a change of wind and the smell of the night was ordinary.

He frowned at the island and the dark water that slid towards the lip, then yawned. He could not hold a new thought when there seemed no danger in it. The fire was sinking to a red eye that lit nothing but itself and the people were still and rock-coloured. He settled down and leaned forward to sleep, pressing his nostrils in with one hand so that the stream of cold air was diminished. He drew his knees to his chest and presented the least possible surface to the night air. His left arm stole up and insinuated the fingers in the hair at the back of his neck. His mouth sank on his knees.

Over the sea in a bed of cloud there was a dull orange

light that expanded. The arms of the clouds turned to gold and the rim of the moon nearly at the full pushed up among them. The sill of the fall glittered, lights ran to and fro along the edge or leapt in a sudden sparkle. The trees on the island acquired definition, the birch trunk that overtopped them was suddenly silver and white. Across the water on the other side of the gap the cliff still harboured the darkness but everywhere else the mountains exhibited their high snow and ice. Lok slept, balanced on his hams. A hint of danger would have sent him flying along the terrace like a sprinter from his mark. Frost twinkled on him like the twinkling ice of the mountain. The fire was a blunted cone containing a handful of red over which blue flames wandered and plucked at the unburnt ends of branches and logs.

The moon rose slowly and almost vertically into a sky where there was nothing but a few spilled traces of cloud. The light crawled down the island and made the pillars of spray full of brightness. It was watched by green eyes, it discovered grey forms that slid and twisted from light to shadow or ran swiftly across the open spaces on the sides of the mountain. It fell on the trees of the forest so that a scatter of faint ivory patches moved over the rotting leaves and earth. It lay on the river and the wavering weed-tails; and the water was full of tinsel loops and circles and eddies of liquid cold fire. There came a noise from the foot of the fall, a noise that the thunder robbed of echo and resonance, the form of a noise. Lok's ears twitched in the moonlight so that the frost that lay along their upper edges shivered. Lok's ears spoke to Lok.

"?"

But Lok was asleep.

43

THREE

L ok was aware of the old woman moving earlier than
any of them, busy about the fire in the first dawn
light. She built up a pile of wood and in his sleep
he heard the wood begin to burst and crackle. Fa was
still crouched and the old man's head stirred on her
shoulder restlessly. Ha moved and stood up. He went
down the terrace and made water, then came back and
looked at the old man. Mal was not waking like the
others. He sat heavily on his hams, turning his head from
side to side in Fa's hair and breathing quickly as a doe
when she is heavy with young. His mouth was open wide
to the hot fire; but another fire that was invisible was
melting him away; it lay everywhere on the sunken flesh
of his limbs and round the hollows of his eyes. Nil ran
down to the river and brought water in her cupped
hands. Mal sucked the water in before his eyes were open.
The old woman put more wood on the fire. She pointed
into the recess and jerked her head at the forest. Ha
touched Nil on the shoulder.

"Come!"

The new one woke too, scrambled over Nil's
shoulder, mewed at her a moment, then was at her
breast. Nil padded after Ha towards the quick way down
to the forest while the new one milked her. They edged
round the corner and disappeared into the morning mist
that lay almost level with the top of the fall.

Mal opened his eyes. They had to lean down to him before they could hear what he said.

"I have a picture."

The three people waited. Mal raised a hand and put it flat on top of his head above the eyebrows. Though two fires were shaking in his eyes he was not looking at them but at something far away across the water. So intent and fearful was this attention that Lok turned to see if he could find what Mal was frightened of. There was nothing: only a log, moved from some creeky shore of the river by the spring flood slid past them and up-ended noiselessly over the lip of the fall.

"I have a picture. The fire is flying away into the forest and eating up the trees."

His breathing was quicker now he was awake.

"It is burning. The forest is burning. The mountain is burning——"

His head turned to each of them. There was panic in his voice.

"Where is Lok?"

"Here."

Mal screwed up his eyes at him, frowning and bewildered.

"Who is this? Lok is on his mother's back and the trees are eaten."

Lok shifted his feet and laughed foolishly. The old woman took Mal's hand and raised it to her cheek.

"That is a picture of long ago. That is all done. You have seen it in your sleep."

Fa patted his shoulder. Then her hand stayed against the skin and her eyes opened wide. But she spoke to Mal gently as she might have spoken to Liku.

"Lok is standing on his feet before you. See! He is a man."

Relieved to understand at last, Lok spoke quickly to all of them.

"Yes, I am a man." He spread out his hands. "Here I am, Mal."

Liku woke, yawning, and the little Oa fell off her shoulder. She put it to her chest.

"I am hungry."

Mal turned so quickly that he nearly fell away from Fa and she had to grab him.

"Where are Ha and Nil?"

"You sent them," said Fa. "You sent them for wood. And Lok and Liku and me for food. We will bring some for you quickly."

Mal rocked to and fro, his face in his hands.

"That is a bad picture."

The old woman put her arms round him.

"Now sleep."

Fa drew Lok away from the fire.

"It is not good that Liku should come out on the plain with us. Let her stay by the fire."

"Mal said."

"He is sick in his head."

"He saw all things burning. I was afraid. How can the mountain burn?"

Fa spoke defiantly.

"To-day is like yesterday and to-morrow."

Ha and Nil with the new one laboured through the entry to the terrace. They bore armfuls of broken branches. Fa ran to them.

"Must Liku come with us because Mal said so?"

Ha pulled at his lip.

"That is a new thing. But it was spoken."

"Mal saw the mountain burning."

Ha looked up at the great dim height above them.

"I do not see this picture."

Lok giggled nervously.

"To-day is like yesterday and to-morrow."

Ha twitched his ears at them and smiled gravely.

"It was spoken."

All at once the indefinable tension broke and Fa, Lok and Liku ran swiftly along the terrace. They leapt at the cliff and began to clamber up. Directly they were high enough to see the line of smoky spray at the foot of the fall the noise of it hit them. When the cliff leaned back a little, Lok went down on one knee, and shouted.

"Up!"

The light was brighter now. They could see the shining river where it lay in the gap through the mountains and the vast stretches of fallen sky where the mountains dammed back the lake. Below them the mist hid the forest and the plain and rested quietly against the side of the mountain. They began to run along the steep side, flitting down towards the mist. They passed across the bare rock and reached high screes of broken and sharp stones, clambered down crazy gullies until they came to rounded rocks where there was a scant fledging of grass and a few bushes that leaned away from the wind. The grass was wet and spiders' webs hitched across the blades broke and clung to their ankles. The slope decreased, the bushes were more frequent. They were coming down to the limit of the mist.

"The sun will drink up the mist."

Fa paid no attention. She was questing, head down, so that the curls by her cheek brushed drops of water from the leaves. A bird squawked and blundered heavily away into the air. Fa pounced on the nest and Liku beat her feet against Lok's belly.

"Eggs! Eggs!"

She slipped from his back and danced among the tufts of grass. Fa broke a thorn from a bush and pierced the egg at both ends. Liku snatched it from her hands and began to suck noisily. There was an egg for Fa and one for Lok. All three were empty between two breathings. When they had eaten them the people knew how hungry they were and began to search busily. They went forward, bent and questing. Though they did not look up they knew that they were following the retreating mist down on to the level ground and that towards the sea the luminous opacity contained the first rays of the sun. They parted leaves and peered into bushes, they found the un-awakened grubs, the pale shoots that lay under a load of stone. As they worked and ate Fa consoled them.

"Ha and Nil will bring a little food from the forest."

Lok was finding grubs, soft delicacies full of strength.

"We cannot go back with a single grub. And back. And then a single grub."

Then they came into an open space. A stone had fallen from the mountain and struck another from its place. The patch of bare earth had been invaded by fat white shoots that had broken into the light, yet were so short and thick that they snapped at a touch. Side by side they concentrated on the circle, eating in. There was so much that they talked as they ate, brief ejaculations of pleasure and excitement, there was so much that for a while they

48

ceased to feel famished and were only hungry. Liku said nothing but sat with her legs stretched out and ate with both hands.

Presently Lok made an embracing gesture.

"If we eat at this end of the patch then we can bring the people to eat at that end."

Fa spoke indistinctly.

"Mal will not come and she will not leave him. We shall come back this way when the sun goes the other side of the mountain. We will take to the people what we can carry in our arms."

Lok belched at the patch and looked at it affectionately.

"This is a good place."

Fa frowned and munched.

"If the patch were nearer——"

She swallowed her mouthful with a gulp.

"I have a picture. The good food is growing. Not here. It is growing by the fall."

Lok laughed at her.

"No plant like this grows near the fall!"

Fa put her hands wide apart, watching Lok all the time. Then she began to bring them together. But though the tilt of her head, the eyebrows moved slightly up and apart asked a question she had no words with which to define it. She tried again.

"But if—— See this picture. The overhang and the fire is down here."

Lok lifted his face away from his mouth and laughed.

"This place is down here. And the overhang and the fire is there."

He broke off more shoots, stuffed them into his mouth

49

and went on eating. He looked into the clearer sunlight and read the signs of the day. Presently Fa forgot her picture and stood up. Lok stood up too and spoke for her.

"Come!"

They padded down among the rocks and bushes. All at once the sun was through, a round of dulled silver, racing slantwise through the clouds yet always staying in the same place. Lok went first, then Liku, serious and eager on this her first proper food hunt. The slope eased and they reached the cliff-like border that gave on to the heathery sea of the plain. Lok poised and the others stilled behind him. He turned, looked a question at Fa, then raised his head again. He blew out air through his nose suddenly, then breathed in. Delicately he sampled this air, drawing a stream into his nostrils and allowing it to remain there till his blood had warmed it and the scent was accessible. He performed miracles of perception in the cavern of his nose. The scent was the smallest possible trace. Lok, if he had been capable of such comparisons, might have wondered whether the trace was a real scent or only the memory of one. So faint and stale was this scent that when he looked his question at Fa she did not understand him. He breathed the word at her.

"Honey?"

Liku jumped up and down till Fa hushed her. Lok tried the air again but this time a new coil of it came to him and this was empty. Fa waited.

Lok did not need to think where the wind was coming from. He clambered on to an apron of rock that held its area out to the sun and began to cast across it. The direction of the wind changed and the scent touched him again. The scent became excitingly real and soon he was following it to a little cliff that frost and sun had fissured and rain worn into a mesh of crevices. There were stains round one of these like the marks of brown fingers, and a single bee, hardly alive, though the sun shone full on the rock-face, was clinging perhaps a hand's-breadth from the opening. Fa jerked her head.

"There will be little honey."

Lok reversed his thorn bush and pushed the torn butt into the crack. A few bees began to hum dully, drugged by cold and hunger. Lok levered the butt about in the crack. Liku was hopping.

"Is there honey, Lok? I want honey!"

Bees crawled out of the crack and lumbered round them. Some fell heavily to the ground and crawled with fanning wings. One hung in Fa's hair. Lok drew the stick back. There was a little honey and wax on the end. Liku stopped jumping and began to lick the butt clean. Now that the others had dulled the point of their hunger they could enjoy watching Liku eat.

Lok chattered.

"Honey is best. There is strength in honey. See how Liku likes honey. I have a picture of the time when honey will run out of this crack in the rock so that you can taste honey off your fingers—so!"

He smeared his hand down the rock, licked his fingers and tasted the memory of honey. Then he thrust the butt into the crack again so that Liku might eat. Presently Fa became restless.

"This is old honey from the time when we went down to the sea. We must find more food for the others. Come!"

But Lok was thrusting the butt in again for joy of

Liku's eating, the sight of her belly and the memory of honey. Fa went away down the apron of rock, following the mist as it sucked back to the plain. She lowered herself over the edge and was out of sight. Then they heard her cry out. Liku scrambled up on Lok's back and he flitted down the apron towards the cry with his thorn bush at the ready. At the edge of the apron was a jagged gully that led out to the open country. Fa was crouching in the mouth of this gully, looking out over the grass and heather of the plain. Lok raced to her. Fa was trembling slightly and raised on her toes. There were two yellowish creatures out there, their legs hidden by the brown bushes of heather, near enough for her to see their eyes. They were prick-eared animals, roused by her voice from their business and standing now at gaze. Lok slid Liku from his back.

"Climb."

Liku scrambled up the side of the gully and squatted, higher in the air than Lok could reach. The yellow creatures showed their teeth.

"Now!"

Lok stole forward holding his thorn bush sideways. Fa circled out to his left. She carried a natural blade of stone in either hand. The two hyenas moved closer together and snarled. Fa suddenly jerked her right hand round and the stone thumped the bitch in the ribs. The bitch yelped then ran howling. Lok shot forward, swinging the thorn bush, and thrust the spines at the dog's snarling muzzle. Then the two beasts were out of reach, talking evilly and afraid. Lok stood between them and the kill.

"Be quick, I smell cat."

Fa was already down on her knees, struggling with the limp body.

"A cat has sucked all her blood. There is no blame. The yellow ones have not even reached the liver."

She was tearing fiercely at the doe's belly with the flake of stone. Lok brandished his thorn bush at the hyenas.

"There is much food for all the people."

He could hear how Fa grunted and gasped as she tore at the furred skin and the guts.

"Be quick."

"I cannot."

The hyenas, having finished their evil talk, were circling forward to left and right. Shadows flitted across Lok as he faced them from two great birds that were floating in the air.

"Take the doe to the rock."

Fa began to lug at the doe, then cried out in anger at the hyenas. Lok backed to her, bent down, seized the doe by the leg. He began to drag the body heavily towards the gully, brandishing the thorn bush the while. Fa seized a foreleg and hauled too. The hyenas followed them, keeping always just out of reach. The people got the doe into the narrow entrance to the gully just below Liku and the two birds floated down. Fa began to slash again with her splinter of stone. Lok found a boulder which he could use hammer-wise. He began to pound at the body, breaking out the joints. Fa was grunting with excitement. Lok talked as his great hands tore and twisted and snapped the sinews. All the time the hyenas ran to and fro. The birds drifted in and settled on the rock opposite Liku so that she slithered down to Lok and Fa.

The doe was wrecked and scattered. Fa split open her belly, slit the complicated stomach and spilt the sour cropped grass and broken shoots on the earth. Lok beat in the skull to get at the brain and levered open the mouth to wrench away the tongue. They filled the stomach with tit-bits and twisted up the guts so that the stomach became a floppy bag.

All the while, Lok talked between his grunts.

"This is bad. This is very bad."

Now the limbs were smashed and bloodily jointed Liku crouched by the doe eating the piece of liver that Fa had given her. The air between the rocks was forbidding with violence and sweat, with the rich smell of meat and wickedness.

"Quick! Quick!"

Fa could not have told him what she feared; the cat would not come back to a drained kill. It would be already half a day's journey away over the plain, hanging round the skirts of the herd, perhaps racing forward to sink its sabres in the neck of another victim and suck the blood. Yet there was a kind of darkness in the air under the watching birds.

Lok spoke loudly, acknowledging the darkness.

"This is very bad. Oa brought the doe out of her belly."

Fa muttered through her clenched teeth as her hands tore.

"Do not speak of that one."

Liku was still eating, unmindful of the darkness, eating the rich warm liver till her jaws ached. After Fa's rebuke, Lok no longer chattered but muttered instead.

"This is bad. But a cat killed you so there is no blame."

54

And as he moved his wide lips he dribbled.

The sun had cleared the mist now and they could see beyond the hyenas the heathery undulations of the plain and beyond it the lower level of light green tree-tops and the flash of water. Behind them the mountains sloped up, austere. Fa squatted back and got her breath. She rubbed the back of one hand across her brows.

"We must go high where the yellow ones cannot follow."

There was little left of the doe but torn hide, bones and hoofs. Lok handed his thorn bush to Fa. She swished it in the air and shouted rude things at the hyenas. Lok laced the haunches together with twisted gut then wound the end round his wrist so that he could hold them with one hand. He bent down and took the tail of the stomach in his teeth. Fa had an armful and he a double embrace of torn and quivering fragments. He began to retreat, grunting and fierce. The hyenas moved into the mouth of the gully, the buzzards flapped up and circled just out of reach of the bush. Liku, very bold between the man and woman, flopped her piece of liver at the buzzards.

"Go away, beaks! This is Liku's meat!"

The buzzards screamed, gave up, and went to argue with the hyenas who were crunching the split bones and the bloody hide. Lok could not talk. The food from the doe was as much as he could have carried on level ground as a proper load over the shoulder. Now it hung from him, bearing mostly against the grip of his fingers and his clenched teeth. Before they reached the top of the apron he was bending and there was pain in his wrists. But Fa understood this without sharing a picture. She came to him and took away the floppy stomach so that

55

he could gasp easily. Then she and Liku climbed on ahead, leaving him to follow. He arranged the meat in three different ways before he could labour after them. There was such a mixture of darkness and joy in his head that he heard his heart beating. He talked to the darkness that had lain over the mouth of the gully.

"There is little food when the people come back from the sea. There are not yet berries nor fruit nor honey nor almost anything to eat. The people are thin with hunger and they must eat. They do not like the taste of meat but they must eat."

Now he was padding along the side of the mountain on a slope of smooth rock where he depended on the grip of his feet. Still dribbling as he swayed along the high rocks he added a brilliant thought.

"The meat is for Mal who is sick."

Fa and Liku found a fault in the mountain side and began to trot onward to the gap. Lok was left far behind, labouring along and looking for a rock on which he might rest his meat as the old woman had rested the fire. He found one where the fault began, a table spread and emptiness on the other side. He squatted and let the meat slither till it bore its own weight. Below and behind, the buzzards had been joined by others and an angry party was in progress. He turned away from the gully and its darkness and looked for Fa and Liku. They were far ahead, still trotting towards the gap where they would tell the others of the food and perhaps send Ha back to help him carry it. He was disinclined to go forward again and rested for a while watching the busy world. The sky was light blue and the distant bar of the sea not much darker. The darkest things to be seen were patches of

56

deep blue shadow moving towards him over the grass and stone and heather, over the grey outcroppings of the plain. Where they rested on the trees of the forest they damped down the green mists of spring foliage and took the flash out of the river. As they came nearer the mountain they widened in extent and dragged over the crest. He looked along towards the fall where Fa and Liku were tiny figures about to duck out of sight. Then he began to frown at the air over the fall and his mouth opened. The smoke of the fire had moved and changed in quality. For a moment he thought that the old woman had shifted it but then the folly of this picture made him laugh. Neither would the old woman make smoke like that. It was a coil of yellow and white, the smoke that comes from wet wood or a green branch loaded with leaves; no one but a fool or some creature too unacquainted with the nature of fire would use it so unwisely. The idea of two fires came to him. Fire sometimes fell from the sky and flared in the forest for a while. It woke magically on the plain among the heather when the flowers had died away and the sun was too hot.

Lok laughed again at his picture. The old woman would not make such smoke and fires never woke of their own accord in the wet spring. He watched the smoke uncoil and drift away through the gap, thinning as it went. Then he smelt meat and forgot the smoke and his picture. He gathered up the lumps and staggered after Fa and Liku along the fault. The weight of the meat, and the thought of bringing all this food back to the people and their respect for the bringer kept the pictures of the smoke out of his head. Fa came running back along the fault. She took some of the lumps from his arms and

57

they half-climbed, half-slithered down the last slope.

Smoke was rolling heavily from the overhang, blue, hot smoke. The old woman had lengthened the bed of the fire so that a pocket of warm air lay between the flames and the rock. The flames of the fire and the smoke were a wall that interrupted any attempt of the light wind to penetrate the overhang. Mal lay on the earth in this pocket. He was curled up, grey against the brown, his eyes were shut and his mouth was open. He was breathing so quickly and shallowly that his chest seemed to beat like a heart. His bones showed plainly and his flesh was like fat that the fire was melting. Nil, the new one and Ha were just moving away down to the forest as Lok came in sight. They ate as they went and Ha waved a congratulatory hand at Lok. The old woman was standing by the fire, picking at the stomach which Fa had left with her.

Fa and Lok dropped down to the terrace and ran to the fire. As he piled his meat on the scattered rocks Lok shouted across the flames to Mal.

"Mal! Mal! We have meat!"

Mal opened his eyes and got himself on one elbow. He looked across the fire at the swinging stomach and panted a grin at Lok. Then he turned to the old woman. She smiled at him and began to beat the free hand on her thigh.

"That is good, Mal. That is strength."

Liku was jumping up and down beside her.

"I ate meat. And little Oa ate meat. I frightened the beaks away, Mal."

Mal was grinning round at them and panting.

"Then after all, Mal saw a good picture."

Lok tore out a scrap of meat and chewed it. He began to laugh, staggering along the terrace in mime of the load as he had mimed the night before. He spoke indistinctly with his mouth full.

"And Lok saw a true picture. Honey for Liku and the little Oa. And armfuls of meat that a cat had killed."

They laughed with him and beat their thighs. Mal lay back, the grin faded from his face and he was silent, concentrating on his pulsing breath. Fa and the old woman sorted the meat and laid some aside on shelves of rock or in the recesses. Liku took another piece of liver and edged round the fire into the pocket where Mal lay. Then the old woman lowered the stomach gently on to a rock, untwisted the mouth and began to poke about inside.

"Bring earth."

Fa and Lok went through the entry to the terrace where rocks and bushes sloped down to the forest. They tore out lumps of coarse grass with the earth still hanging to them and brought the loads back to the old woman. She took the stomach and laid it on the ground. She scraped up fire ash with a flat stone. Lok squatted on the terrace and began to break up earth with a stick. As he worked he talked.

"Ha and Nil have brought many days' wood back. Fa and Lok have brought many days' food back. And soon the warm days will be here."

As he collected the dry, broken earth, Fa wetted it with water from the river. She carried it to the old woman who plastered it round the stomach. Then she quickly raked out the hottest ashes of the fire and piled them round the plastered earth. The ashes lay thick and the

59

air over them shivered with heat. Fa brought more earth and sods. The old woman built these into a pile round the ashes and shut them in. Lok stopped work and stood, looking down at the food. He could see the puckered mouth of the stomach and plastered earth, then the sods. Fa nudged him aside, bent down and poured water from her cupped hands into the mouth. The old woman watched critically as Fa ran back and forth. Again and again she came from the sliding river until the surface of the water in the stomach lay level with the mouth, flat and scummy. Little bubbles bulged out of the scum, wandered and blipped out. The grass on the sods that covered the red-hot ashes began to curl. It writhed and began to blacken and smoulder. Little flames popped out of the earth and ran about in the grass or moved in balls of consuming yellow from the base of a stem to the end. Lok stepped back and reached for scraps of earth. As he poured them over the burning sods he talked to the old woman.

"It is easy to keep the fire in. The flames will not crawl away. There is nothing here for them to eat."

The old woman smiled wisely at him, saying nothing, and this made him feel silly. He tore a strip of muscle from a flabby haunch and wandered down the terrace. The sun was over the gap through the mountains and he adjusted himself without thinking to the fact that now the end part of the day was coming. Part of the day had gone so quickly that he felt he had lost something. He began to picture confusedly the overhang when he and Fa had not been in it. Mal and the old woman had waited, she pondering Mal's sickness, Mal panting, waiting for Ha with wood and Lok with food. Suddenly he

60

understood that Mal had not been certain that they would find food. Yet Mal was wise. Though Lok felt important again at the thought of the meat, yet the knowledge that Mal had not been certain was like a cold wind. Then the knowledge, so nearly like thinking, made a tiredness in his head and he shook it off, returning to be the comfortable and happy Lok whose betters told him what to do and looked after him. He remembered the old woman, so close to Oa, knowing so indescribably much, the doorkeeper to whom all secrets were open. He felt awed and happy and witless again.

Fa was sitting by the fire toasting scraps of meat on a twig. The scraps spat and trickled as the twig burned and she stung her fingers every time she took meat off to eat. The old woman was pouring water from her hands over Mal's face. Liku sat with her back against the rock and the little Oa was on her shoulder. Liku was eating slowly now, her legs were stretched out straight in front of her and her belly was beautifully round. The old woman came back and squatted by Fa and watched the wisp of steam that rose from the bubbles in the stomach. She snatched a floating titbit, juggled with it and popped it in her mouth.

The people were silent. Life was fulfilled, there was no need to look farther for food, to-morrow was secure and the day after that so remote that no one would bother to think of it. Life was exquisitely allayed hunger. Soon Mal would eat of the soft brain. The strength and fleetness of the doe would begin to grow in him. With the wonder of this gift present in their minds they felt no need for speech. They sank then into a settled silence that might have been mistaken for abstracted melancholy, were it not for the steady movement of the muscles that ran up from their jaws and moved the curls gently on the sides of their vaulted heads.

Liku's head nodded and the little Oa fell off her shoulder. The bubbles rose busily in the mouth of the stomach, slipped to the edge and a cloud of steam puffed upwards to be sucked sideways into the rising air of the bigger fire. Fa took a twig, dipped it in the seething mess, tasted the end and turned to the old woman.

"Soon."

The old woman tasted too.

"Mal must drink of the hot water. There is strength in the water from the meat."

Fa was frowning at the stomach. She put her right hand flat on top of her head.

"I have a picture."

She scrambled out of the overhang and pointed back towards the forest and the sea.

"I am by the sea and I have a picture. This is a picture of a picture. I am——" She screwed up her face and scowled—"thinking." She came back and squatted by the old woman. She rocked to and fro a little. The old woman rested the knuckles of one hand on the earth and scratched under her lip with the other. Fa went on speaking. "I have a picture of the people emptying the shells by the sea. Lok is shaking bad water out of a shell."

Lok began to chatter but Fa stopped him.

"—There is Liku and Nil——" She paused, frustrated by the vivid detail of her picture, not knowing how to extract from it the significance she felt was there. Lok laughed. Fa brushed at him as at a fly.

"—water out of a shell."

She looked at the old woman hopefully. She sighed, and started again.

"Liku is in the forest——"

Lok pointed, laughing, to Liku who lay against a rock, sleeping. Fa struck at him this time as though she had a baby on her back.

"It is a picture. Liku is coming through the forest. She carries the little Oa——"

She was gazing earnestly at the old woman. Then Lok saw the strain go out of her face and knew that they were sharing a picture. It came to him too, a meaningless jumble of shells and Liku and water, and the overhang. He began to speak.

"There are no shells by the mountains. Only shells of the little snail people. They are caves for them."

The old woman was leaning towards Fa. Then she swayed back, lifted both hands off the earth and poised on her skinny hams. Slowly, deliberately, her face changed to that face she would make suddenly if Liku strayed too near the flaunting colours of the poison berry. Fa shrank before her and put her hands up to her face. The old woman spoke.

"That is a new thing."

She left Fa who bowed her face over the stomach and began to stir it with a twig.

The old woman laid a hand on Mal's foot and shook it gently. Mal opened his eyes but did not move. There was a tiny patch of dark saliva-stained earth on the ground by his mouth. The sunlight slanted into the overhang from the night side of the gap and lit him brightly so that shadows stretched from him to the other end of the fire. The old woman put her mouth close to his head.

"Eat, Mal."

Mal got up on one elbow, panting.

"Water!"

Lok ran down to the river and came back with water in his hands, and Mal sucked it up. Then Fa knelt on the other side and let him lean against her while the old woman dipped a stick in the broth more times than there were fingers in the whole world and put it to his mouth. There was hardly time between his breathings for him to swallow. At last he began to turn his head from side to side, avoiding the stick. Lok brought him water. Fa and the old woman laid him carefully on his side. He withdrew from them. They could see how private his thought was and how trapped. The old woman stood by the fire looking down at him. They could see that something of his privacy had reached her and lay in her face like a cloud. Fa broke away from them and ran down to the river. Lok read her lips.

"Nil?"

He went after her into the evening light and together they peered along the cliff over the river. Neither Nil nor Ha was to be seen and the forest beyond the fall was already darkening.

"They are carrying too much wood."

Fa made an agreeing noise.

"But they will bring big wood up the slope. Ha has many pictures. To carry wood on the cliff is bad."

Then they knew that the old woman was looking at them and thinking that she was the only one who understood about Mal. They came back to share the cloud in her face. The child Liku was asleep against the rock, her

64

round belly glowing in the firelight. Mal had not even moved a finger but his eyes were still open. Suddenly the sunlight was level. There was a flapping noise from the cliff over the river and then the scrape of someone edging round the corner. Nil hurried to them along the terrace, her hands empty. She cried her words out.

"Where is Ha?"

Lok gaped at her stupidly.

"He is carrying wood with Nil and the new one."

Nil jerked at them. All at once she was shivering, though she stood within an arm's-length of the fire. Then she began talking quickly to the old woman.

"Ha is not with Nil. See!"

She ran round on the terrace demonstrating its emptiness. She came back. She peered into the overhang, caught up a piece of meat and began to tear at it. The new one woke under her hair and put out his head. After a moment she took the meat from her mouth and looked closely at each of them in turn.

"Where is Ha?"

The old woman pressed her hands on her head, considered this fresh problem for a moment and gave up. She crouched by the stomach and began to fish out meat.

"Ha was gathering wood with you."

Nil became violent.

"No! No! No!"

She bounced up and down on her feet. Her breasts bobbed and milk showed in the nipples. The new one sniffed and scrambled over her shoulder. She held him fiercely with both hands so that he mewed before he sucked. She crouched on the rock and gathered them urgently with her eyes.

"See the picture. We bring wood into a pile. Where the big dead tree is. In the open space. We talk about the doe that Fa and Lok have brought. We laugh together."

She looked across the fire and stretched out a hand.

"Mal!"

His eyes turned towards her. He went on panting. Nil talked at him, while the new one sucked at her breast and behind her the sunlight left the water.

"Then Ha goes toward the river to drink and I stay by the wood." She looked as Fa had looked when the details of the picture were too much for her. "Also he goes to ease himself. And I stay by the wood. But he cries out: 'Nil!' When I stand up"—she was miming—"I see Ha running up towards the cliff. He is running after something. He looks back and he is glad and then he is frightened and glad—so! Then I cannot see him any more." They followed her gaze up a cliff and could not see him any more. "I wait and wait. Then I go to the cliff for Ha and to come back for the wood. There is no sun on the cliff."

Her hair bristled and her teeth showed.

"There is a smell on the cliff. Two. Ha and another. Not Lok. Not Fa. Not Liku. Not Mal. Not her. Not Nil. There is another smell of a nobody. Going up the cliff and coming back. But the smell of Ha stops. There is Ha going up the cliff over the weed-tails when the sun has gone down; and then nothing."

The old woman began to move the sods from the stomach. She spoke over her shoulder.

"That is a picture in a dream. There is no other."

Nil started again in anguish.

"Not Lok. Not Mal——" She went sniffing over the

rock, found herself too near the corner that gave on to the cliff and came bristling back. "There is the end of the Ha scent. Mal——!"

The others considered this picture gravely. The old woman opened the steaming bag. Nil jumped over the fire and knelt by Mal. She touched his cheek.

"Mal! Do you hear?"

Mal answered her between gasps.

"I hear."

The old woman held out meat to Nil who took it without eating. She waited for Mal to speak again, but the old woman spoke for him.

"Mal is very sick. Ha has many pictures. Eat now and be happy."

Nil screamed at her so fiercely that the people stopped eating too.

"There is no Ha. The Ha scent has ended."

For a moment no one moved. Then the people turned and looked down at Mal. With much labour he raised his body, and balanced himself on his hams. The old woman opened her mouth to speak, then shut it. Mal put his hands flat on top of his head. This made his balance even more difficult. He began to jerk.

"Ha went to the cliffs."

He coughed and lost what breath he had. They waited while the fast rhythm of his breath evened.

"There is the scent of another."

He pulled down with both hands. His body began to quiver. One leg shot out and the heel stayed him from a fall. The others waited, red in the sunset and firelight, while the steam from the broth poured up with the reek to be hidden by darkness.

"There is the scent of others."

For a moment he held his breath. Then they saw the wasted muscles of his body relax and he fell sideways as if he did not care how he struck himself against the earth. They saw him whisper.

"I cannot see this picture."

Even Lok was silent. The old woman went to the recesses and fetched wood as if she were walking in her sleep. She did things by touch and her eyes looked beyond the people. Because they could not see what she saw they stood still and meditated formlessly the picture of no Ha. But Ha was with them. They knew his every inch and expression, his individual scent, his wise and silent face. His thorn bush lay against the rock, part of the shaft water-smooth from his hot grip. The accustomed rock waited for him, there before them was the worn mark of his body on the earth. All these things came together in Lok. They made his heart swell, gave him strength as if he might will Ha to them out of the air.

Suddenly Nil spoke.

"Ha is gone."

FOUR

stonished, Lok watched the water run out of her
eyes. It lingered at the rim of her eye-hollows,
then fell in great drops on her mouth and the
new one. She ran down to the river and howled into the
night. He saw the drops from Fa's eyes flash in the firelight too and then she was with Nil, howling at the river.
The feeling that Ha was still present by his many
evidences grew so strong in Lok that it overwhelmed
him. He ran after them, seized Nil by the wrist and
swung her round.

"No!"

She was clutching the new one so fiercely that he was
whimpering. The water still dropped from her face. She
shut her eyes and opened her mouth and howled again
high and long. Lok shook her in rage.

"Ha is not gone! See——"

He ran back to the overhang and pointed to the thorn
bush, the rock and the print in the soil. Ha was everywhere. Lok chattered at the old woman.

"I have a picture of Ha. I will find him. How could
Ha meet another? There is no other in the world——"

Fa began to talk eagerly. Nil was sniffing noisily and
listening.

"If there is another then Ha has gone with him. Let
Lok and Fa go——"

The old woman made a gesture that stopped her.

"Mal is very sick and Ha has gone." She looked at each of them in turn. "Now there is only Lok."

"I will find him."

"—and Lok has many words and no pictures. There is no hope in Mal. Therefore let me speak."

She squatted down ceremoniously by the steaming bag. Lok caught her eye and the pictures went from his head. The old woman began to speak with authority as Mal would have done were he not sick.

"Without help Mal will die. Fa must take a present to the ice women and speak for him to Oa."

Fa squatted by her.

"What other man can this be? Is one alive who was dead? Is one come back from Oa's belly as it may be my baby that died in the cave by the sea?"

Nil sniffed again.

"Let Lok go and find him."

The old woman rebuked her.

"A woman for Oa and a man for the pictures in his head. Let Lok speak."

Lok found himself laughing foolishly. He was at the head of the procession, not capering happily at the other end with Liku. The attention of the three women beat at him. He looked down and scratched one foot with the other. He shuffled round until his back was to them.

"Speak, Lok!"

He tried to fix his eyes on some point in the shadows that would draw him away and enable him to forget them. Half-seeing, he glimpsed the thorn bush leant against the rock. All at once the Ha-ness of Ha was with him in the overhang. An extreme excitement filled him. He began to chatter.

"Ha has a mark here under the eye where the stick burned him. He smells—so! He speaks. There is the little patch of hair over his big toe——"

He jumped round.

"Ha has found another. See! Ha falls from the cliff— that is a picture. Then the other comes running. He cries out to Mal: 'Ha has fallen in the water!' "

Fa peered closely in his face.

"The other did not come."

The old woman had her by the wrist.

"Then Ha did not fall. Go quickly, Lok. Find Ha and the other."

Fa frowned.

"Does the other know Mal?"

Lok laughed again.

"Everyone knows Mal!"

Fa made a quick gesture at him, bidding him be silent. She put her fingers to her teeth and tugged at them. Nil was looking at each of them in turn not understanding what they said. Fa whipped the fingers out of her mouth and pointed one in the old woman's face.

"Here is a picture. Someone is—other. Not one of the people. He says to Ha: 'Come! Here is more food than I can eat.' Then Ha says——"

Her voice faded away. Nil began to whimper.

"Where is Ha?"

The old woman answered her.

"He has gone with the other man."

Lok seized Nil and shook her a little.

"They have changed words or shared a picture. Ha

71

will tell us and I will go after him." He looked round at them. "People understand each other."

The people considered this and shook their heads in agreement.

Liku woke up and smiled round at them. The old woman began to busy herself in the overhang. She and Fa muttered together, they compared pieces of meat, hefted bones and came back to the stomach to argue. Nil sat by it, tearful and eating with a mechanical and listless persistence. The new one crawled slowly over her shoulder. He balanced for a moment, looked at the fire and then inserted himself under her hair. Then the old woman looked secretly at Lok so that even the mixed picture of Ha and another went out of his head and he stood first on one foot then the other. Liku came to the stomach and burnt her fingers. The old woman went on looking and at last Nil sniffed and spoke to him.

"Have you a picture of Ha? A true picture?"

The old woman picked up his thorn bush and handed it to him. She was mixed fire and moonlight and Lok's feet carried him out of the overhang.

"I have a true picture."

Fa gave him food quickly from the stomach, food so hot that he had to juggle with it. He looked doubtfully at them and wandered to the corner. Out of the firelight everything was black and silver, black island, rocks and trees carved cleanly out of the sky and silver river with a flashing light rippling back and forth along the lip of the fall. All at once the night was very lonely and the picture of Ha would not come back into his head. He glanced at

72

the overhang to find the picture. It was a flickering hollow in the cliff at the top of the terrace with a curving line of black at the bottom where the earth rose and hid the fire. He could see Fa and the old woman crouched together and they held a bundle of meat between them. He edged out of sight round the corner and the sound of the fall swelled to meet him. He grounded his thorn bush and squatted to eat his food. It was tender and hot and good. He no longer felt the desperate pain of hunger but only zest, so that the food could be enjoyed and not bolted. He held it close to his face and inspected the pallid surface where the moonlight lay more sleekly than on the water. He forgot the overhang and Ha. He became Lok's belly. As he sat above the thunderous fall with the dim expanses of water-riddled forest before him his face shone with grease and serene happiness. To-night was colder than last night though he made no comparisons. There was a diamond glitter in the mist of the fall that was due only to the brightness of the moon but it looked like ice. The wind had died away and the only beings that moved were the hanging ferns that were tugged by the water. He watched the island without seeing it and attended to the sweetness over his tongue, the full clucking swallow and the tightness of his skin.

At last the meat was finished. He cleaned his face with his hands and his teeth with one of the points from the thorn bush. He remembered Ha again and the overhang and the old woman and stood up quickly. He began to use his nose consciously, crouching sideways and sniffing at the rock. The smells were very complex and his nose did not seem to be clever. He knew why that was and lowered himself head downward till he felt the water with

73

his lips. He drank then cleared out his mouth. He clambered back and crouched on the worn rock. Rain had smoothed it but the close passage by the corner was worn down by the innumerable passings of men like himself. He stood for a while over the monstrous booming of the fall and attended to his nose. The scents were a pattern in space and time. Here, by his shoulder, was the freshest scent of Nil's hand on the rock. Below it was a company of smells, smells of the people as they had passed this way yesterday, smells of sweat and milk and the sour smell of Mal in his pain. Lok sorted and discarded these and settled on the last smell of Ha. Each smell was accompanied by a picture more vivid than memory, a sort of living but qualified presence, so that now Ha was alive again. He settled the picture of Ha in his head, intending to keep it there so that he would not forget.

He was standing crouched, holding the thorn bush in one hand. Then slowly he lifted it, took it with both hands. The knuckles paled and he took a cautious step back. There was something else. It was not noticeable when all the people were considered together, but sort and eliminate them and it remained, a smell without a picture. Now that he noticed, it was heavy by the corner. Someone had stood there, his hand on the rock, leaning, peering round at the terrace and the overhang. Without thinking, Lok understood the blank amazement in Nil's face. He began to move forward along the cliff, slowly at first, then running till he was flitting across the rock-face. A confusion of pictures flickered through his head as he ran: here was Nil, bewildered, frightened, here the other, here came Ha, moving fast——

Lok turned and ran back. On that platform where he

himself had so inexplicably fallen, the scent of Ha broke off as if the cliff ended.

Lok leaned out and looked down. He could see the weed-tails waving under the brilliance of the river. He felt the sounds of mourning about to break from his throat and clapped a hand over his mouth. The weed-tails waved, the river rolled a tide of twisted silver along the dark shore of the island. There came to him a picture of Ha struggling in the water, borne by the current towards the sea. Lok began to track along the rock, following the scent of Ha and the other down towards the forest. He passed the bushes where Ha had found berries for Liku, withered berries, and he still lived there, caught in the bushes. The palm of his hand had pulled along the twigs, forcing the berries off them. He was alive in Lok's head, but backwards, moving through time towards their spring coming from the sea. Lok bounded down the slope between the rocks and under the trees of the forest. The moon that shone so brightly on the river was broken here by the high buds and motionless branches. The tree trunks made great bars of darkness but when he moved between them the moon dropped a net of light over him. Here was Ha and his excitement. Here he went towards the river. There, by the abandoned pile of wood was the patch where Nil had waited patiently till her feet made prints that were black now in a splash of light. Here she had followed Ha, puzzled, worried. The mingling tracks ran back up the rocks towards the cliff.

Lok remembered Ha in the river. He began to run, keeping as near the bank as he could. He came to the open patch where the dead tree stood and ran down to

75

the water. Bushes grew out of the water and hung over it. The branches trailing in the current made it visible by combing moon out of the blackness. Lok began to call out.

"Ha! Where are you."

The river did not answer. Lok called again and waited while the picture of Ha became dim and disappeared so that he understood that Ha had gone. Then there came a cry from the island. Lok shouted again and jumped up and down. But as he jumped he began to feel that Ha's voice had not called. This was a different voice; not the voice of the people. It was the voice of other. Suddenly he was filled with excitement. It was of desperate importance that he should see this man whom he smelt and heard. He ran round the clearing, aimlessly, crying out at the top of his voice. Then the smell of other came to him from the damp earth and he followed it away from the river towards the slope up to the mountain. He followed it, bent, flickering under the moon. The smell curved away from the river under the trees and came to the tumbled rocks and bushes. Here was possible danger, cats or wolves or even the great foxes, red as Lok himself, that the spring hunger made savage. But the trail of other was simple and not even crossed by an animal's scent. It kept away from the path up to the overhang, preferring for choice the beds of gullies rather than the steeper rocks at the side. The other had paused here and there, had paused unaccountably long, his feet turned back. Once where the going was smooth and steep the other had walked backwards for more steps than there were fingers in a hand. He had turned again and started to run up the gully, and his feet had kicked up earth, or rather forced it out wherever they had fallen on a patch. He had paused again, climbed the side of the gully, lain for a while at the lip. There built up in Lok's head a picture of the man, not by reasoned deduction but because in every place the scent told him—do this! As the smell of cat would evoke in him a cat-stealth of avoidance and a cat-snarl; as the sight of Mal tottering up the slope had made the people parody him, so now the scent turned Lok into the thing that had gone before him. He was beginning to know the other without understanding how it was that he knew. Lok-other crouched at the lip of the cliff and stared across the rocks of the mountain. He threw himself forward and was running with legs and back bent. He threw himself into the shadow of a rock, snarling and waiting. He moved cautiously forward, he got down on hands and knees, crawled forward slowly and looked over the edge of the cliff into the river-filled gap.

He was looking down at the overhang. The rock projected above it and he could not see any of the people; but from under the rock a semicircle of ruddy light danced on the terrace, diminishing outward till it was indistinguishable from the moonlight. A little smoke was pouring up and drifting away through the gap. Lok-other began to edge down the rock from ledge to ledge. As he approached the overhang itself he went even more slowly and pressed his body flat against the rock. He pushed himself forward, leaned out and looked down. At once his eye was dazzled by a tongue of flame from the fire; he was Lok again, at home with the people, and the other was gone. Lok stayed where he was, looking blankly at the earth and stones and the sane, comfortable terrace. Fa spoke just beneath him. They were strange words and

77

meant nothing to him. Fa appeared, carrying a bundle and trotted away along the terrace to the dizzy suggestion of a path that led up to the ice women. The old woman came out, looked after her, then turned back under the rock. Lok heard wood scrape, then a shower of sparks floated upwards past his face and the firelight on the terrace spread more widely and began to dance.

Lok sat back and stood up slowly. His head was empty. He had no pictures. Along the terrace Fa had left the flat rock and earth and had started to climb. The old woman came out of the overhang, ran down to the river and came back with a double handful of water. She was so close that Lok could see the drops that fell from her fingers and the twin fires reflected in her eyes. She passed under the rock and he knew that she had not seen him. All at once Lok was frightened because she had not seen him. The old woman knew so much; yet she had not seen him. He was cut off and no longer one of the people; as though his communion with the other had changed him he was different from them and they could not see him. He had no words to formulate these thoughts but he felt his difference and invisibility as a cold wind that blew on his skin. The other had tugged at the strings that bound him to Fa and Mal and Liku and the rest of the people. The strings were not the ornament of life but its substance. If they broke, a man would die. All at once he was hungry for someone's eyes to meet his and recognize him. He turned to run along the ledges and drop down to the overhang; but here was the scent of other again. No longer viciously a part of Lok, its strangeness and power drew him. He followed the scent along the ledges that lay above the terrace until it led to the place where the terrace petered out by the water and the way to the ice women lay above him.

The scattered rocks of the island swept in here and broke up the current not the length of many men away. The scent went down to the water and Lok went with it. He stood, shivering slightly at the loneliness of the water and looking at the nearer rock. A picture began to form in his head of the leap that had cleared this gap to land the other on the rock, and then, leap by leap over the deadly water to the dark island. The moon was caught round the rocks and they were outlined. As he watched, one of the farther rocks began to change shape. At one side a small bump elongated then disappeared quickly. The top of the rock swelled, the hump fined off at the base and elongated again then halved its height. Then it was gone.

Lok stood and let the pictures come and go in his head. One was a picture of a cave bear that he had once seen rear itself out of the rock and heard roar like the sea. Lok did not know much more about the bear than that because after the bear had roared the people had run for most of a day. This thing, this black changing shape, had something of the bear's slow movement in it. He screwed up his eyes and peered at the rock to see if it would change again. There was a single birch tree that overtopped the other trees on the island, and was now picked out against the moon-drenched sky. It was very thick at the base, unduly thick, and as Lok watched, impossibly thick. The blob of darkness seemed to coagulate round the stem like a drop of blood on a stick. It lengthened, thickened again, lengthened. It moved up the birch tree with sloth-like deliberation, it hung in the air high above the island

and the fall. It made no noise and at last hung motionless. Lok cried out at the top of his voice; but either the creature was deaf or the ponderous fall erased the words that he said.

"Where is Ha?"

The creature did not move. A little wind pushed through the gap and the top of the birch swayed, its arc made wide and sedate by the black weight that clung to it. The hair rose on Lok's body and some of the unease of the mountainside returned to him. He felt the need for the protection of human beings, yet memory of the old woman who had not seen him kept him from the overhang. He stayed therefore while the lump swung down the birch tree and vanished into the anonymous shadows that made up this part of the island. Then the lump appeared again, changing shape over the farthest rock. In a panic Lok scrambled in the moonlight at the side of the mountain. Before he could see a clear picture in his head he was scrambling up the suggestion of a track where Fa had gone. He paused when he was as high above the gap-water as a tree is tall and looked down. The creature was visible for an instant as it leapt from rock to rock. Lok shivered and set himself to climb.

This rock did not lean back; it stretched up, becoming steeper as it went and in places sheer. He came to a kind of slit in the cliff and water was falling from it to slide along and dive into the gap. This water was so cold that it bit him when a drop splashed on his face. He could smell Fa and meat on the rock and climbed into the slit. This led straight upward, with a slice of moony sky at the top. The rock was slippery with water and sought to be rid of him. The scent of Fa led him on. When he reached the place where the sky was, he found that the slit became a wide gully that appeared to lead straight into the mountain. He looked down and the river was thin in the gap and everything changed in shape. He wanted Fa more than ever and ducked into the gully. Behind him and across the gap the mountains were horns of ice that shone. He could hear Fa only a little way in front of him and cried out. She came back fast down the gully, leaping on the stones where the water clattered. Boulders grated by her feet and the noise rebounded from the cliffs so that she sounded like a whole party of people. Then she was close to him, her face convulsed with rage and fear.

"Be silent!"

Lok did not hear. He was babbling.

"I have seen the other. Ha fell in the river. The other came and watched the overhang."

Fa seized him by the arm. The bundle was clutched against her breast.

"Be silent! Oa will let the ice women hear and they will fall!"

"Let me stay with you!"

"You are a man. There is terror. Go back!"

"I will not see or hear. I will stay behind you. Let me come."

The drone of the fall had diminished to a sigh like the sound of the sea at a great distance, but in bad weather. Their words had flown away from them like a flock of birds that circled and multiplied mysteriously. The cliffs of the deep gully were singing. Fa clapped her hand over his mouth and they stood so while the birds flew farther and farther away and there was no sound but the water by their feet and the sighing of the fall. Fa turned and began to climb the gully and Lok hastened after her. She stopped and motioned him back fiercely but when she went on he followed. Then Fa stopped again, and ran to and fro between the cliffs making silent mouths at Lok and showing her teeth but he would not leave her. The way back led to the Lok-other who had been unutterably alone. At last she gave up and ignored him. She padded up the gully and Lok followed her, his teeth rattling with the cold.

For here at last there was no water by their feet. There were instead, congealed trunks of ice that were fixed solidly against the cliff; and under the unsunned side of every stone lay a bank of snow. He felt all the misery of winter again and the terror of the ice women so that he followed Fa close as though she were a warm fire. The sky was a narrow strip above him, a freezing sky, that was pricked all over with stars and dashed with strokes of cloud that trapped the moonlight. He could see now that the ice clung to the sides of the gully like ivy, broad below and dividing higher up into a thousand branches and tendrils and the leaves were a glittering white. There was ice under his feet so that they burned and then were numbed. Soon he was using his hands as well and they were numbed like his feet. Fa's rump bobbed in front of him and he followed. The gully widened and more light spilled in and he could see that they were facing a sheer wall of rock. Down the left side there was a line of deepest black. Fa crept towards this line and vanished into it. Lok followed her. He was in an entry so narrow that he could touch both sides with his elbows. Then he was through.

Light hit him. He ducked and brought both hands up to his eyes. Blinking, looking down, he could see stones that flashed, lumps of ice and deep blue shadows. He could see Fa's feet in front of him, whitened, dusted with glitter and her shadow changing shape over the ice and stones. He began to look forward at eye-level and he saw the clouds of their breathing hanging round them like the spray clouds of the fall. He stayed where he was and Fa dimmed into her own breath.

The place was huge and open. It was walled with rock; and everywhere the ice ivy-plants reached upwards until they were spread out high above his head on the rock. Where they met the floor of the sanctuary they swelled till they were like the boles of old oaks. Their high branches vanished into caverns of ice. Lok stood back and looked up at Fa who had gone higher towards the other end of the sanctuary. She crouched on the stones and lifted up the parcel of meat. There was no sound, not even the noise of the fall.

Fa began to speak in little more than a whisper. At first he could hear individual words, "Oa" and "Mal": but walls rejected the words so that they bounded back and were thrown again. "Oa" said the wall and the great ivy, and the wall behind Lok sang "Oa Oa Oa". They ceased to utter the separate words and sang "O" and "A" at the same moment. The sound rose like water in a tidal pool, smoothed like water, became a ringing "A" that beat on him, drowned him. "Sick, sick," said the wall at the end of the sanctuary; "Mal" said the rocks behind him, and the air sang with the interminable and rising tide of "Oa". The hair lifted on his skin. He made with his mouth as if to say "Oa". He looked up, and saw the ice women. The caverns where the ivy branches led were their loins. Their thighs and bellies rose out of the cliff above. They impended so that the sky was smaller than the floor of the sanctuary. Body linked with body they leaned out, arching over and their pointed heads flashed in the light of the moon. He saw that their loins were like caverns, blue and terrible. They were detached rom the rock and the ivy was their water, seeping down between the rock and the ice. The pool of sound had risen to their knees.

"Aaaa" sang the cliff, "Aaaa———"

Lok was lying with his face against ice. Though the frost twinkled on his hair sweat had burst through his skin. He could feel the ravine moving sideways. Fa was shaking his arm.

"Come!"

His belly felt as though he had eaten grass and would be sick. He could see nothing but green lights that moved with merciless persistence through a void of blackness. The sound of the sanctuary had entered his head and was living there like the sound of the sea in a shell. Fa's lips moved against his ear.

"Before they see you."

He remembered the ice women. He kept his eyes on the ground lest he should see the awful light and began to crawl away. His body was a dead thing and he could not make it work. He stumbled after Fa and then they were through the crack in the wall and the gully led down in front of them and another crack was the new arrangement of the gap. He fled past Fa and began to fight his way downward. He fell and rolled, stumbled, leapt clumsily among snow and stones. Then he stopped, weak and shaken and whimpering like Nil. Fa came to him. She put her arm round him and he leaned, looking down at the thread-like water of the gap. Fa spoke softly in his ear.

"It is too much Oa for a man."

He turned inward and got his head between her breasts.

"I was afraid."

For a time they were silent. But the cold was in them and their bodies shuddered apart.

In less panic but still crippled by the cold they began to feel their way down the steepening slope where the sound of the fall rose to meet them. This brought pictures of the overhang to Lok. He began to explain to Fa.

"The other is on the island. He is a mighty leaper. He was on the mountain. He came to the overhang and looked down."

"Where is Ha?"

"He fell into the water."

She left a cloud of breath behind her and he heard her voice out of it.

"No man falls in water. Ha is on the island."

For a while she was silent. Lok thought as best he could of Ha leaping the gap across to the rock. He could not see this picture. Fa spoke again.

"The other must be a woman."

"He smells of man."

"Then there must be another woman. Can a man come out of a man's belly? Perhaps there was a woman and then a woman and then a woman. By herself."

Lok digested this. As long as there was a woman there was life. But what use was a man save for smelling things out and having pictures? Confirmed in his humility he did not like to tell Fa that he had seen the other or that he had seen the old woman and known himself invisible. Presently even pictures and the thought of speech went from his head for they had reached the vertical part of the trail. They clambered down in silence and the roar of water came at them. Only when they were on the terrace and trotting towards the overhang did he remember that he had set out to find Ha and was coming back without him. As if the terror of the sanctuary was pursuing them the two people broke into a run.

But Mal was not the new man they expected. He lay collapsed and his breathing was so shallow that his chest hardly moved. They could see that his face was olive dark and shone with sweat. The old woman had kept the fire blazing and Liku had moved outside it. She was eating more liver, slowly and gravely, and watching Mal. The two women were crouched, one on either side of him, Nil bent and brushing the sweat off his forehead with her hair. There seemed no place in the underhang for Lok's news of the other. When she heard them, Nil looked up, saw no Ha and bent to dry the old man's forehead again. The old woman patted his shoulder.

"Be well and strong, old man. Fa has taken an offering to Oa for you."

At that, Lok remembered his terror beneath the ice women. He opened his mouth to chatter but Fa had shared his picture and she clapped her hand across his lips. The old woman did not notice. She took another morsel from the steaming bag.

"Sit up now and eat."

Lok spoke to him.

"Ha is gone. There are other people in the world."

86

Nil stood up and Lok knew that she was going to mourn but the old woman spoke as Fa had done.

"Be silent!"

She and Fa lifted Mal carefully until he was sitting, leaning back in their arms, his head rolling on Fa's breast. The old woman placed the morsel between his lips but they mumbled it out again. He was speaking.

"Do not open my head and my bones. You would only taste weakness."

Lok glanced round at each of the women, his mouth open. An involuntary laugh came from it. Then he chattered at Mal.

"But there is other. And Ha has gone."

The old woman looked up.

"Fetch water."

Lok ran down to the river and brought back two handfuls. He dripped it slowly over Mal's face. The new one appeared, yawning on Nil's shoulder, clambered over and began to suck. They could see that Mal was trying to speak again.

"Put me in the warm earth by the fire."

In the noise of the waterfall there came a great silence. Even Liku ceased to eat and stood staring. The women did not move, but kept their eyes on Mal's face. The silence filled Lok, turned to water that stood suddenly in his eyes. Then Fa and the old woman laid Mal gently on his side. They pushed the great gaunt bones of his knees against his chest, tucked in his feet, lifted his head off the earth and put his two hands under it. Mal was very close to the fire and his eyes looked into the flames. The hair on his brows began to crinkle but he did not seem to notice. The old woman took a splinter of wood and drew

87

a line in the earth round his body. Then they lifted him to one side with the same solemn quiet.

The old woman chose a flat stone and gave it to Lok. "Dig!"

The moon was through to the sunset side of the gap, but its light was hardly noticeable on the earth for the ruddy brilliance of the firelight. Liku began to eat again. She stole round behind the grown-ups and sat against the rock at the back of the overhang. The earth was hard and Lok had to lean his weight on the stone before he could shift any. The old woman gave him a sharp splinter of bone from the doe meat and he found he could break up the surface much more easily with this. Underneath it was softer. The top layer of earth came up like slate, but below it crumbled in his hands and he could scrape it out with the stone. So he continued as the moon moved. There came into his head the picture of a younger and stronger Mal doing this but on the other side of the hearth. The clay of the hearth was a bulging round on one side of the irregular shaped hole that he was digging. Soon he came to another hearth beneath it and then another. There was a little cliff of burnt clay. Each hearth seemed thinner than the one above it, until as the hole deepened the layers were stone hard and not much thicker than birch bark. The new one finished sucking, yawned, and scrambled down to the earth. He took hold of Mal's leg, hauled himself up, leaning forward and gazed unblinkingly and brightly at the fire. Then he dropped back, scuttled round Mal and investigated the hole. He overbalanced into it and scrambled mewing in the soft earth by Lok's hands. He extracted himself arse-upward and fled back to Nil and crouched in her lap.

Lok sat back with a gasp. The perspiration was running down his body. The old woman touched him on the arm.

"Dig! There is only Lok!"

Wearily he returned to the hole. He pulled out an ancient bone and flung it far into the moonlight. He heaved again on the stone, then fell forward.

"I cannot."

Then, though this was a new thing, the women took stones and dug. Liku watched them and the deepening and darkening hole and said nothing. Mal was beginning to tremble. The clay pillar of hearths narrowed as they dug. It was rooted far down in a forgotten depth of the overhang. As each clay layer appeared the earth became easier to work. They began to have difficulty in keeping the sides straight. They came on dry and scentless bones, bones so long divorced from life that they had no meaning to them and were tossed on one side, bones of the legs, rib-bones, the crushed and opened bones of a head. There were stones too, some with edges that would cut or points that would bore and these they used for a moment where they were useful but did not keep. The dug earth grew into a pyramid by the hole and little avalanches of brown grains would run back as they lifted the new earth out by the handful. There were bones scattered over the pyramid. Liku played idly with the bones of the head. Then Lok got his strength back and dug too so that the hole sank more quickly. The old woman made up the fire again and the morning was grey beyond the flames.

At last the hole was finished. The women poured more water over Mal's face. He was skin and bone now. His mouth was wide as if to bite the air he could not breathe. The people knelt in a semicircle round him. The old woman gathered them with her eyes.

"When Mal was strong he found much food."

Liku squatted against the rock at the back of the overhang, holding the little Oa to her chest. The new one slept under Nil's hair. Mal's fingers were moving aimlessly and his mouth was opening and closing. Fa and the old woman lifted the upper part of his body and held his head. The old woman spoke softly in his ear.

"Oa is warm. Sleep."

The movements of his body became spasmodic. His head rolled sideways on the old woman's breast and stayed there.

Nil began to keen. The sound filled the overhang, pulsed out across the water towards the island. The old woman lowered Mal on his side and folded his knees to his chest. She and Fa lifted him and lowered him into the hole. The old woman put his hands under his face and saw that his limbs lay low. She stood up and they saw no expression in her face. She went to a shelf of rock and chose one of the haunches of meat. She knelt and put it in the hole by his face.

"Eat, Mal, when you are hungry."

She bade them follow her with her eyes. They went down to the river, leaving Liku with the little Oa. The old woman took handfuls of water and the others dipped their hands too. She came back and poured the water over Mal's face.

"Drink when you are thirsty."

One by one the people trickled water over the grey, dead face. Each repeated the words. Lok was last, and as the water fell he was filled with a great feeling for Mal. He went back and got a second gift.

"Drink, Mal, when you are thirsty."

The old woman took handfuls of earth and cast them on his head. Last of the people came Liku, timidly, and did as the eyes bid her. Then she went back to the rock. At a sign from the old woman, Lok began to sweep the pyramid of earth into the hole. It fell with a soft swishing sound and soon Mal was blurred out of shape. Lok pressed the earth down with his hands and feet. The old woman watched the shape alter and disappear expressionlessly. The earth rose and filled the hole, rose still until where Mal had been was a little mound in the overhang. There was still some left. Lok swept it away from the mound and then trampled the mound down as firmly as he could.

The old woman squatted down by the freshly stamped earth and waited till they were all looking at her.

She spoke:

"Oa has taken Mal into her belly".

FIVE

After their silence the people ate. They began to find that tiredness lay on them like mist. There was a blankness of Ha and Mal in the overhang. The fire still burned and the food was good; but a sick weariness fell on them. One by one they curled up in the space between the fire and the rock and fell asleep. The old woman went to the recess and brought wood. She built up the fire until it roared like the water. She collected what was left of the food and placed it out of harm's reach in the recesses. Then she squatted by the mound of earth where Mal had been and looked out over the water.

The people did not dream very often, but while the light of the dawn brightened over them they were beset by a throng of phantoms from the other place. The old woman could see out of the corner of her eye how they were enmeshed, exalted and tormented. Nil was talking. Lok's left hand was scrabbling up a handful of dirt. Muttered words, inarticulate cries of pleasure and fear were coming from them all. The old woman did nothing but gazed steadily at a picture of her own. Birds began to cry and the sparrows dropped down and pecked about the terrace. Lok flung out a hand suddenly that struck her thigh.

When the water was already glittering she stood up

92

and brought wood from the recesses. The fire welcomed the wood with a noisy crackle. She stood close by it, looking down.

"Now, is like when the fire flew away and ate up all the trees."

Lok's hand was too near the fire. She bent down and moved it back to his face. He rolled right over and cried out.

Lok was running. The scent of the other was pursuing him and he could not get away. It was night and the scent had paws and a cat's teeth. He was on the island where he had never been. The fall roared by on either side. He was running along the bank, knowing that presently he would drop from exhaustion and the other would have him. He fell and there was an eternity of struggle. But the strings that bound him to the people were still there. Pulled by his desperate need they were coming, walking, running easily over the water, borne inevitably by necessity. The other was gone and the people were all about him. He could not see them clearly for the darkness but knew who they were. They came in, closer and closer, not as they would come into the over-hang, recognizing home and being free of the whole space; they drove in until they were being joined to him, body to body. They shared a body as they shared a picture. Lok was safe.

Liku woke up. The little Oa had fallen from her shoulder and she took it up. She yawned, saw the old woman and said that she was hungry. The old woman went to a recess and brought her the last of the liver. The new one was playing with Nil's hair. He pulled it, swung on it and she was awake and whimpering again. Fa sat up,

Lok rolled back again and nearly went into the fire. He leapt away from it chattering. He saw the others and talked to them foolishly.

"I was asleep."

The people went down to the water, drank and eased themselves. When they came back there was the feeling of much to be said in the overhang and they left two places empty as though one day those who had sat there might come back again. Nil suckled the new one and combed out her curls with her fingers.

The old woman turned from the fire and spoke to them.

"Now there is Lok."

He looked at her blankly. Fa bent her head. The old woman came to him, took him firmly by the hand and led him to one side. Here was the Mal place. She made Lok sit down, his back against the rock, his hams in the smooth earthen dip that Mal had worn. The strangeness of this overcame Lok. He looked sideways at the water, then back at the people and laughed. There were eyes everywhere, and they waited for him. He was at the head of the procession not at the back of it, and every picture went right out of his head. The blood made his face hot and he pressed his hands over his eyes. He looked through his fingers at the women, at Liku, then down at the mound where the body of Mal was buried. He wished urgently to talk to Mal, to wait quietly before him to be told what to do. But no voice came from the mound and no picture. He grasped at the first picture that came into his head.

"I dreamed. The other was chasing me. Then we were together."

Nil lifted the new one on her breast.

"I dreamed. Ha lay with me and with Fa. Lok lay with Fa and with me."

She began to whimper. The old woman made a gesture that startled and silenced her.

"A man for pictures. A woman for Oa. Ha and Mal have gone. Now there is Lok."

Lok's voice came out small, like Liku's.

"To-day we shall hunt for food."

The old woman waited pitilessly. There was still food piled in the recess, though little enough was left. What people would hunt for food when they were not hungry and there was food left to eat?

Fa squatted forward. While she was speaking some of the confusion died away in Lok's head. He did not listen to Fa.

"I have a picture. The other is hunting for food and the people are hunting——"

She looked the old woman daringly in the eye.

"Then the people are hungry."

Nil rubbed her back against the rock.

"That is a bad picture."

The old woman shouted over them.

"Now there is Lok!"

Lok remembered. He took his hands from his face.

"I have seen the other. He is on the island. He jumps from rock to rock. He climbs in the trees. He is dark. He changes shape like a bear in a cave."

The people looked outward to the island. It was full of sunlight and a mist of green leaves. Lok called them back.

"And I followed his scent. He was there"—and he

pointed to the roof of the overhang so that they all looked up—"he stayed and watched us. He is like a cat and he is not like a cat. He is also like, like——"

The pictures went out of his head for a while. He scratched himself under the mouth. There were so many things to be said. He wished he could ask Mal what it was that joined a picture to a picture so that the last of many came out of the first.

"Perhaps Ha is not in the river. Perhaps he is on the island with the other. Ha was a mighty jumper."

The people looked along the terrace to the place where the detached rocks of the island swept in towards the bank. Nil pulled the new one from her breast and let him crawl on the earth. The water fell from her eyes.

"That is a good picture."

"I will speak with the other. How can he be always on the island? I will hunt for a new scent."

Fa was tapping her palm against her mouth.

"Perhaps he came out of the island. Like out of a woman. Or out of the fall."

"I do not see this picture."

Now Lok found how easy it was to speak words to others who would heed them. There need not even be a picture with the words.

"Fa will look for a scent and Nil and Liku and the new one——"

The old woman would not interrupt him. She seized a great bough instead and hurled it into the fire. Lok sprang to his feet with a cry, and then was silent. The old woman spoke for him.

"Lok will not want Liku to go. There is no man. Let Fa and Lok go. This is what Lok says."

He looked at her in bewilderment and her eyes told him nothing. He began to shake his head.

"Yes," he said, "Yes."

Fa and Lok ran together to the end of the terrace.

"Do not tell the old woman that you have seen the ice women."

"When I came down the mountain on the trail of other she did not see me."

He remembered the old woman's face. "Who can tell what she sees or does not see?"

"Do not tell her."

He tried to explain.

"I have seen the other. He and I, we crawled over the mountain-side and we stalked the people."

Fa stopped and they looked at the gap between the island rock and the terrace. She pointed.

"Could even Ha jump that?"

Lok pondered the gap. The confined waters swirled and sent a tail of glistening streaks down the river. Eddies broke out of the green surface in humps. Lok began to mime his pictures.

"With the scent of other I am other. I creep like a cat. I am frightened and greedy. I am strong." He broke out of the mime and ran rapidly past Fa, then turned and faced her. "Now I am Ha and the other. I am strong."

"I do not see this picture."

"The other is on the island——"

He spread his arms as wide as he could. He flapped them like a bird. Fa grinned and then laughed. Lok laughed too, more and more delightedly to be approved. He ran round on the terrace, quacking like a duck, and

Fa laughed at him. He was about to run flapping back to the overhang to share this joke with the people when he remembered. He skidded and stopped.

"Now there is Lok."

"Find the other, Lok, and speak to him."

This reminded him of the scent. He began to nose round on the rock. No rain had fallen and the scent was very faint. He remembered the mixture of scents on the cliff over the fall.

"Come."

They ran back along the terrace past the overhang. Liku shouted to them and held up the little Oa. Lok crept round the corner and felt the touch of Fa's body on his back.

"The log killed Mal."

He turned back to her, and twitched his ears in surprise.

"I mean the log that was not there. It killed Mal."

He opened his mouth, prepared to debate but she pushed at him.

"On."

They could not miss seeing the signs of the other immediately. His smoke was rising from the middle of the island. There were many trees on the island and some of them leaned out till their branches dipped and the people could not see the shore. There were thick bushes among the trees, growing in unvisited profusion so that the rock soil was covered thick and had as many leaves as it could hold. The smoke rose in a dense coil that spread and faded. There was no doubt about it. The other had a fire and he must use logs so thick and wet that the people themselves could never have lifted them.

Fa and Lok considered the smoke without finding any picture they could share. There was smoke on the island, there was another man on the island. There was nothing in life as a point of reference.

At last Fa turned away and Lok saw that she was shivering.

"Why?"

"I am afraid."

He thought about this.

"I shall go down to the forest. That is nearest to the smoke."

"I do not want to go."

"Return to the overhang. Now there is Lok."

Fa looked again at the island. Then suddenly she was writhing herself round the corner and was gone.

Lok flitted down the cliff through the pictures of the people until he came to the place where the forest began. Here the river was only to be seen occasionally for the bushes not only hung out over where the bank had been, but the water had risen so that many bushes stood with their feet in it. Where the ground was low were incursions of water over drowning grass. The trees stood on higher ground and Lok's feet made a pattern that expressed both his horror of water and his desire to see the new man or the new people. The nearer he came to the part of the shore opposite the smoke the more his excitement grew. Now he even dared water above his ankles, shuddering and prancing through it. When he found that he could not see the river or get close to it he ground his teeth and struck to the right and floundered. There was mire under the water and the bleached points of bulbs. Normally his feet would have seized these and handed them up to him but now they were nothing but a brief firmness against his shuddering skin. There was a whole covert of bushes dimmed with buds between him and the river. He began to put his faith in armfuls of boughs which came together and sagged under his weight, so that he swayed terrifyingly forward off his feet. There was really not enough strength in the sappy branches to bear him unless he sprawled spread-eagled among buds and thorns. Then he saw that there was water under him, not a handful over brown mud but deeper water into which the stems of the bushes sank out of sight. He swayed down and the bushes began to escape from his grip; he glimpsed a shining expanse at eye-level so that he cried out and scrambled with a sort of anguished levitation back to the safe, unpleasant mire. There was no way here to the river for any people but the busy moorhens. He hurried away downstream, circling into the forest where the ground was firmer and came out in the open space by the dead tree. He went down to the little earthen cliff where the deep water came swirling in: but across the water the smoke still rose out of a mystery of trees and undergrowth. A picture came into his head of the other climbing the birch tree and peering through the gap. He hurried away along the trail where the scent of the people still hung faintly until he was by the marsh water, but the new log across it had gone. The tree on which he had swung Liku was still there on the other side of the water. He looked about him and settled on a beech tree that grew so huge he might think the clouds were really caught in its branches. He seized a bough and ran up it quickly. The bole divided and there was rainwater lying in the crutch. He went up the thicker

bough hand after foot until he could feel the grave movement of the tree itself beneath the wind and his weight.
The buds were not yet out but in their green thousands
they were an obscurity like tears in the eyes so that Lok
felt impatient with them. He swung higher still until he
was in the very crown, then began to bend and wrench
away the branches between himself and the island. Now
he looked down through a hole that altered shape every
moment as the swarming buds bowed or swung sideways.
The hole contained part of the island.

There were buds everywhere on the island too, drifts
of them like clouds of bright green smoke. They drifted
all along the shore and the larger trees beyond were like
puffs rising vertically then rolling out. The background
to all this greenness was the black of trunks and branches
and there was no earth. But there was a bright eye where
the fire blazed at the base of the real smoke and it
twinkled and winked at him as the branches moved
across it. Concentrating on the fire he could at last see
the earth near it, very brown and firmer than the earth
near this side of the river. It must be full of bulbs and
fallen nuts and grubs and fungi. There was undoubtedly
good food there for the other to eat.

The fire blinked sharply. Lok blinked back. The fire
had blinked, not because of the boughs but because
someone had moved in front of it, someone as dark as the
branches.

Lok shook the top of the beech tree.

"Hoé man!"

The fire blinked twice. Suddenly Lok understood from
these passings that there was more than one person. The
heady excitement of the scent came to him again. He

shook the top of the tree as though he would break it off.

"Hoé new people!"

A great strength entered into Lok. He could have flown across the invisible water between them. He dared a desperate acrobatic in the thin boughs of the beech top, then shouted as loudly as he could.

"New people! New people!"

Suddenly he froze in the swaying branches. The new people had heard him. He could see by the blinking of the fire and the shaking of the thick bushes that they would come into sight. The fire twinkled again, but a track among the green smoke began to twist and sway down towards the river. He could hear branches cracking. He leaned out.

Then there was nothing more. The green smoke steadied or pulsed gently under the wind. The fire twinkled.

So still was Lok that he began to hear the noise of the fall, ponderous, unending. The grip which held his mind to the new people began to loosen. Other pictures came into his head.

"New people! Where is Ha?"

A spray of green down by the water's edge quivered. Lok looked closely. He followed the suggestions of twigs down to the main stem and screwed up the skin in the hollows of his eyes. There was a forearm or perhaps an upper arm across the bough and it was dark and hairy. The spray of green quivered again and the dark arm vanished. Lok blinked the water out of his eyes. A new picture of Ha on the island came to him, Ha with a bear, Ha in danger.

"Ha! Where are you?"

The bushes on the other bank shook and twisted. A trail of movement showed in them, moving quickly from the bank back among the trees. The fire blinked again. Then the flames vanished and a great cloud of white smoke shot up through the green, the base thinned, disappeared, the white cloud rose slowly, turning inside out as it went. Lok leaned foolishly sideways to look round the trees and bushes. The urgency gripped him. He swung himself down the branches till he could see the next tree down river. He leapt at a branch, was on it, and moving like a red squirrel from tree to tree. Then he ran up a trunk again, tore branches away and peered down.

The roar of the fall was a little dulled now and he could see the columns of spray. They brooded over the upper end of the island so that the trees there were obscured. He let his eye run from them down the island to where the bushes had moved and the fire blinked. He could see, though not clearly, into an open space among the trees. The reek from the dead fire still hung over it, slowly dispersing. There were no people in sight but he could see where the bushes had been broken and a track of torn earth made between the shore and the open space. At the inner end of this track, tree-trunks, huge, dead things with the decay of years about them, had gathered themselves together. He inspected the logs, his mouth hanging open and a free hand pressed flat on top of his head. Why should the people bring all this food—he could see the pale fungi clear across the river—and the useless wood with it? They were people without pictures in their heads. Then he saw that there was a dirty smudge in the earth where the fire had been and logs as huge had been used to build it. Without any warning fear flooded into him, fear as complete and unreasoning as Mal's when he had seen the fire burning the forest in his dream. And because he was one of the people, tied to them with a thousand invisible strings, his fear was for the people. He began to quake. The lips writhed back from his teeth, he could not see clearly. He heard his voice crying out through a roaring noise in his ears.

"Ha! Where are you? Where are you?"

Someone thick-legged ran clumsily across the clearing and disappeared. The fire stayed dead and the bushes were combed by a breeze from down river and then were quite still.

Desperately:

"Where are you?"

Lok's ears spoke to Lok.

"?"

So concerned was he with the island that he paid no attention to his ears for a time. He clung swaying gently in the tree-top while the fall grumbled at him and the space on the island remained empty. Then he heard. There were people coming, not on the other side of the water but on this side, far off. They were coming down from the overhang, their steps careless on the stones. He could hear their speech and it made him laugh. The sounds made a picture in his head of interlacing shapes, thin, and complex, voluble and silly, not like the long curve of a hawk's cry, but tangled like line weed on the beach after a storm, muddled as water. This laugh-sound advanced through the trees towards the river. The same sort of laugh-sound began to rise on the island, so that it flitted back and forth across the water. Lok half-fell, half-scrambled down the tree and was on the trail. He ran along it through the ancient smell of the people. The laugh-sound was close by the river bank. Lok reached the place where the log had lain across water. He had to climb a tree, swing and drop down before he was on the trail again. Then among the laugh-sound on this side of the river Liku began to scream. She was not screaming in anger or in fear or in pain, but screaming with that mindless and dreadful panic she might have shown at the slow advance of a snake. Lok spurted, his hair bristling. Need to get at that screaming threw him off the trail and he floundered. The screaming tore him inside. It was not like the screaming of Fa when she was bearing the baby that died, or the mourning of Nil when Mal was buried; it was like the noise the horse makes when the cat sinks its curved teeth into the neck and hangs there, sucking blood. Lok was screaming himself without knowing it and fighting with thorns. And his senses told him through the screaming that Liku was doing what no man and no woman could do. She was moving away across the river.

Lok was still fighting with bushes when the screaming stopped. Now he could hear the laugh-noise again and the new one mewing. He burst the bushes and was out in the open by the dead tree. The clearing round the trunk stank of other and Liku and fear. Across the water there was a great bowing and ducking and swishing of green sprays. He caught a glimpse of Liku's red head and the new one on a dark, hairy shoulder. He jumped up and down and shouted.

"Liku! Liku!"

The green drifts twitched together and the people on the island disappeared. Lok ran up and down along the river-bank under the dead tree with its nest of ivy. He was so close to the water that he thrust chunks of earth out that went splash into the current.

"Liku! Liku!"

The bushes twitched again. Lok steadied by the tree and gazed. A head and a chest faced him, half-hidden. There were white bone things behind the leaves and hair. The man had white bone things above his eyes and under the mouth so that his face was longer than a face should be. The man turned sideways in the bushes and looked at Lok along his shoulder. A stick rose upright and there was a lump of bone in the middle. Lok peered at the stick and the lump of bone and the small eyes in the bone things over the face. Suddenly Lok understood that the man was holding the stick out to him but neither he nor Lok could reach across the river. He would have laughed if it were not for the echo of the screaming in his head. The stick began to grow shorter at both ends. Then it shot out to full length again.

The dead tree by Lok's ear acquired a voice.

"Clop!"

His ears twitched and he turned to the tree. By his face there had grown a twig: a twig that smelt of other, and of goose, and of the bitter berries that Lok's stomach told him he must not eat. This twig had a white bone at the end. There were hooks in the bone and sticky brown stuff hung in the crooks. His nose examined this stuff and did not like it. He smelled along the shaft of the twig. The leaves on the twig were red feathers and reminded him of goose. He was lost in a generalized astonishment and excitement. He shouted at the green drifts across the glittering water and heared Liku crying out in answer but

106

could not catch the words, They were cut off suddenly as though someone had clapped a hand over her mouth. He rushed to the edge of the water and came back. On either side of the open bank the bushes grew thickly in the flood; they waded out until at their farthest some of the leaves were opening under water; and these bushes leaned over.

The echo of Liku's voice in his head sent him trembling at this perilous way of bushes towards the island. He dashed at them where normally they would have been rooted on dry land and his feet splashed. He threw himself forward and grabbed at the branches with hands and feet. He shouted:

"I am coming!"

Half-lying, half-crawling, grinning all the time with fear he moved out over the river. He could see the wetness down there, mysterious and pierced everywhere by the dark and bending stems. There was no place that would support his whole weight. He had to spread it not only through all his limbs and body but be always in two places, moving, moving as the boughs gave. The water under him darkened. There were ripples on the surface behind each bough, weed caught and fluttering lengthwise, random flashes of the sun below and above. He came to the last tall bushes that were half-drowned and hung over the bed of the river itself. For a moment he saw a stretch of water and the island. He glimpsed the pillars of spray by the fall, saw the rocks of the cliff. Then, because he no longer moved, the branches began to bend under him. They swayed outwards and down so that his head was lower than his feet. He sank, gibbering, and the water rose, bringing a Lok-face with it. There was a tremble of light over the Lok-face but he could see the teeth. Below the teeth, a weed-tail was moving backwards and forwards, more than the length of a man each time. But everything else under the teeth and the ripple was remote and dark. A breeze blew along the river and the bushes swayed gently sideways. His hands and feet gripped painfully of themselves and every muscle of his body was knotted. He ceased to think of the old people or the new people. He experienced Lok, upside down over deep water with a twig to save him.

Lok had never been so near the middle of water before. There was a skin on it and under the skin specks of dark stuff rose towards the surface, turned over and over, floated in circles or sank away out of sight. There were stones down there that glimmered greenly and wavered in the water Regularly the weed-tail eclipsed and revealed them. The breeze died away; the bushes bowed and lifted rhythmically as the weed-tail, so that the shining skin moved to and from his face. Pictures had gone from his head. Even fear was a dullness like the ache of hunger. Each hand and foot clung implacably to a sheaf of branches and the teeth grinned in the water.

The weed-tail was shortening. The green tip was withdrawing up river. There was a darkness that was consuming the other end. The darkness became a thing of complex shape, of sluggish and dreamlike movement. Like the specks of dirt, it turned over but not aimlessly. It was touching near the root of the weed-tail, bending the tail, turning over, rolling up the tail towards him. The arms moved a little and the eyes shone as dully as the stones. They revolved with the body, gazing at the surface, at the width of deep water and the hidden bottom with no trace of life or speculation. A skein of weed drew across the face and the eyes did not blink. The body turned with the same smooth and heavy motion as the river itself until its back was towards him rising along the weed-tail. The head turned towards him with dreamlike slowness, rose in the water, came towards his face.

Lok had always been awed by the old woman though she was his mother. She lived too near the great Oa in heart and head for a man to look upon her without dread. She knew so much, she had lived so long, she felt things they could only guess at, she was the woman. Though she wrapped them all in her understanding and compassion there was sometimes a remote stillness in what she did that left them humble and abashed. Therefore they loved her and dreaded her without fear, and they dropped their eyes before her. But now Lok saw her face to face and eye to eye, close. She was ignoring the injuries to her body, her mouth was open, the tongue showing and the specks of dirt were circling slowly in and out as though it had been nothing but a hole in a stone. Her eyes swept across the bushes, across his face, looked through him without seeing him, rolled away and were gone.

SIX

Lok's feet unclenched themselves from the bushes. They slid down and he was hanging by his arms and up to the waist in water. He raised his knees and his hair pricked. He was past screaming. The terror of the water was only a background. He flung himself round, grabbed more branches and floundered through the bushes and the water to the bank. He stood there, his back to the river, and shivered like Mal. His teeth were showing and he had his arms raised and tensed as though he were still holding himself above the water. He was looking slightly up and his head was turning from side to side. Behind him the laugh-noises began again. Little by little they took his attention though the posture and grin of strain stayed in his body. There were many laugh-noises as though the new people had gone mad and there was one louder than the rest, a man's voice, shouting. The other voices ceased and the man went on shouting. A woman laughed, shrill and excited. Then there was silence.

The sun was making a stipple of bright spots over the undergrowth and the wet brown ground. At intervals a breeze would wander up river, making the new and vivid foliage turn slightly to a new direction so that the spots were sifted and resprinkled. A fox barked sharply among the rocks. A pair of woodpigeons spoke to each other of nesting time monotonously.

Slowly his head and arms came down. He no longer grinned. He took a step forward and turned. Then he began to run down river, not fast, but keeping as near to the water as he could. He peered seriously into the bushes, walked, stopped. His eyes unfocused and the grin came back. He stood, his hand resting on the curved bough of a beech and looked at nothing. He examined the bough, holding it with both hands. He began to sway it, backwards and forwards, backwards and forwards, faster and faster. The great fan of branches on the end went swishing over the tops of the bushes, Lok hurled himself backwards and forwards, he was gasping and the sweat of his body was running down his legs with the water of the river. He let go, sobbing, and stood again, arms bent, head tilted, his teeth clenched as if every nerve in his body were burning. The woodpigeons went on talking and the spots of sunlight sifted over him.

He moved from the beech, back along the trail, faltered, stopped, then began to run. He flashed into the open space where the dead tree was and the sun was bright on the tuft of red feathers. He looked towards the island, saw the bushes move, then one of the twigs came twirling across the river and vanished beyond him in the forest. He had a confused idea that someone was trying to give him a present. He would have smiled across at the bone-faced man but no one was visible there and the open space was still full of the faint excruciating echo of Liku screaming. He wrenched the twig from the tree and started to run again. He came to the slope up to the mountain and the terrace and checked at the scent of other and Liku; and then he was following the scent back through time towards the overhang. He moved so fast, pressing down with the knuckles, that were it not for the arrow he held in his left hand he would have seemed to be running on all fours. He put the twig crosswise in his mouth between his teeth, reached out with both hands, half-ran, half-clambered up the slope. When he was near the entry to the terrace he could see over the rock down to the island. One of the bone-faced men was visible there from the chest up, the rest of him hidden by bushes. The new people had never shown up at such a distance before in daylight, and now the face looked like the white patch on a deer's rump. There was smoke behind the new man among the trees, but blue and transparent. The pictures in Lok's head were very confused and too many —worse than no pictures at all. He took the twig from his teeth, He did not know what he shouted.

"I am coming with Fa!"

He ran through the entry and was on the terrace, and no one was about, he saw that, felt it as a coldness coming from the overhang where the fire had been. He went quickly up the earthen rise and stood looking in. The fire had been thrown about and the only one of the people left was Mal under his hump. But there were smells and signs in plenty. He heard a noise on the top of the overhang, leapt out of the circle of ashes and there was Fa coming down the ledges of rock. She saw him and they flew together. She was shuddering and she held him tightly with both her arms. They babbled at each other.

"The bone-face men gave it me. I ran up the slope. Liku screamed across the water."

"When you went down the rock. I am climbing the rocks because I am frightened. Men came to the overhang."

They were silent, clinging and shuddering. The pack of unsorted pictures that flickered between them tired them both. They looked in each other's eyes helplessly and then Lok began to turn his head restlessly from side to side.

"The fire is dead."

They went to the fire, holding each other. Fa squatted and poked about among the charred ends of branches. The hand of habit was on them. They squatted each in the appropriate place and looked out dumbly at the water and the silver line where it poured over the cliff. There was evening sun slanting into the overhang now but no ruddy, flickering light for it to contend with. Fa stirred and spoke at last.

"Here is the picture. I am looking down. The men come and I hide. As I hide I see the old woman go to meet them."

"She was in the water. She looked at me out of the water. I was upside down."

Again they gazed at each other helplessly.

"I come down to the terrace when the men go away. They have Liku and the new one."

The air round Lok echoed with the phantom screaming.

"Liku screamed across the river. She is on the island."

"I do not see this picture."

Neither did Lok. He spread his arms wide and grinned at the memory of the screaming.

"This twig came to me from the island."

Fa examined the twig closely from the barbed bone-point to the red feathers and the smooth nock at the end. She returned to the barbs and wrinkled up her face at the brown gum. Lok's pictures were a little better sorted.

"Liku is on the island with the other people."

"The new people."

"They threw this twig across the river into the dead tree."

"?"

Lok tried to make her see a picture with him but his head was too tired and he gave up.

"Come!"

They followed the scent from the blood to the edge of the river. There was blood on the rock by the water too and a little milk. Fa pressed her hands on her head and gave her picture words.

"They killed Nil and threw her into the water. And the old woman."

"They have taken Liku and the new one."

Now they shared a picture that was a purpose. They ran together along the terrace. At the corner Fa held back but when Lok climbed round she followed him and they stood on the rock-face looking down at the island. They could see the faint blue smoke still spreading in the evening light; but very soon there would be the shadow of the mountains on the forest. Pictures fitted together in Lok's head. He saw himself turning out on the cliff to speak to the old woman because he had smelt fire when she was not there. But this was only another complication in a day of total newness and he let the picture be. The bushes were shaking on the shore of the island. Fa seized Lok by the wrist and they shrank down against the rock. The shaking was prolonged and excited.

Then the two people became nothing but eyes that looked and absorbed and were without thought. There was a log under the bushes floating in the water and one end of it was swinging out into the stream. It was dark and smooth, and hollow. One of the bone-face men sat in it at the end that was swinging out. The branches that hid the other end dragged on a sort of lump; and there it was, free of the bushes, floating, and a man at either end. The log pointed up towards the fall and a little across the river. The current was beginning to take it back downstream. The two men lifted sticks that ended in great brown leaves which they stuck into the water. The log steadied, remained in the same place with the river moving under it. Patches of white foam and swirling green were tailing away down river from the brown leaves. The log sidled out and there was a stretch of uncrossable deep water on either side. The people could see how the men peered at the bank by the dead tree and into the undergrowth on either side through the little holes in their masks of bone.

The man in the front of the log put his stick down and took up a bent one instead. There was a bunch of red feathers by his waist. He held this stick by the middle as he had done when the twig flew across the river to Lok. The log sidled into the bank and the man in the front jumped forward so that he was hidden by the bushes. The log stayed where it was and the man in the back end dug his brown leaf into the water every now and then. The shadow from the fall was reaching him. They could see how the hair grew on his head above the bone. It made a massive clump like a rook's nest in a tall tree and every time he tugged at the leaf, it bobbed and quivered.

Fa was quivering too.

"Will he come to the terrace?"

But then the first man appeared. The end of the log

nosed out of sight against the bank and when it reappeared the first man was sitting again, and he held
another twig in his hand with red feathers at the end.
The log turned out towards the fall, both men were
dipping their leaves together. The log sidled out into
deep water.

Lok began to babble.

"Liku crossed the river in the log. Where does such a
log grow? Now Liku will come back in the log and we
shall be together."

He pointed down to the men in the log.

"They have twigs."

The log was returning to the island. It was nosing at
the bushes by the shore like a water-rat examining something to eat. The man in the front end stood up carefully.
He parted the bushes and hauled himself and the log
through. The other end swung slowly downstream, then
drew forward until the hanging branches covered it so
that the man at the back ducked and laid down his
stick.

Suddenly Fa seized Lok by his right arm and shook
him. She was staring into his face.

"Give the twig back!"

He shared some of the fright in her face. Behind her
the sun made a slope of shadow stretch from the lip of
the fall to the end of the island. Beyond her right
shoulder he glimpsed a trunk of wood, upending and
disappearing without noise over the fall. He lifted the
twig and examined it.

"Throw it. Now."

He jerked his head violently.

"No! No! The new people threw it to me."

Fa took two steps back and forth on the rock. She looked quickly towards the cold overhang, then at the island. She took him by both shoulders and shook him.

"The new people have many pictures. And I have many pictures too."

Lok laughed, uncertainly.

"A man for pictures. A woman for Oa."

Her fingers tightened on his flesh. Her face looked as though she hated him.

She spoke fiercely:

"What will the new one do without Nil's milk? Who will find food for Liku?"

He scratched in the hair under his open mouth. She took her hands away and waited for a moment. Lok continued to scratch and there was an aching emptiness in his head. She jerked twice.

"Lok has no pictures in his head."

She became very solemn and there was the great Oa, not seen but sensed like a cloud round her. Lok felt himself diminish. He clasped his twig with both hands nervously and looked away. Now that the forest was dark he could see the eye of the new peoples' fire blinking at him. Fa spoke to the side of his head.

"Do what I say. Do not say: 'Fa do this.' I will say: 'Lok do this.' I have many pictures."

He diminished a little more, glanced quickly at her, then at the distant fire.

"Throw the twig."

He swung back his right arm and hurled the twig feathers foremost into the air. The feathers dragged, the shaft swung round, the twig hung for a moment in the sunlight, then the point dropped and the whole twig entered the shadows as smoothly as a stooping hawk, slid down and vanished in the water.

He heard Fa make a choking sound, a kind of dry sob: then she was holding him and her head was against his neck and she was laughing and sobbing and shaking as though she had done something difficult but good. She became Fa without much Oa and he put his arms round her for comfort. The sun was right down in the gap and the river flamed so that the edge of the fall was burning bright as the ends of sticks in the fire. There were dark logs coming down river, black against the flaming water. There were whole trees, their roots behaving like strange creatures of the sea. One was turning towards the fall beneath them; roots and branches lifting, dragging, going down. It hung for a moment on the lip; the burning water made a great heap of light over the end and then the tree was going down the air to vanish as smoothly as the twig.

Lok spoke over Fa's shoulder.

"The old woman was in the water."

Presently Fa pushed him away from her.

"Come!"

He followed her round the corner into the level light of the terrace and their bodies wove a parallel skein of shadows as they walked so that a lifted arm seemed to lift a long weight of darkness with it. They went by habit up the rise to the overhang but it was empty of comfort. The recesses were there, dark eyes, and between them the pillar rock, lit redly. The sticks and ashes were so much earth. Fa sat on the ground by the hearth and frowned at the island. Lok waited while she pressed her hands on her head but he could not share her pictures. He remembered the meat in the recesses.

"Food."

Fa said nothing, so Lok, a little timidly, as if he might still have to meet the old woman's eye, felt his way into a recess. He smelled at the meat and brought enough for both of them. When he returned he heard the hyenas yelping on the rocks above the overhang. Fa took meat without seeing Lok and began to eat, still looking at her pictures.

Once he had begun to eat, Lok was reminded of his hunger. He tore the muscle in long strips from the bone and stuffed it in his mouth. There was much strength in the meat.

Fa spoke indistinctly.

"We throw stones at the yellow ones."

"?"

"The twig."

They ate again in silence as the hyenas whined and yelped. Lok's ears told him they were hungry and his nose assured him that they were alone. He picked in the bone for marrow, then took up an unburnt stick from by the dead fire and thrust it in as far as he could. He had a sudden picture of Lok thrusting a stick into a crack for honey. A feeling rushed into him like a wave of the sea, swallowing his contentment in the food, swallowing even the companionship of Fa. He crouched there, the stick still in the hollow bone, and the feeling went through him and over him. It came from nowhere like the river, and like the river it would not be denied. Lok was a log in the river, a drowned animal that the waters treat as they will. He raised his head as Nil had raised her head and the sound of mourning broke from him while the sunlight lifted from the gap and the dusk came welling through. Then he was close to Fa and she was holding him.

The moon had risen when they moved. Fa stood up and squinted at it then looked at the island. She went down to the river and drank and stayed there, kneeling. Lok stood by her.

"Fa."

She made a motion with her hand of not to be disturbed and went on looking at the water. Then she was up and running along the terrace.

"The log! The log!"

Lok ran after her but could not understand. She was pointing at a slim trunk that was sliding towards them and turning as it went. She threw herself on her knees and grabbed a long splinter from the bigger end. The log turned and pulled at her. Lok saw her slip on the rock and dived at her feet. He got her round the knee; and then they were straining landward and the other end of the log was circling round. Fa had one hand wound in his hair and was pulling it without mercy so that the water stood in his eyes, swelled and ran down to his mouth. The other end of the log swung in, and it was floating by the terrace, pulling at them only gently. Fa spoke over her back.

"I have a picture of us crossing to the island on the log."

Lok's hair bristled.

"But men cannot go over the fall like a log!"

"Be silent!"

She puffed for a while and got her breath back.

"Up at the other end of the terrace we can rest the log across to the rock." She blew her breath out hugely.

"The people cross the water on the trail by running along a log."

Then Lok was frightened.

"We cannot go over the fall!"

Fa explained again, patiently.

They towed the log upstream to the end of the terrace. This was a difficult and hair-bristling job because the terrace was not at an even height above the water and there were gaps and outcrops along the edge of it. They had to learn as they went: and all the time the water tugged, now gently, now with sudden strength as though they were robbing it of food. The log was not as dead as firewood. Sometimes it twisted in their hands and the broken branches of the slenderer end would twitch over the rock like legs. Long before they had reached the end of the terrace Lok had forgotten why they were towing it. He only remembered the sudden enlargement of Fa and the wave of misery that had drowned him. Working at the log, frightened of the water, the misery receded to a point where it could be examined and he did not like it. The misery was connected with the people and with strangeness.

"Liku will be hungry."

Fa said nothing.

By the time they had worked the log to the end of the terrace the moon was their only light. The gap was blue and white, and the flat river laced all over with silver.

"Hold the end."

While he held it, Fa pushed the other end away from

her into the river but the current brought it back. Then she squatted for a long time with her hands over her head and Lok waited in obedient dumbness. He yawned widely, licked his lips and looked at the sheer blue cliff on the other side of the gap. There was no terrace on that side of the river but only a sharp drop into deep water. He yawned again and put up both hands to wipe the tears out of his eyes. He blinked awhile at the night, inspected the moon, and scratched himself under his lip.

Fa cried out:

"The log!"

He peered down past his feet but the log had gone; he looked this way and that and flinchingly into the air; then he saw it drifting by Fa and turning away slightly. She scrambled along the rock and grabbed at the leg-like branches. The trunk dragged her, checked, then the end that Lok had forgotten began to swing outward. He made motions of catching hold but the log was out of reach. Fa was chattering and screaming at him in rage. He backed away from her sheepishly. He was saying "The log, the log——" to himself without meaning. The misery had withdrawn like the tide but it was there still.

The other end of the log thumped against the tail of the island. The water of the river pushed sideways against it and the log turned, grinding, pulling the branch out of Fa's hand. The branch scarred down the terrace, bent, flicked, bent again and gave with a long crackle. The log was jammed, the thicker end bumped on the rock, bump, bump, bump; the water made a sluice over the middle, and the crown was crushed in the uneven side of the terrace. The middle of the log, though it was nearly as thick as Lok, bent under the pressure of the water for it was many times as long as a man.

Fa came close to him and looked doubtfully in his face. Lok remembered her anger when the log had seemed to go away from them. He patted her shoulder anxiously.

"I have many pictures."

She looked silently. Then she grinned and patted him back. She put both hands on her thighs and beat them softly, laughing at him so that he patted and laughed with her. The moon was so bright now that two grey-blue shadows imitated them at their feet.

A hyena whined by the overhang. Lok and Fa scuttered over the terrace toward them. Without a word their pictures were one picture. By the time they were near enough to see the hyenas each had stones in either hand and they were wide apart. They began to snarl and yell together and then the prick-eared shapes had fled up the rock to slink and sidle there, grey, with four eyes like green sparks.

Fa took the rest of the food from the recess and the hyenas snarled after them as they ran back along the terrace. By the time they reached the log they were eating mechanically. Then Lok took the bone from his lips.

"It is for Liku."

The log was not alone. Another smaller one lay alongside it, bumping and grinding and the water flowed over both. Fa went forward in the moonlight and laid a foot on the shoreward end. Then she came back and grimaced at the water. She walked away up the terrace, glanced downstream to where the lip of the fall was flickering and then raced forward. She baulked, checked, stopped. A large stick, turning in the water, added itself to the two logs. She tried again with a shorter run and stopped to gibber at the dazzling water. She began to run round by the logs, not speaking proper words but sounding fierce and desperate. This was another new thing and it frightened Lok so that he edged away over the terrace. But then he remembered his own antics by the log in the forest and made himself laugh at her, though there was an emptiness on her back. She ran at him and her teeth grinned in his face as though she would bite him and strange sounds were coming out of her mouth. His body jumped back.

She was silent, clinging to him and trembling, they were one shadow on the rock. She muttered to him in a voice that had no Oa in it:

"Go first on the log."

Lok put her to one side. Now they made no noise the misery was back. He looked at the log, found there was outside of Lok and inside and that outside was better. He hung the meat for Liku firmly from his teeth. She was not riding him and with Fa trembling and the river moving sideways, he did not care to be funny. He inspected the log from end to end, noted a broad bit on this side of the sluice where there had once been the division of a limb and walked away up the terrace. He measured the distance, leaned and rushed forward. The log was under his foot and slippery. It was trembling like Fa, it was moving sideways up the river so that he swayed to the right to retrieve himself. Unaccountably he was falling. His foot came down full force on the other log which sank and he stumbled. His left leg thrust, he was up and the sluice was pushing with more force than a great wind at the crooks of his knees and cold as ice women. He leapt frantically, stumbled, leapt and then he was clawing at the rock, reaching up, holding the top of it with his face pressed in Liku's meat. His feet walked away from each other up the rock until he felt that his crutch would split. He hitched himself painfully round the rock and faced back at Fa. He found that a sound had been coming out of his mouth for all the meat, high and sustained as Nil's sound when she ran on the log in the forest. He fell silent, breathing jerkily. There was another log adding itself to the pile. It lay alongside, bumping, and the sluice broke into foam and sparkling places. Fa tried this log with her feet. She walked carefully along over the water, straddling, with a foot on each log. She reached the rock where he lay and climbed up beside him. She shouted to him over the noise of the water:

"I did not make a noise."

Lok straightened up and tried to pretend that the rock was not moving with them up river. Fa gauged the leap and landed neatly on the next one. He followed her, empty-headed for the noise and newness. They jumped and clambered until they came to a rock that had bushes at the top, and when they reached this Fa lay down and gripped her fingers in the earth while Lok waited patiently with his hands full of meat. They were on the island, and on either side of them the lip of the fall ran and flickered like summer lightning. There was also a new noise, the voice of the main fall beyond the island which was nearer to them than ever before. There was no competing with it. Even the sketch of sound that the smaller fall left of their voices was taken clean away.

Presently Fa sat up. She went forward until she was looking down the shin of the island and Lok went to her.

The foot spread and by the ankle the drifts of water smoke ate inward so that they left only a narrowing way down. Lok crouched and looked over.

Ivy and roots, scars of earth and knobs of jagged rock —the cliff leaned over so that the top with its plume of birch was looking straight down on to the island. The rocks that had fallen were still jumbled against the cliff at the bottom and their dark shapes, always wet, contrasted with the grey gleam of the leaves and the cliff. Trees still lived at the top, though perilously after the rock had torn most of their roots away. What remained were clutched into the crevices in the lip or writhed down the cliff or ended pointlessly in the wet air. The water poured out and down on either side, foamed and flashed, and the solid earth quivered. The moon, nearly full, fronted the cliff high up and the fire glowed in the farthest reach of the island.

The people made no comment on the dizzy height. They leaned out and searched the face of the cliff for a pathway. Fa slid over the edge, her blue shadow more visible than her body, and let herself hand over foot down the roots and the ivy. Lok followed, the meat in his teeth once more, squinting when he could at the glow of the fire. He felt a great impulse to hurry towards it as though there were some remedy by it for his misery. Nor was this remedy only Liku and the new one. The other people with their many pictures were like water that at once horrifies and at the same time dares and invites a man to go near it. He was obscurely aware of this attraction without definition and it made him foolish. He found himself at the end of a huge broken root in a wilderness of glittering, cavernous water. The root was swinging with his weight so that the meat flopped on his chest. He had to jump sideways to the tangle of roots and ivy before he could follow Fa again.

She led the way over the rocks and into the forest of the island. There was little here that might be called a trail. The other people had left their scent among smashed bushes and that was all. Fa followed the scent without reason. She knew the fire must be at the other end but to say why, she would have had to stop and wrestle with pictures, holding her hands to her head. There were many birds nesting on the island and they resented the people so that Fa and Lok began to move with great care. They ceased to pay direct attention to the new scent and adjusted themselves to threading the forest with as little noise and disturbance as possible. Their pictures were shared busily. In the almost total darkness under the coverts they saw with night sight; they avoided the invisible, lifted aside the clinging ivy, undid the draped brambles and sidled through. Soon they could hear the new people.

They could see the fire too; or rather they could see the reflection of the fire and a flicker. The light made the rest of the island impenetrable dark and clouded their night sight so that they were slower. The fire was much bigger than before and the lighted patch was surrounded with a fringe of new leaves that were pale green as though there was some sort of sunlight behind them. The people were making a rhythmic noise like the beat of a heart. Fa stood up in front of Lok so that she became a densely black shape.

The trees were tall at this end of the island and in the centre the bushes were spaced so that there was room to move among them. Lok followed her until they were standing with bent knees and toes flexed for flight behind one of the bushes at the very edge of the firelight. They could just see over into the patch of open ground that the people had chosen. There were too many things to see at once. To begin with, the trees had reorganized themselves. They had crouched down and woven their branches closely so that they made caverns of darkness on either side of the fire. The new people sat on the ground between Lok and the light and no two heads were the same shape. They were pulled out sideways into horns, or spired like a pine tree or were round and huge. Beyond the fire he could see the ends of the pile of logs that was waiting to be burnt and for all their weight the light seemed to make them move.

Then, incredibly, a rutting stag belled by the trunks. The noise was harsh and furious, full of pain and desire. It was the voice of the greatest of all stags and the world was not wide enough for him. Fa and Lok gripped each other and stared at the logs without a picture. The new people bent so that their shapes changed and the heads were hidden. The stag appeared. He moved springily on his two hind legs and his forelegs were stretched out sideways. His antlered head was among the leaves of the trees, he was looking up, past the new people, past Fa and Lok, and it swayed from side to side. The stag began to turn and they saw that his tail was dead and flapped against the pale, hairless legs. He had hands.

In one of the caverns they heard the new one mew. Lok jumped up and down behind the bush.

"Liku!"

Fa had him by the mouth and was holding him still.

The stag stopped dancing. They heard Liku calling. "Here I am, Lok. Here I am!"

There was a sudden clamour of the laugh-noise, dive and twist and scribble of bird-noise, all voices, shouting, a woman screaming. The fire gave a sudden hiss and white steam shot out of it while the light dulled. The new people were flitting to and fro. There was anger and fear.

"Liku!"

The stag was swaying violently in the dim light. Fa was tugging at Lok and muttering at him. The people were coming with sticks, bent and straight.

"Quickly!"

A man was beating savagely at the bush to the right. Lok swung back his arm.

"The food is for Liku!"

He hurled it into the clearing. The lump fell by the stag's feet. Lok had just time to see the stag bend towards it in the steam and then he was stumbling while Fa pulled him. The clamour of the new people was sinking into a purposeful series of shouts, questions and answers, orders—burning branches were racing through the clearing, so that fans of spring foliage leapt into being and disappeared. Lok put down his head and thrust against the soft earth with his feet. There was a hiss as of suddenly indrawn breath close over his head. Fa and Lok swerved among the bushes and slowed. They began to perform their miracle of sensitive ingenuity with the brambles and branches; but this time Lok caught desperation from Fa and her hard breathing. They hurled themselves along and the torches flared under the trees behind them. They heard the new people calling to each other and making a great noise in the undergrowth. Then a single voice cried out loudly. The crashing stopped.

Fa scrabbled at the wet rocks.

"Quickly! Quickly!"

He could just hear her for all the thunder of the glittering skeins of water. Obediently he followed her, astonished at her speed, but with no picture in his head unless it was the meaningless one of the stag dancing.

Fa threw herself over the lip of the cliff and lay down on her shadow. Lok waited. She gasped at him.

"Where are they?"

Lok peered down at the island but she interrupted him.

"Are they climbing?"

Half-way down the cliff a root was swaying slowly from the tug that she had given it but the rest of the cliff was motionless, looking at the moon.

"No!"

They were silent for a time. Lok noticed the noise of the water again and as he did so the noise became something so loud that he could not speak through it. He wondered idly whether they had shared pictures or spoken with their mouths and then he examined the feeling of heaviness in his head and body. There was no doubt at all. The feeling was connected with Liku. He yawned, wiped his eye-hollows with his fingers and licked his lips. Fa got to her feet.

"Come!"

They trotted between the birches over the island, jumped from stone to stone. The log had gathered others so that they lay close together, more than the fingers of a hand they were, and tangled with all the drifting stuff of this side of the river. The water was spurting between them and flowering over. It was as broad a trail as the one through the forest. They reached the terrace easily and stood without speech.

There was a scuffling noise coming from the overhang. They ran quickly and the grey hyenas fled away. The moon shone clear into the overhang so that even the recesses were lighted and the only dark thing was the hole where Mal had been buried. They knelt and swept back the dirt, the ashes and bones over the part of his body they could see. Now the earth did not rise in a hump but was level with the topmost hearth again. Still without speech they rolled a stone and made Mal safe.

Fa muttered.

"How will they feed the new one without milk?"

Then they were holding on to each other, breast against breast. The rocks round them were like any other rocks; the firelight had died out of them. The two pressed themselves against each other, they clung, searching for a centre, they fell, still clinging face to face. The fire of their bodies lit, and they strained towards it.

SEVEN

Fa pushed him to one side. They stood up together and looked round the overhang. The bleak air of first dawn poured round them. Fa went into a recess and came back with an almost meatless bone and some scraps that the hyenas had not been able to reach. The people were red again, copper red and sandy for the blue and grey of the night had left them. They said nothing but picked away and shared the scraps with a passion of pity for each other. Presently they wiped their hands on their thighs and went down to the water and drank. Then still without speaking or sharing a picture they turned to the left and went to the corner round which lay the cliff.

Fa stopped.

"I do not want to see."

Together they turned and looked at the empty over-hang.

"I will take fire when it falls from the sky or wakes among the heather."

Lok considered the picture of fire. Otherwise there was an emptiness in his head and only the tidal feeling, deep and sure, was noticeable inside him. He began to walk towards the logs at the other end of the terrace. Fa caught him by the wrist.

"We shall not go again on the island."

Lok faced her, his hands up.

"There must be food found for Liku. So that she will be strong when she comes back."

Fa looked deeply at him and there were things in her face that he could not understand. He took a step sideways shrugged, gesticulated. He stopped and waited anxiously.

"No!"

She held him by the wrist and lugged him. He resisted, talking all the time. He did not know what he said. She stopped pulling and faced him again.

"You will be killed."

There was a pause. Lok looked at her, then at the island. He scratched his left cheek. Fa came close.

"I shall have children that do not die in the cave by the sea. There will be a fire."

"Liku will have children when she is a woman."

She let go of his wrist again.

"Listen. Do not speak. The new people took the log and Mal died. Ha was on the cliff and a new man was on the cliff. Ha died. The new people came to the overhang. Nil and the old woman died."

The light was much stronger behind her. There was a fleck of red in the sky over her head. She grew in his sight. She was the woman. Lok shook his head at her, humbly. Her words had made the feeling rise.

"When the new people bring Liku back I shall be glad."

Fa made a high, angry sound, she took a step to the water and came back again. She grabbed him by his shoulders.

"How can they give the new one milk? Does a stag give milk? And what if they do not bring back Liku?"

He answered humbly out of an empty head.

"I do not see this picture."

She left him in her anger, turned away and stood with a hand on the corner where the cliff began. He could see how she was bristling and how the muscles of her shoulder twitched. She was bent, leaning forward, right hand on right knee. He heard her mutter at him with her back still turned.

"You have fewer pictures than the new one."

Lok put the heels of his hands in his eyes and pressed so that spokes of light flashed in them like the river.

"There has not been a night."

That was real. Where the night should have been was a greyness. Not only his ears and his nose had been awake after they had lain together, but the Lok inside them, watching the feeling rise and ebb and rise. There was stuffed inside the bones of his head the white flock of the autumn creepers, their seeds were in his nose, making him yawn and sneeze. He put his hands apart and blinked at where Fa had been. Now she was backed on this side of the rock and peering round it at the river. Her hand beckoned.

The log was out again. It was near the island and the same two bone faces were sitting at either end. They were digging the water and the log was sidling across the river. When it was near the bank and the swarming bushes it straightened into the current and the men stopped digging. They were looking closely at the clear patch by the water where the dead tree was. Lok could see how one turned and spoke to the other.

Fa touched his hand.

"They are looking for something."

The log drifted gently downstream with the current and the sun was rising. The farther reaches of the river burst into flame, so that for a time the forest on either side was dark by contrast. The indefinable attraction of the new people pushed the flock out of Lok's head. He forgot to blink.

The log was smaller, drifting down away from the fall. When it turned askew, the man in the back would dig again and the log would point straight at Lok's eyes. Always, the two men looked sideways at the bank.

Fa muttered:

"There is another log."

The bushes by the island shore were shaking busily. They parted for a moment and now that he knew where to look Lok could see the end of another log hidden close in. A man thrust his head and shoulders through the green leaves and waved an arm angrily. The two men in the log began to dig quickly until it had moved right up to where the man waved opposite the dead tree. Now they were no longer looking at the dead tree but at the man, and nodding their heads at him. The log brought them to him and nosed under the bushes.

Curiosity overcame Lok; he began to run towards the new way on to the island so excitedly that Fa shared his picture. She got him again, and grabbed him.

"No! No!"

Lok jabbered. Fa shouted at him.

"I say 'No!' "

She pointed at the overhang.

"What did you say? Fa has many pictures——"

At last he was silent and waiting for her. She spoke solemnly.

"We shall go down into the forest. For food. We shall watch them across the river."

They ran down the slope away from the river, keeping the rocks between them and the new people. In the skirts of the forest there was food; bulbs that just showed a point of green, grubs and shoots, fungi, the tender inside of some kinds of bark. The meat of the doe was still in them and they were not hungry as the people counted hunger. They could eat, where there was food; but without it they could go for to-day easily and for to-morrow if they had to. For this reason there was no urgency in their searching so that presently the enchantment of the new people drew them again to the bushes at the edge of the water. They stood, toes gripped in the mire, and listened for the new people through the noise of the fall. An early fly buzzed at Lok's nose. The air was warm and the sun softly bright so that he yawned again. Then he heard the new people making their bird-noises of conversation and a number of other unexplained sounds, bumps and creakings. Fa sneaked to the edge of the clearing by the dead tree and lay on the earth.

There was nothing to be seen across the water, yet the bumps and creaks continued.

"Fa. Climb the dead trunk, to see."

She turned her face and looked at him doubtfully. All at once he realized that she was going to say no, was going to insist that they went away from the new people and put a great gap of time between them and Liku; and this became a knowledge that was unbearable. He sneaked quickly forward on all fours and ran up the concealed side of the dead tree. In a moment he was burrowing through the shock-head among the dusty, dark, sour-smelling ivy leaves. He had hardly lifted his last limb into the hollow top before Fa's head broke through behind him.

The top of the tree was empty like a great acorn cup. It was white, soft wood that gave and moulded to their weight and was full of food. The ivy spread upwards and downwards in a dark tangle so that they might have been sitting in a bush on the ground. The other trees over-topped them but there was open sky towards the river and the green drifts of the island. Parting the leaves cautiously as if he were looking for eggs, Lok found that he could make a hole no bigger than the eye-part of his face; and though the edges of the hole moved a little he could see the river and the other banks, all the brighter for the dark green leaves round the hole—as though he had cupped his hands and was looking through them. On his left Fa was making herself a lookout, and the edge of the cup even gave her something to rest her elbows on. The heavy feeling sank in Lok as it always did when he had the new people to watch. He sagged luxuriously. Then suddenly they forgot everything else and were very still.

The log was sliding out of the bushes by the island. The two men were digging carefully and the log was turning. It did not point at Lok and Fa but upstream, though it began to move across river towards them. There were many new things in the hollow of the log; shapes like rocks and bulging skins. There were all kinds of stick, from long poles without leaves or branches to sprays of withering green. The log came close.

At last they saw the new people face to face and in sun-light. They were incomprehensibly strange. Their hair was black and grew in the most unexpected ways. The bone-face in the front of the log had a pine-tree of hair that stood straight up so that his head, already too long, was drawn out as though something were pulling it upward without mercy. The other bone-face had hair in a huge bush that stood out on all sides like the ivy on the dead tree.

There was hair growing thickly over their bodies about the waist, the belly and the upper part of the leg so that this part of them was thicker than the rest. Yet Lok did not look immediately at their bodies; he was far too absorbed in the stuff round their eyes. A piece of white bone was placed under them, fitting close, and where the broad nostrils should have shown were narrow slits and between them the bone was drawn out to a point. Under that was another slit over the mouth, and their voices came fluttering through it. There was a little dark hair jutting out under the slit. The eyes of the face that peered through all this bone were dark and busy. There were eyebrows above them, thinner than the mouth or the nostrils, black, curving out and up so that the men looked menacing and wasp-like. Lines of teeth and seashells hung round their necks, over grey, furry skin. Over the eyebrows the bone bulged up and swept back to be hidden under the hair. As the log came closer, Lok could see that the colour was not really bone white and shining but duller. It was more the colour of the big fungi, the ears that the people ate, and something like them in texture. Their legs and arms were stick-thin so that the joints were like the nodes in a twig.

Now that Lok was looking almost into the log he saw that it was much broader than before; or rather that it was the two logs moving side by side. There were more bundles and curious shapes in this log and a man lay among them on his side. His body and bone was like the others but his hair grew on his head in a mass of sharp points that glistened and looked hard as the points on a chestnut case. He was doing something to one of the sharp twigs and his curved stick lay beside him.

The logs sidled right into the bank. The man at the back—Lok thought of him as Pine-tree—spoke softly. Bush laid down his wooden leaf and caught hold of the grass of the bank. Chestnut-head took his curved stick and twig and stole across the logs until he was crouched on the earth itself. Lok and Fa were almost directly above him. They could smell his individual scent, a sea-smell, meat-smell, fearsome and exciting. He was so close that any moment he might wind them for all he was below them and Lok inhibited his own scent in sudden fear, though he did not know what he did. He reduced his breathing till it was the merest surface and the very leaves were more lively.

Chestnut-head stood under them in the sun pattern. The twig was across the curved stick. He looked this way and that round the dead tree, he inspected the ground, he looked forward again into the forest. He spoke sideways to the others in the boat out of his slit; soft twittering speech; the whiteness quivered.

Lok felt the shock of a man who has trusted to a bough that is not there. He understood in a kind of upside-down sensation that there was no Mal face, Fa face, Lok face concealed under the bone. It was skin.

Bush and Pine-tree had done something with strips of hide that joined the logs to the bushes. They got quickly out of the log and ran forward out of sight. Presently there was the sound of someone striking stone against wood. Chestnut-head crept forward too and was hidden.

There was nothing of interest now but the logs. They were very smooth and shiny inside where the wood could be seen and outside there were long smears like the whiteness on a rock when the sea has gone back and the sun has dried it. The edges were rounded, depressed in places where the hands of the bone-faces had rested. The shapes inside them were too various and numerous to be sorted. There were round stones, sticks, hides, there were bundles bigger than Lok, there were patterns of vivid red, bones that had grown into live shapes, the very ends of the brown leaves where the men held them were shaped like brown fish, there were smells, there were questions and no answers. Lok looked without seeing and the picture slid apart and came together again. Across the water there was no movement on the island.

Fa touched him on the hand. She was turning herself in the tree. Lok followed her carefully and they made themselves spy-holes that looked down into the clearing.

Already the familiar had altered. The tangle of bush and stagnant water to the left of the clearing was the same and so was the impenetrable marsh to the right. But where the trail through the forest touched the clearing thorn bushes were now growing thickly. There was a gap in these bushes and as they watched they saw Pine-tree come through the gap with another thorn bush over his shoulder. The stem was clean white and pointed. In the forest behind him the noise of chopping went on.

Fear was coming from Fa. It was not a shared picture but a general sense, a bitter smell, a dead silence and

agonized attention, a motionlessness and tensed awareness that began to call forth the same in him. Now, more
clearly than ever before there were two Loks, outside and
inside. The inner Lok could look for ever. But the outer
that breathed and heard and smelt and was awake always,
was insistent and tightening on him like another skin. It
forced the knowledge of its fear, its sense of peril on him
long before his brain could understand the picture. He
was more frightened than ever before in his life, more
than when he had crouched on a rock with Ha and a cat
had paced to and fro by a drained kill, looking up and
wondering whether they were worth the trouble.

Fa's mouth crept to his ear.

"We are shut in."

The thorn bushes spread. They were very thick where
there was an easy way into the clearing; but there were
others now, two lines of them by the stagnant water and
by the marsh. The clearing was a half-ring open only to
the water of the river. The three bone-faces came
through the last gap, with more thorn bushes. With these
they closed the way behind them.

Fa whispered in his ear.

"They know we are here. They do not want us to go
away."

All the same the bone-faces ignored them. Bush and
Pine-tree went back and the logs bumped each other.
Chestnut-head began to pace slowly round the line of
thorn bushes, keeping his face to the forest. Always the
bent stick was held with a twig across it. The thorn
bushes were up to his chest and when a bull bellowed
far off on the plains he froze, face lifted and the stick unbent a little. The woodpigeons were talking again and the

sun looked down into the top of the dead tree and breathed warmly on the two people.

Someone dug noisily in the water and the logs bumped. There were wooden knockings, draggings and bird speech; then two other men came from under the tree into the clearing. The first man was like the others. His hair gathered into a tuft on top of his head then spread so that it bobbed as he moved. Tuft went straight to the thorn bushes and began to watch the forest. He also had a bent stick and a twig.

The second man was unlike the others. He was broader and shorter. There was much hair on his body and his head-hair was sleek as if fat had been rubbed in it. The hair lay in a ball at the back of his neck. He had no hair on the front of his head at all so that the sweep of bone skin, daunting in its fungoid pallor, came right over above his ears. Now for the first time, Lok saw the ears of the new men. They were tiny and screwed tightly into the sides of their heads.

Tuft and Chestnut-head were crouching down. They were shifting leaves and blades of grass from the footprints that Fa and Lok had made. Tuft looked up and spoke:

"Tuami."

Chestnut-head followed the prints with outstretched hand. Tuft spoke to the broad man.

"Tuami!"

The broad man turned to them from the pile of stones and sticks which had occupied him. He threw a quick bird-noise, incongruously delicate, and they answered. Fa spoke in Lok's ear.

"It is his name——"

Tuami and the others were bent and nodding over the prints. Where the ground hardened towards the tree the footprints were invisible and when Lok expected the new men to put their noses to the ground they straightened up and stood. Taumi began to laugh. He was pointing towards the fall, laughing and twittering. Then he stopped, struck his palms loudly against each other, said one word and returned to the pile.

As though the one word had changed the clearing, the new men began to relax. Although Chestnut-head and Tuft still watched the forest, they stood, each at a side of the clearing, looking over the thorns and their sticks unbent. Pine-tree did not move any of the bundles for a while; he put one hand to his shoulder, pulled a piece of hide and stepped out of his skin. This hurt Lok like the sight of a thorn under a man's nail; but then he saw that Pine-tree did not mind, was glad in fact, was cool and comfortable in his own white skin. He was naked now like Lok, except that he had a piece of deerskin wound tightly round his thin waist and loins.

Now Lok could see two other things. The new people did not move like anything he had ever seen before. They were balanced on top of their legs, their waists were so wasp-thin that when they moved their bodies swayed backwards and forwards. They did not look at the earth but straight ahead. And they were not merely hungry. Lok knew famine when he saw it. The new people were dying. The flesh was sunken to their bones as Mal's flesh had sunken. Their movements, though they had in their bodies the bending grace of a young bough, were dream-slow. They walked upright and they should be dead. It was as though something that Lok could not see were supporting them, holding up their heads, thrusting them slowly and irresistibly forward. Lok knew that if he were as thin as they, he would be dead already.

Tuft had thrown his skin on the ground below the dead tree and was heaving at a great bundle. Chestnut-head came quickly to help him and they lifted together. Lok saw their faces crease as they laughed at each other and a sudden gush of affection for them pushed the heavy feeling down in his body. He could see how they shared the weight, felt in his own limbs the drag and desperate effort. Tuami came back. He took off his skin, stretched, scratched himself and knelt on the ground. He swept a patch bare of leaves until the brown earth showed. He had a little stick in his right hand and he talked to the other men. There was much nodding. The logs bumped and there was a noise of voices by the water. The men in the clearing stopped talking. Tuft and Chestnut-head began to move round the thorns again.

Then a new man appeared. He was tall and not as thin as the others. The hair under his mouth and above the head was grey and white like Mal's. It frizzed in a cloud and under it a huge cat-tooth hung from either ear. They could not see his face for his back was to them. In their heads they called him the old man. He stood looking down at Tuami and his harsh voice dived and struggled.

Tuami made more marks. They joined; and suddenly Lok and Fa shared a picture of the old woman drawing a line round the body of Mal. Fa's eyes flickered sideways at Lok and she made a tiny down-stabbing motion with one finger. Those men who were not on watch gathered round Tuami and talked to each other and to the old man. They did not gesticulate much nor dance

144

out their meanings as Lok and Fa might have done but their thin lips puttered and flapped. The old man made a movement with his arm and bent down to Tuami. He said something to him.

Tuami shook his head. The men went a little way from him and sat down in a row with only Tuft still on watch. Fa and Lok watched what Tuami was doing over the row of hairy heads. Tuami scrambled round the other side of the patch and they could see his face. There were upright lines between his eyebrows and the point of his tongue was moving after the line as he drew it. The line of heads began to twitter again. A man picked some small sticks and broke them. He shut them in his hand and each of the others took one from him.

Tuami got up, went to a bundle and pulled out a bag of leather. There were stones and wood, and shapes in it and he arranged them by the mark on the ground. Then he squatted down in front of the men, between them and the marked patch. Immediately the men began to make a noise with their mouths. They struck their hands together and the noise went with the sharp smacks. The noise swept and plunged and twisted yet always remained the same shape, like the hummocks at the foot of the fall that were rushing water yet always the same in the same place. Lok's head began to fill with the fall as though he had looked at it too long and it was sending him to sleep. The tightness of his skin had relaxed a little since he saw the new people liking each other. Now the flock was coming back into his head as the voices and the smack! smack! went on.

The shattering call of a rutting stag blared just under the tree. The flock left Lok's head. The men had bent till their various heads of hair swept the ground. The stag of all stags was dancing out into the clearing. He came round the line of heads, danced to the other side of the marks, turned and stood still. He blared his call again. Then there was silence in the clearing, while the woodpigeons talked to each other.

Tuami became very busy. He began to throw things on to the marks. He reached forward and made important movements. There was colour on the bare patch, colour of autumn leaves, red berries, the white of frost and the dull blackness that fire will leave on rock. The men's hair still lay on the ground and they said nothing.

Tuami sat back.

The skin that had tightened over Lok's body went wintry chill. There was another stag in the clearing. It lay where the marks had been, flat on the ground; it was racing along and yet, like the men's voices and the water below the fall, it stayed in the same place. Its colours were those of the breeding season, but it was very fat, its small dark eye spied Lok's eye through the ivy. He felt caught and cowered down in the soft wood where the food ran and tickled. He did not want to look.

Fa had his wrist and was drawing him up again. Fearfully he put his eye to the leaves and looked back at the flat stag; but it was hidden for men were standing in front of it. Pine-tree was holding a piece of wood in his left hand and it was polished and there was a branch or a piece of a branch sticking out of the farther side of it. One of Pine-tree's fingers was stretched along this branch. Tuami stood opposite him. He took hold of the other end of the wood. Pine-tree was talking to the standing stag and the flat stag. They could hear that he was pleading. Tuami raised his right hand in the air. The stag blared. Tuami struck hard and there was now a glistening stone biting into the wood. Pine-tree stood still for a moment or two. Then he removed his hand carefully from the polished wood and a finger remained stretched out on the branch. He turned away and came to sit with the others. His face was more like bone than it had been before, and he moved very slowly and with a stagger. The other men held up their hands and helped him down among them. He said nothing. Chestnut-head took out some hide and bound up his hand and both the stags waited until he had finished.

Tuami turned the wooden thing over and the finger lingered, then dropped off with a little plop. It lay on the foxy red of the stag. Tuami sat down again. Two of the men had their arms round Pine-tree who was leaning sideways. There was a great stillness so that the fall sounded nearer.

Chestnut-head and Bush stood up and went near the lying stag. They held their curved sticks in one hand and the red-feathered twigs in the other. The standing stag moved his man's hand as though he were sprinkling them with something, then he reached out and touched them each on the cheek with a frond of fern. They began to bend over the stag on the ground, stretching their arms down and their right elbows were rising behind them. Then there was a flick! flick! and two twigs were sticking in the stag by its heart. They bent down, pulled the twigs out and the stag made no movement. The seated men beat their hands together and made the water-hump sounds over and over till Lok yawned and licked

147

his lips. Chestnut-head and Bush were still standing with their sticks. The stag blared, the men bent till their hair was on the ground. The stag began to dance again. His dance prolonged the sound of voices. He came near; he passed under the tree and out of sight and the voices ceased. Behind them, between the dead tree and the river, the stag blared once more.

Tuami and Bush ran quickly to the thorns across the trail and pulled one aside. They stood each side of the opening, pulling back, and Lok could see that now their eyes were shut. Chestnut-head and Bush stole forward softly, their bent sticks raised. They passed through the opening, disappeared noiselessly into the forest and Tuami and Tuft let the thorns fall back.

The sun had moved so that the stag that Tuami had made was smelling at the shadow of the dead tree. Pine-tree was sitting on the ground under the tree and shivering a little. The men began to move slowly in the dream sloth of hunger. The old man came out from under the dead tree and began to talk to Tuami. Now his hair was tied tightly to his head and spots of sun slid over it. He walked forward and looked down at the stag. He reached out a foot and began to rub it round in the stag's body. The stag did nothing but allowed itself to be hidden. In a moment or two there was nothing on the ground but patches of colour and a head with a tiny eye. Tuami turned away, talking to himself, went to a bundle and rummaged. He brought out a spike of bone, heavy and wrinkled at one end like the surface of a tooth and fined down at the other to a blunt point. He knelt and began to rub this blunt point with a little stone and Lok could hear it scrape. The old man came close to him, pointed

148

to the bone, laughed in a roaring voice and pretended to thrust something into his chest. Tuami bent his head and went on rubbing. The old man pointed to the river and then to the ground and began to make a long speech. Tuami thrust the bone and stone into the hide by his waist, got up and passed under the dead tree out of sight.

The old man stopped talking. He sat carefully on a bundle near the centre of the clearing. The stag's head with its tiny eye was at his feet.

Fa spoke in Lok's ear:

"He went away before. He fears the other stag."

Lok had an immediate and vivid picture of the standing stag that had danced and blared. He shook his head in agreement.

EIGHT

F a shifted herself with great care and settled again. Lok, glancing sideways, saw her red tongue pass along her lips. A pause linked them and for a moment Lok saw two Fas who slid apart and could only be brought together by great firmness. The inside of the ivy was full of flying things that sang thinly or settled on his body so that the skin twitched. The shadows between the bars and patches of sunlight detached themselves and sank until the sunlight was on a different level. Odd sayings of Mal or the old woman swam up with pictures and mixed with the voices of the new people until he hardly knew which was which. It could hardly be the old man below them who was talking in Mal's voice of the summer land where the sun was as warm as a fire and fruit ripened all year long, nor could the overhang mix as it now did with the thorn bushes and bundles of the clearing. The feeling that was so unpleasant had sunk and spread like a pool. Lok was almost used to it.

There was a pain in his wrist. He opened his eyes and looked down irritably. Fa had her fingers round it and his flesh was raised painfully on either side of them. Then quite clearly he heard the new one mew. The bird-chatter and high laughter of the new people was lifted to a new height as though they had all become children. Fa was turning in the tree back to the river. For a while Lok

lay bemused by the sun and his mixture of waking
dreams and new people. Then the new one mewed again
so that Lok himself turned with Fa and peered through
to the river.

One of the two logs was moving in to the bank. Tuami
sat at the back, digging, and the remainder of the log was
full of people. They were women, for he could see their
naked and empty breasts. They were much smaller than
the men and they carried less of the removable fur on
their bodies. Their hair was less astonishing and elaborate than the men's. There was a crumpled look about
their faces and they were very thin. Between Tuami and
the bundles and crumpled women sat a creature who
caught Lok's eye so firmly that he had little time to inspect the others. She was a woman, too, she carried shining fur round her waist that rose and was looped over
either arm and formed a pouch at the back of her head.
Her hair gleamed black and was arranged round the bone
white of her face like the petals of a flower. Her shoulders
and breast were white, startlingly white by contrast, for
the new one was struggling over them. He was trying to
get away from the water and climbing over her shoulder
to that pouch of fur behind her, and she was laughing,
her face crumpled, mouth open, so that Lok could see
her strange, white teeth. There was too much to see and
he became eyes again that registered and perhaps would
later remember what now he was not aware of. The
woman was fatter than the others, as the old man had
been fatter; but she was not as old as he and there was
milk standing in the points of her breasts. The new one
had hold of her shining hair and was pulling himself up
while she tried to drag him down; her head was leaning

sideways, face up. The laughter rose like the charm of starlings. The log slid under the limit of his spy-hole and Lok heard the bushes sigh by the bank.

He turned to Fa. There was silent laughter in her face and she was shaking her head. She looked at him and he saw that there was water standing in her eyes so full that at any moment it might spill out into the hollows. She stopped laughing; her face crumpled till it looked as though she were bearing the pain of a long thorn in her side. Her lips came together, parted, and though she did not give it breath he knew she had spoken the word.

"Milk——"

The laughter faded and a babble of speech took its place. There were the heavy sounds of things being lifted out of the log and thrown on the bank. Lok stirred another hole into the ivy and looked down. By his side he knew that Fa had already done so.

The fat woman had calmed the new one. She stood by the water and he was sucking her breast. The other women were moving about, pulling at bundles or opening them with clever twists and flutters of their hands. One of them, Lok could see, was only a child, tall and thin, with deerskin wrapped round her waist. She was looking down at a bag that lay on the ground by her feet. One of the other women was opening it. As Lok watched he saw the bag change shape convulsively. The mouth opened, then Liku tumbled out. She fell on all fours, and leapt. He saw that there was a long piece of skin that led from her neck and as she leapt the woman fell on this and grabbed it. Liku turned over in the air and landed on her back with a thump. The starlings charmed again. Liku tugged, ran round, then squatted under the great tree.

Lok could see her round belly and how she was holding the little Oa against it. The woman who had opened the bag led the long skin round the tree and twisted it together. Then she went away. The fat woman moved towards Liku so that Lok could see the shiny top of her head and the thin white line where her hair divided. She spoke to Liku, knelt down, spoke again, laughing and the new one was at her breast. Liku said nothing but moved the little Oa up from her belly to her chest. The woman stood up and went away.

The girl came, hunger-slow, and squatted down about her own length away from Liku. She said nothing but watched her. For a while the two children looked at each other. Liku stirred. She picked something off the tree and put it in her mouth. The girl watched, straight lines appeared between her brows. She shook her head. Lok and Fa looked at each other and shook their heads eagerly. Liku took another piece of fungus from the tree and held it out to the girl, who backed away. Then she came forward, reached gingerly, and snatched the food. She hesitated, put the food to her mouth and began to chew. She looked quickly from side to side at the places where the other women had disappeared, then swallowed. Liku gave her another piece, so small that only children could eat it. The girl swallowed again. Then they were silent and looking at each other.

The girl pointed to the little Oa and asked a question, but Liku said nothing and for a time there was silence. They could see how she examined Liku from head to foot, and perhaps, though they could not see her face, Liku was doing the same. Liku took the little Oa from her chest and balanced her on her shoulder. Suddenly the girl laughed, showing her teeth and then Liku laughed and they were laughing together.

Lok and Fa were laughing too. The feeling in Lok had turned warm and sunny. He felt like dancing were it not for the outside-Lok who insisted on listening for danger.

Fa put her head to his.

"When it is dark we will take Liku and run away."

The fat woman came down to the water. She spread the furs and sat down and they saw that the new one was no longer with her. The furs slid down from her arms till she was naked to the waist, hair and skin gleaming in the sunlight. She lifted her arms to the back of her head, bowed, and began to work at the pattern in her hair. All at once the petals fell in black snakes that hung over her shoulders and breasts. She shook her head like a horse and the snakes flew back till they could see her breasts again. She took thin white thorns out of her head and put them in a little pile by the water. Then she felt in her lap and picked up a piece of bone that was divided like the fingers of a hand. She lifted the hand and passed the bone fingers through her hair again and again till the hair was no longer snakes, but a fall of shining black and the white line lay neatly along the top. She stopped playing with her hair and watched the two girls for a while, speaking to them every now and then. The thin girl was putting twigs together on the ground and joining them at the top. Liku was on all fours, watching her and saying nothing. The fat woman began to work at her hair; she twisted and pulled through, she smoothed, she passed the bone hand here and there, she bowed and ducked; and the hair was building into another pattern that humped up and then coiled close.

Lok heard Tuami speak. The fat woman took her fur quickly and slid it up to her shoulders so that her navel and the wide, white rump was hidden. Her breast only showed and the fur cradled them. She looked sideways under the tree and he knew she was talking to Tuami. She spoke with much laughter.

The old man spoke loudly from the clearing and now that Lok had attention for more than the children he understood how many new sounds there were. Some wood was being broken and a fire was crackling and people were beating things. Not only the old man but the others too were giving orders in their high bird-voices. Lok yawned happily. There would be darkness and a swift flight through the dark with Liku on his back.

Tuami went back under the tree and talked with the old man. Pine-tree came into sight in the back of a log. There was wood piled high in it and in the water behind it swam a group of the heavy logs from the clearing on the island. His shadow was before him now for the sun was just declining from the highest point of its flight through the sky. It blazed up at Lok from the broken water round the logs and made him blink. Pine-tree and the fat woman touched their heads of hair and talked to each other for a moment. Then the old man appeared under Lok and began to gesticulate and talk loudly. The fat woman laughed up at him, her chin lifted, she looked sideways at him and the reflections from the river plucked apart and quivered over her white skin. The old man went away again.

The children were close together. The thin girl was bending over her cave of twigs and Liku was squatting by her as far away from the dead tree as the strip of skin would reach. The thin girl was holding the little Oa in her hands, turning her over and over and examining her curiously. She spoke to Liku then put the little Oa carefully into the cave so that she lay down on her back. Liku gazed at the thin girl with eyes of adoration.

The fat woman stood up, smoothing her furs. She had hung a bright, glittering thing round her neck so that it lay between her breasts. Lok saw that it was one of the pretty, bending yellow stones that the people sometimes picked up and played with until they tired of them and threw them away. The fat woman stepped, swaying on her hips, and passed out of sight into the clearing. Liku was talking to the thin girl. They were pointing at each other.

"Liku!"

The thin girl laughed all over her face. She clapped her hands.

"Liku! Liku!"

She pointed to her own chest.

"Tanakil."

Liku regarded her solemnly.

"Liku."

The thin girl was shaking her head and Liku was shaking her head.

"Tanakil."

Liku spoke very carefully.

"Tanakil."

The thin girl leapt to her feet, shouted and clapped and laughed. One of the crumpled women came and stood looking down at Liku. Tanakil jabbered at her, pointed, nodding, then stopped and spoke to Liku carefully.

"Tanakil."

Liku screwed up her face.

"Tanakil."

They all three laughed. Tanakil went to the dead tree, examined it, talked, and picked off a piece of the yellow fungus that Liku had given her. She put it in her mouth. The crumpled woman screamed so that Liku fell over. The crumpled woman struck Tanakil's shoulder fiercely, screaming and shouting. Tanakil quickly put her hand to her mouth and pulled the fungus out. The woman smacked it out of her hand so that it fell in the river. She screamed at Liku who bolted back to the tree. The woman bent down to her, keeping out of reach and made fierce noices at her.

"Ah!" she said. "Ah!"

She turned on Tanakil, talking all the time and pushed her with one hand while she kept the other on her hip. She pushed and talked, urging Tanakil towards the clearing. Tanakil moved unwillingly, looking back. Then she too was out of sight. Liku crept to the cave of twigs, snatched up the little Oa and scuttled back to the tree again with the little Oa at her chest. The crumpled woman came back and looked at her. Some of the crumples smoothed out of her face. For a time she said nothing. Then she bent down, keeping the length of the skin away from Liku.

"Tamakil."

Liku did not move. The woman picked up a twig and held it out gingerly. Liku took it doubtfully, smelt it and dropped it on the ground. The woman spoke again.

"Tanakil?"

The woodpigeons talked for answer and the water light shivered up and down the woman's face.

"Tanakil!"

Liku said nothing. Presently the woman went away. Fa took her hand from Lok's mouth.

"Do not speak to her."

She frowned at him. The twitching of his skin diminished now that the woman was no longer near Liku. Outside-Lok reminded him to be careful.

There were raised voices in the clearing. Lok and Fa shifted round again. They could see great alterations. A good bright fire burned in the centre and its heavy smoke went straight up into the sky. There were caves built on either side of the clearing, overhangs of branches that the new people had brought with them in their logs. Most of the bundles had disappeared so that there was plenty of room near the fire. The people were gathered there and they were all talking. They were facing the old man who was talking back. They held out their arms to him all except Tuami who was standing to one side as though he were of a different people. The old man was shaking his head and shouting. The people turned inwards until they were a knot of backs and they muttered to each other. Then they were at the old man again, shouting. He shook his head, turned his back on them and bent into the overhang on the left. The people swarmed round Tuami, shouting still. He held up one hand and they were silent. He pointed to the stag's head that still lay on the ground, sticking out beyond the logs of the fire. He jerked his head at the forest, while the people clamoured again. The old man came out of the cave and held up a hand like Tuami. The people stilled for a moment.

The old man said one word, very loudly. Immediately there was a great shout from the people. Even their slow

158

movements quickened a little. The fat woman brought a curious bundle out of the cave. It was the whole skin of an animal but it wobbled as if the animal were made of water. The people brought hollow pieces of wood and held them under the animal which immediately made water in them. It filled each, for Lok could see the water flash when it fell in the wood. The fat woman was happy with the animal as she had been happy with the new one; all the people were happy, even the old man who grinned and laughed. The people carried their pieces of wood away to the fire, carefully holding them so that they would not spill, though there was much water in the river. They knelt or sat slowly and put the wood to their mouths and drank. Tuami knelt down grinning, by the fat woman, and the animal made water in his mouth. Fa and Lok cowered down in the tree with twisted faces. A lump was going up and down in Lok's throat. The food of the tree crawled over him and he grimaced as he absently popped them one after another in his mouth. He licked his lips, grimaced, and yawned again. Then he looked down at Liku.

The thin girl was back again. She smelt different, sour, but she was cheerful. She began to talk to Liku in the high bird language and presently Liku came a little way from the tree. Tanakil looked sideways to where the people were gathered round the fire, then came softly to Liku. She laid a hand on the strip of skin where it led round the trunk and began to untwist it. The strip came free. Tanakil twisted it round her wrist, making diving and turning movements like the summer flight of a swallow. She walked right round the tree and the strip came with her. She spoke to Liku, tugged gently and the two girls moved away together.

Tanakil talked all the time. Liku kept close to her and listened with both ears for they could see them twitch. Lok had to stir another hole to see where they went. Tanakil took Liku to look at a bundle.

Sleepily Lok changed his viewpoint until he could see the clearing. The old man was walking about restlessly and he held the grey hair under his mouth with one hand. Those people who were not on guard or arranging the fire were lying down, looking flat as dead men. The fat woman had gone into a cave again.

The old man decided something. Lok could see how his hand came away from his face. He clapped his hands loudly and began to speak. The men who were lying by the fire got up unwillingly. The old man was pointing to the river, urging them. There was silence from the men and then a great shaking of heads and sudden speech. The old man's voice became angry. He walked towards the water, stopped, spoke over his shoulder and pointed to the hollow logs. Slowly the dream men came forward over the tufts of grass and leafy earth. They talked softly to themselves and each other. The old man began to shout as the woman had shouted at Tanakil. The dream men came to the river bank and stood looking into the logs without movement or speech. The sour smell of the drink from the wobbling animal rose up to Lok like the decay of autumn. Tuami walked across the clearing and stood behind them.

The old man made a speech. Tuami, nodding went away, and a few moments later Lok heard chopping noises. The two other men took the strips of hide from the bushes, jumped into the water, pushed the back end of the first log out into the river and brought the other to the bank. They stood on either side of the end and began to lift. Then they both bowed into the log, gasping. The old man shouted again with both hands high in the air. Then he pointed. The men heaved again. Tuami came with a piece of a branch that was smoothly trimmed. The men began to tear away the soft earth of the bank. Lok turned round in his nest to look for Liku. He could see that Tanakil was showing her all manner of wonderful things, a line of sea shells that hung on a thread and an Oa so lifelike that at first Lok thought it was only asleep or perhaps dead. She held the strip of skin in her hand but it was slack, for Liku was keeping close to the bigger girl, looking up as she looked at Lok when he swung her or clowned for her. The straight lines of sunlight were slanting into the clearing from over the gap. The old man began to shout and at his voice the women came crawling and yawning out of the caves. He shouted again so that they shambled under the tree talking to each other as the men had done. Soon there was no one in sight but the guard and the two children.

A new sort of shouting started between the tree and the river. Lok turned round to see what was happening.

"A-ho! A-ho! A-ho!"

The new people, men and women, were leaning back. The log was looking at them, its snout resting on the log that Tuami had brought. Lok knew that this end was its snout because the log had eyes on either side. He had not seen them before because they had been under the white stuff which was now darkend and half washed off. The people were joined to the log by strips of skin. The old man was urging them and they leaned back, gasping, their feet pushing lumps of earth out of the soft ground.

They moved jerkily and the log followed them, watching all the time. Lok could see the lines in their faces and the sweat as they passed under the tree and out of sight. The old man followed them and the shouting went on.

Tanakil and Liku came back to the tree. Liku was holding Tanakil's wrist with one hand and the little Oa with the other. The shouting stopped and all the people trudged gloomily into sight and lined up by the river. Tuami and Pine-tree got into the water by the second log. Tanakil walked forward to see but Liku pulled away from her. Tanakil explained to her but Liku would not go near the water. Tanakil began to pull the strip of skin. Liku held on to the earth with hands and feet. Suddenly Tanakil began to scream at her like the crumple-faced woman. She picked up a stick, spoke in a biting sharp voice and began to pull again. Liku still held on and Tanakil hit her across the back with the stick. Liku howled and Tanakil pulled and beat.

"A-ho! A-ho! A-ho!"

The second log had its snout on the bank but this time it did not climb any further. It slipped back and the people fell over. The old man shouted at the top of his voice. He pointed furiously down the river, then at the fall, then into the forest and his voice raved all the time. The people shouted back at him. Tanakil stopped hitting Liku and watched the grown-ups. The old man was moving round stirring the people with his foot. Tuami was standing to one side, watching him like a log and saying nothing. Slowly the people got to their feet and laid hold of the strips again. Tanakil lost interest, turned away and knelt by Liku. She picked up small stones, threw them in the air and tried to catch them on the narrow back of her hand. Soon Liku was watching her again. The log climbed out on the bank, wagged and was firmly ashore. The people leant back and moved out of sight.

Lok looked down on Liku, happy in the sight of her round belly and the quiet now that Tanakil was no longer using her stick. He thought of the new one at the fat woman's breast and smiled sideways at Fa. Fa grinned at him wryly. She did not seem to be as happy as he was. The feeling inside him had sunk away and disappeared like the frost when the sun finds it on a flat rock. The people who were so miraculously endowed with possessions no longer seemed to him the immediate menace they had been earlier. Even outside-Lok was lulled and not so sharp on sounds and smells. He yawned hugely and pressed his palms into his eye-sockets. The flock was swarming, drifting along as when in high summer a wind cards it out of the bushes of the plain and the air is full of drifting streamers. He could hear Fa whispering outside him.

"Remember that we shall take them when it is dark."

A picture came to him of the fat woman laughing and giving milk.

"How will you feed him?"

"I will half-eat for him. And perhaps the milk will come."

He thought of this. Fa spoke once more.

"Presently the new people will sleep."

The new people were not yet asleep or anything near it. They were making more noise than ever. Both logs were in the clearing, lying across thick, round branches. The people were grouped round the last one and screaming at the old man. He was pointing fiercely at the way into the forest and making his bird-noises flutter and twist. The people were shaking their heads, freeing themselves from the lines of skin, moving away towards the caves. The old man was shaking his fists at the sky where the air was darkest blue, was beating his head with his fists; but the people moved in their dream of walking to the fire and the caves. When he was quite alone by the trunks of wood he fell silent. There was the beginning of darkness under the trees and the sunlight was lifting from the ground.

The old man walked very slowly towards the river. Then he stopped and they could see no expression on his face, but he went back quickly to his cave and disappeared inside. Lok heard the fat woman speak and then the old man came out. He walked towards the river slowly, in the same footsteps, and this time he did not pause by the logs but came straight on. He passed under the tree, stood between the tree and the river, looking down at the children.

Tanakil was teaching Liku to catch, the stick forgotten. When she saw the old man she stood up, put her hands behind her and rubbed one foot over the other. Liku did this too as well as she could. The old man said nothing for a while. Then he jerked his head at the clearing and spoke sharply. Tanakil took the end of the strip of skin in her hand and walked under the tree with Liku following. Turning carefully in the tree, Lok saw them go into a cave. When he looked back on the river side the old man was standing and making water over the edge of the bank. The sunlight had left the river and was caught in the treetops on the other side. There was a great redness over the fall and the gap and the water sounded very loud. The old man came back to the tree, stood under it and peered carefully towards the thorns where the guard was standing. Then he went to the other side of the tree and looked again, and all round. He came back, and leaned against the tree facing the water. He put his hand inside the skin of his chest and pulled out a lump. Lok smelt, saw and recognized. The old man was eating the meat that had been intended for Liku. They could hear him as he leaned there, head bent, elbows out, tearing, pulling and chewing. He sounded busy at his meat as a beetle in dead wood.

Someone was coming. Lok heard him but the old man, caught between the sounds of his two jaws, did not. The man came round the tree, saw the old man, stopped, howled with fury. It was Pine-tree. He ran back to the clearing, stood by the fire and began to shout at the top of his voice. Figures pulled themselves out of the dark caves, men and women. The darkness was swarming over the ground and Pine-tree kicked the fire so that sparks and flames shot up. Then there was a flood of firelight to wrestle with the swarm of darkness under the still, bright sky. The old man was shouting by the logs; Pine-tree was shouting and pointing at him and the fat woman came out of a cave with the new one squirming over her shoulder. All at once the people made a rush. The old man jumped into one of the logs, picked up a wooden leaf and brandished it. The fat woman began to scream at the people and the noise was so great that birds flapped in the trees. Now the old man's voice had the dusk to itself. The people were a little quieter. Tuami who had said nothing, but stood by the fat woman, said something now and the people took up and repeated what he said. Their voices were louder again. The old man was pointing at the stag's head where it lay by the fire but the noise of the people saying one word over and over again sounded as if they were coming nearer. The fat woman ducked into her cave and Lok could see the people fasten their eyes on the entrance. She came out not with the new one but with the animal that wobbled. At this the people shouted and clapped their hands. They moved away quickly and brought the hollow pieces of wood and the animal on the fat woman's shoulder made water into them. The people drank and Lok could see how the bones of their throats moved in the firelight. The old man was waving them back to their caves but they would not go. They came back to the fat woman and got more to drink. The fat woman was not laughing now but looking from the old man to the people and then to Tuami. He was close to her and his face was smiling. The fat woman tried to take the animal back into the cave but Pine-tree and a woman would not let her. At that the old man rushed forward and the knot of them began to struggle together. Tuami stood by the struggle watching as though the people were something he had drawn in the air with his stick. More of the people joined in. The crowd was turning round and round and the fat woman was screaming. The wobbling animal slid off her shoulder and disappeared. Some of the people fell on top of it. Lok heard a watery sound and then the heap of people sank a little. They staggered apart and there was the animal flat on the ground, flat as the stag that Tuami had made, but far more dead-looking.

The old man made himself very tall.

Lok yawned. These sights would not join together. His eyes closed, jerked open. The old man had both arms stretched up in the air. He was facing the people and the voice he used was frightening them. They had moved a little back. The fat woman sneaked into a cave. Tuami had disappeared. The old man's voice rose, finished, his hands fell. There was silence and fear and a sour smell from the dead animal.

For a while the people said nothing but stayed, crouched a little, leaning away. Suddenly one of the women rushed forward. She screamed up at the old man, she rubbed her belly, she held out her breasts for him to look at, she spat at him. The people began to move again. There was nodding and shouting. The old man shouted the others down and pointed to the head of the stag. Then there was silence. The people's eyes turned in and down to the stag that still watched Lok with its little eye through the spy-hole.

There was a noise in the forest outside the clearing. Gradually the people became aware of it. Someone was howling. The thorns moved, opened; Chestnut-head, blood glistening all down his left leg, hopped through, holding on to Bush. When he saw the fire, he lay down, and a woman ran to him. Bush came forward towards the people.

Lok's eyelids fell and bounced open again. For a dreamy moment he saw himself in a picture telling all this to Liku who would not understand it any more than he did.

The fat woman appeared by the cave and she had the new one sucking at her breast. Bush was asking a question. A shout answered him. The woman who had held out her empty breast was pointing to the old man, the dead tree, and to the people. Chestnut-head spat at the stag's head and the people shouted again, moving forward. The old man lifted up his hands and began that same high, menacing speech but the people jeered and laughed. Chestnut-head stood by the stag's head. They could see his eyes gleaming in the firelight like two stones. He began to draw a twig from his waist and he held the bent stick in his other hand. He and the old man watched each other.

The old man took a step sideways and talked rapidly. He reached the fat woman, put out his hands and tried to take the new one from her. She bent quickly and snapped at his hand with her mouth as any woman would, so that the old man danced and howled. Chestnut-head put the twig across the bent stick and pulled the red feathers back. The old man stopped dancing and went towards him, hands out, palms facing the twig. He stood still almost within reach of Chestnut-head, curled the fingers of his right hand all except the long one. This one he moved sideways until it was pointing at one of the caves. All the people were very silent. The fat woman laughed in a high voice and was still again. Tuami was watching the old man's back. The old man glanced round the clearing, peered out to where the darkness was crowded under the trees and then back at the people. None of them said anything.

Lok yawned and backed down into the hollow of the treetop where he was protected from the sight of the people and their whole camp was nothing but a flicker of reflected light over the trees. He looked up at Fa, inviting her to sleep at his side but she did not notice him.

He could see her face and her eyes peering through the ivy and unblinkingly open. So concentrated was she that even when he touched her leg with his hand she did nothing but went on staring. He saw her mouth open and her breathing quicken. She gripped the rotten wood of the dead trunk so that it crunched and crumbled into wet pulp. Despite his tiredness this interested Lok and frightened him a little. He had a picture of one of the people climbing the tree, so he struggled back and began to stir the leaves open. Fa glanced sideways quickly and her face was like the face of a sleeper who wrestles with a terrible dream. She grabbed his wrist and forced him down. She gripped him by the shoulders and burrowed her face against his chest. Lok put his arm round her and outside-Lok felt a warm pleasure in the touch. But Fa had no wish to play. She knelt up again, pulled him towards her and held his head against her breast while her face looked downwards through the leaves and her heart beat urgently against his cheek. He tried to see what it was that made her so afraid but when he struggled she held him close and all he could see was the angle of her jaw and her eyes, open, open for ever, watching.

The flock came back and her body was warm. Lok yielded, knowing that she would wake him when the people slept and they could run away with the children. He burrowed close, holding, pillowed over the thumping heart with the tight arms round him so that the flock, swarming now in the darkness became a whole world of exhausted sleep.

NINE

He awoke to fight with arms that were pressing him down, arms holding his shoulder and a hand smothering his face. He talked and bubbled against the fingers, ready almost to bite them from the new habit of terror. Fa's face was close to his and she was holding him down as he threshed against the leaves and moulded tinder wood.

"Quiet!"

She had spoken louder than ever before in the tree, had spoken in more than an ordinary voice as though the people were no longer all round them. He ceased to struggle and was properly awake, noticing how the light was leaping over the dark leaves making spots in their darkness that jumped this way and that together. There were many stars over the tree and they were small and dying by contrast. Sweat was streaming down Fa's face and the skin of her body where he touched it was wet. As he noticed her he heard the new people also for they were noisy as a pack of wolves in cry. They were shouting, laughing, singing, babbling in their bird speech, and the flames of their fire were leaping madly with them. He turned over and poked his fingers into the leaves to see what was happening.

The clearing was full of firelight. They had pulled ashore the great logs that had swum across the river behind Pine-tree and stood them on end over the fire so that they leaned against each other. There was nothing warm and comfortable about this fire—it was like the fall, like a cat. He could see part of the log that had killed Mal leaning against the pile and the hard, ear-like fungi were red hot. The flames came squirting out of the top of the pile as though they were being squeezed from below, they were red and yellow and white and they shot small sparks straight up out of sight. The tops of the flames where they faded out were level with Lok and the blue smoke round them was almost invisible. From the pile with its fountain of flame, light beat round the clearing, not warm light but fierce, white-red and blinding. This light pulsed like a heart so that even the trees round the clearing with their drifts of curling leaves seemed to jump sideways like the holes between the leaves of ivy.

The people were like the fire, made of yellow and white, for they had thrown off their furs and wore nothing but the binding of skin round their waists and loins. They jumped sideways in time with the trees and their hair was fallen or awry so that Lok could not easily tell the difference between the men among them. The fat woman was leaning against one of the hollow logs, her hands braced on either side of her and she was naked to the waist so that her body was yellow and white. Her head was back, throat curved, mouth open and laughing while her loose hair swung down into the hollow of the log. Tuami was crouched by her, his face against her left wrist; and he was moving, not only jerkily back and forth with the firelight but up, his mouth creeping, his fingers playing, moving up as though he were eating her flesh, moving up towards her naked shoulder. The old man was lying in the other hollow log, his feet sticking out either side. He held a round stone thing in his hand which he put to his mouth every now and then and in between whiles he was singing. The other men and women were scattered round the clearing. They held more of these round stones and now Lok saw that they were drinking from them. His nose caught the scent of what they drank. It was sweeter and fiercer than the other water, it was like the fire and the fall. It was a bee-water, smelling of honey and wax and decay, it drew toward and repelled, it frightened and excited like the people themselves. There were other stones nearer the fire with holes in their tops and the smell seemed to come particularly strongly from them. Now Lok saw that when the people had finished their drink they came to these and lifted them and took more to drink. The girl Tanakil was lying in front of one of the caves, flat on her back as if she were dead. A man and a woman were fighting and kissing and screeching and another man was crawling round and round the fire like a moth with a burnt wing. Round and round he went, crawling, and the other people took no notice of him but went on with their noise.

Tuami had reached the fat woman's neck. He was pulling her and she was laughing and shaking her head and squeezing his shoulder with her hand. The old man sang and the people fought, the man crawled round the fire, Tuami burrowed at the fat woman and all the time the clearing jumped back and forth, sideways.

There was plenty of light for Lok to see Fa. The jerking tired his eyes for they tried to follow it, so he turned his head and looked at her instead. She too was jerking but not so much; and apart from the light her face was very still. Her eyes looked as though they had neither blinked nor shifted since before he fell asleep. The pictures in his head came and went like the firelight. They meant nothing and they began to spin till his head felt as if it would split. He found words for his tongue but his tongue hardly knew how to use them.

"What is it?"

Fa did not move. A kind of half-knowledge, terrible in its very formlessness, filtered into Lok as though he were sharing a picture with her but had no eyes inside his head and could not see it. The knowledge was something like that sense of extreme peril that outside-Lok had shared with her earlier; but this was for inside-Lok and he had no room for it. It pushed into him, displacing the comfortable feeling of after sleep, the pictures and their spinning, breaking down the small thoughts and opinions, the feeling of hunger and the urgency of thirst. He was possessed by it and did not know what it was.

Fa turned her head sideways slowly. The eyes with their twin fires came round like the eyes of the old woman moving up through the water. A movement round her mouth—not a grimace or preparation for speech—set her lips fluttering like the lips of the new people; and then they were open again and still.

"Oa did not bring them out of her belly."

At first the words had no picture connected with them but they sank into the feeling and reinforced it. Then Lok peered through the leaves again for the meaning of the words and he was looking straight at the fat woman's mouth. She was coming towards the tree, holding on to Tuami, and she staggered and screeched with laughter so that he could see her teeth. They were not broad and useful for eating and grinding; they were small and two were longer than the others. They were teeth that remembered wolf.

The fire collapsed with a roar and a torrent of sparks. The old man was no longer drinking but lying still in the hollow log and the other people were sitting or flat and the singing noise was dying like the fire. Tuami and the fat woman passed erratically under the tree and disappeared so that Lok moved round to watch them. The fat woman made for the water but Tuami caught her arm and pulled her round. They stood like that looking at each other, the fat woman pale on one side from the moon, ruddy on the other from the fire. She laughed up at Tuami and stuck her tongue out while he spoke quickly to her. Suddenly he grabbed her with both hands and pulled her against his chest and they wrestled, gasping without speech. Tuami shifted his grip, got her by a hank of long hair and dragged it down till her face lifted, contorted with pain. She stuck the nails of her right hand into his shoulder and dragged down as her hair was dragged. Tuami thrust his face against hers and lurched so that one knee was behind her. He shifted his hand up until it was gripping the back of her head. The hand that was gripped into the flesh of his shoulder slackened, fumbled, reached round him and suddenly they were bound together, straining together, loins against loins and mouth against mouth. The fat woman began to slide down so that Tuami was bending over. He fell clumsily on one knee and her arms were round his neck. She lay back in the moonlight, her eyes shut, her body limp and her breast moving up and down. Tuami was kneeling and fumbling in the fur about her waist. He made a kind of snarling sound and threw himself upon her. Now Lok could see the wolf teeth again. The fat woman was moving her face from side to side and it was contorted as it had been when she struggled against Tuami.

He turned back to Fa. She was still kneeling, looking out into the clearing at the red-hot heap of wood and the sweat on her skin glistened faintly. He had a sudden and brilliant picture of himself and Fa taking the children and racing away through the clearing. He became alert. He put his head by her mouth and whispered.

"Shall we take the children now?"

She leaned away from him so that she was far enough off to see him clearly in the now dim light. She shuddered suddenly as though the moonlight that fell on the tree were wintry.

"Wait!"

The two people beneath the tree were making noises fiercely as though they were quarrelling. In particular the fat woman had begun to hoot like an owl and Lok could hear Tuami gasping like a man who fights with an animal and does not think he will win. He looked down at them and saw that Tuami was not only lying with the fat woman but eating her as well for there was black blood running from the lobe of her ear.

Lok was excited. He reached out and laid a hand on Fa but she had only to turn her eyes of stone upon him and she was immediately surrounded by that same incomprehensible feeling, that worse than Oa feeling which he recognized but could not understand. He took his hand hurriedly from her body and began to stir with it in the leaves until he had a spy-hole that looked at the fire and the clearing. Most of the people had gone into the caves. The old man's feet were the only part of him that was to be seen resting on the sides of the hollow logs. The man who had crawled round the fire was lying on his face among the round stones that held the bee-water, and the hunter who had been on guard was still standing by the thorn fence, leaning on a stick. As Lok watched, this man began to slip down the stick until he collapsed near the thorns and lay still with the moonlight gleaming dully on his bare skin. Tanakil had gone and the crumpled women with her so that the clearing was little but a space round a dull red heap of wood.

He turned round and looked down at Tuami and the fat woman who had risen to a rowdy climax and now lay still, glistening with sweat and smelling of flesh and the honey from the stones. He glanced at Fa who was still silent and terrible and who looked at a picture that was not there in the darkness of the ivy. He dropped his eyes and automatically began to feel over the rotten wood for something to eat. But suddenly as he did so he discovered his thirst and once discovered it would not be ignored. Restlessly he peered down at Tuami and the fat woman for of all the astonishing and inexplicable events that had taken place in the clearing they were at once the most understandable and at the same time the most interesting.

Their fierce and wolflike battle was ended. They had fought it seemed against each other, consumed each other rather than lain together so that there was blood on the woman's face and the man's shoulder. Now, the fighting done and peace restored between them, or whatever state it was that was restored, they played together. Their play was complicated and engrossing. There was no animal on the mountain or the plain, no lithe and able creature of the bushes or forest that had the subtlety and imagination to invent games like these, nor the leisure and incessant wakefulness to play them. They hunted down pleasure as the wolves will follow and run down horses; they seemed to follow the tracks of the invisible prey, to listen, head tilted, faces concentrated and withdrawn in the pale light for the first steps of its secret approach. They sported with their pleasure when they had it fast, as a fox will play with the fat bird she has caught, postponing the death because she has the will to put off and enjoy twice over the pleasure of eating. They were silent now except for little grunts and gasps and an occasional gurgle of secret laughter from the fat woman.

A white owl swept over the tree and a moment later Lok heard his note that always sounded farther away than it was. The sight of Tuami and the fat woman was not as rousing as it had been when they fought together and they were powerless to put down the presence of his thirst. He dared not speak to Fa not only because of her strange remoteness but also because Tuami and the fat woman made so little noise now that speech was dangerous again. He became restless to take the children and run.

The fire was a very dull red and its light hardly reached to the wall of branches buds and twigs round the clearing so that they had begun to be a pattern of darkness against the brighter sky behind them. The ground of the clearing was so sunken in gloom that Lok had to use his night sight to see it. The fire was isolated and seemed to float. Tuami and the fat woman came from beneath the tree unsteadily and they did not walk together but made their way waist deep in shadows to separate caves. Now the fall roared and the voices of the forest, crepitations and scuttering of unseen feet were audible. Another white owl drifted through the clearing and away across the river.

Lok turned to Fa and whispered.

"Now?"

She came close. There was in her voice the same urgency and command as when she had bidden him obey her on the terrace.

"I shall take the new one and jump the thorns. When I have gone, follow."

Lok thought but no picture would come.

"Liku——"

Her hands tightened on his body.

"Fa says 'Do this!' "

He moved quickly so that the ivy leaves brushed each other harshly.

"But Liku——"

"I have many pictures in my head."

Her hands left him. He lay in the treetop and all the pictures of the day began to spin once more. He heard her breathing pass by him and sink into the ivy that rustled again so that he looked quickly into the clearing, but no one stirred. He could just make out the old man's feet sticking out of the hollow log and the holes of deep black where the branch caves were. The fire floated, dull red for the most part, but with a brighter heart where blue flames wandered over the wood. Tuami came out of the cave, stood by the fire, looking down at it. Fa was already half out of the ivy and clinging to the thick branches in the river side of the tree. Tuami took a branch and began to rake the hot ashes together so that they sparkled and sent up a puff of smoke and winking points. The crumpled woman crept out and took the branch from him and for a moment or two they stood swaying and talking. Tuami went away into a cave and the moment after Lok heard a crash as he fell among dry leaves. He waited for the woman to go; but first she dug earth round the fire until there was nothing but a black hummock with a glowing mouth at the top. She carried a sod to the fire and dumped it on the mouth so that the grass flared and crackled while a wave of light shook out over the clearing. She stood, quivering at the end of her long shadow, the light faltered and went out. He half heard, half sensed her as she went feeling towards the cave, fell on hands and knees and crawled inside.

His night-sight came back to him. The clearing was very still again and he heard the noise of Fa's skin scraping against the old bark of the tree as she let herself down. An immediacy of danger came to him; the knowledge that they were about to cheat these strange people and all their inscrutable works, the awful knowledge of Fa creeping towards them caught him by the throat so that he could not breathe and his heart began to shake him. He gripped the rotten wood and cowered behind the ivy with his eyes shut, seeking without knowing for those hours when the dead tree was relatively safe. The scent of Fa rose up to him from the fireward side of the tree and he shared a picture with her of a cave with a great bear standing at the mouth of it. The scent ceased to rise, the picture disappeared and he knew that she had become eyes and ears and nose crawling noiselessly towards the cave by the fire.

His heart slowed a little and his breathing so that he could look again at the clearing. The moon soared from the edge of a thick cloud and poured a grey blue light over the forest. He could see Fa, flattened by the light, clutched down to the ground and not more than twice her length from the dark mound of the fire. The cloud was succeeded by another and the clearing was full of darkness. Over by the thorns that blocked the entry to the trail he heard the guard choke and struggle to his feet. There came the sound of vomiting and then a long moan. Feelings mixed themselves in Lok. He had a half-thought that the new people might choose suddenly to be as they were; to stand up, talk and be wary or infinitely knowing and secure in their strength. With this was mixed a picture of Fa not daring to run first across the log by the terrace; and this feeling of warmth and urgent desire to be with her was part of it. He moved in the ivy cup, parted the leaves towards the river and felt for the branches on the trunk. He let himself down quickly before the feelings had time to change and make an obedient Lok of him; he stood in the long grass at the foot of the dead tree. Now the thought of Liku possessed him and he crept past the tree and tried to see which cave contained her. Fa was moving towards the cave on the right of the fire. Lok moved to the left, he sank on all fours and crept towards the cave that had grown beyond the logs and the pile of unsorted bundles. The hollow logs were lying where the people had left them as though they too had drunk of the honey drink and the old man's feet still stuck out of the nearer one. Lok cowered under the height of the log and sniffed cautiously at the foot above him. It had no toes or rather—now he was able to get so close to it—it was covered in hide like the peoples' waists and it smelt strongly of cow and sweat. Lok lifted his eyes above his nose and looked over the edge of the log. The old man was lying full length in it, his mouth open, and he was snoring through his thin, pointed nose. The hair prickled on Lok's body and he ducked down as though the old man's eyes had been open. He cowered in the torn earth and grass by the log, and now that his nose was adjusted to the old man, it discounted him, for there were many other bits of information coming to it. The logs, for example, were connected with the sea. The white on their sides was sea-white, bitter and evocative of beaches and the ceaseless progression of the waves. There was the smell of pine-tree gum, of a peculiarly thick and fiery sort of mud that his nose could identify as different but not name. There were the smells of many men and women and children and, finally, most obscurely but none the less powerfully, there was the smell compounded of many that had sunk beneath the threshold of separate identification into the one smell of extreme age.

Lok stilled his flesh and the pricking of his hair and crawled along by the log until he came to where the round stones had been left a little way from the hot but lightless fire. They maintained their own atmosphere, a smell so powerful that his mind could see it like a glow or a cloud round the holes in the top. The smell was like the new people, it repelled and attracted, it daunted and enticed, it was like the fat woman and at the same time like the terror of the stag and the old man. Lok was reminded of the stag so strongly that he cowered again; but he could not remember where the stag had gone nor where it came from except that it approached the clearing from behind the dead tree. He turned then, looked up and saw the dead tree with its ivy, vast, shock-headed and impending from the clouds like a cave-bear. He crawled quickly to the hut on the left. The guard over by the thorns groaned again.

Lok smelt his way along the leaning branches at the back of the cave and found a man and a man and another man. There was no smell of Liku unless a sort of generalized smell in his nostrils so faint as to be nothing but an awareness might be connected with her. Wherever he cast over the ground the awareness persisted and would not be tracked down to a source. He grew bold. He gave up his random and fruitless casting and made for the open side of the cave. First the people had set up two sticks and laid one other long stick across the top. Then they had leaned innumerable branches against the long stick so that they formed a leafy overhang in the clearing. There were three of these, one to the left, one to the right, and one between the fire and the thorns where the guard was. The cut ends of the branches had been forced into the earth in a curving line. Lok crawled to the end of the line and put his head round it cautiously. The noise of breathing and snoring that came from the shapes inside was irregular and loud. Someone was asleep not an arm's length from his face. The someone grunted, belched, turned and an arm fell over so that the open palm of the hand brushed Lok's face. He jerked back, quivering, then leant forward and smelt the hand. It was pale, glistening slightly, helpless and innocent as Mal's hand. But it was narrower and longer and of a different colour in its fungoid whiteness.

There was a narrow space between the arm and the place where the ends of the branches slanted into the earth. The picture of Liku so maddeningly present and so hidden drove him forward. He did not know what this feeling required him to do but knew that he must do something. He began to draw his body forward slowly into the narrow space like a snake sliding into a hole. He felt breath on his face and froze. There was a face not a hand's length from his own. He could feel the tickle of the fantastic hair, could see the long, useless cliff of bony skull that prolonged the head above the eyebrows. He could see the dull gleam of an eye beneath a lid that was not tightly shut, see the irregular wolf's teeth, feel now the honey-sour breath on his cheek. Inside-Lok shared a picture of terror with Fa but outside-Lok was coldly brave and still as ice.

Lok passed his arm over the sleeping man and felt space, then leaves and earth on the other side. He put the palm of his hand firmly in the space and prepared to pass his body over on hand and foot, arching away from the sleeper. As he did so the man spoke. The words were deep in his throat as though he had no tongue and they interfered with his breathing. His chest began to rise and fall quickly. Lok whipped his arm back and crouched again. The man threshed about in the leaves; his clenched fist smacked a shower of lights out of Lok's eye. Lok shrank back and the man arched so that his belly was higher than his head. All the time the tongueless words were struggling and the arms beat about among the sloping branches. The man's head turned to Lok and he could see that his eyes were staring wide open, staring at nothing, turning with the head like the eyes of the old woman in the water. They looked through him and the fear contracted on his skin. The man was jerking his body higher and higher, the words had become a series of croaks that grew louder and louder. There was a noise coming from one of the other huts, the shrill chatter of women and then a terrified screech. The man by Lok fell over on his side, staggered up and struck away the branches so that they fell in a pile. The man staggered forward and his croaks became a shout that someone answered. Other men were struggling in the cave, knocking down the boughs and shouting. By the thorns the guard was stumbling round and fighting with shadows. A figure stood up out of the wreckage by Lok, saw the first man dimly and swung a great stick at him. All at once the darkness of the clearing was full of people who fought and screamed. Someone was kicking the sods of earth away from the fire so that a dim glow and then a burst of flame lit up the crowded ground and ring of trees. The old man was standing there, his grey hair swirling round his head and face. Fa was there, running and empty-handed. She saw the old man and swerved. A figure by Lok swung a huge stick with so much purpose that Lok grabbed it. Then he was rolling with a tangle of limbs and teeth and claws. He pulled away and the tangle went on fighting and snarling. He saw Fa rise and dive at the top of the thorns and vanish over them, saw the old man, a demented picture of hair and gleaming eyes, swing a stick with a lump on the end into the heap of struggling men. As Lok flung himself over the thorns he saw the guard fighting to get through them. He landed on his hands and ran till bushes clutched at him. He saw the guard fly past, with bent stick and twig ready, duck

184

under the curved bough of a beech tree and disappear into the forest.

There was a fire burning brightly now in the clearing. The old man was standing by it and the other men were picking themselves up. The old man shouted and pointed until one of the men staggered to the thorns and ran after the guard. The women were crowding round the old man and the child Tanakil was among them with the backs of her hands to her eyes. The two men came running back, shouted at the old man and fought their way through the thorns into the clearing. Now Lok could see that the women were throwing branches on the fire, the branches that had made them a cave. The fat woman was there, twisting one hand over the other and wailing with the new one on her shoulder. Tuami was talking urgently to the old man, pointing to the forest and then down at the ground where the stag's head was. The fire grew; whole sprays of leaves burst into light with an explosive crackle so that the trees of the clearing were to be seen as clearly as by day. The people crowded round the fire, keeping their backs to it, and facing outward at the darkness of the forest. They went quickly to the caves and hurried back with branches and the fire pulsed out light with each addition. They began to bring whole skins of animals and wrap them round their bodies. The fat woman had ceased to wail for she was feeding the new one. Lok could see how the women stroked him fearfully, talked to him, offered him the shells from their necks and always looked outward to the dark ring of trees that trapped the firelight. Tuami and the old man were still talking urgently to each other with much nodding. Lok felt himself secure in the darkness but understood the impervious power of the people in the light. He called out:

"Where is Liku?"

He saw the people still their bodies and shrink. Only the child Tanakil began to scream until the crumpled woman seized her by the arm and shook her into silence.

"Give me Liku!"

Chestnut-head was listening sideways in the firelight, searching for the voice with his ear and his bent stick was rising.

"Where is Fa?"

The stick shrank and straightened suddenly. A moment later something brushed by in the air like the wing of a bird; there came a dry tap, then a wooden bounce and clatter. A woman rushed to the cave where Lok had crawled and brought a whole sheaf of branches and dumped them on the fire. The dark silhouettes of the people gazed into the forest inscrutably.

Lok turned away and trusted to his nose. He cast across the trail, found the scent of Fa and the scent of the two men who had followed her. He trotted forward, nose to the ground, along the scent that would bring him back to Fa. He had a great desire to hear her speak again and to touch her with his body. He moved faster through the darkness that preceded dawn and his nose told him, pace by pace, the whole story. Here were Fa's prints, far apart as she fled, the grip of her toes forcing back a little half-moon of earth out of the ground. He found that he could see more clearly now that he was away from the firelight for the dawn was breaking behind the trees. Once more the thought of Liku came to him. He turned back, swung himself into the cleft trunk of a beech tree and looked through the branches at the clearing. The guard who had run after Fa was dancing in front of the new people. He crawled like a snake, he went to the wreck of the caves; he stood; he came back to the fire snapping like a wolf so that the people shrank from him. He pointed; he created a running, crouching thing, his arms flapped like the wings of a bird. He stopped by the thorn bushes, sketched a line in the air over them, a line up and up towards the trees till it ended in a gesture of ignorance. Tuami was talking rapidly to the old man. Lok saw him kneel by the fire, clear a space and begin to draw on it with a stick. There was no sign of Liku and the fat woman was sitting in one of the hollow logs with the new one on her shoulder.

Lok let himself down to the ground, found Fa's tracks once more and ran along them. Her steps were full of terror so that his own hair rose in sympathy. He came to a place where the hunters had stopped and he could see how one of them had stood sideways till his toeless feet made deep marks in the earth. He saw the gap between steps where Fa had leapt in the air and then her blood, dropping thickly, leading in an uneven curve back from the forest to the swamp where the tree-trunk had been. He followed her into a tangle of briar that the hunters had threshed over. He went in deeper than they, heedless of the thorns that tore his skin. He saw where her feet like his own had plunged terribly in the mud and left an open hole that was filling now with stagnant water. Before him the surface of the marsh was polished and awesome. The bubbles had ceased to rise from the bottom and any brown mud that had been whipped up to make coils in the top water had sunk again as if nothing had happened. Even the scum and the weed and clustering frog's spawn had drifted back and lay motionless in the dead water under the dirty boughs. The steps and the blood came thus far; there was the scent of Fa and her terror; and after that, nothing.

TEN

The drab light increased, silvered, and the black water of the marshes shone. A bird squawked among the islands of reed and briar. Far off, the stag of all stags blared and blared again. The mud round Lok's ankles tightened so that he had to balance with his arms. There was an astonishment in his head and beneath the astonishment a dull, heavy hunger that strangely included the heart. Automatically his nose inquired of the air for food and his eyes turned this way and that among the mud and tangles of briar. He lurched, bent his toes and drew his feet out of the mud and staggered to firmer land. The air was warm and tiny flying things sang thinly like the note that comes in the ears after a blow on the head. Lok shook himself but the high thin note continued and the heavy feeling weighed on his heart.

Where the trees began were bulbs with green points that just broke the ground. He turned these up with his feet, lifted them to his hand and put them to his mouth. Outside-Lok did not seem to want them, though inside-Lok made his teeth grind them and his throat rise and swallow. He remembered that he was thirsty and ran back to the marsh but the mud had changed; it was daunting now as it had not been before when he was following the scent of Fa. His feet would not enter it.

Lok began to bend. His knees touched the ground, his hands reached down and took his weight slowly, and with all his strength he clutched himself into the earth. He writhed himself against the dead leaves and twigs, his head came up, turned, and his eyes swept round, astonished eyes over a mouth that was strained open. The sound of mourning burst out of his mouth, prolonged, harsh, pain-sound, man-sound. The high note of the flying things continued and the fall droned at the foot of the mountain. Far off, the stag blared again.

There was pink in the sky and a new green in the tops of the trees. The buds that had been no more than points of life had opened into fingers so that their swarms had thickened against the light and only the larger branches were visible. The earth itself seemed to vibrate as though it were working to force the sap up the trunks. Slowly as the sounds of his mourning died away Lok attended to this vibration and was minutely comforted. He crawled, he took up bulbs with his fingers and chewed them, his throat rose and swallowed. He remembered his thirst again and went crouched and questing for firm ground by the water. He let himself head down from a raking branch, held with one hand and sucked at the dark onyx surface.

There was the sound of feet in the forest. He scrambled back to the firm earth and saw two of the new people flitting past the trunks with bent sticks in their hands. There were noises coming from the remainder of the people in the clearing; noises of logs moving over each other, and of trees being cut. He remembered Liku and ran away towards the clearing until he could peer over the bushes and see what the people were doing.

"A-ho! A-ho! A-ho!"

All at once he had a picture of the hollow logs nosing up the bank and coming to rest in the clearing. He crept forward and crouched. There were no more logs in the river, so no more would come out of it. He had another picture of the logs moving back into the river and this picture was so clearly connected in some way with the first one and the sounds from the clearing that he understood why one came out of the other. This was an upheaval in the brain and he felt proud and sad and like Mal. He spoke softly to the briars with their chains of new buds.

"Now I am Mal."

All at once it seemed to him that his head was new, as though a sheaf of pictures lay there to be sorted when he would. These pictures were of plain grey daylight. They showed the solitary string of life that bound him to Liku and the new one; they showed the new people towards whom both outside- and inside-Lok yearned with a terrified love, as creatures who would kill him if they could.

He had a picture of Liku looking up with soft and adoring eyes at Tanakil, guessed how Ha had gone with a kind of eager fearfulness to meet his sudden death. He clutched at the bushes as the tides of feeling swirled through him and howled at the top of his voice.

"Liku! Liku!"

The cutting noises stopped and became a long, grinding crackle instead. In front of him he saw Tuami's head and shoulders move quickly aside and then a whole tree with arms that bent and shattered in a mass of greenery came smashing down. As the green of the tree swept sideways he could see the clearing again for the thorn bushes had been torn down and the hollow logs were coming through. The people were heaving at the logs, inching them forward. Tuami was shouting and Bush was struggling to get his bent stick off his shoulder. Lok raced away until the people were small at the beginning of the trail.

The logs were not going back to the river but coming towards the mountain. He tried to see another picture that came out of this but could not; and then his head was Lok's head again and empty.

Tuami was hacking at the tree, not cutting the trunk itself but at the thin end where the arms stuck out, for Lok could hear the difference in the note. He could hear the old man too.

"A-ho! A-ho! A-ho!"

The log nosed along the trail. It rode on other logs, rollers that sank into the soft earth so that the people were gasping and crying out in their exhaustion and terror. The old man, though he did not touch the logs, was working harder than anybody. He ran round, commanded, exhorted, mimed their struggles, gasped with them; and his high bird-voice fluttered all the time. The women and Tanakil were ranged on either side of the hollow log and even the fat woman was heaving at the back. There was only one person in the log; the new one stood in the bottom, holding on to the side and gazing over at the uproarious commotion.

Tuami came back from the side of the trail dragging a great section of the tree-trunk. When he got it on to smooth ground he began to roll it towards the hollow log. The women gathered round the staring eyes, heaved up and forward and the log was rolling easily over the soft ground with the tree-trunk turning under it. The eyes dipped and Bush and Tuami came from behind with a smaller roller so that the log never touched the ground. There was a ceaseless movement and swirl like bees round a cleft in the rock, an ordered desperation. The log moved along the trail towards Lok with the new one swaying, bobbing up and down, mewing occasionally, but most of the time fastening his gaze on the nearest or most energetic of the people. As for Liku, she was nowhere to be seen; but Lok with a flash of Mal thinking remembered that there was another log and many bundles.

Just as the new one did nothing but look, so Lok was absorbed in their approach as a man who watches the tide come in may not remember to move until the spray washes at his feet. Only when they were so close to him that he could see how the grass flattened in front of the roller did he remember that the people were dangerous and flit away into the forest. He stopped when they were hidden from sight but still within earshot. The women were crying with the strain of pushing the log along and the old man was getting hoarse. Lok had so many feelings in his body that they bewildered him. He was frightened of the new people and sorry for them as for a woman who has the sickness. He began to roam about under the trees, picking at what food he could find but not minding if he did not find it. Pictures went from his head again and he became nothing but a vast well of feeling that could not be examined or denied. He thought at first he was hungry and crammed anything he could find into his mouth. Suddenly he found himself cramming in young branches, sour and useless inside their slippery bark. He was stuffing and gulping and then he was crouching on all fours, vomiting all the branches up again.

The noise of the people diminished a little until he could hear no more than the voice of the old man when it rose in command or fury. Down here where the forest changed to marsh and the sky opened over bushes, straggling willow and water, there was no other sign of their passage. The woodpigeons talked, preoccupied with their mating; nothing was changed, not even the great bough where a red-haired child had swung and laughed. All things profited and thrived in a warm windlessness. Lok got to his feet and wandered along by the marshes towards the mere where Fa had disappeared. To be Mal was proud and heavy. The new head knew that certain things were gone and done with like a wave of the sea. It knew that the misery must be embraced painfully as a man might hug thorns to him and it sought to comprehend the new people from whom all changes came.

Lok discovered "Like". He had used likeness all his life without being aware of it. Fungi on a tree were ears, the word was the same but acquired a distinction by circumstances that could never apply to the sensitive things on the side of his head. Now, in a convulsion of the understanding Lok found himself using likeness as a tool as surely as ever he had used a stone to hack at sticks or meat. Likeness could grasp the white-faced hunters with a hand, could put them into the world where they were thinkable and not a random and unrelated irruption.

He was picturing the hunters who went out with bent sticks in skill and malice.

"The people are like a famished wolf in the hollow of a tree."

He thought of the fat woman defending the new one from the old man, thought of her laughter, of men working at a single load and grinning at each other.

"The people are like honey trickling from a crevice in the rock."

He thought of Tanakil playing, her clever fingers, her laughter, and her stick.

"The people are like honey in the round stones, the new honey that smells of dead things and fire."

They had emptied the gap of its people with little more than a turn of their hands.

"They are like the river and the fall, they are a people of the fall; nothing stands against them."

He thought of their patience, of the broad man Tuami creating a stag out of coloured earth.

"They are like Oa."

There came a confusion in his head, a darkness; and then he was Lok again, wandering aimlessly by the marshes and the hunger that food would not satisfy was back. He could hear the people running along the trail to the clearing where the second log lay and they did not speak, but betrayed themselves by the thump and rustle of their steps. He shared a picture like a gleam of sunlight in winter that was gone before he had time to see it properly. He stopped, head up and nostrils flared. His ears took over the business of living, they discounted the noise of the people and concentrated on the moorhens that were driving their smooth breasts so furiously through the water. They came towards him in a wide angle, saw him and sheared off abruptly and all together to the right. A water rat followed them, nose up, body jerking inside the wave that it made. There was a washing sound, a swish and lap among the bushes of briar that dotted the marshes. Lok ran away then came back. He crouched through the mud and began to unlace the brambles that hid his view. The washing had stopped and the ripples from it were lapping the bushes, splashing into his footprints. He sought in the air with his nose, fought with the bushes and was through. He took three steps in the water and sank in mud crookedly. The washing began again and Lok, laughing and talking, took drunken steps towards it. The hair of outside-Lok rose at the touch of the cold stuff round his thighs and the grip of the unseen mud sucking at his feet. The heaviness, the hunger was rising, became a cloud that filled him, a cloud that the sun fills with fire. There was no heaviness any more but only the lightness that set him talking and laughing like the honey people, laughing and blinking water out of his eyes. Already they shared a picture.

"Here I am! I am coming!"

"Lok! Lok!"

Fa's arms were up, her fists doubled, her teeth clenched, she was leaning and forcing her way through the water. They were still covered to the thigh when they clung to each other and made clumsily for the bank. Before they could see their feet again in the squelching mud Lok was laughing and talking.

"It is bad to be alone. It is very bad to be alone."

Fa limped as she held him.

"I am hurt a little. The man did it with a stone on the end of a stick."

Lok touched the front of her thigh. The wound was no longer bleeding but black blood lay in it like a tongue.

"It is bad to be alone——"

"I ran into the water after the man hit me."

"The water is a terrible thing."

"The water is better than the new people."

Fa took her arm from his shoulder and they squatted down under a great beech. The people were returning from the clearing with the second hollow log. They were sobbing and gasping as they went. The two hunters who had gone off earlier were shouting down from the rocks of the mountain.

Fa stuck her wounded leg straight out in front of her.

"I ate eggs and reeds and the frog jelly."

Lok found that his hands kept reaching out and touching her. She smiled at him grimly. He remembered the instant connection that had made daylight of the disconnected pictures.

"Now I am Mal. It is heavy to be Mal."

"It is heavy to be the woman."

"The new people are like a wolf and honey, rotten honey and the river."

"They are like a fire in the forest."

Quite suddenly Lok had a picture from so deep down in his head he had not known it was there. For a moment the picture seemed to be outside him so that the world changed. He himself was the same size as before but everything else had grown suddenly bigger. The trees were mountainous. He was not on the ground but riding on a back and he was holding to reddish-brown hair with hands and feet. The head in front of him, though he could not see the face was Mal's face and a greater Fa fled ahead of him. The trees above were flailing up flames and the breath from them was attacking him. There was urgency and that same tightening of the skin—there was terror.

"Now is like when the fire flew away and ate up the trees."

The sounds of the people and their logs were far in the distance. Runners came thumping back along the trail to the clearing. There came a moment of bird-speech, then silence. The steps thumped back along the trail and faded again. Fa and Lok stood up and went towards the trail. They did not speak but in their cautious, circling approach was the unspoken admission that the people could not be left alone. Terrible they might be as the fire or the river but they drew like honey or meat. The trail had changed like everything else that the people had touched. The earth was gouged and scattered, the rollers had depressed and smoothed a way broad enough for Lok and Fa and another to walk abreast.

"They pushed their hollow logs on trees that rolled along. The new one was in a log. And Liku will be in the other."

Fa looked mournfully at his face. She pointed to a smear on the smoothed earth that had been a slug.

"They have gone over us like a hollow log. They are like a winter."

The feeling was back in Lok's body; but with Fa standing before him it was a heaviness that could be borne.

"Now there are only Fa and Lok and the new one and Liku."

For a while she looked at him in silence. She put out a hand and he took it. She opened her mouth to speak but no sound came. She gave a shake of her whole body and then started to shudder. He could see her master this shudder as if she were leaving the comfort of the cave in a morning of snow. She took her hand away.

"Come!"

The fire was still smouldering in a great ring of ash. The shelters were torn apart though the uprights still stood. As for the ground in the clearing it had been churned up as though a whole herd of cattle had stampeded there. Lok crept to the edge of the clearing while Fa hung back. He began to circle. In the centre of the clearing were the pictures and the gifts.

When Fa saw these she moved inward behind Lok, and they approached them spirally, ears cocked for the return of the new people. The pictures were confused by the fire where the stag's head still watched Lok inscrutably. There was a new stag now, spring-coloured and fat, but another figure lay across it. This figure was red, with enormous spreading arms and legs and the face glared up at him for the eyes were white pebbles. The hair stood out round the head as though the figure were in the act of some frantic cruelty, and through the figure, pinning it to the stag, was a stake driven deep, its end split and furred over. The two people retreated from it in awe, for they had never seen any thing like it. Then they returned timidly to the presents.

The whole haunch of a stag, raw but comparatively bloodless, hung from the top of the stake and an opened stone of honey-drink stood by the staring head. The scent of the honey rose out of it like the smoke and flame from a fire. Fa put out her hand and touched the meat which swung so that she snatched her hand back. Lok fetched another circle round the figure, his feet avoiding the outstretched limbs while his hand moved out slowly. In a moment they were tearing at the present, ripping apart the muscle and cramming the raw meat into their mouths. They did not stop till they were skin tight with food and a shining white bone hung from the stake by a strip of hide.

At last Lok stood back and wiped his hands on his thighs. Still with nothing said they turned in towards each other and squatted by the pot. From far off on the slope leading to the terrace they could hear the old man.

"A-ho! A-ho! A-ho!"

The reek from the open mouth of the pot was thick. A fly meditated on the lip, then as Lok's breathing came closer, shuffled its wings, flew for a moment and landed again.

Fa put her hand on Lok's wrist.

"Do not touch it."

But Lok's mouth was close to the pot, his nostrils wide, his breathing quick. He spoke in a loud cracked voice.

"Honey."

All at once he ducked, thrust his mouth into the pot and sucked. The rotten honey burnt his mouth and tongue so that he somersaulted backwards and Fa fled from the pot round the ashes of the fire. She stood looking fearfully at him while he spat and began to crawl back stalking the pot that waited for him, reeking. He lowered himself cautiously and sipped. He smacked his lips and sucked again. He sat back and laughed in her face.

"Drink."

Uncertainly she bent to the mouth of the pot and put her tongue in the stinging, sweet stuff. Lok suddenly knelt forward, talking, and pushed her away so that she was astonished and squatted, licking her lips and spitting. Lok burrowed into the pot and sucked three times; but at the third suck the surface of the honey slid out of reach so that he sucked air and choked explosively. He rolled on the ground, trying to get back his breath. Fa tried for the honey but could not reach it with her tongue and spoke bitterly to him. She stood silent for a moment then picked up the pot and held it to her mouth as the new people did. Lok saw her with the great stone at her face and laughed and tried to tell her how funny she was. He remembered the honey in time, leapt up and tried to take the stone from her face. But it was stuck, glued, and as he dragged it down her face came with it. Then they were pulling and shouting at each other. Lok heard his voice coming out, high and loud and savage. He let go to examine this new voice and Fa staggered away with the pot. He found that the trees were moving very gently sideways and upwards. He had a magnificent picture that would put everything right and tried to describe it to Fa who would not listen. Then he had nothing but the picture of having had a picture and this made him furiously angry. He reached out after the picture with his voice and he heard it, disconnected from inside-Lok, laughing and quacking like a duck. But there was one word that was the beginning of the picture even though the picture itself had gone out of sight. He held on to the word. He stopped laughing and spoke very solemnly to Fa who was still standing with the stone at her face.

"Log!" he said. "Log!"

Then he remembered the honey and indignantly pulled the stone from her. Immediately her red face came out of the pot she started to laugh and talk. Lok held the pot as the new people had held it and the honey flowed over his chest. He writhed his body until his face was under the pot and contrived to get the trickle into his mouth. Fa was shrieking with laughter. She fell over, rolled, and lay back kicking her legs in the air. Lok and the honey fire responded to this invitation clumsily. Then they both remembered the pot and were pulling and arguing once more. Fa managed to drink a little but the honey turned sulky and would not come out. Lok snatched the pot, wrestled with it, beat it with his fist, shouted; but there was no more honey. He hurled the pot at the ground in fury and it grinned open into two pieces. Lok and Fa flung themselves at the pieces, squatted, each licking and turning a piece over to find where the honey had gone. The fall was roaring in the clearing, inside Lok's head. The trees were moving faster. He sprang to his feet and found that the ground was as perilous as a log. He struck at a tree as it came past to keep it still and then he was lying on his back with the sky spinning over him. He turned over, and got up rump first, swaying like the new one. Fa was crawling round the ashes of the fire like a moth with a burnt wing. She was talking to herself about hyenas. All at once Lok discovered the power of the new people in him. He was one of them, there was nothing he could not do. There were many branches left in the clearing and unburnt logs. Lok ran sideways to a log and commanded it to move. He shouted.

"A-ho! A-ho! A-ho!"

The log was sliding like the trees but not fast enough.

He went on shouting but the log would not move any faster. He seized a branch and struck again and again at the log as Tanakil had struck at Liku. He had a picture of people on either side of the log, straining, mouths open. He shouted at them like the old man

Fa was crawling past. She was moving slowly, deliberately as the log and the trees. Lok swung the stick at her rump with a great yell and the splintered end of the branch flew off and bounded among the trees. Fa screeched and staggered to her feet so that Lok struck again and missed. She swung round and they were standing face to face, shouting and the trees were sliding. He saw her right breast move, her arm come up, her open palm in the air, a palm somehow of importance that any moment now would become a thing he must attend to. Then the side of his face was struck by lightning that dazzled the world and the earth stood up and hit his right side a thunderous blow. He leaned against this vertical ground while the side of his face opened and shut and flames burst out of it. Fa was lying down, receding and coming close. Then she was pulling him up or down, there was solid earth under his feet again and he was hanging on to her. They were weeping and laughing at each other and the fall was roaring in the clearing while the shock head of the dead tree was climbing away into the sky, only getting larger instead of smaller. He became frightened in a detached way, he knew it would be good to get close to her. He put aside the strangeness and sleepiness of his head; he peered for her, bored at her face which kept receding like the shock-headed tree. The trees were still sliding but steadily as though it had always been their nature to do so.

He spoke to her through the mists.

"I am one of the new people."

This made him caper. Then he walked through the clearing with what he thought was the slow swaying carriage of the new people. The picture came to him that Fa must cut off his finger. He lumbered round the clearing, trying to find her and tell her so. He found her behind the tree near the edge of the river and she was being sick. He told her about the old woman in the water but she took no notice so he went back to the broken pot and licked the traces of decaying honey off it. The figure on the ground became the old man and Lok told him that there was now an addition to the new people. Then he felt very tired so that the ground became soft and the pictures in his head went round and round. He explained to the man that now Lok must go back to the overhang but that reminded him even with his spinning head that there was no overhang any more. He began to mourn, loudly and easily and the mourning was very pleasant. He found that when he looked at the trees they slid apart and could only be induced to come together with a great effort that he was not disposed to make. All at once there was nothing but sunlight and the voice of the woodpigeons over the drone of the fall. He lay back, his eyes open, watching the strange pattern that the doubled branches made against the sky. His eyes closed themselves and he fell down as over a cliff of sleep.

ELEVEN

Fa was shaking him.

"They are going away."

Hands not Fa's hands were gripped round his head, producing a hot pain. He groaned and rolled away from the hands but they held on, squeezing until the pain was inside his head.

"The new people are going away. They are taking their hollow logs up the slope to the terrace."

Lok opened his eyes and yelped with pain for he seemed to be looking straight into the sun. Water ran out of his eyes and blazed fiercely between the lids. Fa shook him again. He felt for the ground with his hands and feet and lifted himself a little way from it. His stomach contracted and all at once he was sick. His stomach had a life of its own; it rose in a hard knot, would have nothing to do with this evil, honey-smelling stuff and rejected it. Fa was taking by his shoulder.

"My stomach has been sick too."

He turned over again, and squatted laboriously without opening his eyes. He could feel the sunlight burning down one side of his face.

"They are going away. We must take back the new one."

Lok prised open his eyes, looked out cautiously between gummed-up lids to see what had happened to the world. It was brighter. The earth and the trees were made of nothing but colour and swayed so that he shut his eyes again.

"I am ill."

For a while she said nothing. Lok discovered that the hands holding his head were inside it and they squeezed so tightly that he could feel blood pulsing through his brain. He opened his eyes, blinked, and the world settled a little. There were still the blazing colours but they were not swaying. In front of him the earth was rich brown and red, the trees were silver and green and the branches were covered with spurts of green fire. He squatted, blinking, feeling the tenderness of his face while Fa went on speaking.

"I was sick and you would not wake up. I went to see the new people. Their hollow logs have moved up the slope. The new people are frightened. They stand and move like people who are frightened. They heave and sweat and watch the forest over their backs. But there is no danger in the forest. They are frightened of the air where there is nothing. Now we must get the new one from them."

Lok put his hands to the earth on either side of him. The sky was bright and the world blazed with colour, but it was still the world he knew.

"We must take Liku from them."

Fa stood up and ran round the clearing. She came back and looked down at him. He got up carefully.

"Fa says 'Do this!' "

He waited obediently. Mal had gone out of his head.

"Here is a picture. Lok goes up the path by the cliff where the people cannot see him. Fa goes round and climbs to the mountain above the people. They will follow. The men will follow. Then Lok takes the new one from the fat woman and runs."

She took hold of him by the arms and looked imploringly into his face.

"There will be a fire again. And I shall have children."

A picture came into Lok's head.

"I will do so," he said sturdily, "and when I see Liku I will take her also."

There were things in Fa's face, not for the first time, that he could not understand.

They parted at the foot of the slope where the bushes still hid them from the new people. Lok went to the right and Fa flitted away along the skirts of the forest to make a great circle round the slope. When Lok glanced back he could see her, red as a squirrel, running mostly on all fours in the cover of the trees. He began to climb, listening for voices. He came out on the track above the water, with the fall roaring ahead of him. There was more water coming over than ever. There was a profounder thunder from the basin at the foot and the smoke was spread far over the island. The sheets of falling water shook out into milky skeins, unspun into a creamy substance that was hard to distinguish from the leaping spray and mist that rose to meet it. Beyond the island he could see great trees in all their spring foliage sliding over the lip. They would vanish into the spray and then appear again beyond it, shattered and leaning in the water of the river, jerking as if a gigantic hand were plucking at them beneath. But on this side of the island no trees came over; only a ceaseless abundance of shining water and creamy milk falling into noise and white, drifting smoke.

Then, through all the noise of the water he heard the voices of the new people. They were on the right, hidden by the rising rock where the ice woman had hung. He paused and heard them screaming at each other.

Here, with the so familiar sights about him, with the history of his people still hanging round the rocks, his misery returned with a new strength. The honey had not killed the misery but put it to sleep for a while so that now it was refreshed. He groaned at emptiness and had a great feeling for Fa on the other side of the slope. There was Liku too somewhere among the people and his need of either or both became urgent. He set himself to climb up the crack where the ice woman had hung and the sounds of the new people were louder. Presently he was lying at the lip of the cliff, looking over a hand's breadth of earth and straggling grass and stunted bushes.

Once more the new people were performing for him. They had done meaningless things with logs. Some were wedged in rocks with others lying across them. The scarred earth of the slope led right on to the terrace so that he understood that the other log had reached the overhang. The one the people were working at now was pointing up the slope between the wedged logs. There were strips of thick and twisted hide leading from it. There was a log wedged crosswise behind the hollow log, balanced at its mid-point against an outcrop and this nearer end was bending with the weight of a boulder that wanted to roll downhill. As Lok caught sight of it, he saw the old man pull a strip of twisted hide and the boulder was free. It pushed against the log, forcing it down the slope and the hollow log slid in the other direction towards the terrace. The boulder did all its work and went bumping away down to the forest. Tuami had jammed a stone behind the hollow log and the people were shouting. There were no more boulders between the log and the terrace so that now the people did the boulder's work. They laid hold of the log and heaved. The old man stood by them and a dead snake hung from his right hand. He began to cry—a-ho! and the people strained till their faces crumpled. The old man raised the snake in the air and struck with it at the shuddering backs. The log moved onwards.

After a while Lok noticed the other people. The fat woman was not pushing. She was standing well to one side between Lok and the hollow log and she was holding the new one. Now Lok could see what Fa meant by the fright of the new people, for the fat woman was glancing round all the time and her face was even paler than it had been in the clearing. Tanakil stood close by her so that she was partly hidden. As if his eyes had been opened Lok could see how the frantic heaving at the log was made strong by this fear. The people consented to the dead snake if it would call from their bodies, already so thin, the strength they could not command themselves. There was a hysterical speed in the efforts of Tuami and in the screaming voice of the old man. They were retreating up the slope as though cats with their evil teeth were after them, as though the river itself were flowing uphill. Yet the river stayed in its bed and the slope was bare of all but the new people.

"They are frightened of the air."

Pine-tree yelled and slipped and instantly Tuami had

209

the rock jammed against the back of the log. The people gathered round Pine-tree, babbling, and the old man flourished his snake. Tuami was pointing up the mountainside. He ducked and a stone struck the hollow log with a thump. The babble became a shriek. Tuami, leaning with all his strength, was holding the log on a single length of hide while it ground sideways. He fastened the hide to a rock and then the men spread out in a line facing the mountain. Fa was visible, a small red figure dancing on the rock above them. Lok saw her swing her arm and another stone came humming through the line. The men were bending their sticks and letting them straighten suddenly. Lok saw twigs fly up the rock, falter before they reached Fa, turn and come back again. Another stone broke on the rock by the log and the fat woman came running to the cliff where Lok was. She stopped and turned back but Tanakil came on, right to the lip. She saw him and screeched. He was up, had grabbed her before the fat woman had time to turn again. He seized Tanakil by her thin arms and talked to her urgently.

"Where is Liku! Tell me, where is Liku?"

At the sound of Liku's name Tanakil began to struggle and scream as though she had fallen into deep water. The fat woman was screaming too and the new one had scrambled to her shoulder. The old man was running along the lip of the cliff. Chestnut-head was coming from where the log was. He rushed straight at Lok and his teeth were bare. The screaming and the teeth terrified Lok. He let Tanakil go so that she reeled back. Her foot struck Chestnut-head's knee just as he launched himself at Lok. He travelled through the air past Lok, grunting aintly and went over the cliff. He just fitted the delicate curve of the descent so that he seemed to skim down on his belly, never more than a hand's breadth away from rock but never touching it. He vanished and did not even leave a scream behind him. The old man flung a stick at Lok who could see that there was a sharp stone on the end and avoided it. Then he was running between the fat woman with her mouth open and Tanakil flat on her back. The men who had thrown twigs at Fa had turned and were watching Lok. He went very fast across the slope until he reached the strip of hide that held the log. He ran through this and it took most of the skin off his shin before it gave. The log began to slide backwards. The people ceased to watch Lok and watched the log instead so that he turned his head as he ran to see what they were looking at. The log got up speed on two rollers but after that they were not necessary. It left the slope where the descent steepened and travelled on through the air. The back end hit a point of rock and the log opened in two halves all along its length. The two halves went on, turning round and round until they smashed into the forest. Lok leapt into a gully and the people were out of sight.

Fa was jumping about at the head of the gully and he ran towards her as fast as he could. The men were advancing across the rocks with their bent sticks but he reached her first. They were about to climb further when the men stopped for the old man was shouting at them. Even without knowing the words Lok could understand his gestures. The men ran down the rock and were lost to view.

Fa was showing her teeth too.

She came at Lok brandishing her arms and there was still a sharp stone in one hand.

"Why did you not snatch the new one?"

Lok put out his hands defensively.

"I asked for Liku. I asked Tanakil."

Fa's arms came down slowly.

"Come!"

The sun was sinking towards the gap and making a whirl of gold and red. They could see the new people hurrying about on the terrace as Fa led the way towards the cliff above the overhang. The new people had shifted the hollow log to the upriver end of the terrace and were trying to get it past the jam of tree-trunks that now lay where Lok and Fa had crossed to the island. They slid it from the terrace and it lay in the water with logs all round it. The men were heaving at the tree-trunks, trying to deflect them to the other side of the rock where they would be swept away over the fall. Fa ran about on the mountainside.

"They will take the new one with them."

She began to run down the steep rock as the sun sank into the gap. There was red now over the mountains and the ice women were on fire. Lok shouted suddenly and Fa stopped and looked down at the water. There was a tree coming towards the jam; not a small trunk or a splintered fragment but a whole tree from some forest over the horizon. It was coming along this side of the gap, a colony of budding twigs and branches, a vast, half-hidden trunk, and roots that spread above the water and held enough earth between them to make a hearth for all the people in the world. As it came into sight the old man began to yell and dance. The women looked up from the bundles they were lowering into the hollow log and the men scrambled back across the jam. The roots struck the jam and splintered logs leapt into the air or stood up slowly. They caught the roots and hung. The tree stopped moving and swung sideways until it lay along the cliff beyond the terrace. Now there was a tangle of logs between the hollow log and the open water like a huge line of thorns. The jam had become an impassable barrier.

The old man stopped shouting. He ran to one of the bundles and began to open it. He shouted to Tuami who ran, holding Tanakil by the hand. They were coming along the terrace.

"Quickly!"

Fa fled away down the side of the mountain towards the entrance to the terrace and the overhang. As she ran she shouted to Lok:

"We will take Tanakil. Then they will give back the new one."

The rock was different. The colours that had drenched the world when Lok awoke from his honey sleep were richer, deeper. He seemed to leap and scamper through a tide of red air and the shadows behind the rocks were mauve. He dropped down the slope.

Together they stopped at the entrance to the terrace and crouched. The river was running crimson and there were golden flashes on it. The mountains on the other side of the river had become so dark that Lok had to peer at it before he discovered that it was dark blue. The jam and the tree and the toiling figures on it were black. But the terrace and the overhang were still brightly lit by the red light. The stag was dancing again, dancing on the slope of earth that led up to the overhang and he faced into the space where Mal had died before the right-hand recess. He was black against the fire where the sun was sinking and as he moved he wielded long rays of sunlight that dazzled the eyes. Tuami was working in the over-hang, smearing colour on a shape that stood between the two recesses against the pillar. Tanakil was there, a small, thin, black figure crouching where the fire had been.

From the other end of the terrace came a rhythmic clop! clop! Two of the men were cutting at the log that Lok had jammed. The sun buried itself in cloud, red shot up to the top of the sky and the mountains were black.

The stag blared. Tuami came running out of the over-hang, running towards the jam where the men were working and Tanakil started to scream. The clouds swarmed over the sun and the pressure went out of the redness so that it seemed to float in the gap like a thinner water. Now the stag was bounding away towards the jam and the men were struggling with the log like beetles on a dead bird.

Lok ran forward and Tanakil's scream echoed the screams of Liku crossing the water so that they frightened him. He stood in the entrance to the overhang, gibbering.

"Where is Liku? What have you done with Liku?"

Tanakil's body straightened, arched, and her eyes rolled. She stopped screaming and lay on her back and there was blood between her grinning teeth. Fa and Lok crouched in front of her.

The overhang had altered like everything else. Tuami had made a figure for the old man and it stood there against the pillar and glared at them. They could see how quickly, savagely he had worked for the figure was smeared and not filled in as carefully as the figures in the clearing. It was some kind of man. Its arms and legs were contracted as though it were leaping forward and it was red as the water had been. There was hair standing out on all sides of the head as the hair of the old man had stood out when he was enraged or frightened. The face was a daub of clay but the pebbles were there, staring blindly. The old man had taken the teeth from his neck and stuck them in the face and finished them off with the two great cat's teeth from his ears. There was a stick driven into a crack in the creature's breast and to this stick was fastened a strip of hide; and to the other end of the hide was fastened Tanakil

Fa began to make noises. They were not words and they were not screams. She seized the stick and began to heave but it would not come for the end was furred where Tuami had driven it in. Lok pushed her to one side and pulled but the stick stayed where it was. The red light was lifting from the water and the overhang was full of shadow through which the creature glared with eyes and teeth.

"Pull!"

He swung all his weight on the stick and felt it bend. He lifted his feet, planted them in the figure's red belly and thrust until his muscles ached. The mountain seemed to move and the figure slid so that its arms were about to grasp him. Then the stick whipped out of the crack and he was rolling with it on the ground.

"Bring her quickly."

Lok staggered to his feet, picked up Tanakil and ran

after Fa along the terrace. There came a screaming from the figures by the hollow log and a loud bang from the jam. The tree began to move forward and the logs were lumbering about like the legs of a giant. The crumple-faced woman was struggling with Tuami on the rock by the hollow log; she burst free and came running towards Lok. There was movement everywhere, screaming, de-moniac activity; the old man was coming across the tumbling logs. He threw something at Fa. Hunters were holding the hollow log against the terrace and the head of the tree with all its weight of branches and wet leaves was drawing along them. The fat woman was lying in the log, the crumpled woman was in it with Tanakil, the old man was tumbling into the back. The boughs crashed and drew along the rock with an agonized squealing. Fa was sitting by the water holding her head. The branches took her. She was moving with them out into the water and the hollow log was free of the rock and drawing away. The tree swung into the current with Fa sitting limply among the branches. Lok began to gibber again. He ran up and down on the terrace. The tree would not be cajoled or persuaded. It moved to the edge of the fall, it swung until it was lying along the lip. The water reared up over the trunk, pushing, the roots were over. The tree hung for a while with the head facing upstream. Slowly the root end sank and the head rose. Then it slid forward soundlessly and dropped over the fall.

The red creature stood on the edge of the terrace and did nothing. The hollow log was a dark spot on the water towards the place where the sun had gone down. The air in the gap was clear and blue and calm. There was no noise at all now except for the fall, for there was no wind and the green sky was clear. The red creature turned to the right and trotted slowly towards the far end of the terrace. Water was cascading down the rocks beyond the terrace from the melting ice in the mountains. The river was high and flat and drowned the edge of the terrace. There were long scars in the earth and rock where the branches of a tree had been dragged past by the water. The red creature came trotting back to a dark hollow in the side of the cliff where there was evidence of occupation. It looked at the other figure, dark now, that grinned down at it from the back of the hollow. Then it turned away and ran through the little passage that joined the terrace to the slope. It halted, peering down at the scars, the abandoned rollers and broken ropes. It turned again, sidled round a shoulder of rock and stood on an almost imperceptible path that ran along the sheer rocks. It began to sidle along the path, crouched, its long arms swinging, touching, almost as firm a support as the legs. It was peering down into the thunderous waters but there was nothing to be seen but the columns of glimmering haze where the water had scooped a bowl out of the rock. It moved faster, broke into a queer loping run that made the head bob up and down and the forearms alternate like the legs of a horse. It stopped at the end of the path and looked down at the long streamers of weed that were moving backwards and forwards under the water. It put up a hand and scratched under its chinless mouth. There was a tree, far away in the gleaming reaches of the river, a tree in leaf that was rolling over and over as the current thrust it towards the sea. The red creature, now grey and blue in the twilight, loped down the slope and dived into the forest. It followed a track broad and scarred as a cart-track, until it came to a clearing by the river beneath a dead tree. It scrambled about by the water, clambered up the tree, peered through the ivy after the tree in the river. Then it came down, raced along a trail that led through the bushes by the river until it came to an arm that broke the trail. Here it paused, then ran to and fro by the water. It seized a great swinging beech bough and lugged it back and forwards until its breathing was fierce and uneven. It ran back to the clearing, began to circle round and between the thorn bushes that had been laid there in heaps. It made no sound. There were stars pricking out and the sky was no longer green, but dark blue. A white owl floated through the clearing to its nest among the trees of the island on the other side of the river. The creature paused and looked down at some smears by what had been a fire.

Now that the sunlight had gone completely, no longer even throwing light into the sky from below the horizon, the moon took over. Shadows began to sharpen, leading from every tree and tangling behind the bushes. The red creature began to sniff round by the fire. Its weight was on its knuckles and it worked with its nose lowered almost to the ground. A water rat returning to the river glimpsed the four legs and flashed sideways under a bush to lie there waiting. The creature stopped between the ashes of the fire and the forest. It shut its eyes, and breathed in quickly. It began to scramble in the earth, its nose always searching. Out of the churned-up earth the right forepaw picked a small, white bone.

It straightened up a little and stood, not looking at the bone but at a spot some distance ahead. It was a strange

218

creature, smallish, and bowed. The legs and thighs were bent and there was a whole thatch of curls on the outside of the legs and the arms. The back was high, and covered over the shoulders with curly hair. Its feet and hands were broad, and flat, the great toe projecting inwards to grip. The square hands swung down to the knees. The head was set slightly forward on the strong neck that seemed to lead straight on to the row of curls under the lip. The mouth was wide and soft and above the curls of the upper lip the great nostrils were flared like wings. There was no bridge to the nose and the moon-shadow of the jutting brow lay just above the tip. The shadows lay most darkly in the caverns above its cheeks and the eyes were invisible in them. Above this again, the brow was a straight line fledged with hair; and above that there was nothing.

The creature stood and the splashes of moonlight stirred over it. The eye-hollows gazed not at the bone but at an invisible point towards the river. Now the right leg began to move. The creature's attention seemed to gather and focus in the leg and the foot began to pick and search in the earth like a hand. The big toe bored and gripped and the toes folded round an object that had been almost completely buried in the churned soil. The foot rose, the leg bent and presented an object to the lowered hand. The head came down a little, the gaze swept inward from that invisible point and regarded what was in the hand. It was a root, old and rotted, worn away at both ends but preserving the exaggerated contours of a female body.

The creature looked again towards the water. Both hands were full, the bar of its brow glistened in the moon-light, over the great caverns where the eyes were hidden.

There was light poured down over the cheek-bones and the wide lips and there was a twist of light caught like a white hair in every curl. But the caverns were dark as though already the whole head was nothing but a skull.

The water rat concluded from the creature's stillness that it was not dangerous. It came with a quick rush from under the bush and began to cross the open space, it forgot the silent figure and searched busily for something to eat.

There was light now in each cavern, lights faint as the starlight reflected in the crystals of a granite cliff. The lights increased, acquired definition, brightened, lay each sparkling at the lower edge of a cavern. Suddenly, noiselessly, the lights became thin crescents, went out, and streaks glistened on each cheek. The lights appeared again, caught among the silvered curls of the beard. They hung, elongated, dropped from curl to curl and gathered at the lowest tip. The streaks on the cheeks pulsed as the drops swam down them, a great drop swelled at the end of a hair of the beard, shivering and bright. It detached itself and fell in a silver flash, striking a withered leaf with a sharp pat. The water rat scurried away and plopped into the river.

Stealthily the moonlight moved the blue shadows. The creature pulled its right foot out of the mire and took a lurching step forward. It staggered in a half-circle until it reached the gap between the thorn bushes where the broad track began. It started to run along the track and it was blue and grey in the moonlight. It went laboriously, slowly, with much bobbing up and down of the head. It limped. When it reached the slope up to the top of the fall it was on all fours.

On the terrace the creature moved faster. It ran to the far end where the water was coming down from the ice in a cascade. It turned, came back, and crept on all fours into the hollow where the other figure was. The creature wrestled with a rock that was lying on a mound of earth but was too weak to move it. At last it gave up and crawled round the hollow by the remains of a fire. It came close to the ashes and lay on its side. It pulled its legs up, knees against the chest. It folded its hands under its cheek and lay still. The twisted and smoothed root lay before its face. It made no noise, but seemed to be growing into the earth, drawing the soft flesh of its body into a contact so close that the movements of pulse and breathing were inhibited.

There were eyes like green fires above the hollow and grey dogs that slid and sidled through the moon-shadows. They descended to the terrace and approached the overhang. They sniffed curiously and cautiously at the earth outside the hollow but did not dare to approach nearer. Slowly the procession of stars sank behind the mountain and the night waned. There was grey light on the terrace and a little wind of dawn, blowing through the gap in the mountains. The ashes stirred, lifted, turned over and scattered themselves across the motionless body. The hyenas sat, tongues lolling, panting rapidly.

The sky over the sea turned to pink and then to gold. Light and colour came back. They showed the two red shapes, the one glaring from the rock the other, moulded into the earth, sandy, and chestnut and red. The water from the ice increased in volume, sparkling out into the gap in a long curved fall. The hyenas lifted their hind-quarters off the earth, separated and approached the interior of the hollow from either hand. The ice crowns of the mountains were a-glitter. They welcomed the sun. There was a sudden tremendous noise that set the hyenas shivering back to the cliff. It was a noise that engulfed the water noises, rolled along the mountains, boomed from cliff to cliff and spread in a tangle of vibrations over the sunny forests and out towards the sea.

TWELVE

Tuami sat in the stern of the dug-out, the steering
paddle under his left arm. There was plenty of
light and the patches of salt no longer looked like
holes in the skin sail. He thought bitterly of the great
square sail they had left bundled up in that last mad hour
among the mountains; for with that and the breeze
through the gap he need not have endured these hours
of strain. He need not have sat all night wondering
whether the current would beat the wind and bear them
back to the fall while the people or as many as were left
of them slept their collapsed sleep. Still, they had moved
on, the walls of rock folding back until this lake became
so broad that he had been able to find no transits for
judging their motion but had sat, guessing, with the
mountains looming over the flat water and his eyes red
with the tears of strain. Now he stirred a little for the
rounded bilge was hard and the pad of leather that many
steersmen had moulded to a comfortable seat was lost on
the slope up from the forest. He could feel the slight
pressure transmitted to his forearm along the loom of the
paddle and knew that if he were to trail his hand over the
side the water would tinkle against the palm and heap up
over his wrist. The two dark lines spreading on either
bow were not laid back at a sharp angle but led out almost
at right angles to the line of the boat. If the breeze

changed or faltered those lines would creep ahead and fade and the pressure in the paddle would slacken and they would begin to slide astern towards the mountains.

He shut his eyes and passed a hand wearily over his forehead. The breeze might die away and then they would be forced to paddle with what strength the journey had left them in order to reach a shore before the current bore them back. He jerked his hand away and glanced at the sail. It was full but pulsing gently, the double sheets that led aft here to the belaying pins were moving together, moving apart, moving up and down. He looked away at the miles of now visible grey water and there was a monster sliding past, not half a cable to starboard, the root lifted above the surface like a mammoth's tusk. It was sliding towards the fall and the forest devils. The dug-out was hanging still, waiting for the wind to die away. He tried to perform a calculation in his aching head, tried to balance the current, the wind, the dug-out but he could come to no conclusion.

He shook himself irritably and parallel lines rippled out from the sides of the boat. A fair wind, steerage-way, and plenty of water all round—what more could a man want? Those hardening clouds on either hand were hills with trees on them. Forrard there under the sail was what looked like lower land, plains perhaps where men could hunt in the open, not stumble among dark trees or on hard, haunted rocks. What more could a man want?

But this was confusion. He rested his eyes on the back of his left hand and tried to think. He had hoped for the light as for a return to sanity and the manhood that seemed to have left them; but here was dawn—past dawn —and they were what they had been in the gap, haunted, bedevilled, full of strange irrational grief like himself, or emptied, collapsed, and helplessly asleep. It seemed as though the portage of the boats—or boat rather, now she was gone—from that forest to the top of the fall had taken them on to a new level not only of land but of experience and emotion. The world with the boat moving so slowly at the centre was dark amid the light, was untidy, hopeless, dirty.

He waggled the paddle in the water and the sheets tossed. The sail made a sleepy remark and then was attentively full again. Perhaps if they squared off the boat, stowed things properly——? Partly to assess the job and partly to turn his eyes outwards from his own mind, Tuami examined the hollow hull before him.

The bundles lay where the women had thrown them. Those two on the port side amidships made a tent for Vivani though with her usual contrariness she preferred a shelter of leaves and branches. There was a bundle of spears under them and they were being spoiled because Bata was sleeping on them face down. He would find the shafts bent or cracked and the good flint-points broken. To starboard was a jumble of skins that was of little use to anyone, but the women had thrown it in when they might have kept the sail instead. One of the empty pots was broken and the other lay on its side with the clay plug still in place. There would be little to drink but water. Vivani lay curled on the useless skins—had she made them place the skins there for comfort, not bothering with the precious sail? It would be like her. She was covered with a magnificent skin, the cave-bear skin that had cost two lives to get and was the price her first man paid for her. What was a sail, thought Tuami bitterly, when Vivani wanted to be comfortable? What a fool Marlan was, at his age, to have run off with her for her great heart and wit, her laughter and her white, incredible body! And what fools we were to come with him, forced by his magic, or at any rate forced by some compulsion there are no words for! He looked at Marlan, hating him, and thought of the ivory dagger that he had been grinding so slowly to a point. Marlan sat facing aft, his legs stretched in the bottom, his head resting against the mast. His mouth was open and his hair and beard were like a grey bush. Tuami could see in the growing light how strength had gone out of him. There had been lines before round the mouth, deep channels from the nostrils downwards but now the face behind the hair was not only lined but thin. There was utter exhaustion in the slanted fall of the head and in the jaw pulled down and sideways. Not long now, thought Tuami, when we are safe and out of the devil's country I shall dare to use the ivory-point.

Even so to watch Marlan's face and intend to kill him was daunting. He turned his eyes away, glimpsed the huddle of bodies in the bow beyond the mast and then looked down past his own feet. Tanakil lay there, flat on her back. She was not drained of life like Marlan but rather had life in abundance, a new life, not her own. She did not move much and her quick breathing fluttered a scrap of dried blood that hung on her lower lip. The eyes were neither asleep nor awake. Now he could see them clearly he saw that the night was going on in them for they were sunken and dark, opaquenesses without intelligence. Though he leaned forward where she must have seen him her eyes did not focus on his face but continued to strain inward towards the night. Twal, who lay by her, had one arm stretched protectively across her. Twal's body looked like the body of an old woman, though she was younger than he and was Tanakil's mother.

Tuami rubbed a hand across his forehead again. If I could drop this paddle and work at my dagger or if I had charcoal and a flat stone—he looked desperately round the boat for something on which to fasten his attention—I am like a pool, he thought, some tide has filled me, the sand is swirling, the waters are obscured and strange things are creeping out of the cracks and crannies in my mind.

The skin at Vivani's feet stirred, lifted and he thought she was waking up. Then a small leg, red, covered with curls and no longer than his hand stretched itself in the air. It felt round, tried the surface of the pot and rejected it, touched skin, moved again and rubbed a tuft of hair between its thumb and toe. Satisfied, it laid hold of the bear skin, clenched its toes firmly round a curl or two and was still. Tuami was jerking like a man in a fit, the paddle was jerking and the parallel lines were spreading from the boat. The red leg was one of six that were creeping out of a crevice.

He cried out:

"What else could we have done?"

The mast and sail slid into focus. He saw that Marlan's eyes were open and could not tell how long they had been watching him.

Marlan spoke from deep inside his body.

"The devils do not like the water."

That was true, that was comfort. The water was miles wide and bright. Tuami looked imploringly at Marlan out of his pool. He forgot the dagger that was so nearly ground to a point.

"If we had not we should have died."

Marlan shifted restlessly, easing his bones from the hard wood. Then he looked at Tuami and nodded gravely.

The sail glowed red-brown. Tuami glanced back at the gap through the mountain and saw that it was full of golden light and the sun was sitting in it. As if they were obeying some signal the people began to stir, to sit up and look across the water at the green hills. Twal bent over Tanakil and kissed her and murmured to her. Tanakil's lips parted. Her voice was harsh and came from far away in the night.

"Liku!"

Tuami heard Marlan whisper to him from by the mast.

"That is the devil's name. Only she may speak it."

Now Vivani was really waking. They heard her huge, luxurious yawn and the bear skin was thrown off. She sat up, shook back her loose hair and looked first at Marlan then at Tuami. At once he was filled again with lust and hate. If she had been what she was, if Marlan, if her man, if she had saved her baby in the storm on the salt water——

"My breasts are paining me."

If she had not wanted the child as a plaything, if I had not saved the other as a joke——

He began to talk high and fast.

"There are plains beyond those hills, Marlan, for they grow less; and there will be herds for hunting. Let us steer in towards the shore. Have we water—but of course we have water! Did the women bring the food? Did you bring the food, Twal?"

228

Twal lifted her face towards him and it was twisted with grief and hate.

"What have I to do with food, master? You and he gave my child to the devils and they have given me back a changeling who does not see or speak."

The sand was swirling in Tuami's brain. He thought in panic: they have given me back a changed Tuami; what shall I do? Only Marlan is the same—smaller, weaker but the same. He peered forrard to find the changeless one as something he could hold on to. The sun was blazing on the red sail and Marlan was red. His arms and legs were contracted, his hair stood out and his beard, his teeth were wolf's teeth and his eyes like blind stones. The mouth was opening and shutting.

"They cannot follow us, I tell you. They cannot pass over water."

Slowly the red mist faded and became a sail glowing in the sun. Vakiti crawled round the mast, still carefully preserving the magnificent hair of which he was so proud from contact with the sheets which would have disarranged it. He slid round Marlan, conveying as much as the narrow boat would allow his respect for him and his regret for having to come so close. He picked his way past Vivani and came aft to Tuami, grinning ruefully.

"I am sorry, master. Now sleep."

He took the steering paddle under his left arm and settled down in Tuami's place. Released, Tuami crawled over Tanakil and knelt by the full pot, yearning at it. Vivani was doing her hair, arms up, comb drawing across, down, out. She had not changed, or at least only in respect of the little devil who owned her. Tuami remembered the night in Tanakil's eyes and put aside the thought of sleep. Presently perhaps, when he had to, but with the pot to help him. His restless hands felt at his belt and drew out the sharpening ivory with the shapeless haft. He found the stone in his pouch and began to grind, and there was silence. The wind freshened a little and the paddle made a rushing sound in their wake. The dug-out was so heavy that it would not lift or keep up with the wind as boats sometimes did if they were made of bark. So the wind blew round them warmly and took with it some of the confusion in his mind. He worked unhappily at the blade of his dagger and did not care whether he finished it or not but it was something to do.

Vivani finished with her hair and looked round at them all. She gave a little laugh that would have been nervous in anyone but Vivani. She pulled the cord that held the leathern cradle of her breasts and let the sun shine on them. Behind her Tuami could see the low hills and the green of trees with the darkness under them. The darkness stretched along above the water like a thin line and above it the trees were green and lively.

Vivani bent down and twitched aside the fold of bearskin. The little devil was there on a pelt, hands and feet holding tight. As the light poured over him he lifted his head off the fur and blinked his eyes open. He got up on his forelegs and looked round, brightly, solemnly, with quick movements of his neck and body. He yawned so that they could see how his teeth were coming and then a pink tongue whipped along his lips. He sniffed, turned, ran at Vivani's leg and scrambled up to her breast. She was shuddering and laughing as if this pleasure and love were also a fear and a torment. The devil's hands and feet had laid hold of her. Hesitating, half-ashamed, with

230

that same frightened laughter, she bent her head, cradled him with her arms and shut her eyes. The people were grinning at her too as if they felt the strange, tugging mouth, as if in spite of them there was a well of feeling opened in love and fear. They made adoring and submissive sounds, reached out their hands, and at the same time they shuddered in replusion at the too-nimble feet and the red, curly hair. Tuami, his head full of swirling sand, tried to think of the time when the devil would be full grown. In this upland country, safe from pursuit by the tribe but shut off from men by the devil-haunted mountains, what sacrifice would they be forced to perform to a world of confusion? They were as different from the group of bold hunters and magicians who had sailed up the river towards the fall as a soaked feather is from a dry one. Restlessly he turned the ivory in his hands. What was the use of sharpening it against a man? Who would sharpen a point against the darkness of the world?

Marlan spoke hoarsely out of some meditation.

"They keep to the mountains or the darkness under the trees. We will keep to the water and the plains. We shall be safe from the tree-darkness."

Without being conscious of what he did, Tuami looked again at the line of darkness that curved away under the trees as the shore receded. The devil brat had had enough. He climbed down Vivani's wincing body and dropped into the dry bilges. He began to crawl inquisitively, propped on his forearms and peering about through eyes full of sunlight. The people shrank and adored, giggled and clenched their fists. Even Marlan shifted his feet and tucked them under him.

The morning was in full swing and the sun poured down at them from over the mountains. Tuami gave up his rubbing of stone against bone. He felt under his hand the shapeless lump that would be the haft of the knife when it was finished. There was no power in his hands and no picture in his head. Neither the blade nor the haft was important in these waters. For a moment he was tempted to throw the thing overboard.

Tanakil opened her mouth and made her mindless syllables.

"Liku!"

Twal flung herself howling across her daughter, holding the body close as if trying to reach the child who had left it.

The sand was back in Tuami's brain. He squatted, moving himself from side to side and turning the ivory aimlessly in his hand. The devil examined Vivani's foot.

There came a sound from the mountains, a tremendous noise that boomed along them and spread in a tangle of vibrations across the glittering water. Marlan was crouched, making stabbing motions at the mountains with his fingers, and his eyes were glaring like stones. Vakiti had ducked so that the paddle had swung them off the wind and the sail was rattling. The devil shared in all this confusion. He climbed rapidly up Vivani's body, through her hands that were spread instinctively to ward off, and then was burrowing into the hood of fur that lay behind her head. He fell in and was confined. The hood struggled.

The noise from the mountains was dying away. The people, released as if a lifted weapon had been lowered, turned their relief and laughter on the devil. They shrieked at the struggling lump. Vivani's back was arched and she was writhing as though a spider had got inside her furs. Then the devil appeared, arse-upward, his little rump pushing against the nape of her neck. Even the sombre Marlan twisted his weary face into a grin. Vakiti could not straighten course for his wild laughing and Tuami let the ivory drop from his hands. The sun shone on the head and the rump and quite suddenly everything was all right again and the sands had sunk back to the bottom of the pool. The rump and the head fitted each other and made a shape you could feel with your hands. They were waiting in the rough ivory of the knife-haft that was so much more important than the blade. They were an answer, the frightened, angry love of the woman and the ridiculous, intimidating rump that was wagging at her head, they were a password. His hands felt for the ivory in the bilges and he could feel in his fingers how Vivani and her devil fitted it.

At last the devil was turned round and settled. He poked his head over her shoulder, keeping close, he nestled it against her neck. And the woman rubbed her cheek sideways against the curly hair, giggling and looking defiantly at the people. Marlan spoke in the silence.

"They live in the darkness under the trees."

Holding the ivory firmly in his hands, feeling the onset of sleep, Tuami looked at the line of darkness. It was far away and there was plenty of water in between. He peered forward past the sail to see what lay at the other end of the lake, but it was so long, and there was such a flashing from the water that he could not see if the line of darkness had an ending.

Pincher Martin

〖The Two Deaths of Christopher Martin〗

1

He was struggling in every direction, he was the centre of the writhing and kicking knot of his own body. There was no up or down, no light and no air. He felt his mouth open of itself and the shrieked word burst out.

"Help!"

When the air had gone with the shriek, water came in to fill its place—burning water, hard in the throat and mouth as stones that hurt. He hutched his body towards the place where air had been but now it was gone and there was nothing but black, choking welter. His body let loose its panic and his mouth strained open till the hinges of his jaw hurt. Water thrust in, down, without mercy. Air came with it for a moment so that he fought in what might have been the right direction. But the water reclaimed him and spun so that knowledge of where the air might be was erased completely. Turbines were screaming in his ears and green sparks flew out from the centre like tracer. There was a piston engine too, racing out of gear and making the whole universe shake. Then for a moment there was air like a cold mask against his face and he bit into it. Air and water mixed, dragged down into his body like gravel. Muscles,

7

nerves and blood, struggling lungs, a machine in the head, they worked for one moment in an ancient pattern. The lumps of hard water jerked in the gullet, the lips came together and parted, the tongue arched, the brain lit a neon track.

"Moth——"

But the man lay suspended behind the whole commotion, detached from his jerking body. The luminous pictures that were shuffled before him were drenched in light but he paid no attention to them. Could he have controlled the nerves of his face, or could a face have been fashioned to fit the attitude of his consciousness where it lay suspended between life and death that face would have worn a snarl. But the real jaw was contorted down and distant, the mouth was slopped full. The green tracer that flew from the centre began to spin into a disc. The throat at such a distance from the snarling man vomited water and drew it in again. The hard lumps of water no longer hurt. There was a kind of truce, observation of the body. There was no face but there was a snarl.

A picture steadied and the man regarded it. He had not seen such a thing for so many years that the snarl became curious and lost a little intensity. It examined the picture.

The jam jar was standing on a table, brightly lit from O.P. It might have been a huge jar in the centre of a stage or a small one almost touching the face, but it was interesting because one could see into a little world there which was quite separate but which one could control. The jar was nearly full of clear water and a tiny glass figure floated upright in it. The top of the jar was covered with a thin mem-

8

brane—white rubber. He watched the jar without moving or thinking while his distant body stilled itself and relaxed. The pleasure of the jar lay in the fact that the little glass figure was so delicately balanced between opposing forces. Lay a finger on the membrane and you would compress the air below it which in turn would press more strongly on the water. Then the water would force itself farther up the little tube in the figure, and it would begin to sink. By varying the pressure on the membrane you could do anything you liked with the glass figure which was wholly in your power. You could mutter,—sink now! And down it would go, down, down; you could steady it and relent. You could let it struggle towards the surface, give it almost a bit of air then send it steadily, slowly, remorselessly down and down.

The delicate balance of the glass figure related itself to his body. In a moment of wordless realization he saw himself touching the surface of the sea with just such a dangerous stability, poised between floating and going down. The snarl thought words to itself. They were not articulate, but they were there in a luminous way as a realization.

Of course. My lifebelt.

It was bound by the tapes under that arm and that. The tapes went over the shoulders—and now he could even feel them—went round the chest and were fastened in front under the oilskin and duffle. It was almost deflated as recommended by the authorities because a tightly blown-up belt might burst when you hit the water. Swim away from the ship then blow up your belt.

With the realization of the lifebelt a flood of connected images came back—the varnished board on which the in-

9

structions were displayed, pictures of the lifebelt itself with the tube and metal tit threaded through the tapes. Suddenly he knew who he was and where he was. He was lying suspended in the water like the glass figure; he was not struggling but limp. A swell was washing regularly over his head.

His mouth slopped full and he choked. Flashes of tracer cut the darkness. He felt a weight pulling him down. The snarl came back with a picture of heavy seaboots and he began to move his legs. He got one toe over the other and shoved but the boot would not come off. He gathered himself and there were his hands far off but serviceable. He shut his mouth and performed a grim acrobatic in the water while the tracer flashed. He felt his heart thumping and for a while it was the only point of reference in the formless darkness. He got his right leg across his left thigh and heaved with sodden hands. The seaboot slipped down his calf and he kicked it free. Once the rubber top had left his toes he felt it touch him once and then it was gone utterly. He forced his left leg up, wrestled with the second boot and got it free. Both boots had left him. He let his body uncoil and lie limply.

His mouth was clever. It opened and shut for the air and against the water. His body understood too. Every now and then it would clench its stomach into a hard knot and sea water would burst out over his tongue. He began to be frightened again—not with animal panic but with deep fear of death in isolation and long drawn out. The snarl came back but now it had a face to use and air for the throat. There was something meaningful behind the snarl which would not waste the air on noises. There was a purpose which had not yet had time and experience to discover how relentless it was. It could not use the mechanism for regular breathing but it took air in gulps between the moments of burial.

He began to think in gulps as he swallowed the air. He remembered his hands again and there they were in the darkness, far away. He brought them in and began to fumble at the hard stuff of his oilskin. The button hurt and would hardly be persuaded to go through the hole. He slipped the loop off the toggle of his duffle. Lying with little movement of his body he found that the sea ignored him, treated him as a glass figure of a sailor or as a log that was almost ready to sink but would last a few moments yet. The air was regularly in attendance between the passage of the swells.

He got the rubber tube and drew it through the tapes. He could feel the slack and uninflated rubber that was so nearly not holding him up. He got the tit of the tube between his teeth and unscrewed with two fingers while the others sealed the tube. He won a little air from between swells and fuffed it through the rubber tube. For uncounted numbers of swell and hollow he taxed the air that might have gone into his lungs until his heart was staggering in his body like a wounded man and the green tracer was flicking and spinning. The lifebelt began to firm up against his chest but so slowly that he could not tell when the change came. Then abruptly the swells were washing over his shoulders and the repeated burial beneath them had become a wet and splashing slap in the face. He found he had no need to play catch-as-catch-can for air. He blew deeply and regularly into the tube until the lifebelt rose

11

and strained at his clothing. Yet he did not stop blowing at once. He played with the air, letting a little out and then blowing again as if frightened of stopping the one positive action he could take to help himself. His head and neck and shoulders were out of the water now for long intervals. They were colder than the rest of his body. The air stiffened them. They began to shake.

He took his mouth from the tube.

"Help! Help!"

The air escaped from the tube and he struggled with it. He twisted the tit until the air was safe. He stopped shouting and strained his eyes to see through the darkness but it lay right against his eyeballs. He put his hand before his eyes and saw nothing. Immediately the terror of blindness added itself to the terror of isolation and drowning. He began to make vague climbing motions in the water.

"Help! Is there anybody there? Help! Survivor!"

He lay shaking for a while and listened for an answer but the only sound was the hissing and puddling of the water as it washed round him. His head fell forward.

He licked salt water off his lips.

"Exercise."

He began to tread water gently. His mouth mumbled.

"Why did I take my sea boots off? I'm no better off than I was." His head nodded forward again.

"Cold. Mustn't get too cold. If I had those boots I could put them on and then take them off and then put them on——"

He thought suddenly of the boots sinking through water towards a bottom that was still perhaps a mile remote from them. With that, the whole wet immensity

12

seemed to squeeze his body as though he were sunk to a great depth. His chattering teeth came together and the flesh of his face twisted. He arched in the water, drawing his feet up away from the depth, the slopping, glutinous welter.

"Help! Help——"

He began to thresh with his hands and force his body round. He stared at the darkness as he turned but there was nothing to tell him when he had completed the circle and everywhere the darkness was grainless and alike. There was no wreckage, no sinking hull, no struggling survivors but himself, there was only darkness lying close against the balls of the eyes. There was the movement of water.

He began to cry out for the others, for anyone.

"Nat! Nathaniel! For Christ's sake! Nathaniel! Help!"

His voice died and his face untwisted. He lay slackly in his lifebelt, allowing the swell to do what it would. His teeth were chattering again and sometimes this vibration would spread till it included his whole body. His legs below him were not cold so much as pressed, squeezed mercilessly by the sea so that the feeling in them was not a response to temperature but to weight that would crush and burst them. He searched for a place to put his hands but there was nowhere that kept the ache out of them. The back of his neck began to hurt and that not gradually but with a sudden stab of pain so that holding his chin away from his chest was impossible. But this put his face into the sea so that he sucked it into his nose with a snoring noise and a choke. He spat and endured the pain in his neck for a while. He wedged his hands between his life-belt and his chin and for a swell or two this was some relief but then the pain returned. He let his hands fall

13

away and his face dipped in the water. He lay back, forcing his head against the pain so that his eyes if they had been open would have been looking at the sky. The pressure on his legs was bearable now. They were no longer flesh, but had been transformed to some other substance, petrified and comfortable. The part of his body that had not been invaded and wholly subdued by the sea was jerking intermittently. Eternity, inseparable from pain was there to be examined and experienced. The snarl endured. He thought. The thoughts were laborious, disconnected but vital.

Presently it will be daylight.

I must move from one point to another.

Enough to see one move ahead.

Presently it will be daylight.

I shall see wreckage.

I won't die.

I can't die.

Not me——

Precious.

He roused himself with a sudden surge of feeling that had nothing to do with the touch of the sea. Salt water was coming fast out of his eyes. He snivelled and gulped.

"Help, somebody—help!"

His body lifted and fell gently.

If I'd been below I might have got to a boat even. Or a raft. But it had to be my bloody watch. Blown off the bloody bridge. She must have gone on perhaps to starboard if he got the order in time, sinking or turning over. They'll be there in the darkness somewhere where she sank asking each other if they're down-hearted, knots and stipples of heads in the water and oil and drifting stuff.

14

When it's light I must find them, Christ I must find them. Or they'll be picked up and I'll be left to swell like a hammock. Christ!

"Help! Nathaniel! Help——!"

And I gave the right order too. If I'd done it ten seconds earlier I'd be a bloody hero—Hard a-starboard for Christ's sake!

Must have hit us bang under the bridge. And I gave the right order. And I get blown to buggery.

The snarl fixed itself, worked on the wooden face till the upper lip was lifted and the chattering teeth bared. The little warmth of anger flushed blood back into the tops of the cheeks and behind the eyes. They opened.

Then he was jerking and splashing and looking up. There was a difference in the texture of the darkness; there were smears and patches that were not in the eye itself. For a moment and before he remembered how to use his sight the patches lay on the eyeballs as close as the darkness had been. Then he firmed the use of his eyes and he was inside his head, looking out through the arches of his skull at random formations of dim light and mist. However he blinked and squinted they remained there outside him. He bent his head forward and saw, fainter than an after-image, the scalloped and changing shape of a swell as his body was lifted in it. For a moment he caught the inconstant outline against the sky, then he was floating up and seeing dimly the black top of the next swell as it swept towards him. He began to make swimming motions. His hands were glimmering patches in the water and his movements broke up the stony weight of his legs. The thoughts continued to flicker.

15

We were travelling north-east. I gave the order. If he began the turn she might be anywhere over there to the east. The wind was westerly. That's the east over there where the swells are running away down hill.

His movements and his breathing became fierce. He swam a sort of clumsy breast-stroke, buoyed up on the inflated belt. He stopped and lay wallowing. He set his teeth, took the tit of the lifebelt and let out air till he was lying lower in the water. He began to swim again. His breathing laboured. He stared out of his arches intently and painfully at the back of each swell as it slunk away from him. His legs slowed and stopped; his arms fell. His mind inside the dark skull made swimming movements long after the body lay motionless in the water.

The grain of the sky was more distinct. There were vaporous changes of tone from dark to gloom, to grey. Near at hand the individual hillocks of the surface were visible. His mind made swimming movements.

Pictures invaded his mind and tried to get between him and the urgency of his motion towards the east. The jam jar came back but robbed of significance. There was a man, a brief interview, a desk-top so polished that the smile of teeth was being reflected in it. There was a row of huge masks hung up to dry and a voice from behind the teeth that had been reflected in the desk spoke softly.

"Which one do you think would suit Christopher?"

There was a binnacle-top with the compass light just visible, there was an order shouted, hung up there for all heaven and earth to see in neon lighting.

"Hard a-starboard, for Christ's sake!"

Water washed into his mouth and he jerked into consciousness with a sound that was half a snore and half a choke. The day was inexorably present in green and grey. The seas were intimate and enormous. They smoked. When he swung up a broad, hilly crest he could see two other smoking crests then nothing but a vague circle that might be mist or fine spray or rain. He peered into the circle, turning himself, judging direction by the run of the water until he had inspected every part. The slow fire of his belly, banked up to endure, was invaded. It lay defenceless in the middle of the clothing and sodden body.

"I won't die! I won't!"

The circle of mist was everywhere alike. Crests swung into view on that side, loomed, seized him, elevated him for a moment, let him down and slunk off, but there was another crest to take him, lift him so that he could see the last one just dimming out of the circle. Then he would go down again and another crest would loom weltering towards him.

He began to curse and beat the water with the flat of his white hands. He struggled up the swells. But even the sounds of his working mouth and body were merged unnoticed in the thin innumerable sounds of travelling water. He hung still in his belt, feeling the cold search his belly with its fingers. His head fell on his chest and the stuff slopped weakly, persistently over his face. Think. My last chance. Think what can be done.

She sank out in the Atlantic. Hundreds of miles from land. She was alone, sent north-east from the convoy to break WT silence. The U-boat may be hanging round to pick up a survivor or two for questioning. Or to pick off any ship that comes to rescue survivors. She may surface

17

at any moment, breaking the swell with her heavy body like a half-tide rock. Her periscope may sear the water close by, eye of a land-creature that has defeated the rhythm and necessity of the sea. She may be passing under me now, shadowy and shark-like, she may be lying down there below my wooden feet on a bed of salty water as on a cushion while her crew sleeps. Survivors, a raft, the whaler, the dinghy, wreckage may be jilling about only a swell or two away hidden in the mist and waiting for rescue with at least bully and perhaps a tot.

He began to rotate in the water again, peering blearily at the mist, he squinted at the sky that was not much higher than a roof; he searched the circle for wreckage or a head. But there was nothing. She had gone as if a hand had reached up that vertical mile and snatched her down in one motion. When he thought of the mile he arched in the water, face twisted, and began to cry out.

"Help, curse you, sod you, bugger you—Help!"

Then he was blubbering and shuddering and the cold was squeezing him like the hand that had snatched down the ship. He hiccupped slowly into silence and started to rotate once more in the smoke and green welter.

One side of the circle was lighter than the other. The swell was shouldering itself on towards the left of this vague brightness; and where the brightness spread the mist was even more impenetrable than behind him. He remained facing the brightness not because it was of any use to him but because it was a difference that broke the uniformity of the circle and because it looked a little warmer than anywhere else. He made swimming movements again without thought and as if to follow in the wake of that brightness was an inevitable thing to do. The light made the sea-smoke seem solid. It penetrated the water so that between him and the very tops of the restless hillocks it was bottle green. For a moment or two after a wave had passed he could see right into it but the waves were nothing but water—there was no weed in them, no speck of solid, nothing drifting, nothing moving but green water, cold, persistent idiot water. There were hands to be sure and two forearms of black oilskin and there was the noise of breathing, gasping. There was also the noise of the idiot stuff, whispering, folding on itself, tripped ripples running tinkling by the ear like miniatures of surf on a flat beach; there were sudden hisses and spats, roars and incompleted syllables and the soft friction of wind. The hands were important under the bright side of the circle but they had nothing to seize on. There was an infinite drop of the soft, cold stuff below them and under the labouring, dying body.

The sense of depth caught him and he drew his dead feet up to his belly as if to detach them from the whole ocean. He arched and gaped, he rose over the chasm of deep sea on a swell and his mouth opened to scream against the brightness.

It stayed open. Then it shut with a snap of teeth and his arms began to heave water out of the way. He fought his way forward.

"Ahoy—for Christ's sake! Survivor! Survivor! Fine on your starboard bow!"

He threshed with his arms and legs into a clumsy crawl. A crest overtook him and he jerked himself to the chest out of water.

19

"Help! Help! Survivor! For God's sake!"

The force of his return sent him under but he struggled up and shook the wave from his head. The fire of his belly had spread and his heart was thrusting the sluggish blood painfully round his body. There was a ship in the mist to port of the bright patch. He was on her starboard bow—or —and the thought drove him to foam in the water—he was on her port quarter and she was moving away. But even in his fury of movement he saw how impossible this was since then she would have passed by him only a few minutes ago. So she was coming towards, to cut across the circle of visibility only a few yards from him.

Or stopped.

At that, he stopped too, and lay in the water. She was so dull a shape, little more than a looming darkness that he could not tell both her distance and her size. She was more nearly bows on than when he had first seen her and now she was visible even when he was in a trough. He began to swim again but every time he rose on a crest he screamed.

"Help! Survivor!"

But what ship was ever so lop-sided? A carrier? A derelict carrier, deserted and waiting to sink? But she would have been knocked down by a salvo of torpedoes. A derelict liner? Then she must be one of the Queens by her bulk—and why lop-sided? The sun and the mist were balanced against each other. The sun could illumine the mist but not pierce it. And darkly in the sun-mist loomed the shape of a not-ship where nothing but a ship could be.

He began to swim again, feeling suddenly the desperate

20

exhaustion of his body. The first, fierce excitement of sighting had burned up the fuel and the fire was low again. He swam grimly, forcing his arms through the water, reaching forward under his arches with sight as though he could pull himself into safety with it. The shape moved. It grew larger and not clearer. Every now and then there was something like a bow-wave at the forefoot. He ceased to look at her but swam and screamed alternately with the last strength of his body. There was green force round him, growing in strength to rob, there was mist and glitter over him; there was a redness pulsing in front of his eyes—his body gave up and he lay slack in the waves and the shape rose over him. He heard through the rasp and thump of his works the sound of waves breaking. He lifted his head and there was rock stuck up in the sky with a sea-gull poised before it. He heaved over in the sea and saw how each swell dipped for a moment, flung up a white hand of foam then disappeared as if the rock had swallowed it. He began to think swimming motions but knew now that his body was no longer obedient. The top of the next swell between him and the rock was blunted, smoothed curiously, then jerked up spray. He sank down, saw without comprehension that the green water was no longer empty. There was yellow and brown. He heard not the formless mad talking of uncontrolled water but a sudden roar. Then he went under into a singing world and there were hairy shapes that flitted and twisted past his face, there were sudden notable details close to of intricate rock and weed. Brown tendrils slashed across his face, then with a destroying shock he hit solidity. It was utter difference, it was under his body, against his knees and face, he could close

21

fingers on it, for an instant he could even hold on. His mouth was heedlessly open and his eyes so that he had a moment of close and intent communion with three limpets, two small and one large that were only an inch or two from his face. Yet this solidity was terrible and apocalyptic after the world of inconstant wetness. It was not vibrant as a ship's hull might be but merciless and mother of panic. It had no business to interrupt the thousands of miles of water going about their purposeless affairs and therefore the world sprang here into sudden war. He felt himself picked up and away from the limpets, reversed, tugged, thrust down into weed and darkness. Ropes held him, slipped and let him go. He saw light, got a mouthful of air and foam. He glimpsed a riven rock face with trees of spray growing up it and the sight of this rock floating in mid-Atlantic was so dreadful that he wasted his air by screaming as if it had been a wild beast. He went under into a green calm, then up and was thrust sideways. The sea no longer played with him. It stayed its wild movement and held him gently, carried him with delicate and careful motion like a retriever with a bird. Hard things touched him about the feet and knees. The sea laid him down gently and retreated. There were hard things touching his face and chest, the side of his forehead. The sea came back and fawned round his face, licked him. He thought movements that did not happen. The sea came back and he thought the movements again and this time they happened because the sea took most of his weight. They moved him forward over the hard things. Each wave and each movement moved him forward. He felt the sea run down to smell at his feet then come back and nuzzle under his arm. It no

22

longer licked his face. There was a pattern in front of him that occupied all the space under the arches. It meant nothing. The sea nuzzled under his arm again.

He lay still.

2

The pattern was white and black but mostly white. It existed in two layers, one behind the other, one for each eye. He thought nothing, did nothing while the pattern changed a trifle and made little noises. The hardnesses under his cheek began to insist. They passed through pressure to a burning without heat, to a localized pain. They became vicious in their insistence like the nag of an aching tooth. They began to pull him back into himself and organize him again as a single being.

Yet it was not the pain nor the white and black pattern that first brought him back to life, but the noises. Though the sea had treated him so carefully, elsewhere it continued to roar and thump and collapse on itself. The wind too, given something to fight with other than obsequious water was hissing round the rock and breathing gustily in crevices. All these noises made a language which forced itself into the dark, passionless head and assured it that the head was somewhere, somewhere—and then finally with the flourish of a gull's cry over the sound of wind and water, declared to the groping consciousness: wherever you are, you are here!

Then he was there, suddenly, enduring pain but in deep communion with the solidity that held up his body. He remembered how eyes should be used and brought the two lines of sight together so that the patterns fused and made a distance. The pebbles were close to his face, pressing against his cheek and jaw. They were white quartz, dulled and rounded, a miscellany of potato-shapes. Their whiteness was qualified by yellow stains and flecks of darker material. There was a whiter thing beyond them. He examined it without curiosity, noting the bleached wrinkles, the blue roots of nails, the corrugations at the finger-tips. He did not move his head but followed the line of the hand back to an oilskin sleeve, the beginnings of a shoulder. His eyes returned to the pebbles and watched them idly as if they were about to perform some operation for which he was waiting without much interest. The hand did not move.

Water welled up among the pebbles. It stirred them slightly, paused, then sank away while the pebbles clicked and chirruped. It swilled down past his body and pulled gently at his stockinged feet. He watched the pebbles while the water came back and this time the last touch of the sea lopped into his open mouth. Without change of expression he began to shake, a deep shake that included the whole of his body. Inside his head it seemed that the pebbles were shaking because the movement of his white hand forward and back was matched by the movement of his body. Under the side of his face the pebbles nagged.

The pictures that came and went inside his head did not disturb him because they were so small and remote. There was a woman's body, white and detailed, there was a boy's

25

body; there was a box office, the bridge of a ship, an order picked out across a far sky in neon lighting, a tall, thin man who stood aside humbly in the darkness at the top of a companion ladder; there was a man hanging in the sea like a glass sailor in a jam jar. There was nothing to choose between the pebbles and the pictures. Sometimes one was uppermost, sometimes the other. The individual pebbles were no bigger than the pictures. Sometimes a pebble would be occupied entirely by a picture as though it were a window, a spy-hole into a different world or other dimension. Words and sounds were sometimes visible as shapes like the shouted order. They did not vibrate and disappear. When they were created they remained as hard enduring things like the pebbles. Some of these were inside the skull, behind the arch of the brow and the shadowy nose. They were right in the indeterminate darkness above the fire of hardnesses. If you looked out idly, you saw round them.

There was a new kind of coldness over his body. It was creeping down his back between the stuffed layers of clothing. It was air that felt like slow fire. He had hardly noticed this when a wave came back and filled his mouth so that a choke interrupted the rhythm of shaking.

He began to experiment. He found that he could haul the weight of one leg up and then the other. His hand crawled round above his head. He reasoned deeply that there was another hand on the other side somewhere and sent a message out to it. He found the hand and worked the wrist. There were still fingers on it, not because he could move them but because when he pushed he could feel the wooden tips shifting the invisible pebbles. He moved his four limbs in close and began to make swimming

26

movements. The vibrations from the cold helped him. Now his breath went in and out quickly and his heart began to race again. The inconsequential pictures vanished and there was nothing but pebbles and pebble noises and heart-thumps. He had a valuable thought, not because it was of immediate physical value but because it gave him back a bit of his personality. He made words to express this thought, though they did not pass the barrier of his teeth.

"I should be about as heavy as this on Jupiter."

At once he was master. He knew that his body weighed no more than it had always done, that it was exhausted, that he was trying to crawl up a little pebble slope. He lifted the dents in his face away from the pebbles that had made them and pushed with his knees. His teeth came together and ground. He timed the expansion of his chest against the pebbles, the slow shaking of his body till they did not hold up the leaden journey. He felt how each wave finished farther and farther down towards his feet. When the journey became too desperate he would wait, gasping, until the world came back. The water no longer touched his feet.

His left hand—the hidden one—touched something that did not click and give. He rolled his head and looked up under the arch. There was greyish yellow stuff in front of his face. It was pock-marked and hollowed, dotted with red lumps of jelly. The yellow tents of limpets were pitched in every hole. Brown fronds and green webs of weed hung over them. The white pebbles led up into a dark angle. There was a film of water glistening over everything, drops falling, tiny pools caught at random, lying and shuddering

27

or leaking down among the weed. He began to turn on the pebbles, working his back against the rock and drawing up his feet. He saw them now for the first time, distant projections, made thick and bear-like by the white, seaboot stockings. They gave him back a little more of himself. He got his left hand down beneath his ear and began to heave. His shoulder lifted a little. He pushed with feet, pulled with hands. His back was edging into the angle where the pools leaked down. His head was high. He took a thigh in both hands and pulled it towards his chest and then the other. He packed himself into the angle and looked down at the pebbles over his knees. His mouth had fallen open again.

And after all, as pebbles go there were not very many of them. The length of a man or less would measure out the sides of the triangle that they made under the shadow of the rock. They filled the cleft and they were solid.

He took his eyes away from the pebbles and made them examine the water. This was almost calm in comparison with the open sea; and the reason was the rock round which the waves had whirled him. He could see the rock out there now. It was the same stuff as this, grey and creamy with barnacles and foam. Each wave tripped on it so that although the water ran and thumped on either side of the cleft, there was a few yards of green, clear water between him and the creamy rock. Beyond the rock was nothing but a smoking advance of sea with watery sunlight caught in it.

He let his eyes close and ignored the pictures that came and went behind them. The slow movement of his mind settled on a thought. There was a small fire in his body

28

that was almost extinguished but incredibly was still smouldering despite the Atlantic. He folded his body consciously round that fire and nursed it. There was not more than a spark. The formal words and the pictures evolved themselves.

A seabird c ied over him with a long sound descending down wind. He removed his attention from the spark of fire and opened his eyes again. This time he had got back so much of his personality that he could look out and grasp the whole of what he saw at once. There were the dark walls of rock on either side that framed the brighter light. There was sunlight on a rock with spray round it and the steady march of swells that brought their own fine mist along with them under the sun. He turned his head sideways and peered up.

The rock was smoother above the weeds and limpets and drew together. There was an opening at the top with daylight and the suggestion of cloud caught in it. As he watched, a gull flicked across the opening and cried in the wind. He found the effort of looking up hurt him and he turned to his body, examined the humps that were his knees under the oilskin and duffle. He looked closely at a button.

His mouth shut then opened. Sounds came out. He readjusted them and they were uncertain words.

"I know you. Nathaniel sewed you on. I asked him to. Said it was an excuse to get him away from the mess-deck for a bit of peace."

His eyes closed again and he fingered the button clumsily.

"Had this oilskin when I was a rating. Lofty sewed on the buttons before Nathaniel."

His head nodded on his knees.

"All the blue watch. Blue watch to muster."

The pictures were interrupted by the solid shape of a snore. The shiverings were less dramatic but they took power from his arms so that presently they fell away from his knees and his hands lay on the pebbles. His head shook. Between the snores the pebbles were hard to the feet, harder to the backside when the heels had slid slowly from under. The pictures were so confused that there was as much danger that they would destroy the personality as that the spark of fire would go out. He forced his way among them, lifted his eyelids and looked out.

The pebbles were wavering down there where the water welled over them. Higher up, the rock that had saved him was lathered and fringed with leaping strings of foam. There was afternoon brightness outside but the cleft was dripping, dank and smelly as a dockside latrine. He made quacking sounds with his mouth. The words that had formed in his mind were: Where is this bloody rock? But that seemed to risk something by insult of the dark cleft so that he changed them in his throat.

"Where the hell am I?"

A single point of rock, peak of a mountain range, one tooth set in the ancient jaw of a sunken world, projecting through the inconceivable vastness of the whole ocean—and how many miles from dry land? An evil pervasion, not the convulsive panic of his first struggles in the water, but a deep and generalized terror set him clawing at the rock with his blunt fingers. He even got half-up and leaned or crouched against the weed and the lumps of jelly.

"Think, you bloody fool, think."

The horizon of misty water stayed close, the water leapt from the rock and the pebbles wavered.

"Think."

He crouched, watching the rock, not moving but trembling continually. He noted how the waves broke on the outer rock and were tamed, so that the water before the cleft was sloppily harmless. Slowly, he settled back into the angle of the cleft. The spark was alight and the heart was supplying it with what it wanted. He watched the outer rock but hardly saw it. There was a name missing. That name was written on the chart, well out in the Atlantic, eccentrically isolated so that seamen who could to a certain extent laugh at wind and weather had made a joke of the rock. Frowning, he saw the chart now in his mind's eye but not clearly. He saw the navigating commander of the cruiser bending over it with the captain, saw himself as navigator's yeoman standing ready while they grinned at each other. The captain spoke with his clipped Dartmouth accent—spoke and laughed.

"I call that name a near miss."

Near miss whatever the name was. And now to be huddled on a near miss how many miles from the Hebrides? What was the use of the spark if it winked away in a crack of that ludicrous isolation? He spat his words at the picture of the captain.

"I am no better off than I was."

He began to slide down the rocks as his bones bent their hinges. He slumped into the angle and his head fell. He snored.

But inside, where the snores were external, the consciousness was moving and poking about among the

31

pictures and revelations, among the shape-sounds and the disregarded feelings like an animal ceaselessly examining its cage. It rejected the detailed bodies of women, slowly sorted the odd words, ignored the pains and the insistence of the shaking body. It was looking for a thought. It found the thought, separated it from the junk, lifted it and used the apparatus of the body to give it force and importance.

"I am intelligent."

There was a period of black suspension behind the snores; then the right hand, so far away, obeyed a command and began to fumble and pluck at the oilskin. It raised a flap and crawled inside. The fingers found cord and a shut clasp-knife. They stayed there.

The eyes blinked open so that the arch of brows was a frame to green sea. For a while the eyes looked, received impressions without seeing them. Then the whole body gave a jump. The spark became a flame, the body scrambled, crouched, the hand flicked out of the oilskin pocket and grabbed rock. The eyes stared and did not blink.

As the eyes watched, a wave went clear over the outer rock so that they could see the brown weed inside the water. The green dance beyond the pebbles was troubled. A line of foam broke and hissed up the pebbles to his feet. The foam sank away and the pebbles chattered like teeth. He watched, wave after wave as bursts of foam swallowed more and more of the pebbles and left fewer visible when they went back. The outer rock was no longer a barrier but only a gesture of defence. The cleft was being connected more and more directly with the irresistible progress of the green, smoking seas. He jerked away from the open water and turned towards the rock. The dark, lavatorial cleft,

32

with its dripping weed, with its sessile, mindless life of shell and jelly was land only twice a day by courtesy of the moon. It felt like solidity but it was a sea-trap, as alien to breathing life as the soft slop of the last night and the vertical mile.

A gull screamed with him so that he came back into himself, leaned his forehead against the rock and waited for his heart to steady. A shot of foam went over his feet. He looked down past them. There were fewer pebbles to stand on and those that had met his hands when he had been washed ashore were yellow and green beneath a foot of jumping water. He turned to the rock again and spoke out loud.

"Climb!"

He turned round and found handholds in the cleft. There were many to choose from. His hands were poor, sodden stuff against their wet projections. He leaned a moment against the rock and gathered the resources of his body together. He lifted his right leg and dropped the foot in an opening like an ash-tray. There was an edge to the ash-tray but not a sharp one and his foot could feel nothing. He took his forehead away from a weedy surface and heaved himself up until the right leg was straight. His left leg swung and thumped. He got the toes on a shelf and stayed so, only a few inches off the pebbles and spreadeagled. The cleft rose by his face and he looked at the secret drops of the stillicide in the dark angle as though he envied them their peace. Time went by drop by drop. The two pictures drifted apart.

The pebbles rattled below him and a last lick of water flipped into the crevice. He dropped his head and looked

33

down over his lifebelt, through the open skirt of the oilskin to where the wetted pebbles lay in the angle of the cleft. He saw his seaboot stockings and thought his feet back into them.

"I wish I had my seaboots still."

He changed the position of his right foot cautiously and locked his left knee stiffly upright to bear his weight without effort. His feet were selective in a curious way. They could not feel rock unless there was sharpness. They only became a part of him when they were hurting him or when he could see them.

The tail end of a wave reached right into the angle and struck in the apex with a plop. A single string of spray leapt up between his legs, past the lifebelt and wetted his face. He made a sound and only then found how ruinous an extension of flesh he carried round him. The sound began in the throat, bubbled and stayed there. The mouth took no part but lay open, jaw lying slack on the hard oilskin collar. The bubbling increased and he made the teeth click. Words twisted out between them and the frozen stuff of his upper lip.

"Like a dead man!"

Another wave reached in and spray ran down his face. He began to labour at climbing. He moved up the intricate rock face until there were no more limpets nor mussels and nothing clung to the rock but his own body and tiny barnacles and green smears of weed. All the time the wind pushed him into the cleft and the sea made dispersed noises.

The cleft narrowed until his head projected through an opening, not much wider than his body. He got his elbows jammed on either side and looked up.

Before his face the rock widened above the narrowest part of the cleft into a funnel. The sides of the funnel were not very smooth; but they were smooth enough to refuse to hold a body by friction. They sloped away to the top of the rock like a roof angle. The track from his face to the cliff-like edge of the funnel at the top was nearly twice the length of a man. He began to turn his head, slowly, searching for handholds, but saw none. Only at about half-way there was a depression, but too shallow for a hand-hold. Blunted fingers would never be safe on the rounded edge.

There came a thud from the bottom of the angle. Solid water shot into the angle, burst and washed down again. He peered over his lifebelt, between his two feet. The pebbles were dimmed, appeared clearly for a moment, then vanished under a surge of green water. Spray shot up between his body and the rock.

He pulled himself up until his body from the waist was leaning forward along the slope. His feet found the holds where his elbows had been. His knees straightened slowly while he breathed in gasps and his right arm reached out in front of him. Fingers closed on the blunted edge of the depression. Pulled.

He took one foot away from a hold and edged the knee up. He moved the other.

He hung, only a few inches from the top of the angle, held by one hand and the friction of his body. The fingers of his right hand quivered and gave. They slipped over the rounded edge. His whole body slid down and he was back at the top of the crevice again. He lay still, not seeing the rock by his eyes and his right arm was stretched above him.

35

The sea was taking over the cleft. Every few seconds there came the thump and return of a wave below him. Heavy drops fell and trickled on the surface of the funnel before his face. Then a wave exploded and water cascaded over his legs. He lifted his face off the rock and the snarl wrestled with his stiff muscles.

"Like a limpet."

He lay for a while, bent at the top of the crevice. The pebbles no longer appeared in the angle. They were a wavering memory of themselves between bouts of spray. Then they vanished, the rock vanished with them and with another explosion the water hit him from head to foot. He shook it from his face. He was staring down at the crevice as though the water were irrelevant.

He cried out.

"Like a limpet!"

He put his feet down and felt for holds, lowered himself resolutely, clinging each time the water hit him and went back. He held his breath and spat when each wave left him. The water was no longer cold but powerful rather. The nearer he lowered his body to the pebbles the harder he was struck and the heavier the weight that urged him down at each return. He lost his hold and fell the last few inches and immediately a wave had him, thrust him brutally into the angle then tried to tear him away. Between waves when he staggered to his feet the water was knee-deep over the pebbles and they gave beneath him. He fell on all fours and was hidden in a green heap that hit the back of the angle and climbed up in a tree-trunk of spray. He staggered round the angle then gripped with both hands. The water tore at him but he held on. He got his knife free and opened the

36

blade. He ducked down and immediately there were visions of rock and weed in front of his eyes. The uproar of the sea sank to a singing note in the ears. Then he was up again, the knife swinging free, two limpets in his hands and the sea knocked him down and stood him on his head. He found rock and clung against the backwash. When the waves left him for a moment he opened his mouth and gasped in the air as though he were winning territory. He found holds in the angle and the sea exploded, thrust him up so that now his effort was to stay down and under control. After each blow he flattened himself to escape the descent of the water. As he rose the seas lost their quality of leaden power but became more personal and vicious. They tore at his clothing, they beat him in the crutch, they tented up his oilskin till the skirt was crumpled above his waist. If he looked down the water came straight at his face, or hit him in the guts and thrust him up.

He came to the narrowest part and was shoved through. He opened his eyes after the water gushed back and breathed wetly as the foam streamed down his face. A lock of hair was plastered just to the bridge of his nose and he saw the end of it, double. The chute struck him again, the waterfall rushed back and he was still there, wedged by his weight in the narrowest part of the crevice where the funnel began and his body was shaking. He lay forward on the slope and began to straighten his legs. His face moved up against the rock and a torrent swept back over him. He began to fumble in the crumples of his oilskin. He brought out a limpet and set it on the rock by his waist. Water came again and went. He reversed his knife and tapped the limpet on the top with the haft. The limpet gave a tiny sideways lurch and sucked itself down against the rock. A weight pressed on him and the man and the limpet firmed down against the rock together.

His legs were straight and stiff and his eyes were shut. He brought his right arm round in a circle and felt above him. He found the blunted dent that was too smooth for a handhold. His hand came back, was inundated, fumbled in oilskin. He pulled it out and when the hand crawled round and up there was a limpet in the palm. The man was looking at the rock an inch or two from his face but without interest. What life was left was concentrated in the crawling right hand. The hand found the blunted hollow, and pitched the limpet beyond the edge. The body was lifted a few inches and lay motionless waiting for the return of the water. When the chute had passed the hand came back, took the knife, moved up and tapped blindly on rock. The fingers searched stiffly, found the limpet, hit with the haft of the knife.

He turned his face, endured another wave and considered the limpet above him gravely. His hand let the knife go, which slid and clattered and hung motionless by his waist. He took the tit of the lifebelt and unscrewed the end. The air breathed out and his body flattened a little in the funnel. He laid the side of his head down and did nothing. Before his mouth the wet surface of the rock was blurred a little and regularly the blur was erased by the return of the waterfall. Sometimes the pendant knife would clatter.

Again he turned his face and looked up. His fingers closed over the limpet. Now his right leg was moving. The toes searched tremulously for the first limpet as the fingers had searched for the second. They did not find the limpet

38

but the knee did. The hand let go, came down to the knee and lifted that part of the leg. The snarl behind the stiff face felt the limpet as a pain in the crook of the knee. The teeth set. The whole body began to wriggle; the hand went back to the higher limpet and pulled. The man moved sideways up the slope of the roof. The left leg came in and the seaboot stocking pushed the first leg away. The side of the foot was against the limpet. The leg straightened. Another torrent returned and washed down.

The man was lying with one foot on a limpet, held mostly by friction. But his foot was on one limpet and the second one was before his eyes. He reached up and there was a possible handhold that his fingers found, provided the other one still gripped the limpet by his face. He moved up, up, up and then there was an edge for his fingers. His right arm rose, seized. He pulled with both arms, thrust with both legs. He saw a trench of rock beyond the edge, glimpsed sea, saw whiteness on the rocks and jumble. He fell forward.

3

He was lying in a trench. He could see a weathered wall of rock and a long pool of water stretching away from his eye. His body was in some other place that had nothing to do with this landscape. It was splayed, scattered behind him, his legs in different worlds, neck twisted. His right arm was bent under his body and his wrist doubled. He sensed this hand and the hard pressure of the knuckles against his side but the pain was not intense enough to warrant the titanic effort of moving. His left arm stretched away along the trench and was half-covered in water. His right eye was so close to this water that he could feel a little pluck from the surface tension when he blinked and his eyelashes caught in the film. The water had flattened again by the time he saw the surface consciously but his right cheek and the corner of his mouth were under water and were causing a tremble. The other eye was above water and was looking down the trench. The inside of the trench was dirty white, strangely white with more than the glossy reflection from the sky. The corner of his mouth pricked. Sometimes the surface of the water was pitted for a moment or two and faint, interlacing circles spread over

40

it from each pit. His left eye watched them, looking through a kind of arch of darkness where the skull swept round the socket. At the bottom and almost a straight line, was the skin colour of his nose. Filling the arch was the level of shining water.

He began to think slowly.

I have tumbled in a trench. My head is jammed against the farther side and my neck is twisted. My legs must be up in the air over the other wall. My thighs are hurting because the weight of my legs is pushing against the edge of the wall as a fulcrum. My right toes are hurt more than the rest of my leg. My hand is doubled under me and that is why I feel the localized pain in my ribs. My fingers might be made of wood. That whiter white under the water along there is my hand, hidden.

There was a descending scream in the air, a squawk and the beating of wings. A gull was braking wildly over the wall at the end of the trench, legs and claws held out. It yelled angrily at the trench, the wide wings gained a purchase and it hung flapping only a foot or two above the rock. Wind chilled his cheek. The webbed feet came up, the wings steadied and the gull side-slipped away. The commotion of its passage made waves in the white water that beat against his cheek, the shut eye, the corner of his mouth. The stinging increased.

There was no pain sharp enough to compel action. Even the stinging was outside the head. His left eye watched the whiter white of his hand under water. Some of the memory pictures came back. They were new ones of a man climbing up rock and placing limpets.

The pictures stirred him more than the stinging. They

41

made his left hand contract under the surface and the oilskin arm roll in the water. His breathing grew suddenly fierce so that waves rippled away along the trench, crossed and came back. A ripple splashed into his mouth.

Immediately he was convulsed and struggling. His legs kicked and swung sideways. His head ground against rock and turned. He scrabbled in the white water with both hands and heaved himself up. He felt the too-smooth wetness running on his face and the brilliant jab of pain at the corner of his right eye. He spat and snarled. He glimpsed the trenches with their thick layers of dirty white, their trapped inches of solution, a gull slipping away over a green sea. Then he was forcing himself forward. He fell into the next trench, hauled himself over the wall, saw a jumble of broken rock, slid and stumbled. He was going down hill and he fell part of the way. There was moving water round flattish rocks, a complication of weedy life. The wind went down with him and urged him forward. As long as he went forward the wind was satisfied but if he stopped for a moment's caution it thrust his unbalanced body down so that he scraped and hit. He saw little of the open sea and sky or the whole rock but only flashes of intimate being, a crack or point, a hand's breadth of yellowish surface that was about to strike a blow, unavoidable fists of rock that beat him impersonally, struck bright flashes of light from his body. The pain in the corner of his eye went with him too. This was the most important of all the pains because it thrust a needle now into the dark skull where he lived. The pain could not be avoided. His body revolved round it. Then he was holding brown weed and the sea was washing over his head and shoulders. He pulled

42

himself up and lay on a flat rock with a pool across the top. He rolled the side of his face and his eye backwards and forwards under water. He moved his hands gently so that the water swished. They left the water and reached round and gathered smears of green weed.

He knelt up and held the smears of green against his eye and the right side of his face. He slumped back against rock among the jellies and scalloped pitches and encampments of limpets and let the encrusted barnacles hurt him as they would. He set his left hand gently on his thigh and squinted sideways at it. The fingers were half-bent. The skin was white with blue showing through and wrinkles cut the surface in regular shapes. The needle reached after him in the skull behind the dark arch. If he moved the eyeball the needle moved too. He opened his eye and it filled immediately with water under the green weed.

He began to snort and make sounds deep in his chest. They were like hard lumps of sound and they jerked him as they came out. More salt water came out of each eye and joined the traces of the sea and the solution on his cheeks. His whole body began to shiver.

There was a deeper pool on a ledge farther down. He climbed slowly and heavily down, edged himself across and put his right cheek under again. He opened and closed his eye so that the water flushed the needle corner. The memory pictures had gone so far away that they could be disregarded. He felt round and buried his hands in the pool. Now and then a hard sound jerked his body.

The sea-gull came back with others and he heard them sounding their interlacing cries like a trace of their flight over his head. There were noises from the sea too, wet gurgles below his ear and the running thump of swells, blanketed by the main of the rock but still able to sidle round and send offshoots sideways among the rocks and into the crannies. The idea that he must ignore pain came and sat in the centre of his darkness where he could not avoid it. He opened his eyes for all the movement of the needle and looked down at his bleached hands. He began to mutter.

"Shelter. Must have shelter. Die if I don't."

He turned his head carefully and looked up the way he had come. The odd patches of rock that had hit him on the way down were visible now as part of each other. His eyes took in yards at a time, surfaces that swam as the needle pricked water out of him. He set himself to crawl back up the rock. The wind was lighter but dropping trails of rain still fell over him. He hauled himself up a cliff that was no higher than a man could span with his arms but it was an obstacle that had to be negotiated with much arrangement and thought for separate limbs. He lay for a while on the top of the little cliff and looked in watery snatches up the height of the rock. The sun lay just above the high part where the white trenches had waited for him. The light was struggling with clouds and rain-mist and there were birds wheeling across the rock. The sun was dull but drew more water from his eyes so that he screwed them up and cried out suddenly against the needle. He crawled by touch, and then with one eye through trenches and gullies where there was no whiteness. He lifted his legs over the broken walls of trenches as though they belonged to another body. All at once, with the diminishing of the pain in his eye, the cold and exhaustion came back. He fell flat in a gully and

44

let his body look after itself. The deep chill fitted close to him, so close it was inside the clothes, inside the skin.

The chill and the exhaustion spoke to him clearly. Give up, they said, lie still. Give up the thought of return, the thought of living. Break up, leave go. Those white bodies are without attraction or excitement, the faces, the words, happened to another man in another place. An hour on this rock is a lifetime. What have you to lose? There is nothing here but torture. Give up. Leave go.

His body began to crawl again. It was not that there was muscular or nervous strength there that refused to be beaten but rather that the voices of pain were like waves beating against the sides of a ship. There was at the centre of all the pictures and pains and voices a fact like a bar of steel, a thing—that which was so nakedly the centre of everything that it could not even examine itself. In the darkness of the skull, it existed, a darker dark, self-existent and indestructible.

"Shelter. Must have shelter."

The centre began to work. It endured the needle to look sideways, put thoughts together. It concluded that it must crawl this way rather than that. It noted a dozen places and rejected them, searched ahead of the crawling body. It lifted the luminous window under the arch, shifted the arch of skull from side to side like the slow shift of the head of a caterpillar trying to reach a new leaf. When the body drew near to a possible shelter the head still moved from side to side, moving more quickly than the slow thoughts inside.

There was a slab of rock that had slipped and fallen sideways from the wall of a trench. This made a triangular

45

hole between the rock and the side and bottom of the trench. There was no more than a smear of rainwater in this trench and no white stuff. The hole ran away and down at an angle following the line of the trench and inside there was darkness. The hole even looked drier than the rest of the rock. At last his head stopped moving and he lay down before this hole as the sun dipped from view. He began to turn his body in the trench, among a complication of sodden clothing. He said nothing but breathed heavily with open mouth. Slowly he turned until his white seaboot stockings were towards the crevice. He backed to the triangular opening and put his feet in. He lay flat on his stomach and began to wriggle weakly like a snake that cannot cast its skin. His eyes were open and unfocused. He reached back and forced the oilskin and duffle down on either side. The oilskin was hard and he backed with innumerable separate movements like a lobster backing into a deep crevice under water. He was in the crack up to his shoulders and rock held him tightly. He hutched the lifebelt up till the soft rubber was across the upper part of his chest. The slow thoughts waxed and waned, the eyes were empty except for the water that ran from the needle in the right one. His hand found the tit and he blew again slowly until the rubber was firmed up against his chest. He folded his arms, a white hand on either side. He let the left side of his face fall on an oilskinned sleeve and his eyes were shut —not screwed up but lightly closed. His mouth was still open, the jaw fallen sideways. Now and then a shudder came up out of the crack and set his head and arms shaking. Water ran slowly out of his sleeves, fell from his hair and his nose, dripped from the rucked-up clothing round

46

his neck. His eyes fell open like the mouth because the needle was more controllable that way. Only when he had to blink them against water did the point jab into the place where he lived.

He could see gulls swinging over the rock, circling down. They settled and cried with erect heads and tongues, beaks wide open on the high point of the rock. The sky greyed down and sea-smoke drifted over. The birds talked and shook their wings, folded them one over the other, settled like white pebbles against the rock and tucked in their heads. The greyness thickened into a darkness in which the few birds and the splashes of their dung were visible as the patches of foam were visible on the water. The trenches were full of darkness for down by the shelter for some reason there was no dirty white. The rocks were dim shapes among them. The wind blew softly and chill over the main rock and its unseen, gentle passage made a continual and almost inaudible hiss. Every now and then a swell thumped into the angle by the safety rock. After that there would be a long pause and then the rush and scramble of falling water down the funnel.

The man lay, huddled in his crevice, left cheek pillowed on black oilskin and his hands were glimmering patches on either side. Every now and then there came a faint scratching sound of oilskin as the body shivered.

4

The man was inside two crevices. There was first the rock, close and not warm but at least not cold with the coldness of sea or air. The rock was negative. It confined his body so that here and there the shudders were beaten; not soothed but forced inward. He felt pain throughout most of his body but distant pain that was sometimes to be mistaken for fire. There was dull fire in his feet and a sharper sort in either knee. He could see this fire in his mind's eye because his body was a second and interior crevice which he inhabited. Under each knee, then, there was a little fire built with crossed sticks and busily flaring like the fire that is lighted under a dying camel. But the man was intelligent. He endured these fires although they gave not heat but pain. They had to be endured because to stand up or even move would mean nothing but an increase of pain—more sticks and more flame, extending under all the body. He himself was at the far end of this inner crevice of flesh. At this far end, away from the fires, there was a mass of him lying on a lifebelt that rolled backwards and forwards at every breath. Beyond the mass was the round, bone globe of the world and himself hang-

48

ing inside. One half of this world burned and froze but with a steadier and bearable pain. Only towards the top half of this world there would sometimes come a jab that was like a vast needle prying after him. Then he would make seismic convulsions of whole continents on that side and the jabs would become frequent but less deep and the nature of that part of the globe would change. There would appear shapes of dark and grey in space and a patch of galactic whiteness that he knew vaguely was a hand connected to him. The other side of the globe was all dark and gave no offence. He floated in the middle of this globe like a waterlogged body. He knew as an axiom of existence that he must be content with the smallest of all small mercies as he floated there. All the extensions with which he was connected, their distant fires, their slow burnings, their racks and pincers were at least far enough away. If he could hit some particular mode of inactive being, some subtlety of interior balance, he might be allowed by the nature of the second crevice to float, still and painless in the centre of the globe.

Sometimes he came near this. He became small, and the globe larger until the burning extensions were interplanetary. But this universe was subject to convulsions that began in deep space and came like a wave. Then he was larger again, filling every corner of the tunnels, sweeping with shrieking nerves over the fires, expanding in the globe until he filled it and the needle jabbed through the corner of his right eye straight into the darkness of his head. Dimly he would see one white hand while the pain stabbed. Then slowly he would sink back into the centre of the globe, shrink and float in the middle of a dark world. This became a rhythm that had obtained from all ages and would endure so.

This rhythm was qualified but not altered in essentials by pictures that happened to him and sometimes to someone else. They were brightly lit in comparison with the fires. There were waves larger than the universe and a glass sailor hanging in them. There was an order in neon lighting. There was a woman, not like the white detailed bodies but with a face. There was the gloom and hardness of a night-time ship, the lift of the deck, the slow cant and bumble. He was walking forward across the bridge to the binnacle and its dim light. He could hear Nat leaving his post as port look-out, Nat going down the ladder. He could hear that Nat had walking shoes on, not seaboots or plimsols. Nat was lowering his un-handy spider-length down the ladder with womanish care, not able now after all these months to wear the right clothes or negotiate a ladder like a seaman. Dawn had found him shivering from inadequate rig, the mess-deck would find him hurt by the language, a butt, humble, obedient and useless.

He looked briefly at the starboard horizon then across to the convoy, bulks just coming into view in the dawn light. They interrupted the horizon like so many bleak iron walls where now the long, blurred tears of rust were nearly visible.

But Nat would be fumbling aft, to find five minutes' solitude by the rail and meet his aeons. He would be picking his diffident way toward the depth-charge thrower on the starboard side not because it was preferable to the port rail but because he always went there. He would be enduring the wind and engine stink, the peculiar dusty dirt and shabbiness of a wartime destroyer because life itself with all its touches, tastes, sights and sounds and smells had been at a distance from him. He would go on enduring until custom made him indifferent. He would never find his feet in the Navy because those great feet of his had always been away out there, attached by accident while the man inside prayed and waited to meet his aeons.

But the deck-watch was ticking on to the next leg of the zigzag. He looked carefully at the second hand.

"Starboard fifteen."

Out on the port bow *Wildebeeste* was turning too. The grey light showed the swirl under her stern where the rudder had kicked across. As the bridge canted under him *Wildebeeste* seemed to slide astern from her position until she was lying parallel and just forrard of the beam.

"Midships."

Wildebeeste was still turning. Connected by the soles of his feet through steel to the long waver and roll of glaucous water he could predict to himself the exact degree of her list to port as she came round. But the water was not so predictable after all. In the last few degrees of her turn he saw a mound of grey, a seventh wave slide by her bows and pass under her. The swing of her stern increased, her stern slid down the slope and for that time she had carried ten degrees beyond her course, in a sudden lurch.

"Steady."

And curse the bloody Navy and the bloody war. He yawned sleepily and saw the swirl under *Wildebeeste's* stern as she came back on course. The fires out there at the end of the second crevice flared up, a needle stabbed

51

and he was back in his body. The fire died down again in the usual rhythm.

The destroyers in a V screen turned back together. Between orders he listened to the shivering ping of the Asdic and the light increased. The herd of merchantmen chugged on at six knots with the destroyers like outriders scouring the way before them, sweeping the sea clear with their invisible brooms, changing course together, all on one string.

He heard a step behind him on the ladder and busied himself to take a bearing because the captain might be coming. He checked the bearing of *Wildebeeste* with elaborate care. But no voice came with the steps.

He turned casually at last and there was Petty Officer Roberts—and now saluting.

"Good morning, Chief."

"Good morning, sir."

"What is it? Wangled a tot for me?"

The close eyes under their peak withdrew a little but the mouth made itself smile.

"Might, sir——"

And then, the calculation made, the advantage to self admitted, the smile widened.

"I'm a bit off me rum these days, somehow. Any time you'd care to——"

"O.K. Thanks."

And what now? A draft chit? Recommend for commission? Something small and manageable?

But Petty Officer Roberts was playing a game too deep. Whatever it was and wherever the elaborate system of obligations might lead to, it required nothing today but a grateful opinion of his good sense and understanding.

"About Walterson, sir."

Astonished laugh.

"My old friend Nat? What's he been doing? Not got himself in the rattle, has he?"

"Oh no, sir, nothing like that. Only——"

"What?"

"Well, just look now, sir, aft on the starboard side."

Together they walked to the starboard wing of the bridge. Nathaniel was still engaged with his aeons, feet held by friction on the corticene, bony rump on the rail just aft of the thrower. His hands were up to his face, his improbable length swaying with the scend of the swells.

"Silly ass."

"He'll do that once too often, sir."

Petty Officer Roberts came close. Liar. There was rum in his breath.

"I could have put him in the rattle for it, sir, but I thought, seeing he's a friend of yours in civvy street——"

Pause.

"O.K., Chief. I'll drop him a word myself."

"Thank you, sir."

"Thank *you*, Chief."

"I won't forget the tot, sir."

"Thanks a lot."

Petty Officer Roberts saluted and withdrew from the presence. He descended the ladder.

"Port fifteen."

Solitude with fires under the knees and a jabbing needle. Solitude out over the deck where the muzzle of X gun was lifted over the corticene. He smiled grimly to himself and reconstructed the inside of Nathaniel's head. He must have laid aft, hopefully, seeking privacy between the crew of the gun and the depth-charge watch. But there was no solitude for a rating in a small ship unless he was knowing enough to find himself a quiet number. He must have drifted aft from the mob of the fo'castle, from utter, crowded squalor to a modified and windy form of it. He was too witless to understand that the huddled mess-deck was so dense as to ensure a form of privacy, like that a man can achieve in a London crowd. So he would endure the gloomy stare of the depth-charge watch at his prayers, not understanding that they would keep an eye on him because they had nothing else to do.

"Midships. Steady."

Zig.

And he is praying in his time below when he ought to be turned in, swinging in his hammock, because he has been told that on watch he must keep a look-out over a sector of the sea. So he kept a look-out, dutiful and uncomprehending.

The dark centre of the head turned, saw the port look-out hunched, the swinging RDF aerial, the funnel with its tremble of hot air and trace of fume, looked down over the break of the bridge to the starboard deck.

Nathaniel was still there. His improbable height, combined with the leanness that made it seem even more incredible, had reduced the rail to an insecure parapet. His legs were splayed out and his feet held him by friction against the deck. As the dark centre watched, it saw Nathaniel take his hands down from his face, lay hold of the rail and get himself upright. He began to work his way forrard over the deck, legs straddled, arms out for balance. He carried his absurd little naval cap exactly level on the

54

top of his head, and his curly black hair—a trifle lank for
the night's dampness—emerged from under it all round.
He saw the bridge by chance and gravely brought his right
hand toward the right side of his head—taking no liberties,
thought the black centre, knowing his place, humble
aboard as in civvy street, ludicrous, unstoppable.

But the balance of the thin figure was disturbed by this
temporary exercise of the right hand; it tottered sideways,
tried for the salute again, missed, considered the problem
gravely with arms out and legs astraddle. A scend made it
rock. It turned, went to the engine casing, tried out the
surface to see if the metal was hot, steadied, turned forrard
and slowly saluted the bridge.

The dark centre made itself wave cheerfully to the foreshortened figure. Nathaniel's face altered even at that distance. The delight of recognition appeared in it, not plastered on and adjusted as Petty Officer Roberts had smiled
under his too-close eyes: but rising spontaneously from
the conjectural centre behind the face, evidence of sheer
niceness that made the breath come short with maddened
liking and rage. There was a convulsion in the substrata of
the globe at this end so that the needle came stabbing and
prying towards the centre that had floated all this while
without pain.

He seized the binnacle and the rock and cried out in an
anguish of frustration.

"Can't anyone understand how I feel?"

Then he was extended again throughout the tunnels of
the inner crevice and the fires were flaring and spitting in
his flesh.

There came a new noise among the others. It was con-

55

nected with the motionless blobs of white out there. They were more definite than they had been. Then he was aware that time had passed. What had seemed an eternal rhythm had been hours of darkness and now there was a faint light that consolidated his personality, gave it bounds and sanity. The noise was a throaty cluck from one of the roosting gulls.

He lay with the pains, considering the light and the fact of a new day. He could inspect his wooden left hand if he was careful about the management of the inflamed corner of his eye. He willed the fingers to close and they quivered, then contracted. Immediately he was back in them, he became a man who was thrust deep into a crevice in barren rock. Knowledge and memory flowed back in orderly succession, he remembered the funnel, the trench. He became a castaway in broad daylight and the necessity of his position fell on him. He began to heave at his body, dragging himself out of the space between the rocks. As he moved out, the gulls clamoured out of sleep and took off. They came back, sweeping in to examine him with sharp cries then sidling away in the air again. They were not like the man-wary gulls of inhabited beaches and cliffs. Nor had they about them the primal innocence of unvisited nature. They were wartime gulls who, finding a single man with water round him, resented the warmth of his flesh and his slow, unwarranted movements. They told him, with their close approach, and flapping hover that he was far better dead, floating in the sea like a burst hammock. He staggered and struck out among them with wooden arms.

"Yah! Get away! Bugger off!"

They rose clamorously wheeling, came back till their

wings beat his face. He struck out again in panic so that one went drooping off with a wing that made no more than a half-beat. They retired then, circled and watched. Their heads were narrow. They were flying reptiles. An ancient antipathy for things with claws set him shuddering at them and thinking into their smooth outlines all the strangeness of bats and vampires.

"Keep off! Who do you think I am?"

Their circles widened. They flew away to the open sea.

He turned his attention back to his body. His flesh seemed to be a compound of aches and stiffnesses. Even the control system had broken down for his legs had to be given deliberate and separate orders as though they were some unhandy kind of stilts that had been strapped to him. He broke the stilts in the middle, and got upright. He discovered new fires—little islands of severer pain in the general ache. The one at the corner of his right eye was so near to him that he did not need to discover it. He stood up, leaning his back against the side of a trench and looked round him.

The morning was dull but the wind had died down and the water was leaping rather than progressing. He became aware of a new thing; sound of the sea that the sailor never hears in his live ship. There was a gentle undertone compounded of countless sloppings of wavelets, there was a constant gurgling and sucking that ranged from a stony smack to a ruminative swallow. There were sounds that seemed every moment to be on the point of articulation but lapsed into a liquid slapping like appetite. Over all this was a definable note, a singing hiss, soft touch of the air on stone, continuous, subtle, unending friction.

A gull-cry swirled over him and he raised an arm and

looked under the elbow but the gull swung away from the rock. When the cry had gone everything was gentle again, non-committal and without offence.

He looked down at the horizon and passed his tongue over his upper lip. It came again, touched experimentally, vanished. He swallowed. His eyes opened wider and he paid no attention to the jab. He began to breathe quickly.

"Water!"

As in the sea at a moment of desperate crisis his body changed, became able and willing. He scrambled out of the trench on legs that were no longer wooden. He climbed across fallen buttresses that had never supported anything but their own weight; he slithered in the white pools of the trenches near the top of the rock. He came to the edge of the cliff where he had climbed and a solitary gull slipped away from under his feet. He worked himself round on his two feet but the horizon was like itself at every point. He could only tell when he had inspected every point by the lie of the rock beneath him. He went round again.

At last he turned back to the rock itself and climbed down but more slowly now from trench to trench. When he was below the level of the white bird-droppings he stopped and began to examine the rock foot by foot. He crouched in a trench, gripping the lower side and looking at every part of it with quick glances as if he were trying to follow the flight of a hover-fly. He saw water on a flat rock, went to it, put his hands on either side of the puddle and stuck his tongue in. His lips contracted down round his tongue, sucked. The puddle became nothing but a patch of wetness on the rock. He crawled on. He came to a horizontal crack in the side of a trench. Beneath the crack a slab of rock was falling away and there was water caught. He put his forehead against the rock then turned sideways until his cheek rested above the crack—but still his tongue could not reach the water. He thrust and thrust, mouth ground against the stone but still the water was beyond him. He seized the cracked stone and jerked furiously until it broke away. The water spilled down and became a film in the bottom of the trench. He stood there, heart thumping and held the broken stone in his hands.

"Use your loaf, man. Use your loaf."

He looked down the jumbled slope before him. He began to work the rock methodically. He noticed the broken stone in his hands and dropped it. He worked across the rock and back from trench to trench. He came on the mouldering bones of fish and a dead gull, its upturned breast-bone like the keel of a derelict boat. He found patches of grey and yellow lichen, traces even of earth, a button of moss. There were the empty shells of crabs, pieces of dead weed, and the claws of a lobster.

At the lower end of the rock there were pools of water but they were salt. He came back up the slope, his needle and the fires forgotten. He groped in the crevice where he had lain all night but the rock was nearly dry. He clambered over the fallen slab of stone that had sheltered him.

The slab was in two pieces. Once there must have been a huge upended layer of rock that had endured while the others weathered away. It had fallen and broken in two. The larger piece lay across the trench at the very edge of the rock. Part of it projected over the sea, and the trench led underneath like a gutter.

He lay down and inserted himself. He paused. Then he

was jerking his tail like a seal and lifting himself forward with his flippers. He put his head down and made sucking noises. Then he lay still.

The place in which he had found water was like a little cave. The floor of the trench sloped down gently under water so that this end of the pool was shallow. There was room for him to lie with his elbows spread apart for the slab had smashed down the wall on the right-hand side. The roof stone lay across at an angle and the farther end of the cave was not entirely stopped up. There was a small hole high up by the roof, full of daylight and a patch of sky. The light from the sky was reflected in and from the water so that faint lines quivered over the stone roof. The water was drinkable but there was no pleasure in the taste. It tasted of things that were vaguely unpleasant though the tastes were not individually identifiable. The water did not satisfy thirst so much as allay it. There seemed to be plenty of the stuff, for the pool was yards long before him and the farther end looked deep. He lowered his head and sucked again. Now that his one and a half eyes were adjusted to the light he could see there was a deposit under the water, reddish and slimy. The deposit was not hard but easily disturbed so that where he had drunk, the slime was coiling up, drifting about, hanging, settling. He watched dully.

Presently he began to mutter.

"Rescue. See about rescue."

He struggled back with a thump of his skull against rock. He crawled along the trench and clambered to the top of the rock and peered round and round the horizon again. He knelt and lowered himself on his hands. The thoughts began to flicker quickly in his head.

"I cannot stay up here all the time. I cannot shout to them if they pass. I must make a man to stand here for me. If they see anything like a man they will come closer."

There was a broken rock below his hands, leaning against the wall from which the clean fracture had fallen. He climbed down and wrestled with a great weight. He made the stone rise on an angle; he quivered and the stone fell over. He collapsed and lay for a while. He left the stone and scrambled heavily down to the little cliff and the scattered rocks where he had bathed his eye. He found an encrusted boulder lying in a rock pool and pulled it up. He got the stone against his stomach, staggered for a few steps, dropped the stone, lifted and carried again. He dumped the stone on the high point above the funnel and came back. There was a stone like a suitcase balanced on the wall of a trench and he pondered what he should do. He put his back against the suitcase and his feet against the other side of the trench. The suitcase grated, moved. He got a shoulder under one end and heaved. The suitcase tumbled in the next trench and broke. He grinned without humour and lugged the larger part up into his lap. He raised the broken suitcase to the wall, turned it end over end, engineered it up slopes of fallen but unmanageable rock, pulled and hauled.

Then there were two rocks on the high part, one with a trace of blood. He looked once round the horizon and climbed down the slope again. He stopped, put a hand to his forehead, then examined the palm. But there was no blood.

He spoke out loud in a voice that was at once flat and throaty.

"I am beginning to sweat."

He found a third stone but could not get it up the wall of the trench. He retreated with it, urged it along the bottom to a lower level until he could find an exit low enough for him to heave it up. By the time he had dragged it to the others his hands were broken. He knelt by the stones and considered the sea and sky. The sun was out wanly and there were fewer layers of cloud. He lay down across the three stones and let them hurt him. The sun shone on his left ear from the afternoon side of the rock.

He got up, put the second stone laboriously on the third and the first on the second. The three stones measured nearly two feet from top to bottom. He sat down and leaned back against them. The horizon was empty, the sea gentle, the sun a token. A sea-gull was drifting over the water a stone's throw from the rock, and now the bird was rounded, white and harmless. He covered his aching eye with one hand to rest it but the effort of holding a hand up was too much and he let the palm fall back on his knee. He ignored his eye and tried to think.

"Food?"

He got to his feet and climbed down over the trenches. At the lower end were cliffs a few feet high and beyond them separate rocks broke the surface. He ignored these for the moment because they were inaccessible. The cliffs were very rough. They were covered with a crust of tiny barnacles that had welded their limy secretions into an extended colony that dipped down in the water as deep as his better eye could see. There were yellowish limpets and coloured sea-snails drying and drawn in against the rock. Each limpet sat in the hollow its foot had worn. There were clusters of blue mussels too, with green webs of weed caught over them. He looked back up the side of the rock —under the water-hole for he could see the roof slab projecting like a diving-board—and saw how the mussels had triumphed over the whole wall. Beneath a defined line the rock was blue with them. He lowered himself carefully and inspected the cliff. Under water the harvest of food was even thicker for the mussels were bigger down there and water-snails were crawling over them. And among the limpets, the mussels, the snails and barnacles, dotted like sucked sweets, were the red blobs of jelly, the anemones. Under water they opened their mouths in a circle of petals but up by his face, waiting for the increase of the tide they were pursed up and slumped like breasts when the milk has been drawn from them.

Hunger contracted under his clothes like a pair of hands. But as he hung there, his mouth watering, a lump rose in his throat as if he were very sad. He hung on the creamy wall and listened to the washing of water, the minute ticks and whispers that came from this abundant, but not quite vegetable, life. He felt at his waist, produced the lanyard, swung it and caught the knife with his free hand. He put the blade against his mouth, gripped with his teeth and pulled the haft away from it. He put the point under a limpet and it contracted down so that he felt its muscular strength as he turned the blade. He dropped the knife to the length of the lanyard and caught the limpet as it fell. He turned the limpet over in his hand and peered into the broad end. He saw an oval brown foot drawn in, drawn back, shutting out the light.

"Bloody hell."

He jerked the limpet away from him and the tent made

a little flip of water in the sea. As the ripples died away he watched it waver down whitely out of sight. He looked for a while at the place where the limpet had disappeared. He took his knife again and began to chisel lines among the barnacles. They wept and bled salty, uretic water. He poked an anemone with the point of the knife and the jelly screwed up tight. He pressed the top with the flat of the blade and the opening pissed in his eye. He jammed the knife against the rock and shut it. He climbed back and sat on the high rock with his back against the three stones —two broken and an encrusted one on top.

Inside, the man was aware of a kind of fit that seized his body. He drew his feet up against him and rolled sideways so that his face was on the rock. His body was jumping and shuddering beneath the sodden clothing. He whispered against stone.

"You can't give up."

Immediately he began to crawl away down hill. The crawl became a scramble. Down by the water he found stones but they were of useless shape. He chose one from just under water and toiled back to the others. He changed the new one for the top stone, grated it into place, then put the encrusted one back. Two feet, six inches.

He muttered.

"Must. Must."

He climbed down to the rock-side opposite the cliff of mussels. There were ledges on this side and water sucking up and down. The water was very dark and there was long weed at the bottom, straps like the stuff travellers some-times put round suitcases when the locks are broken. This brown weed was collapsed and coiled over itself near the surface but farther out it lay upright in the water or moved slowly like tentacles or tongues. Beyond that there was nothing but the blackness of deep water going down to the bottom of the deep sea. He took his eyes away from this, climbed along one of the ledges, but everywhere the rock was firm and there were no separated pieces to be found, though in one place the solid ledge was cracked. He pushed at this part with his stockinged feet but could not move it. He turned clumsily on the ledge and came back. At the lower end of the great rock he found the stones with the wrong shape and took them one by one to a trench and piled them. He pried in crevices and pulled out blocks and rounded masses of yellowing quartz on which the weed was draggled like green hair. He took them to the man he was building and piled them round the bottom stone. Some were not much bigger than potatoes and he knocked these in where the big stones did not fit until the top one no longer rocked when he touched it. He put one last stone on the others, one big as his head.

Three feet.

He stood away from the pile and looked round him. The pile reached in his view from horizon level to higher than the sun. He was astonished when he saw this and looked carefully to establish where west was. He saw the outlying rock that had saved him and the sea-gulls were floating just beyond the backwash.

He climbed down the rock again to where he had prised off the limpet. He made a wry face and pushed his doubled fists into the damp cloth over his belly. He hung on the little cliff and began to tear away the blobs of red jelly with his fingers. He set them on the edge of the cliff and did not

65

look at them for a while. Then he turned his one and a half eyes down to them and inspected them closely. They lay like a handful of sweets only they moved ever so slightly and there was a little clear water trickling from the pile. He sat by them on the edge of the cliff and no longer saw them. His face set in a look of agony.

"Bloody hell!"

His fingers closed over a sweet. He put it quickly in his mouth, ducked, swallowed, shuddered. He took another, swallowed, took another as fast as he could. He bolted the pile of sweets then sat rigid, his throat working. He subsided, grinning palely. He looked down at his left hand and there was one last sweet lying against his little finger in a drip of water. He clapped his hand to his mouth, stared over the fingers and fought with his stomach. He scrambled over the rocks to the water-hole and pulled himself in. Again the coils of red silt and slime rose from the bottom. There was a band of red round the nearer end of the pool that was about half an inch across.

When he had settled his stomach with the harsh water he came out of the hole backwards. The sea-gulls were circling the rock now and he looked at them with hate.

"You won't get me!"

He clambered back to the top of the rock where his three-foot dwarf stood. The horizon was in sight all round and empty. He licked a trace of drinkable water from his lips.

"I have enough to drink——"

He stood, looking down at the slab over his drinking water where it projected like a diving-board. He went slowly to the cliff, got down and peered under the slab.

The seaward end of the pool was held back by a jumble of broken stones that were lodged against each other. Behind the impaired window of his sight he saw the red silt rising and coiling. The stuff must lie over the inner side of these stones, sealing them lightly against the water's escape. He had a quick vision of the hidden surfaces, holes that time had furred with red till they were stopped and the incongruous fresh water held back among all the salt; but held back so delicately that the merest touch would set his life irrevocably flowing——

He backed away with staring eyes and breath that came quick.

"Forget it!"

He began to thrust himself backwards into the sleeping crevice. He got almost to his ears out of sight and filled the hole with his body and heavy clothing. He pulled the sleeves of his duffle out of the oilskin tubes until they came over the backs of his hands. After a little struggling he could grip them with his fingers and double his fists so that they were hidden in the hairy duffle. The lifebelt supported his chest and throat once more and he pillowed his left cheek on his forearm. He lay so, shivering now that the sun had gone down, while the green sky turned blue, dark blue and the gulls floated down. His body yielded to the shivers but between the bouts it lay quite still. His mouth was open and his eyes stared anxiously into the darkness. Once, he jerked and the mouth spoke.

"Forget it!"

A gull moved a little then settled down again.

5

But he could not fall into the pit because he was extended through his body. He was aware dimly of returning strength; and this not only allowed him to savour the cold and be physically miserable but to be irritated by it. Instead of the apocalyptic visions and voices of the other night he had now nothing but ill-used and complaining flesh. The point of the needle in his eye was blunted but instead of enduring anything rather than its stab he had continually to rub one foot over the other or press with his body against the slab of rock in an effort to shut off the chill on that side, only to find that the other side required attention more and more insistently. He would heave the globe of darkness in which he most lived off a hard, wooden surface, rotate it and lay the other hemisphere down. There was another difference between this night and the last. The fires had died down but they were still there now he had the time and the strength to attend to them. The stiffness had become a settled sense of strain as if his body were being stretched mercilessly. The rock too, now that he had a little strength to spare was forcing additional discomfort on him. What the globe had taken in its extreme exhaustion for a smooth surface was in fact undulating with the suggestion of prominences here and there. These suggestions became localized discomforts that changed in turn to a dull ache. Allowed to continue, aches became pains then fires that must be avoided. So he would heave his thigh away or wriggle weakly only to find that the prominence was gone and had left nothing but an undulation. His thigh would flatten down again and wait in the darkness for the discomfort, the ache, the pain, the fire.

Up at the top end now that the window was dark the man found the intermissions of discomfort were again full of voices and things that could not but be seen. He had a confused picture of the passage of the sun below him beyond the central fires of the earth. But both the sun and the fires were too far away to warm him. He saw the red silt holding back the fresh water, a double handful of red sweets, an empty horizon.

"I shall live!"

He saw the sun below him with its snail movement and was confused inside his head by the earth's revolution on its axis and its year-long journey round the sun. He saw how many months a man must endure before he was warmed by the brighter light of spring. He watched the sun for months without thought or identity. He saw it from many angles, through windows of trains or from fields. He confused its fires with other fires, on allotments, in gardens, in grates. One of these fires was most insistent that here was reality and to be watched. The fire was behind the bars of a grate. He found that the grate was in a room and then everything became familiar out of the past and he knew where he was and that the time and the words were significant. There was a tall and spider-thin figure sitting in the chair opposite. It looked up under its black curls, as if it were consulting a reference book on the other side of the ceiling.

"Take us as we are now and heaven would be sheer negation. Without form and void. You see? A sort of black lightning destroying everything that we call life."

But he was laughing and happy in his reply.

"I don't see and I don't much care but I'll come to your lecture. My dear Nathaniel, you've no idea how glad I am to see you!"

Nathaniel looked his face over carefully.

"And I, too. About seeing you, I mean."

"We're showing emotion, Nat. We're being un-English."

Again the careful look.

"I think you need my lecture. You're not happy, are you?"

"I'm not really interested in heaven either. Let me get you a drink."

"No, thanks."

Nathaniel uncoiled from the chair and stood with his arms out on either side, hands bent up. He looked, first at nothing, then round the room. He went to the wall and perched himself absurdly high up with his bony rump on the top of a shelf. He pushed his incredible legs out and splayed them apart till he was held insecurely by the friction of the soles of his feet. He looked up at the reference book again.

"You could call it a talk on the technique of dying."

"You'll die a long time before me. It's a cold night—and look how you're dressed!"

Nathaniel peered at the laughing window then down at himself.

"Is it? Yes. I suppose I am."

"And I'm going to have a damned long life and get what I'm after."

"And that is——?"

"Various things."

"But you're not happy."

"Why do you spill this over me, of all people?"

"There's a connection between us. Something will happen to us or perhaps we were meant to work together. You have an extraordinary capacity to endure."

"To what end?"

"To achieve heaven."

"Negation?"

"The technique of dying into heaven."

"No thanks. Be your age, Nat."

"You could, you know. And I——"

Nat's face was undergoing a change. It turned towards him again. The flush on the cheeks was painful. The eyes loomed and impended.

"—And I, have a feeling. Don't laugh, please—but I feel—you could say that I know." Below the eyes the breath came out in a little gasp. Feet scraped.

"—You could say that I know it is important for you personally to understand about heaven—about dying—because in only a few years——"

For a while there was silence, a double shock—for the bells ceased to toll beyond the windows of the room as though they had stopped with the voice. A vicious sting from his cigarette whipped along the arm into the globe

71

so that he flicked it away and cried out. Then he was flat on the floor, fumbling for the stub under the armchair and the undulations of the floor were a discomfort to the body. Lying there, the words pursued him, made his ears buzz, set up a tumult, pushed his heart to thump with sudden, appalled understanding as though it were gasping the words that Nathaniel had not spoken.

"—because in only a few years you will be dead."

He cried out against the unspoken words in fury and panic.

"You bloody fool, Nat! You awful bloody fool!"

The words echoed in the trench and he jerked his cheek up off the oilskin. There was much light outside, sunlight and the crying of gulls.

He shouted.

"I'm damned if I'll die!"

He hauled himself quickly out of the crevice and stood in the trench. The sea and sky were dark blue and the sun was high enough not to make a dazzle from the water. He felt the sun on his face and rubbed with both hands at the bristles. He looked quickly round the horizon then climbed down to a trench. He began to fumble with his trousers, glancing furtively behind him. Then for the first time on the rock he broke up the bristly, external face with a shout of jeering laughter. He went back to the dwarf and made water in a hosing gesture at the horizon.

"Gentlemen are requested to adjust their dress before leaving."

He began to fumble with the buttons of his oilskin and lugged it off fiercely. He picked and pulled at the tapes that held his lifebelt inside the duffle. He slipped both off and dumped them in a heavy heap and stood there looking down. He glanced at the two wavy lines of gold braid on either arm, the gilt buttons, the black doeskin of his jacket and trousers. He peeled himself, jacket, woollen sweater, black sweater, shirt, vest; pulled off his long stockings, his socks, his pants. He stood still and examined what he could see of his body.

The feet had been so thoroughly sodden that they seemed to have lost their shape. One big toe was blue and black with bruise and drying blood. There were bruises on either knee that ended in lacerations, not cuts or jabs but places the size of a sixpence where the skin and flesh had been worn off. His right hip was blue as though someone had laid a hand dipped in paint on it.

He examined his arms. The right elbow was swollen and stiff and there were more bruises about. Here and there on his body were patches, not of raw flesh but of blood flecks under the skin. He felt the bristles on his face tenderly. His right eye was fogged and that cheek was hot and stiff.

He took his vest and tried to wring out the body but there was water held in the material that would not come free. He put his left foot on one end of the twisted cloth and screwed the other with both hands. Dampness appeared and moistened the rock. He did this in turn to each piece of clothing and spread the lot in the sun to dry. He sat down by the dwarf, fumbled in his jacket and brought out a sodden packet of papers and a small brown booklet. The colour had run from the booklet and stained the papers as if they were rusting. He spread the papers out round him and rummaged through his pockets in turn. He found two pennies and a florin. He laid them by the dwarf in a little heap. He took his knife on its lanyard from the pocket of his oilskin and hung it round his neck. When he had done that he put up his hand and tugged gently at the small brown disc that was tied round his neck by a white thread. He bent his face into a grin. He got up and scrambled over the rocks to the water-hole. He eased himself in and leaned forward. The red coils rose and reminded him of the other tamped end of the pool. He backed out carefully, holding his breath.

He climbed down over the trenches to the lower end of the rock. The water was low and tons of living jelly was spread in armour over the cliffs. Where he stood with his toes projecting over the edge the food was dry, and talked with continual tiny crepitations. The weed was transparent over the shells and only faintly green. He clambered down from handhold to handhold, wincing as he caught the sharp shells with his feet. He pulled at mussels but they would not come away. He had to twist them out as if he were breaking bones away from their tendons, screwing them out of the joints. He jerked them over his head so that they arched up and fell clattering on the rock. He worked among the sharp shells over the wavering water until his legs were trembling with strain. He climbed the cliff, rested, came back and twisted out more. There was a scattered harvest of them on the rock, some of them four inches long. He sat down, breathless in the sun and worked at them. They were not vulnerable like the red sweets; they were gripped and glued tight and there was nowhere to get the blade of the knife in. He put one on the rock and beat it with the haft of his knife until the shell fractured. He took out the complicated body and looked away over the sea.

"The Belgians do."

He gulped the body down. He set his teeth, broke another shell. Soon he had a heap of raw flesh that lay, white and yellow on the dry rock. His jaws moved, he looked away at the horizon. The fogged side of his right eye was pulled slightly as he ate. He felt round with his hand and the heap was gone. He climbed down the cliff and got more. He opened each of these with a sudden downward jab of his knife. When they were gone he forced the red sweets from the rock and popped them in his mouth. He made no distinction between green and red. He took a wisp of green seaweed and chewed it like a leaf of lettuce. He went back to the water-hole, inserted himself and lay for a moment, looking down at the gleaming surface. He moistened his lips, so that the coils of red slime only stirred a little then lay down again. He eased himself out, clambered to the top of the rock and looked round. The horizon was ruled straight and hard in every part. He sat down.

The papers and booklet were still damp but he took up the booklet and opened it. Inside the cover was a transparent guard over a photograph. He peered through the cover and made out a fogged portrait. He could see a carefully arranged head of hair, a strong and smiling face, the white silk scarf round the neck. But detail had gone for ever. The young man who smiled dimly at him through fog and brown stains was distant as the posed portraits of great-grandparents in a faint, brown world.

Even so, he continued to look, searching for the details

he remembered rather than saw, touching his bristled cheek while he divined the smiling smoothness of the one before him, rearranging the unkempt hair, feeling tenderly the painful corner of an eye. Opposite the photograph was writing in a slot but this too was smeared and washed into illegibility. He put the booklet down and felt for the brown disc hanging round his neck. He lifted the disc as far as the string would allow until it was close to his left eye. He strained back and got it far enough away from him.

CHRISTOPHER

HADLEY

MARTIN

TY. LIEUT., R.N.V.R.

C. OF E.

He read the inscription again and again, cut by cut. His lips began to move. He dropped the disc, looked down at his salted legs with their scars, at his belly and the bush of hair over his privates.

He spoke out loud, using his voice hoarsely and with a kind of astonishment.

"Christopher Hadley Martin. Martin. Chris. I am what I always was!"

All at once it seemed to him that he came out of his curious isolation inside the globe of his head and was extended normally through his limbs. He lived again on the surface of his eyes, he was out in the air. Daylight crowded down on him, sunlight, there was a sparkle on the sea. The solid rock was coherent as an object, with layered guano, with fresh water and shell-fish. It was a position in a finite sea at the intersection of two lines, there were real ships passing under the horizon. He got quickly to his feet and laboured round the rock, turning his clothes in the sun. He sniffed the pants and laughed. He went back to the papers and turned them. He took up the coins, chinked them in his hand for a moment and made as if to toss them in the sea. He paused.

"That would be too cracker-motto. Too ham."

He looked at the quiet sea.

"I don't claim to be a hero. But I've got health and education and intelligence. I'll beat you."

The sea said nothing. He grinned a little foolishly at himself.

"What I meant was to affirm my determination to survive. And of course, I'm talking to myself."

He looked round the rock.

"The first thing to do is to survey the estate."

The rock had diminished from an island to a thing. In the sunlight and absence of cold the whole could be inspected not only with eyes but with understanding. He saw at once that the trenches were the worn ends of vertical strata and the walls between them, harder layers that had worn more slowly. They were the broken end of a deep bed of mud that had been compressed by weight until the mud had heated and partly fused. Some convulsion of the upper layers, an unguessable contortion, a gripe of the earth's belly had torn the deep bed and thrust this broken end up vertically through mud and clay until it erupted as the tooth bursts out of the fleshy jaw. Then the less compressed layers had worn away into trenches full of edges like the cut pages of a book. The walls too were broken in places and modified everywhere by local hazard. Some of the walls had fallen and lay jumbled in the trenches. The whole top of the rock tended down, trench by trench, from the west to the east.

The cliff sides of the rock concealed the stratification for they were water-worn and fretted into lace by the plant-animals that clustered so thickly on them. This top was concreted with whiteness under stinking water but down there where the blue and shattered mussel-shells lay scattered, the rock was clean or covered with barnacles and weed. Beyond the rock was a gap of shallow water, then another smaller rock, another and another in a slightly curving line. Then there was a pock that interrupted the pattern of the water and after that, the steep climb of the sea up to the sky.

He looked solemnly at the line of rocks and found himself thinking of them as teeth. He caught himself imagining that they were emerging gradually from the jaw—but that was not the truth. They were sinking; or rather they were being worn away in infinite slow motion. They were the grinders of old age, worn away. A lifetime of the world had blunted them, was reducing them as they ground what food rocks eat.

He shook his head irritably then caught his breath at the sudden pain in his neck.

"The process is so slow it has no relevance to——"

He stopped. He looked up into the air, then round over his shoulder. He repeated the words carefully, with the same intonation and at the same strength.

"The process is so slow——"

There was something peculiar about the sound that came out of his mouth. He discounted the hoarseness as of a man recovering from a cold or a bout of violent shouting. That was explicable.

He sang loudly.

"Alouette, gentille Alouette——"

He held his nose with his right hand and tried to blow through it until the pressure rounded his cheeks. Nothing cracked in his ears. His eyes hurt and water ran round them. He bent down, put his hands on his scarred knees and turned his head sideways. He shook his head violently, ignoring the pain in his neck and hoping to feel the little wobbling weight that would tell of water caught in his ears.

He stood up, facing a whole amphitheatre of water and sang a scale.

"Lah-la, la, la, la, la, la-lah!"

The sound ended at his mouth.

He struck an attitude and declaimed.

> *The weary moon with her lamp before*
> *Knocks even now upon dawn's grey door——*

His voice faltered and stopped. He brought his hand down, turned the wrist, held the palm about a foot in front of his mouth.

"Testing. Testing. I am receiving you, strength——"

He closed his lips, lowered his hand slowly. The blue, igloo-roof over the rock went away to a vast distance, the visible world expanded with a leap. The water lopped round a tiny rock in the middle of the Atlantic. The strain tautened his face. He took a step among the scattered papers.

"My God!"

He gripped the stone dwarf, clutched himself to the

humped shoulders and stared across. His mouth was open again. His heart-beats were visible as a flutter among the ribs. The knuckles of his hands whitened.

There was a clatter from the dwarf. The head stone thumped and went knock, knock, knock down the cliff.

Flumf.

He began to curse. He scrambled down the rock, found a too heavy stone, moved it about a yard and then let go. He threw himself over the stone and went cursing to the water. But there was nothing visible within reach that he could handle. He went quickly to the top again and stood looking at the headless dwarf in terror. He scrambled back to the too heavy stone and fought with it. He moved it, end over end. He built steps to the top of a wall and worked the great stone up. He drew from his body more strength than he had got. He bled. He stood sweating among the papers at last. He dismantled the dwarf and rebuilt him on the stone that after all was not too heavy for education and intelligence and will.

Four feet.

He jammed in the dry, white potatoes.

"Out of this nettle danger——"

The air sucked up his voice like blotting-paper.

Take a grip.

Education and intelligence.

He stood by the dwarf and began to talk like a man who has an unwilling audience but who will have his say whether anyone listens to him or not.

"The end to be desired is rescue. For that, the bare minimum necessary is survival. I must keep this body going. I must give it drink and food and shelter. When I do that it does not matter if the job is well done or not so long as it is done at all. So long as the thread of life is unbroken it will connect a future with the past for all this ghastly interlude. Point one.

"Point two. I must expect to fall sick. I cannot expose the body to this hardship and expect the poor beast to behave as if it were in clover. I must watch for signs of sickness and doctor myself.

"Point three. I must watch my mind. I must not let madness steal up on me and take me by surprise. Already—I must expect hallucinations. That is the real battle. That is why I shall talk out loud for all the blotting-paper. In normal life to talk out loud is a sign of insanity. Here it is proof of identity.

"Point four. I must help myself to be rescued. I cannot do anything but be visible. I have not even a stick to hoist a shirt on. But no one will come within sight of this rock without turning a pair of binoculars on it. If they see the rock they will see this dwarf I have made. They will know that someone built the dwarf and they will come and take me off. All I have to do is to live and wait. I must keep my grip on reality."

He looked firmly at the sea. All at once he found that he was seeing through a window again. He was inside himself at the top end. The window was bounded above by the mixed, superimposed skin and hair of both brows, and divided into three lights by two outlines or shadows of noses. But the noses were transparent. The right-hand light was fogged and all three drew together at the bottom. When he looked down at the rock he was seeing the surface over the scrubby hedge of his unshaven upper lip. The window was surrounded by inscrutable darkness which extended throughout his body. He leaned forward to peer round the window-frame but it went with him. He altered the frame for a moment with a frown. He turned the three lights right round the horizon. He spoke, frowning.

"That is the ordinary experience of living. There is nothing strange in that." He shook his head and busied himself. He turned the windows on his own body and examined the skin critically. Great patches were pink over the scars and he cried out.

"Sunburn!"

He grabbed his vest and pulled it on. The material was so nearly dry that he accepted it as such and shuffled into his pants. The luminous windows became the ordinary way of seeing. He gathered his papers, put them in the identity book and stowed the whole packet in the pocket of his reefer. He padded round the top of the rock, handling his clothes and testing them for dryness. They did not feel damp so much as heavy. There was no moisture that would come off on the fingers or could be wrung out, but where he lifted them from the rock they left their shapes in darker stone that faded slowly in the sun.

He spoke flatly against the blotting-paper.

"I wish I'd kept my seaboots."

He came to his oilskin and knelt, looking at it. Then suddenly he was rummaging through the forgotten pockets. He drew out a sou'wester from which the water ran, and a sodden balaclava. He unfolded the sou'wester and wrung out the balaclava. He spread them and dived at the other pocket. An expression of anxious concentration settled on his face. He fumbled and drew out a greening ha'penny, some string and the crumpled wrapping from a bar of chocolate. He unfolded the paper with great care; but there was nothing left inside. He put his face close to the glittering paper and squinted at it. In one crease there was a single brown grain. He put out his tongue and took the grain. The chocolate stung with a piercing sweetness, momentary and agonizing, and was gone.

He leaned back against the stone dwarf, reached for his socks and pulled them on. He took his seaboot stockings, rolled down the tops and made do with them for boots.

He let his head lie against the dwarf and closed his eyes. The sun shone over his shoulder and the water washed. Inside his head the busy scenes flickered and voices spoke. He experienced all the concomitants of drowsiness but still there did not come the fall and gap of sleep. The thing in the middle of the globe was active and tireless.

"I should like a bed with sheets. I should like a pint or two and a hot meal. I should like a hot bath."

He sat for a while, silent, while the thing jumped from thought to thought. He remembered that speech was proof of identity and his lips began to move again.

"So long as I can want these things without finding the absence of them unendurable; so long as I can tell myself that I am alone on a rock in the middle of the Atlantic and that I have to fight to survive—then I can manage. After all, I am safe compared with those silly sods in H.M. ships. They never know when they're going to be blown up. But I should like to see the brick that could shift this rock."

The thing that could not examine itself danced on in the world behind the eyes.

"And anyway I must not sleep in the daytime. Save that for the miserable nights."

He stood up suddenly and looked round the horizon.

"Dress and eat. Dress for dinner."

He kicked off the seaboot stockings and got into his clothes, all but the duffle and oilskin. He pulled the stockings up over his trousers to the knees. He stood and became voluble in the flat air.

"I call this place the Look-out. That is the Dwarf. The rock out there under the sun where I came swimming is Safety Rock. The place where I get mussels and stuff is Food Cliff. Where I eat them is—The Red Lion. On the south side where the strap-weed is, I call Prospect Cliff. This cliff here to the west with the funnel in it is——"

He paused, searching for a name. A sea-gull came swingings in under the sun, saw the two figures standing on the Look-out, screamed, side-slipped crazily and wheeled away. It came straight back but at a lower level on his right hand and vanished into the cliff. He edged forward and looked down. There was a sheer, almost unbroken descent on the left and then the cleft in the middle of the cliff, and above that, the funnel. To the right the foot of the cliff was hidden for the highest corner of the Look-out leaned out. He went on hands and knees to the edge and looked down. The cliff was visible for a yard and then turned in and hid itself. The rock began again near the bottom and he could see a glint of feather.

"A lump has fallen out of the cliff."

He searched the water carefully and thought he could make out a square shape deep under the surface. He backed away and stood up.

"Gull Cliff."

The horizon was still empty.

He climbed down the rock to the Red Lion.

"I wish I could remember the name of the whole rock. The Captain said it was a near miss and he laughed. I have it on the tip of my tongue. And I must have a name for this habitual clamber of mine between the Look-out and the Red Lion. I shall call it the High Street."

He saw that the rock on which he sat was dark and glanced over his shoulder. The sun was just leaving him, going down behind the Dwarf, so that the piled stones had become a giant. He got up quickly and lowered himself down the plastered Food Cliff. He hung spreadeagled, traversed a couple of yards and twisted out mussels. The deep sea tide was up now and he had much less scope. He had to lean down and work the mussels loose under water. He climbed back to the Red Lion and began to eat. The great shape of the rock had lost detail and become a blotch against the evening sky. The shadow loomed, vast as a mountain peak. He looked the other way and there were the three rocks diminishing into a dark sea.

"I name you three rocks—Oxford Circus, Piccadilly and Leicester Square."

He went to the dark water-hole and pulled himself in. A little light still came from the hole in the jumbled stones at the other end and when he drank he could see ripples faintly but the red coils were invisible. He put his forefinger straight down into the water and felt the slimy bottom. He lay very still.

"It will rain again."

Then he was jumping and shuddering for there was someone else in the hole with him. Or there was a voice that spoke almost with his, from the water and the slab. As his heart eased he could think coherently of the sound as a rare and forgotten thing, a resonance, an echo. Then immediately he could reason that his voice was full-sized in here so he quietened his body and spoke deliberately.

"Plenty of identity in here, Ladies and Gentlemen——"

He cut his voice off sharply and heard the rock say, "—men——"

"It will rain."

"—ain."

"How are you?"

"—u?"

"I am busy surviving. I am netting down this rock with names and taming it. Some people would be incapable of understanding the importance of that. What is given a name is given a seal, a chain. If this rock tries to adapt me to its ways I will refuse and adapt it to mine. I will impose

86

my routine on it, my geography. I will tie it down with names. If it tries to annihilate me with blotting-paper, then I will speak in here where my words resound and significant sounds assure me of my own identity. I will trap rain-water and add it to this pool. I will use my brain as a delicate machine-tool to produce the results I want. Comfort. Safety. Rescue. Therefore to-morrow I declare to be a thinking day."

He backed out of the water-hole, climbed the High Street and stood on the Look-out by the Dwarf. He dressed in everything, pulled on the damp balaclava and drew the sou-wester round his head with the chinstay down. He looked quickly round the horizon, listened to the faint movement from the invisible aery half-way down Gull Cliff. He went down the High Street, came to his crevice. He sat on the wall by the crevice, put his feet in the grey sweater and wrapped it round them. He got down and wormed his way into the crevice, pushing down his duffle and oilskin. He blew the lifebelt up tight and tied the two breast ends of the tube together with the tape. The lifebelt made a pillow big enough for his head and very soft. He lay on his back and rested his head in the sou-wester on the soft pillow. He inched his arms down on either side of him in the crevice. He spoke to the sky.

"I must dry seaweed and line this crevice. I could be as snug as a bug in a rug."

He shut his eyes.

"Rélax each muscle in turn."

Sleep is a condition to be attained by thought like any other.

"The trouble with keeping house on a rock is that

there's so much to do. But I shan't get bored, that's one thing."

Relax the muscles of the feet.

"And what a story! A week on a rock. Lectures——"

How to Survive. By Lieutenant—but why not Lieutenant-Commander? Or Commander? Brass Hat and all.

"You men must remember——"

His eyes fell open.

"And I never remembered! Never thought of it! Haven't had a crap for a week!" Or not since before I was blown off the bloody bridge anyway.

The flaps of his sou-wester prevented him from hearing the flatness of his voice against the sky. He lay and meditated the sluggishness of his bowels. This created pictures of chrome and porcelain and attendant circumstances. He put the toothbrush back, and stood, looking at his face in the mirror. The whole business of eating was peculiarly significant. They made a ritual of it on every level, the Fascists as a punishment, the religious as a rite, the cannibal either as a ritual or as medicine or as a superbly direct declaration of conquest. Killed and eaten. And of course eating with the mouth was only the gross expression of what was a universal process. You could eat with your cock or with your fists, or with your voice. You could eat with hobnailed boots or buying and selling or marrying and begetting or cuckolding——

Cuckolding reminded him. He turned from the mirror, bound his dressing-gown with the cord and opened the bathroom door. And there, coming towards him, as if the rather antiquated expression had conjured him up was Alfred. But it was a different Alfred, pale, sweating, tremb-

88

ling, coming at a run toward. He took the wrist as the fist came at his chest and twisted it till Alfred was gritting his teeth and hissing through them. Secure in his knowledge of the cosmic nature of eating he grinned down at him.

"Hullo, Alfred!"

"You bloody swine!"

"Nosey little man."

"Who've you got in there? Tell me!"

"Now, now. Come along quietly Alfred, we don't want any fuss."

"Don't pretend it's someone else! You bastard! Oh Christ——"

They were by the closed door. Alfred was crying into the lines round his mouth and struggling to get at the door handle.

"Tell me who she is, Chris. I *must* know—for God's sake!"

"Don't ham it, Alfred."

"And don't pretend it's not Sybil, you dirty, thieving bastard!"

"Like to look, Alfred?"

Hiccups. Weak struggles.

"You mean it's someone else? You're not fooling Chris, honestly?"

"Anything to cheer up you old man. Look."

The door opening; Sybil, giving a tiny shriek and pulling the sheet up to her mouth as if this were a bedroom-farce which, of course, in every sense, it was.

"Honestly, Alfred old man, anyone would think you'd married the girl."

89

But there was a connection between eating and the Chinese box. What was a Chinese box? A coffin? Or those carved ivory ornaments, one inside the other? Yet there was a Chinese box in it somewhere——

Astonished, he lay like a stone man, open-mouthed and gazing into the sky. The furious struggle against his chest, the slobbering sobs of the weak mouth were still calling their reactions out of his stronger body when he was back in the crevice.

He cleared his throat and spoke aloud.

"Where the hell am I? Where was I?"

He heaved over and lay face downwards in the crevice, his cheek on the lifebelt.

"Can't sleep."

But sleep is necessary. Lack of sleep was what sent people crazy. He spoke aloud and the lifebelt wobbled under his jaw.

"I was asleep then. I was dreaming about Alfred and Sybil. Go to sleep again."

He lay still and considered sleep. But it was a tantalizingly evasive subject.

Think about women then or eating. Think about eating women, eating men, crunching up Alfred, that other girl, that boy, that crude and unsatisfactory experiment, lie restful as a log and consider the gnawed tunnel of life right up to this uneasy intermission.

This rock.

"I shall call those three rocks out there the Teeth."

All at once he was gripping the lifebelt with both hands and tensing his muscles to defeat the deep shudders that were sweeping through him.

"No! Not the Teeth!"

The teeth were here, inside his mouth. He felt them with his tongue, the double barrier of bone, each known and individual except the gaps—and there they persisted as a memory if one troubled to think. But to lie on a row of teeth in the middle of the sea——

He began to think desperately about sleep.

Sleep is a relaxation of the conscious guard, the sorter. Sleep is when all the unsorted stuff comes flying out as from a dustbin upset in a high wind. In sleep time was divorced from the straight line so that Alfred and Sybil were on the rock with him and that boy with his snivelling, blubbered face. Or sleep was a consenting to die, to go into complete unconsciousness, the personality defeated, acknowledging too frankly what is implicit in mortality that we are temporary structures patched up and unable to stand the pace without a daily respite from what we most think ours——

"Then why can't I sleep?"

Sleep is where we touch what is better left unexamined. There, the whole of life is bundled up, dwindled. There the carefully hoarded and enjoyed personality, our only treasure and at the same time our only defence must die into the ultimate truth of things, the black lightning that splits and destroys all, the positive, unquestionable nothingness.

And I lie here, a creature armoured in oilskin, thrust into a crack, a morsel of food on the teeth that a world's lifetime has blunted.

Oh God! Why can't I sleep?

Gripping the lifebelt in two hands, with face lifted, eyes

staring straight ahead down the gloomy tunnel, he whispered the answer to his own question in a mixture of astonishment and terror.

"I am afraid to."

7

The light changed before the staring eyes but so slowly that they did not notice any difference. They looked, rather, at the jumble of unsorted pictures that presented themselves at random. There was still the silent, indisputable creature that sat at the centre of things, but it seemed to have lost the knack of distinguishing between picture and reality. Occasionally the gate in the lower part of the globe would open against the soft lifebelt and words come out, but each statement was so separated by the glossy and illuminated scenes the creature took part in that it did not know which was relevant to which.

"I said that I should be sick."

"Drink. Food. Sanity. Rescue."

"I shall call them the——"

But the glossy images persisted, changed, not as one cloud shape into another but with sudden and complete differences of time and place.

"Sit down, Martin."

"Sir."

"We're considering whether we should recommend you for a commission. Cigarette?"

"Thank you, sir."

Sudden smile over the clicked lighter.

"Got your nickname on the lower deck yet?"

Smile in return, charming, diffident.

" 'Fraid so, sir. Inevitably, I believe."

"Like Dusty Miller and Nobby Clark."

"Yes, sir."

"How's the life up forrard?"

"It's—endurable, sir."

"We want men of education and intelligence; but most of all, men of character. Why did you join the Navy?"

"One felt one ought to—well, help, sir, if you see what I mean?"

Pause.

"I see you're an actor in civvy street."

Careful.

"Yes, sir. Not a terribly good one, I'm afraid."

"Author?"

"Nothing much, yet, sir."

"What would you have liked to be then?"

"One felt it was—unreal. Not like this. You know, sir! Here in this ship. Here we *are* getting down to the basic business of life—something worth doing. I wish I'd been a sailor."

Pause.

"Why would you like a commission, Martin?"

"As an ordinary seaman, sir, one's the minutest cog in a machine. As an officer one would have more chance of hitting the old Hun for six, sir, actually."

Pause.

"Did you volunteer, Martin?"

94

He's got it all on those papers there if he chooses to look it up.

Frank.

"Actually, no, sir."

He's blushing, under that standard Dartmouth mask of his.

"That will be all, Martin, thank you."

"Aye, aye, sir, thank you, sir."

He's blushing like a virgin of sixteen.

"She's the producer's wife, old man, here where are you going?"

An exceptionally small French dictionary, looking like an exceptionally large red eraser.

A black lacquer cash-box on which the gilt was worn.

The Chinese box was evasive. Sometimes it was the fretted ivories, one inside the other, sometimes it was a single box like a cash-box. But however evasive, it was important and intrusive.

She's the producer's wife, old man. Fat. White. Like a maggot with tiny black eyes. I should like to eat you. I should love to play Danny. I should love to eat you. I should love to put you in a play. How can I put you anywhere if I haven't eaten you? He's a queer. He'd love to eat you. And I should love to eat you too. You're not a person, my sweet, you're an instrument of pleasure.

A Chinese box.

A sword is a phallus. What a huge mountain-shaking

joke! A phallus is a sword. Down, dog, down. Down on all fours where you belong.

Then he was looking at a half-face and crying out. The half-face belonged to one of the feathered reptiles. The creature was perched on the slab and looking down sideways at him. As he cried out the wide wings beat and flapped away and immediately a glossy picture swept the blue sky and the stone out of sight. This was a bright patch, sometimes like a figure eight lying on its side and sometimes a circle. The circle was filled with blue sea where gulls were wheeling and settling and loving to eat and fight. He felt the swing of the ship under him, sensed the bleak stillness and silence that settled on the bridge as the destroyer slid by the thing floating in the water—a thing, humble and abused and still, among the fighting beaks, an instrument of pleasure.

He struggled out into the sun, stood up and cried flatly in the great air.

"I am awake!"

Dense blue with white flecks and diamond flashes. Foam, flowering abundantly round the three rocks.

He turned away from the night.

"Today is a thinking day."

He undressed quickly to his trousers and sweater, spread his clothing in the sun and went down to the Red Lion. The tide was so low that mussels were in sight by the ship load.

Mussels were food but one soon tired of them. He wondered for a moment whether he should collect some sweets but his stomach did not entertain the idea. He thought of chocolate instead and the silver paper came into his mind. He sat there, chewing mechanically while his mind's eye watched silver, flashing bright.

"After all, I may be rescued today."

He examined the thought and found that the whole idea was neutral as the mussels had become, harsh and negative as the fresh water. He climbed to the water-hole and crawled in. The red deposit lay in a band nearly two inches wide at the nearer edge.

He cried out in the echoing hole.

"It will rain again!"

Proof of identity.

"I must measure this pool. I must ration myself. I must force water to come to me if necessary. I must have water."

A well. Boring through rock. A dew pond. Line with clay and straw. Precipitation. Education. Intelligence.

He reached out his hand and prodded down with the finger. When his hand had submerged to the knuckles his finger-tip met slime and slid. Then rock. He took a deep breath. There was darker water farther on under the window.

"A fool would waste water by crawling forward, washing this end about just to see how much there is left. But I won't. I'll wait and crawl forward as the water shrinks. And before that there will be rain."

He went quickly to his clothes, took out the silver paper and the string and climbed back to the Dwarf.

He frowned at the Dwarf and began to talk into the blotting-paper.

"East or west is useless. If convoys appear in either of those quarters they would be moving towards the rock anyway. But they may appear to the south, or less likely, to the north. But the sun does not shine from the north. South is the best bet, then."

He took the Dwarf's head off and laid the stone carefully on the Look-out. He knelt down and smoothed the silver paper until the sheet gleamed under his hand. He forced the foil to lie smoothly against the head and bound it in place with the string. He put the silver head back on the Dwarf, went to the southern end of the Look-out and stared at the blank face. The sun bounced at him from the paper. He bent his knees until he was looking into the paper at eye-level and still he saw a distorted sun. He shuffled round in such arc as the southern end of the Look-out would allow and still he saw the sun. He took the silver head off the Dwarf again, polished the silver on his sea-boot stockings and put it back. The sun winked at him. There stood on the Look-out a veritable man and one who carried a flashing signal on his shoulders.

"I shall be rescued today."

He fortified and deepened the meaningless statement with three steps of a dance but stopped with a grimace.

"My feet!"

He sat down and leaned against the Dwarf on the south side.

Today is a thinking day.

"I haven't done so badly."

He altered the arch over his window with a frown.

"Ideally, of course, the stone should be a sphere. Then no matter where the ship appears in an arc of one hundred and eighty degrees the sun will bounce straight at her from the Dwarf. If a ship is under the horizon then the gleam

98

might fetch her crow's-nest, following it along like a hand of arrest on the shoulder, persisting, nagging, till even the dullest of seamen would notice and the idea sink in."

The horizon remained empty.

"I must get a sphere. Perhaps I could beat the nearest to it with another stone until it rounds. Stone mason as well. Who was it cut stone cannon-balls? Michael Angelo? But I must look for a very round stone. Never a dull moment. Just like Itma."

He got up and went down to the sea. He peered over the edge of the little cliff by the mussels but saw nothing worth having. There was green weed and a mass of stone between him and the three rocks but he turned away from it. He went instead to Prospect Cliff, climbed down the ledges to low water. But here there was nothing but masses of weed that stank. His climb tired him and he clung over the water for a moment, searching the surface of the rock with his eyes for anything of value. There was a coralline substance close to his face, thin and pink like icing and then not pink as though it were for ever changing its mind to purple. He stroked the smooth stuff with one finger. They called that paint Barmaid's Blush and splashed on gallons with the inexpert and casual hand of the wartime sailor. The colour was supposed to merge a ship into the sea and air at the perilous hour of dawn. There were interminable hard acres of the pink round scuttles and on gun shields, whole fields on sides and top hamper, hanging round the hard angles, the utilitarian curves, the grudgingly conceded living quarters of ships on the Northern Patrol, like pink icing or the coral growths on a washed rock. He took his face away from the casing and turned to climb the ladders to the

99

bridge. There must be acres of the stuff spread on the child-time rocks at Tresellyn. That was where Nat had taken her—taken her in two senses, grateful for the tip.

The ship rolled heavily and here was Nat descending the upper ladder like a daddy-longlegs, carefully placing the remote ends of the limbs for security and now faced with a crisis at the sight of the face and the cap. Here is Nat saluting as ever off balance, but this time held in position by one arm and two legs.

"Wotcher, Nat. Happy in your work?"

Dutiful Nat-smile though a little queasy. See the bright side.

"Yes, sir."

Amble aft you drawn-out bastard.

Climb, climb. The bridge, a little wind and afternoon.

"Hallo. Mean course o-nine-o. Now on zag at one-one-o. And I may say, dead in station, not wandering all over the ocean the way you leave her. She's all yours and the Old Man is in one of his moods, so watch out for sparks."

"Zig coming up in ten seconds? I've got her."

"See you again at the witching hour."

"Port fifteen. Midships. Steady."

He looked briefly round the convoy and then aft. Nat was there, tediously in his usual place, legs wide apart, face in hands. The corticened deck lurched under him, re-arranged itself and he swayed on the rail. The luminous window that looked down at him bent at the sides in a snarl that was disguised as a grin.

Christ, how I hate you. I could eat you. Because you fathomed her mystery, you have a right to handle her transmuted cheap tweed; because you both have made a

100

place where I can't get; because in your fool innocence you've got what I had to get or go mad.

Then he found himself additionally furious with Nathaniel, not because of Mary, not because he had happened on her as he might have tripped over a ring-bolt but because he dared sit so, tilting with the sea, held by a thread, so near the end that would be at once so anguishing and restful like the bursting of a boil.

"Christ!"

Wildebeeste had turned seconds ago.

"Starboard thirty! Half-ahead together!"

Already, from the apex of the destroyer screen, a light was stabbing erratically.

"Midships! Steady. Slow ahead together."

There was a clatter from the ladder. The Captain burst at him.

"What the bloody hell are you playing at?"

Hurried and smooth.

"I thought there was wreckage on the starboard bow, sir, and couldn't be sure so I maintained course and speed till we were clear, sir."

The Captain stopped, one hand on the screen of the bridge and lowered at him.

"What sort of wreckage?"

"Baulks of timber, sir, floating just under the surface."

"Starboard look-out!"

"Sir?"

"Did you see any wreckage?"

"No, sir."

"—I may have been mistaken, sir, but I judged it better to make sure, sir."

The Captain bored in, face to face so that his grip on the rock tightened as he remembered. The Captain's face was big, pale and lined, the eyes red-rimmed with sleeplessness and gin. It examined for a moment what the window had to exhibit. The two shadowy noses on either side of the window caught a faint, sweet scent. Then the face changed, not dramatically, not registering, not making obvious, but changing like a Nat-face, from within. Under the pallor and moist creases, in the corners of the mouth and eyes, came the slight muscular shift of complicated tensions till the face was rearranged and bore like an open insult, the pattern of contempt and disbelief.

The mouth opened.

"Carry on."

In a confusion too complete for answer or salute he watched the face turn away and take its understanding and contempt down the ladder.

There was heat and blood.

"Signal, sir, from Captain D. 'Where are you going to my pretty maid?' "

Signalman with a wooden face. Heat and blood.

"Take it to the Captain."

"Aye aye, sir."

He turned back to the binnacle.

"Port fifteen. Midships. Steady."

Looking under his arm he saw Nathaniel pass the bridge messenger in the waist. Seen thus, he was a bat hanging upside down from the roof of a cave. Nat passed on, walking and lurching till the break of the fo'castle hid him.

He found he was cursing an invisible Nat, cursing him

102

for Mary, for the contempt in old Gin-soak's face. The centre, looking in this reversed world over the binnacle, found itself beset by a storm of emotions, acid and inky and cruel. There was a desperate amazement that anyone so good as Nat, so unwillingly loved for the face that was always rearranged from within, for the serious attention, for love given without thought, should also be so quiveringly hated as though he were the only enemy. There was amazement that to love and to hate were now one thing and one emotion. Or perhaps they could be separated. Hate was as hate had always been, an acid, the corroding venom of which could be borne only because the hater was strong.

"I am a good hater."

He looked quickly at the deck watch, across at *Wildebeeste* and gave orders for the new course.

And love? Love for Nat? That was this sorrow dissolved through the hate so that the new solution was a deadly thing in the chest and the bowels.

He muttered over the binnacle.

"If I were that glass toy that I used to play with I could float in a bottle of acid. Nothing could touch me then."

Zag.

"That's what it is. Ever since I met her and she interrupted the pattern, coming at random, obeying no law of life, facing me with the insoluble, unbearable problem of her existence the acid's been chewing at my guts. I can't even kill her because that would be her final victory over me. Yet as long as she lives the acid will eat. She's there. In the flesh. In the not even lovely flesh. In the cheap mind. Obsession. Not love. Or if love, insanely compounded of this jealousy of her very being. *Odi et amo.* Like that thing I tried to write."

There were lace curtains in decorous curves either side of the oak occasional table with its dusty fern. The round table in the centre of the almost unused parlour smelt of polish—might one day support a coffin in state, but until then, nothing. He looked round at the ornaments and plush, took a breath of the air that was trapped this side of the window, smelt of last year and varnish like the vilest cooking sherry. The room would suit her. She would fit it, she was the room at all points except for the mania.

He looked down at the writing-pad on his knee.

Zig.

"And that wasn't the half of it. And the acid still eats. Who could ever dream that he would fall in love—or be trapped—by a front parlour on two feet?"

He began to pace backward and forward on the bridge.

"As long as she lives the acid will eat. There's nothing that can stand that. And killing her would make it worse."

He stopped. Looked back along the deck at the quarter-deck and the empty, starboard rail.

"Christ! Starboard twenty——"

There was a sense in which she could be—or say that the acid flow could be checked. Not to pass Petty Officer Roberts' message on was one thing—but that merely acquiesced in the pattern. But say one nudged circumstances—not in the sense that one throttled with the hands or fired a gun—but gently shepherded them the way they might go? Since it would be a suggestion to circumstances only it could not be considered what a strict moralist might call it——

"And who cares anyway?"

This was to run with a rapier at the arras without more than a hope of success.

"He may never sit there again."

Then the officer of the watch in the execution of his duty gives a helm order to avoid floating wreckage or a drifting mine and no one is any the worse.

"But if he sits there again——"

The corrosive swamped him. A voice cried out in his belly—I do not want him to die! The sorrow and hate bit deep, went on biting. He cried out with his proper voice.

"Does no one understand how I feel?"

The look-outs had turned on their perches. He scowled at them and felt another warmth in his face. His voice came out savagely.

"Get back to your sectors."

He leaned over the binnacle and felt how his body shook.

"I am chasing after—a kind of peace."

Barmaid's blush with hair that was coarse even for a barmaid. He looked at the ledges of rock.

"A kind of peace."

Coral growth.

He shook his head as though he were shaking water out of his hair.

"I came down here for something."

But there was nothing, only weed and rock and water.

He climbed back to the Red Lion, gathered some of the uneaten mussels that he had left from the morning and went up the High Street to the Look-out. He sat under the south side of the winking Dwarf and opened them with his knife. He ate with long pauses between each mouthful. When he had finished the last one he lay back.

"Christ."

They were no different from the mussels of yesterday but they tasted of decay.

"Perhaps I left them too long in the sun."

But they hang in the sun between tides for hours!

"How many days have I been here?"

He thought fiercely, then made three scratches on the rock with his knife.

"I must not let anything escape that would reinforce personality. I must make decisions and carry them out. I have put a silver head on the Dwarf. I have decided not to be tricked into messing about with the water-hole. How far away is the horizon? Five miles? I could see a crow's-nest at ten miles. I can advertise myself over a circle twenty miles in diameter. That's not bad. The Atlantic is about two thousand miles wide up here. Twenty into two thousand goes a hundred."

He knelt down and measured off a line ten inches in length as near as he could judge.

"That makes it a tenth of an inch."

He put the blade of his knife on the line at about two inches from the end and rotated the haft slowly till the point made a white mark in the grey rock. He squatted back on his heels and looked at the diagram.

"With a really big ship I could be seen at fifteen miles."

He put the point of the knife back on the mark and enlarged it. He paused, then went on scraping till the mark was the size of a silver threepenny-bit. He put out his foot and scuffed the seaboot stocking over the mark until it was grey and might have been there since the rock was made.

"I shall be rescued today."

He stood up and looked into the silver face. The sun was still shining back at him. He traced mental lines from the sun to the stone, bounced them out at this part of the horizon and that. He went close to the dwarf and looked down at the head to see if he could find his face reflected there. The sunlight bounced up in his eyes. He jerked upright.

"The air! You fool! You clot! They ferry planes and they must use this place for checking the course—and Coastal Command, looking for U-boats——"

He cupped his hands at his eyes and turned slowly round, looking at the sky. The air was dense blue and interrupted by nothing but the sun over the south sea. He flung his hands away and began to walk hastily up and down by the look-out.

"A thinking day."

The Dwarf was all right for ships—they were looking across at a silhouette. They would see the Dwarf or perhaps the gleam of the head. But to a plane, the Dwarf would be invisible, merged against the rock, and the glint from the silver might be a stray crystal of quartz. There was nothing about the rock to catch the eye. They might circle at a few thousand feet—a mile, two miles—and see nothing that was different. From above, the stone would be a tiny grey patch, that was eye-catching only by the surf that spread round in the sea.

He looked quickly and desperately up, then away at the water.

A pattern.

Men make patterns and superimpose them on nature. At ten thousand feet the rock would be a pebble; but suppose the pebble were striped? He looked at the trenches. The pebble was striped already. The upended layers would be grey with darker lines of trench between them.

He held his head in his hands.

A chequer. Stripes. Words. S.O.S.

"I cannot give up my clothes. Without them I should freeze to death. Besides if I spread them out they would still be less visible than this guano."

He looked down the High Street between his hands.

"Pare away here and here and there. Make all smooth. Cut into a huge, shadowed S.O.S."

He dropped his hands and grinned.

"Be your age."

He squatted down again and considered in turn the material he had with him. Cloth. Small sheets of paper. A rubber lifebelt.

Seaweed.

He paused, lifted his hands and cried out in triumph.

"Seaweed!"

There were tons of the stuff hanging round the rock, floating or coiled down under water by Prospect Cliff.

"Men make patterns."

Seaweed, to impose an unnatural pattern on nature, a pattern that would cry out to any rational beholder— Look! Here is thought. Here is man!

"The best form would be a single indisputable line drawn at right angles to the trenches, piled so high that it will not only show a change of colour but even throw a shadow of its own. I must make it at least a yard wide and it must be geometrically straight. Later I will fill up one of the trenches and turn the upright into a cross. Then the rock will become a hot cross bun."

Looking down towards the three Rocks he planned the line to descend across the trenches, parallel more or less to the High Street. The line would start at the Red Lion and come up to the Dwarf. It would be an operation.

He went quickly down the High Street: and now that he had found a job with point, he was muttering without knowing why.

"Hurry! Hurry!"

Then his ears began to fill with the phantom buzzing of planes. He kept looking up and fell once, cutting himself. Only when he was already pulling at the frondy weed by Food Cliff did he pause.

"Don't be a fool. Take it easy. There's no point in looking up because you can do nothing to attract attention. Only a clot would go dancing and waving his shirt because he thought there was a plane about five miles up."

He craned back his head and searched the sky but found nothing besides blueness and sun. He held his breath and listened and heard nothing but the inner, mingled humming of his own life, nothing outside but the lap and gurgle of water. He straightened his neck and stood there thinking. He went back to the crevice. He stripped naked and spread his clothing in the sun. He arranged each item carefully to one side of where the line of seaweed would lie. He went back to the Red Lion and looked down at the space between the Red Lion and the three rocks. He turned round and lowered himself over the edge. The water was colder than he remembered, colder than the fresh water that he drank. He ground his teeth and forced himself down and the rock was so sharp against his knee that he reopened the wounds of the first day. His waist was on the rock between his hands and he was groaning. He could not feel bottom and the weed round his calves was colder than the water. The cold squeezed as the water had done in the open sea, so that he was panic-stricken at the memory. He made a high, despairing sound, pushed himself clear of the rock and fell. The water took him with a freezing hand. He opened his eyes and weed was lashing

110

before them. His head broke the surface and he struck out frantically for the rock. He hung there, shivering.

"Take a grip."

There was whiteness under the weed. He pushed off and let his feet sink. Under the weed, caught between his own rock and the three others were boulders, quartz perhaps, stacked and unguessable. He stood, crouched in the water, half-supporting his weight with swimming movements of the arms and felt round him with his feet. Carefully he found foothold and stood up. The water reached to his chest and the weed dragged at him. He took a breath and ducked. He seized weed and tried to tear off fronds but they were very tough and he could win no more than a handful before he had to surface again. He began to collect weed without ducking, reaping the last foot of the crop. Sometimes when he pulled there would be a stony turn and slight shock, or the water-slowed movements of re-adjustment. He threw weed up on the rock and the fronds flopped down over the edge, dripping.

Suddenly the weed between his feet tugged and something brushed over his toes. A line of swift and erratic movement appeared in the weed, ceased. He clawed at the cliff and hung there, drawing his legs up.

The water lapped.

"Crab. Lobster."

He kneed his painful way to the Red Lion and lay down by the weed till his heart steadied.

"I loathe it."

He crawled to the edge of the cliff and looked down. At once, as if his eye had created it, he saw the lobster among the weed, different in dragon-shape, different in colour. He

111

knelt, looking down, mesmerized while the worms of loathing crawled over his skin.

"Beast. Filthy sea-beast."

He picked up a mussel shell and threw it with all his strength into the water. At the smack, the lobster clenched like a fist and was gone.

"That line of seaweed's going to take a devil of a time to build."

He shook himself free of the worms on his skin. He lowered himself over Prospect Cliff. The bottom four or five feet was covered with a hanging mass of strap-weed. At the surface of the water, weed floated out so that the sea seemed solid.

"Low water."

He climbed along the rock and began to tug at the weed but it would not come off. The roots clung to the rock with suckers more difficult to remove than limpets or mussels. Some of the weeds were great bushes that ended in dimpled bags full of jelly. Others were long swords but with a fluted and wavered surface and edge. The rest was smooth brown leather like an assembly of sword belts for all the officers in the world. Under the weed the rock was furry with coloured growths or hard and decorative with stuff that looked like uncooked batter. There was also Barmaid's Blush. There were tiny bubblings and pips and splashes.

He tugged at a bunch of weed with one hand while he hung on to the rock with the other. He cursed and climbed back up the rock, walked up the High Street to the Lookout and stood looking at the sea and sky.

He came to with a jump.

"Don't waste time. Be quick."

He went to the crevice, slung the knife round his neck by its lanyard and picked up the lifebelt. He unscrewed the mouth of the tit, let the air out and climbed down the rock. He slung the lifebelt over his arm and went at the weed-roots with the knife. They were not only hard as hard rubber but slippery. He had to find a particular angle and a particular careful sobriety of approach before he could get the edge of his knife into them. He wore the weed like firewood over his shoulder. He held the lifebelt in his teeth and drew fronds of weed through between the lifebelt and the tape. He reversed his position, holding on with his left arm and gathering with his right. The weed made a great bundle on his shoulder that draped down and fell past his knees in a long, brown smear.

He climbed to the Red Lion, and flung down the weed. At a distance of a few feet from him it looked like a small patch. He laid out the separate blades, defining the straight line that would interrupt the trenches. In the trenches themselves the weed had no support.

"I must fill the trenches flush with the wall where the weed crosses them."

When he had used up all the weed the load stretched from the Red Lion to the Look-out. On the average the line was two inches wide.

He went back to Prospect Cliff and got more weed. He squatted in the Red Lion with his forehead corrugated. He shut one eye and considered his handiwork. The line was hardly visible. He climbed round to the cliff again.

There was a sudden plop in the water by the farthest of the three rocks, so that he sprang round. Nothing. No

113

foam, only a dimpled interruption in the pattern of wavelets.

"I ought to catch fish."

He gathered himself another load of weed. The jellied bags burst when he pressed them, and he put one of the bags to his lips but the taste was neutral. He carried another load to the Red Lion and another. When he piled the weed in the first trench it did not come within a foot of the top.

He stood in the trench, looking down at the red and brown weed and felt suddenly listless.

"Twelve loads? Twenty? And then the line to thicken after that——"

Intelligence sees so clearly what is to be done and can count the cost beforehand.

"I will rest for a while."

He went to the Dwarf and sat down under the empty sky. The seaweed stretched away across the rock like a trail.

"Harder than ever in my life before. Worn out for today."

He put his head on his knees and muttered to the ghost of a diagram—a line with a grey blob on it.

"I haven't had a crap since we were torpedoed."

He sat motionless and meditated on his bowels. Presently he looked up. He saw that the sun was on the decline and made a part of the horizon particularly clear and near. Squinting at it he thought he could even see the minute distortions that the waves made in the perfect curve of the world.

There was a white dot sitting between the sun and Safety

Rock. He watched closely and saw that the dot was a gull sitting in the water, letting itself drift. All at once he had a waking vision of the gull rising and flying east over the sea's shoulder. To-morrow morning it could be floating among the stacks and shields of the Hebrides or following the plough on some Irish hill-side. As an intense experience that interrupted the bright afternoon before him he saw the ploughman in his cloth cap hitting out at the squawking bird.

"Get away from me now and the bad luck go with you!"

But the bird would not perch on the boundary-stone, open its bill and speak as in all folk lore. Even if it were more than a flying machine it could not pass on news of the scarred man sitting on a rock in the middle of the sea. He got up and began to pace to and fro on the Look-out. He took the thought out and looked at it.

I may never get away from this rock at all.

Speech is identity.

"You are all a machine. I know you, wetness, hardness, movement. You have no mercy but you have no intelligence. I can outwit you. All I have to do is to endure. I breathe this air into my own furnace. I kill and eat. There is nothing to——"

He paused for a moment and watched the gull drifting nearer; but not so near that the reptile under the white was visible.

"There is nothing to fear."

The gull was being carried along by the tide. Of course the tide operated here too, in mid-Atlantic, a great wave that swept round the world. It was so great that it thrust out tongues that became vast ocean currents, sweeping the water in curves that were ten thousand miles long. So there was a current that flowed past this rock, rising, pausing, reversing and flowing back again eternally and pointlessly. The current would continue to do so if life were rubbed off the skin of the world like the bloom off a grape. The rock sat immovable and the tide went sweeping past.

He watched the gull come floating by Prospect Cliff. It preened its feathers and fluttered like a duck in a pond.

He turned abruptly away and went quickly down to Prospect Cliff. Half the hanging seaweed was covered.

To-morrow.

"Exhausted myself. Mustn't overdo it."

Plenty to do on a rock. Never a dull moment.

He considered the mussels with positive distaste and switched his mind instead to the bags of jelly on the seaweed. He had a vague feeling that his stomach was talking to him. It disliked mussels. As for anemones—the bare thought made the bag contract and send a foul taste to his mouth.

"Overwork. Exposure. Sunburn, perhaps. I mustn't overdo it."

He reminded himself seriously that this was the day on which he was going to be rescued but could not rediscover conviction.

"Dress."

He put on his clothes, walked round the Dwarf then sat down again.

"I should like to turn in. But I mustn't as long as there's light. She might come close for a look, blow her siren and go away again if I didn't show myself. But I thought to some purpose today. To-morrow I must finish the sea-

116

weed. She may be just below the horizon. Or up so high I can't see her. I must wait."

He hunched down by the Dwarf and waited. But time had infinite resource and what at first had been a purpose became grey and endless and without hope. He began to look for hope in his mind but the warmth had gone or if he found anything it was an intellectual and bloodless ghost.

He muttered.

"I shall be rescued. I shall be rescued."

At an end so far from the beginning that he had forgotten everything he had thought while he was there, he lifted his chin and saw that the sun was sinking. He got up heavily, went to the water-hole and drank. The stain of red round the nearer edge was wider.

He echoed.

"I must do something about water."

He dressed as for bed and wrapped the grey sweater round his feet. It made a muffling between them and the rock like the cathedral carpets over stone. That was a particular sensation the feet never found anywhere else particularly when they wore those ridiculous medieval shoes of Michael's all fantasticated but with practically no sole. Beside the acoustics were so bad—wah, wah, wah and then a high whine up among the barrel vault to which one added with every word one spoke as though one were giving a little periodic momentum to a pendulum——

"Can't hear you, old man, not a sausage. Up a bit. Give. I still can't hear you——"

"More? Slower?"

"Not slower for God's sake. Oh, turn it up. That's all for today boys and girls. Wait a bit, Chris. Look, George, Chris isn't coming off here at all——"

"Give him a bit more time, old man. Not your pitch is it, Chris?"

"I can manage, George."

"He'll be better in the other part, old man. Didn't you see the rehearsal list, Chris? You're doubling—but of course——"

"Helen never said——"

"What's Helen got to do with it?"

"She never said——"

"I make out my own lists, old man."

"Of course, Pete, naturally."

"So you're doubling a shepherd and one of the seven deadly sins, old man. Eh, George, don't you think? Chris for one of the seven deadly sins?"

"Definitely, old man, oh, definitely."

"Well, I do think, Pete, after the amount of work I've done for you, I shouldn't be asked to——"

"Double, old man? Everybody's doubling. I'm doubling. So you're wanted for the seven sins, Chris."

"Which one, Pete?"

"Take your pick, old man. Eh, George? We ought to let dear old Chris pick his favourite sin, don't you think?"

"Definitely, old boy, definitely."

"Prue's working on them in the crypt, come and look, Chris——"

"But if we've finished until to-night's house——"

"Come along, Chris. The show must go on. Eh, George?

118

You'd like to see which mask Chris thinks would suit him?"

"Well—yes. Yes by God, Pete. I would. After you, Chris."

"I don't think I——"

"After you, Chris."

"Curious feeling to the feet this carpet over stone, George. Something thick and costly, just allowing your senses to feel the basic stuff beneath. There they are, Chris, all in a row. What about it?"

"Anything you say, old man."

"What about Pride, George? He could play that without a mask and just stylized make-up, couldn't he?"

"Look, Pete, if I'm doubling I'd sooner not make——"

"Malice, George?"

"Envy, Pete?"

"I don't mind playing Sloth, Pete."

"Not Sloth. Shall we ask Helen, Chris? I value my wife's advice."

"Steady, Pete."

"What about a spot of Lechery?"

"Pete! Stop it."

"Don't mind me, Chris, old man. I'm just a bit wrought-up that's all. Now here's a fine piece of work, ladies and gentlemen, guaranteed unworn. Any offers? Going to the smooth-looking gentleman with the wavy hair and profile. Going! Going——"

"What's it supposed to be, old man?"

"Darling, it's simply *you*! Don't you think, George?"

"Definitely, old man, definitely."

"Chris-Greed. Greed-Chris. Know each other."

"Anything to please you, Pete."

"Let me make you two better acquainted. This painted bastard here takes anything he can lay his hands on. Not food, Chris, that's far too simple. He takes the best part, the best seat, the most money, the best notice, the best woman. He was born with his mouth and his flies open and both hands out to grab. He's a cosmic case of the bugger who gets his penny and someone else's bun. Isn't that right, George?"

"Come on, Pete. Come and lie down for a bit."

"Think you can play Martin, Greed?"

"Come on, Pete. He doesn't mean anything, Chris. Just wrought-up. A bit over-excited, eh, Pete?"

"That's all. Yes. Sure. That's all."

"I haven't had a crap for a week."

The dusk came crowding in and the sea-gulls. One sat on the Dwarf and the silver head rocked so that the sea-gull muted and flapped away. He went down to the crevice, blew up the lifebelt, tied the tapes and put it under his head. He got his hands tucked in. Then his head felt unprotected, although he was wearing the balaclava, so that he wriggled out and fetched his sou'wester from the Red Lion. He went through the business of insertion again.

"Good God!"

He hauled himself out.

"Where the hell's my oilskin?"

He went scrambling over the rocks to the Red Lion, the water-hole, the Prospect Cliff——

"It can't be by the Dwarf because I never——"

120

In and out of the trenches, stinking seaweed, clammy, is it underneath?

He found his oilskin where he had left it by the Dwarf. There were white splashes on it. He put on his oilskin over his duffle and inserted himself again.

"That's what they can never tell you, never give you any idea. Not the danger or the hardship but the niggling little idiocies, the damnable repetitions, the days dripping away in a scrammy-handed flurry of small mistakes you wouldn't notice if you were at work or could drop into the Red Lion or see your popsie—Where's my knife? Oh, Christ!"

But the knife was present, had swung round and was a rock-like projection under his left ribs. He worked it free and cursed.

"I'd better do my thinking now. I was wrong to do it when I could have worked. If I'd thought last night instead I could have treated the day methodically and done everything.

Now: problems. First I must finish that line of weed. Then I must have a place for clothes so that I never get into a panic again. I'd better stow them here so that I never forget. Second. No, third. Clothes were second. First clothes in the crevice, then more weed until the line is finished. Third, water. Can't dig for it. Must catch it when it comes. Choose a trench below guano level and above spray. Make a catchment area."

He worked his lower jaw sideways. His bristles were very uncomfortable in the wool of the balaclava. He could feel the slight freezing, prickling sensation of sunburn on his arms and legs. The unevennesses of the rock were penetrating again.

121

"It'll soon rain. Then I'll have too much water. What shall I do about this crack? Musn't get my clothes wet. I must rig a tent. Perhaps to-morrow I'll be rescued."

He remembered that he had been certain of rescue in the morning and that made his heart sink unaccountably as though someone had broken his sworn word. He lay, looking up into the stars and wondering if he could find a scrap of wood to touch. But there was no wood on the rock, not even the stub of a pencil. No salt to throw over the left shoulder. Perhaps a splash of sea-water would be just as effective.

He worked his hand down to his right thigh. The old scar must have caught the sun too, for he could feel the raised place burning gently—a not unpleasant feeling but one that took the attention. The bristles in the balaclava made a scratching sound when he grimaced.

"Four. Make the knife sharp enough to shave with. Five. Make sure I'm not egg-bound to-morrow."

The sunburn pricked.

"I am suffering from reaction. I went through hell in the sea and in the funnel, and then I was so pleased to be safe that I went right over the top. And that is followed by a set-back. I must sleep, must keep quite still and concentrate on the business of sleeping."

The sunburn went on pricking, the bristles scratched and scraped and the unevennesses of the rock lit their slow, smouldering fires. They stayed there like the sea. Even when consciousness was modified they insisted. They became a luminous landscape, they became a universe and he oscillated between moments of hanging in space, observing them and of being extended to every excruciating corner.

He opened his eyes and looked up. He shut them again and muttered to himself.

"I am dreaming."

He opened his eyes and the sunlight stayed there. The light lulled the fires to a certain extent because the mind could at last look away from them. He lay, looking at the daylight sky and trying to remember the quality of this time that had suddenly foreshortened itself.

"I wasn't asleep at all!"

And the mind was very disinclined to hutch out of the crevice and face what must be done. He spoke toneless words into the height of air over him.

"I shall be rescued today."

He hauled himself out of the crevice and the air was warm so that he undressed to trousers and sweater. He folded his clothes carefully and put them in the crevice. When he hutched forward in the water-hole the red deposit made a mark across his chest. He drank a great deal of water and when he stopped drinking he could see that there was a wider space of darkness between the water and the window.

"I must get more water."

He lay still and tried to decide whether it was more important to arrange for catching water or to finish the line of weed. That reminded him how quickly time could pass if you let it out of your sight so he scrambled back to the Look-out. This was a day of colour. The sun burned and the water was deep blue and sparkled gaily. There was

123

colour spilt over the rocks, shadows that were deep purple until you looked straight at them. He peered down the High Street and it was a picture. He shut his eyes and then opened them again but the rock and the sea seemed no more real. They were a pattern of colour that filled the three lights of his window.

"I am still asleep. I am shut inside my body."

He went to the Red Lion and sat by the sea.

"What did I do that for?"

He frowned at the water.

"I meant to get food. But I'm not hungry. I must get weed."

He fetched the lifebelt and knife from the crevice and went to Prospect Cliff. He had to climb farther along the ledges for weed because the nearer part of the cliff was stripped already. He came to a ledge that was vaguely familiar and had to think.

"I came here to get stones for the Dwarf. I tried to shift that stone there but it wouldn't move although it was cracked."

He frowned at the stone. Then he worked his way down until he was hanging on the cliff by it with both hands and the crack was only a foot from his face. Like all the rest of the cliff where the water could reach it was cemented with layers of barnacles and enigmatic growths. But the crack was wider. The whole stone had moved and skewed perhaps an eighth of an inch. Inside the crack was a terrible darkness.

He stayed there, looking at the loose rock until he forgot what he was thinking. He was envisaging the whole rock as a thing in the water, and he was turning his head from side to side.

"How the hell is it that this rock is so familiar? I've never been here before——"

Familiar, not as a wartime acquaintance whom one knows so quickly because one is forced to live close to him for interminable stretches of hours but familiar as a relative, seldom seen, but to be reckoned with, year after year, familiar as a childhood friend, a nurse, some acquaintance with a touch of eternity behind him; familiar now, as the rocks of childhood, examined and reapprized holiday after holiday, remembered in the darkness of bed, in winter, imagined as a shape one's fingers can feel in the air——

There came a loud plop from the three rocks. He scrambled quickly to the Red Lion but saw nothing.

"I ought to fish."

The seaweed in the trenches stank. There came another plop from the sea and he was in time to see the ripples spreading. He put his hands on either cheek to think but the touch of hair distracted him.

"I must have a beard pretty well. Bristles, anyway. Strange that bristles go on growing even when the rest of you is——"

He went quickly to Prospect Cliff and got a load of weed and dumped it in the nearest trench. He went slowly up the High Street to the Look-out and sat down, his opened hands on either side of him. His head sank between his knees. The lap lap of water round Safety Rock was very quieting and a gull stood on the Look-out like an image.

The sounds of the inside body spread. The vast darkness was full of them as a factory is full of the sound of mach-

125

inery. His head made a tiny bobbing motion each time his heart beat.

He was jerked out of this state by a harsh scream. The gull had advanced across the rock, its wings half-open, head lowered.

"What do you want?"

The feathered reptile took two steps sideways then shuffled its wings shut. The beak preened under the wing.

"If I had a crap I'd feel better."

He heaved himself round and looked at the Dwarf who winked at him with a silver eye. The line of the horizon was hard and near. Again he thought he could see indentations in the curve.

The trouble was there were no cushions on the rock, no tussocks. He thought for a moment of fetching his duffle and folding the skirt as a seat but the effort seemed too great.

"My flesh aches inside as though it were bruised. The hardness of the rock is wearing out my flesh. I will think about water."

Water was insinuating, soft and yielding.

"I must arrange some kind of shelter. I must arrange to catch water."

He came to a little, felt stronger and worried. He frowned at the tumbled rocks that were so maddeningly and evasively familiar and followed with his eye the thin line of weed. It shone in places. Perhaps the weed would appear from the air as a shining strip.

"I could catch water in my oilskin. I could make the wall of a trench into a catchment area."

He stopped talking and lay back until the unevenness of

126

the Dwarf as a chair-back made him lean forward again. He sat, hunched up and frowning.

"I am aware of——"

He looked up.

"I am aware of a weight. A ponderous squeezing. Agoraphobia or anyway the opposite of claustrophobia. A pressure."

Water catchment.

He got to his feet and climbed back down the High Street. He examined the next trench to his sleeping crevice.

"Prevailing wind. I must catch water from an area facing south west."

He took his knife and drew a line sloping down across the leaning wall. It ended in a hollow, set back to the depth of his fist where the wall met the bottom of the trench. He went to the Dwarf, carefully extracted a white potato and brought it back. On the end of the clasp knife was a projection about a quarter of an inch long which was intended as a screwdriver. He placed this against the rock about an inch above the slanting line and tapped the other end of his knife with the stone. The rock came away in thin flakes. He put the screwdriver in the slanting line and tapped till the line sank in. Soon he had made a line perhaps an eighth of an inch deep and a foot long. He went to the bottom end of the line.

"Begin at the most important end of the line. Then no matter how soon the rain comes I can catch some of it."

The noise of the taps was satisfactorily repeated in the trench and he felt enclosed as though he were working in a room.

127

"I could spread my duffle or oilskin over this trench and then I should have a roof. That ponderous feeling is not so noticeable here. That's partly because I am in a room and partly because I am working."

His arms ached but the line rose away from the floor and he could work in an easier position. He made a dreamy calculation to see whether increasing ease would overtake tiredness and found that it would not. He sat on the floor with his face a few inches from the rock. He leaned his forehead on stone. His hands fell open.

"I could go to the crevice and lie down for a bit. Or I could roll up in my duffle by the Dwarf."

He jerked his head away from the rock and set to work again. The cut part of the line lengthened. This part met the part he had cut first and he sat back to examine it.

"I should have cut it back at a slant. Damn."

He grimaced at the rock and went back over the cut so that the bottom of the groove trended inward.

"Make it deeper near the end."

Because the amount of water in the cut—but he changed his mind and did the calculation out loud.

"The amount of water in any given length of the cut will consist of all the water collected higher up, and also will be proportional to the area of rock above."

He tapped at the rock and the flakes fell. His hands gave out and he sat on the floor of the trench, looking at his work.

"After this I shall do a real engineering job. I shall find a complex area round a possible basin and cut a network of lines that will guide the water to it. That will be rather interesting. Like sand-castles."

Or like Roman emperors, bringing water to the city from the hills.

"This is an aqueduct. I call it the Claudian."

He began to flake again, imposing purpose on the senseless rock.

"I wonder how long I've been doing that?"

He lay down in the trench and felt his back bruise. The Claudian was a long, whitish scar.

"There is something venomous about the hardness of this rock. It is harder than rock should be. And—familiar."

The ponderous weight squeezed down. He struggled up to a sitting position.

"I should have dried seaweed and lined the crevice. But there are too many things to do. I need another hand on this job of living and being rescued. Perhaps I could find another place to sleep. In the open? I feel warm enough."

Too warm.

"My flesh is perceptible inside—as though it were bruised everywhere to the bone. And big. Tumescent."

The globe of darkness turned a complicated window towards the sky. The voice evaporated at the gate like escaping steam on a dry day.

"I'm working too hard. If I don't watch out I shall exhaust myself. Anyway I'll hand it to you, Chris. I don't think many people would——"

He stopped suddenly, then began again.

"Chris. Christopher! Christopher Hadley Martin——"

The words dried up.

There was an instrument of examination, a point that knew it existed. There were sounds that came out of the lower part of a face. They had no meaning attached to them. They were useless as tins thrown out with the lids buckled back.

"Christopher. Christopher!"

He reached out with both arms as though to grab the words before they dried away. The arms appeared before the window and in complete unreason they filled him with terror.

"Oh, my God."

He wrapped his arms round him, hugged himself close, rocked from side to side. He began to mutter.

"Steady. Steady. Keep calm."

He got up and sat gingerly on the side of the trench. He could feel the separate leaves of rock and their edges through his trousers and pants. He shifted farther down the trench to a place where the leaves were smoothly cut but his backside seemed to fare no better.

"I am who I was."

He examined the shape of his window and the window-box of hair that was flourishing between his two noses. He turned the window down and surveyed all that he could see of himself. The sweater was dragged out into tatters and wisps of wool. It lay in folds beneath his chest and the sleeves were concertina'd. The trousers beneath the sweater were shiny and grey instead of black and beneath them the seaboot stockings drooped like the wads of waste that a stoker wipes his hands on. There was no body to be seen, only a conjunction of worn materials. He eyed the peculiar shapes that lay across the trousers indifferently for a while until at last it occurred to him how strange it was that lobsters should sit there. Then he was suddenly seized with a terrible loathing for lobsters and flung them away so that they cracked on the rock. The dull pain of the blow extended him into them again and they became his hands, lying discarded where he had tossed them.

He cleared his throat as if about to speak in public.

"How can I have a complete identity without a mirror? That is what has changed me. Once I was a man with twenty photographs of myself—myself as this and that with the signature scrawled across the bottom right-hand corner as a stamp and seal. Even when I was in the Navy there was that photograph in my identity card so that every now and then I could look and see who I was. Or perhaps I did not even need to look, but was content to wear the card next to my heart, secure in the knowledge that it was there, proof of me in the round. There were mirrors too, triple mirrors, more separate than the three lights in this window. I could arrange the side ones so that there was a double reflection and spy myself from the side or back in the reflected mirror as though I were watching a stranger. I could spy myself and assess the impact of Christopher Hadley Martin on the world. I could find assurance of my solidity in the bodies of other people by warmth and caresses and triumphant flesh. I could be a character in a body. But now I am this thing in here, a great many aches of bruised flesh, a bundle of rags and those lobsters on the rock. The three lights of my window are not enough to identify me however sufficient they were in the world. But there were other people to describe me to myself—they fell in love with me, they applauded me, they caressed this body they defined it for me. There were the people I got the better of, people who disliked me, people who quarrelled with me. Here I have nothing to quarrel with. I am in danger of losing definition. I am an

132

album of snapshots, random, a whole show of trailers of old films. The most I know of my face is the scratch of bristles, an itch, a sense of tingling warmth."

He cried out angrily.

"That's no face for a man! Sight is like exploring the night with a flashlight. I ought to be able to see all round my head——"

He climbed down to the water-hole and peered into the pool. But his reflection was inscrutable. He backed out and went down to the Red Lion among the littered shells. He found a pool of salt water on one of the sea rocks. The pool was an inch deep under the sun with one green-weeded limpet and three anemones. There was a tiny fish, less than an inch long, sunning itself on the bottom. He leaned over the pool, looked through the displayed works of the fish and saw blue sky far down. But no matter how he turned his head he could see nothing but a patch of darkness with the wild outline of hair round the edge.

"The best photograph was the one of me as Algernon. The one as Demetrius wasn't bad, either—and as Freddy with a pipe. The make-up took and my eyes looked really wide apart. There was the Night Must Fall one. And that one from The Way of the World. Who was I? It would have been fun playing opposite Jane. That wench was good for a tumble."

The rock hurt the scar on the front of his right thigh. He shifted his leg and peered back into the pool. He turned his head sideways again, trying to catch the right angle for his profile—the good profile, the left one, elevated a little and with a half-smile. But first a shadowy nose and then the semicircle of an eye socket got in the way. He turned back to inquire of his full face but his breathing ruffled the water. He puffed down and the dark head wavered and burst. He jerked up and there was a lobster supporting his weight at the end of his right sleeve.

He made the lobster into a hand again and looked down at the pool. The little fish hung in sunshine with a steady trickle of bubbles rising by it from the oxygen tube. The bottles at the back of the bar loomed through the aquarium as cliffs of jewels and ore.

"No, thanks, old man, I've had enough."

"He's had enough. Ju hear that, George? Ju hear?"

"Hear what, Pete?"

"Dear ol' Chris has had enough."

"Come on, Chris."

"Dear ol' Chris doesn't drink 'n doesn't smoke."

"Likes company, old man."

"Likes company. My company. I'm disgusted with my-self. Yur not goin' to say 'Time, Gentlemen, please', miss, are you, gentlemen? He promised his old mother. He said. She said. She said, Chris, my child, let the ten command-ments look after themselves she said. But don't drink and don't smoke. Only foke, I beg your pardon, miss, had I known such an intemperate word would have escaped the barrier of my teeth I would have taken steps to have it indictated in the sex with an obelisk or employed a peri-fris."

"Come on, Pete. Take his other arm, Chris."

"Unhand me, Gentlemen. By heaven I'll make a fish of him that lets me. I am a free and liberal citizen of this company with a wife and child of indifferent sex."

134

"It's a boy, old man."

"Confidently, George, it's not the sex but the wisdom. Does it know who I am? Who we are? Do you love me, George?"

"You're the best producer we've ever had, you drunken old soak."

"I meant soak, miss. George, you're the most divinely angelic director the bloody theatre ever had and Chris is the best bloody juvenile, aren't you, Chris?"

"Anything you say, eh, George?"

"Definitely, old man, definitely."

"So we all owe everything to the best bloody woman in the world. I love you, Chris. Father and mother is one flesh. And so my uncle. My prophetic uncle. Shall I elect you to my club?"

"How about toddling home, now, Pete?"

"Call it the Dirty Maggot Club. You member? You speak Chinese? You open sideways or only on Sundays?"

"Come on, Pete."

"We maggots are there all the week. Y'see when the Chinese want to prepare a very rare dish they bury a fish in a tin box. Presently all the lil' maggots peep out and start to eat. Presently no fish. Only maggots. It's no bloody joke being a maggot. Some of 'em are phototropic. Hey, George—phototropic!"

"What of it, Pete?"

"Phototropic. I said phototropic, miss."

"Finish your maggots, Pete and let's go."

"Oh, the maggots. Yes, the maggots. They haven't finished yet. Only got to the fish. It's a lousy job crawling round the inside of a tin box and Denmark's one of the

135

worst. Well, when they've finished the fish, Chris, they start on each other."

"Cheerful thought, old man."

"The little ones eat the tiny ones. The middle-sized ones eat the little ones. The big ones eat the middle-sized ones. Then the big ones eat each other. Then there are two and then one and where there was a fish there is now one huge, successful maggot. Rare dish."

"Got his hat, George?"

"Come on, Pete! Now careful——"

"I love you, Chris, you lovely big hunk. Eat me."

"Get his arm over your shoulder."

"There's nearly half of me left'n, I'm phototropic. You eat George yet? 'N when there's only one maggot left the Chinese dig it up——"

"You can't sit down here, you silly sot!"

"Chinese dig it up——"

"For Christ's sake, stop shouting. We'll have a copper after us."

"Chinese dig it up——"

"Snap out of it, Pete. How the hell do the Chinese know when to dig it up?"

"They know. They got X-ray eyes. Have you ever heard a spade knocking on the side of a tin box, Chris? Boom! Boom! Just like thunder. You a member?"

There was a round of ripples by the three rocks. He watched them intently. Then a brown head appeared by the rocks, another and another. One of the heads had a silver knife across its mouth. The knife bent, flapped and he saw the blade was a fish. The seal heaved itself on to the

136

rock while the others dived, leaving dimpled water and circles. The seal ate, calmly in the sun, rejected the head and tail and lay quiet.

"I wonder if they know about men?"

He stood up slowly and the seal turned its head towards him so that he found himself flinching from an implacable stare. He raised his arms suddenly in the gesture of a man who points a gun. The seal heaved round on the rock and dived. It knew about men.

"If I could get near I could kill it and make boots and eat the meat——"

The men lay on the open beach, wrapped in skins. They endured the long wait and the stench. At dusk, great beasts came out of the sea, played round them, then lay down to sleep.

"An oilskin rolled up would look enough like a seal. When they were used to it I should be inside."

He examined the thought of days. They were a recession like repeated rooms in mirrors hung face to face. All at once he experienced a weariness so intense that it was a pain. He laboured up to the Look-out through the pressure of the sky and all the vast quiet. He made himself examine the empty sea in each quarter. The water was smoother to-day as though the dead air were flattening it. There was shot silk in swathes, oily-looking patches that became iridescent as he watched, like the scum in a ditch. But the wavering of this water was miles long so that a molten sun was elongated, pulled out to nothing here to appear there in a different waver with a sudden blinding dazzle.

"The weather changed while I was in the Red Lion with George and Pete."

He saw a seal head appear for a moment beyond the three rocks and had a sudden wild sight of himself riding a seal across the water to the Hebrides.

"Oh, my God!"

The sound of his voice, flat, yet high and agonized, intimidated him. He dropped his arms and huddled down in his body by the Dwarf. A stream of muttered words began to tumble through the hole under his window.

"It's like those nights when I was a kid, lying awake thinking the darkness would go on for ever. And I couldn't go back to sleep because of the dream of the whatever it was in the cellar coming out of the corner. I'd lie in the hot, rumpled bed, hot burning hot, trying to shut myself away and know that there were three eternities before the dawn. Everything was the night world, the other world where everything but good could happen, the world of ghosts and robbers and horrors, of things harmless in the daytime coming to life, the wardrobe, the picture in the book, the story, coffins, corpses, vampires, and always squeezing, tormenting darkness, smoke thick. And I'd think of anything because if I didn't go on thinking I'd remember whatever it was in the cellar down there, and my mind would go walking away from my body and go down three stories defenceless, down the dark stairs past the tall, haunted clock, through the whining door, down the terrible steps to where the coffin ends were crushed in the walls of the cellar—and I'd be held helpless on the stone floor, trying to run back, run away, climb up——"

He was standing, crouched. The horizon came back.

"Oh, my God!"

Waiting for the dawn, the first bird cheeping in the

eaves or the tree-tops. Waiting for the police by the smashed car. Waiting for the shell after the flash of the gun.

The ponderous sky settled a little more irresistibly on his shoulders.

"What's the matter with me? I'm adult. I know what's what. There's no connection between me and the kid in the cellar, none at all. I grew up. I firmed my life. I have it under control. And anyway there's nothing down there to be frightened of. Waiting for the result. Waiting for that speech—not the next one after this, I know that, but where I go across and take up the cigarette-box. There's a black hole where that speech ought to be and he said you fluffed too much last night, old man. Waiting for the wound to be dressed. This will hurt a little. Waiting for the dentist's chair.

"I don't like to hear my voice falling dead at my mouth like a shot bird."

He put a hand up to either side of his window and watched two black lines diminish it. He could feel the roughness of bristles under either palm and the heat of cheeks.

"What's crushing me?"

He turned his sight round the horizon and the only thing that told him when he had completed the circle was the brighter waver under the sun.

"I shall be rescued any day now. I must not worry. Trailers out of the past are all right but I must be careful when I see things that never happened, like—I have water and food and intelligence and shelter."

He paused for a moment and concentrated on the feeling

in the flesh round his window. His hands and skin felt lumpy. He swivelled his eyes sideways and saw that there might indeed be a slight distortion of the semicircle of the eye-hollows.

"Heat lumps? When it rains I shall strip and have a bath. If I haven't been rescued by then."

He pressed with the fingers of his right hand the skin round his eyes. There were heat lumps on the side of his face, that extended down beneath the bristles. The sky pressed on them but they knew no other feeling.

"I must turn in. Go to bed. And stay awake."

The day went grey and hot. Dreary.

"I said I should be sick. I said I must watch out for symptoms."

He went down to the water-hole and crawled in. He drank until he could hear the water washing about in his belly. He crawled out backwards and dimensions were mixed up. The surface of the rock was far too hard, far too bright, far too near. He could not gauge size at all.

There was no one else to say a word.

You're not looking too good, old man.

"How the hell can I tell how I look?"

He saw a giant impending and flinched before he could connect the silver head with his chocolate paper. He felt that to stand up would be dangerous for a reason he was not able to formulate. He crawled to the crevice and arranged the clothing. He decided that he must wear everything. Presently he lay with his head out of the crevice on an inflated lifebelt. The sky was bright blue again but very heavy. The opening under his bristles dribbled on.

"Care Charmer Sleep. Cracker mottoes. Old tags. Rag

140

bag of a brain. But don't sleep because of the cellar. How sleep the brave. Nat's asleep. And old gin-soak. Rolled along the bottom or drifting like an old bundle. This is high adventure and anyone can have it. Lie down, rat. Accept your cage. How much rain in this month? How many convoys? How many planes? My hands are larger. All my body is larger and tenderer. Emergency. Action stations. I said I should be ill. I can feel the old scar on my leg tingling more than the rest. Salt in my trousers. Ants in my pants."

He hutched himself sideways in the crevice and withdrew his right hand. He felt his cheek with it but the cheek was dry.

"The tingling can't be sweat, then."

He got his hand back and scratched in his crutch. The edge of the duffle was irritating his face. He remembered that he ought to be wearing the balaclava but was too exhausted to find it. He lay still and his body burned.

He opened his eyes and the sky was violet over him. There was an irregularity in the eye sockets. He lay there, his eyes unfocused and thought of the heat lumps on his face. He wondered if they would close the sockets altogether.

Heat lumps.

The burnings and shiverings of his body succeeded each other as if they were going over him in waves. Suddenly they were waves of molten stuff, solder, melted lead, heated acid, so thick that it moved like oil. Then he was fighting and crying to get out of the crevice.

He knelt, shaking on the rock. He put his hands down and they hurt when he leaned his weight on them. He

141

peered down at them first with one eye then the other. They swelled and diminished with a slow pulsing.

"That's not real. Thread of life. Hang on. That's not real."

But what was real was the mean size of the hands. They were too big even on the average, butcher's hands so full of blood that their flesh was pulpy and swollen. His elbows gave way and he fell between his hands. His cheek was against the uniquely hard rock, his mouth open and he was looking blearily back into the crevice. The waves were still in his body and he recognized them. He gritted his teeth and hung on to himself in the centre of his globe.

"That must mean I'm running a temperature of well over a hundred. I ought to be in hospital."

Smells. Formalin. Ether. Meth. Idioform. Sweet chloroform. Iodine.

Sights. Chromium. White sheets. White bandages. High windows.

Touches. Pain, Pain, Pain.

Sounds. Forces programme drooling like a cretin in the ears from the headphones hitched under the fever chart.

Tastes. Dry lips.

He spoke again with intense solemnity and significance. "I must go sick."

He lugged the clothes off his body. Before he had got down to his vest and pants the burning was intolerable so that he tore off his clothes and threw them anywhere. He stood up naked and the air was hot on his body, but the action of being naked seemed to do something, for his body started to shiver. He sat painfully on the wall by the white scar of the Claudian and his teeth chattered.

"I must keep going somehow."

But the horizon would not stay still. Like his hands, the sea pulsed. At one moment the purple line was so far away that it had no significance and the next, so close that he could stretch out his arm and lay hold.

"Think. Be intelligent."

He held his head with both hands and shut his eyes.

"Drink plenty of water."

He opened his eyes and the High Street pulsed below him. The rock was striped with lines of seaweed that he saw presently were black shadows cast by the sun and not seaweed at all. The sea beyond the High Street was dead flat and featureless so that he could have stepped down and walked on it, only his feet were swollen and sore. He took his body with great care to the water-hole and pulled himself in. At once he was refrigerated. He put his face in the water and half-gulped, half-ate it with chattering teeth. He crawled away to the crevice.

"The squeezing did it, the awful pressure. It was the weight of the sky and the air. How can one human body support all that weight without bruising into a pulp?"

He made a little water in the trench. The reptiles were floating back to the sea round the rock. They said nothing but sat on the flat sea with their legs hidden.

"I need a crap. I must see about that. Now I must wear everything and sweat this heat out of my body."

By the time he had pulled on all his clothing dusk was come and he felt his way into the crevice with his legs. The crevice enlarged and became populous. There were times when it was larger than the rock, larger than the world,

143

times when it was a tin box so huge that a spade knocking at the side sounded like distant thunder. Then after that there was a time when he was back in rock and distant thunder was sounding like the knocking of a spade against a vast tin box. All the time the opening beneath his window was dribbling on like the Forces Programme, cross-talking and singing to people whom he could not see but knew were there. For a moment or two he was home and his father was like a mountain. The thunder and lightning were playing round the mountain's head and his mother was weeping tears like acid and knitting a sock without a beginning or end. The tears were a kind of charm for after he had felt them scald him they changed the crevice into a pattern.

The opening spoke.

"She is sorry for me on this rock."

Sybil was weeping and Alfred. Helen was crying. A bright boy face was crying. He saw half-forgotten but now clearly remembered faces and they were all weeping.

"That is because they know I am alone on a rock in the middle of a tin box."

They wept tears that turned them to stone faces in a wall, masks hung in rows in a corridor without beginning or end. There were notices that said No Smoking, Gentlemen, Ladies, Exit and there were many uniformed attendants. Down there was the other room, to be avoided, because there the gods sat behind their terrible knees and feet of black stone, but here the stone faces wept and had wept. Their stone cheeks were furrowed, they were blurred and only recognizable by some indefinite mode of identity. Their tears made a pool on the stone floor so that his feet

144

were burned to the ankles. He scrabbled to climb up the wall and the scalding stuff welled up his ankles to his calves, his knees. He was struggling, half-swimming, half-climbing. The wall was turning over, curving like the wall of a tunnel in the underground. The tears were no longer running down the stone to join the burning sea. They were falling freely, dropping on him. One came, a dot, a pearl, a ball, a globe, that moved on him, spread. He began to scream. He was inside the ball of water that was burning him to the bone and past. It consumed him utterly. He was dissolved and spread throughout the tear an extension of sheer, disembodied pain.

He burst the surface and grabbed at a stone wall. There was hardly any light but he knew better than to waste time because of what was coming. There were projections in the wall of the tunnel so that though it was more nearly a well than a tunnel he could still climb. He laid hold, pulled himself up, projection after projection. The light was bright enough to show him the projections. They were faces, like the ones in the endless corridor. They were not weeping but they were trodden. They appeared to be made of some chalky material for when he put his weight on them they would break away so that only by constant movement upward was he able to keep up at all. He could hear his voice shouting in the well.

"I am! I am! I am!"

And all the time there was another voice that hung in his ears like the drooling of the Forces Programme. Nobody paid any attention to this voice but the nature of the cretin was to go on talking even though it said the same thing over and over again. This voice had some connection with the lower part of his own face and leaked on as he climbed and broke the chalky, convenient faces.

"Tunnels and wells and drops of water all this is old stuff. You can't tell me. I know my stuff just sexual images from the unconscious, the libido, or is it the id? All explained and known. Just sexual stuff what can you expect? Sensation, all tunnels and wells and drops of water. All old stuff, you can't tell me. I know."

10

A tongue of summer lightning licked right inside the inner crevice so that he saw shapes there. Some were angled and massive as the corners of corridors and between them was the light falling into impenetrable distances. One shape was a woman who unfroze for that instant and lived. The lightning created or discovered her in the act of breathing in; and so nearly was that breath finished that she seemed only to check and breathe out again. He knew without thinking who she was and where she was and when, he knew why she was breathing so quickly, lifting the silk blouse with apples, the forbidden fruit, knew why there were patches of colour on either cheek-bone and why the flush had run as it so uniquely did into the nose. Therefore she presented to him the high forehead, the remote and unconquered face with the three patches of pink arranged across the middle. As for the eyes, they fired an ammunition of contempt and outrage. They were eyes that confirmed all the unworded opinions of his body and fevered head. Seen as a clothed body or listened to, she was common and undistinguished. But the eyes belonged to some other person for they had nothing to do with the irregularity of the face or the aspirations, prudish and social, of the voice. There was the individual, Mary, who was nothing but the intersection of influences from the cradle up, the Mary gloved and hatted for church, the Mary who ate with such maddening refinement, the Mary who carried, poised on her two little feet, a treasure of demoniac and musky attractiveness that was all the more terrible because she was almost unconscious of it. This intersection was so inevitably constructed that its every word and action could be predicted. The intersection would chose the ordinary rather than the exceptional; would fly to what was respectable as to a magnet. It was a fit companion for the pursed-up mouth, the too high forehead, the mousey hair. But the eyes—they had nothing in common with the mask of flesh that nature had fixed on what must surely be a real and invisible face. They were one with the incredible smallness of the waist and the apple breasts, the transparency of the flesh. They were large and wise with a wisdom that never reached the surface to be expressed in speech. They gave to her many silences—so explicable in terms of the intersection—a mystery that was not there. But combined with the furious musk, the little, guarded breasts, the surely impregnable virtue, they were the death sentence of Actaeon. They made her occupy as by right, a cleared space in the world behind the eyes that was lit by flickers of summer lightning. They made her a madness, not so much in the loins as in the pride, the need to assert and break, a blight in the growing point of life. They brought back the nights of childhood, the hot, eternal bed with seamed sheets, the desperation. The things she did became important though they were trivial, the very onyx she wore became a talis-

148

man. A thread from her tweed skirt—though she had bought it off the hook in a shop where identical skirts hung empty and unchanged—that same thread was magicked into power by association. Her surname—and he thumped rock with lifted knees—her surname now abandoned to dead Nathaniel forced him to a reference book lest it should wind back to some distinction that would set her even more firmly at the centre than she was. By what chance, or worse what law of the universe was she set there in the road to power and success, unbreakable yet tormenting with the need to conquer and break? How could she take this place behind the eyes as by right when she was nothing but another step on which one must place the advancing foot? Those nights of imagined copulation, when one thought not of love nor sensation nor comfort nor triumph, but of torture rather, the very rhythm of the body reinforced by hissed ejaculations—take that and that! That for your pursed mouth and that for your pink patches, your closed knees, your impregnable balance on the high, female shoes—and that if it kills you for your magic and your isled virtue!

How can she so hold the centre of my darkness when the only real feeling I have for her is hate?

Pale face, pink patches. The last chance and I know what she is going to say, inevitably out of the intersection. And here it comes, quickly, with an accent immediately elevated to the top drawer.

"No."

There are at least three vowels in the one syllable.

"Why did you agree to come here with me, then?"

Three patches.

149

"I thought you were a gentleman."

Inevitably.

"You make me tired."

"Take me home, please."

"Do you really mean that in the twentieth century? You really feel insulted? You don't just mean 'No, I'm sorry, but no'?"

"I want to go home."

"But look——"

I must, I must, don't you understand you bloody bitch?

"Then I'll take a bus."

One chance. Only one.

"Wait a minute. Our language is so different. Only what I'm trying to say is—well, it's difficult. Only don't you understand that I—Oh Mary, I'll do anything to prove it to you!"

"I'm sorry. I just don't care for you in that way."

And then he, compelled about the rising fury to tread the worn path:

"Then it's still—no?"

Ultimate insult of triumph, understanding and compassion.

"I'm sorry, Chris. Genuinely sorry."

"You'll be a sister to me, I know."

But then the astonishing answer, serenely, brushing away the sarcasm.

"If you like."

He got violently to his feet.

"Come on. Let's get out of here for Christ's sake."

Wait, like a shape in the driving seat. Does she know nothing of me at all? She comes from the road house, one foot swerved in front of the other as in the photographs, walking an invisible tight-rope across the gravel, bearing proudly the invincible banner of virginity.

"That door's not properly shut. Let me."

Subtle the scent, the touch of the cheap, transmuted tweed, hand shaking on the gear, road drawing back, hooded wartime lights, uncontrollable summer lightning ignoring the regulations from beyond that hill to away south in seven-league boots, foot hard down, fringes of leaves jagged like a painted drop, trees touched, brought into being by sidelights and bundled away to the limbo of lost chances.

"Aren't you driving rather fast?"

Tilted cheek, pursed mouth, eyes under the foolish hat, remote, blacked out. Foot hard down.

"Please drive slower, Chris!"

Tyre-scream, gear-whine, thrust and roar——

"Please——!"

Rock, sway, silk hiss of skid, scene film-flicking.

Power.

"Please! Please!"

"Let me, then. Now. To-night, in the car."

"Please!"

Hat awry, road unravelled, tree-tunnel drunk up——

"I'll kill us."

"You're mad—oh, please!"

"Where the road forks at the whitewashed tree, I'll hit it with your side. You'll be burst and bitched."

"Oh God, oh God."

Over the verge, clout on the heap of dressing, bump, swerve back, eating macadam, drawing it in, pushing it

151

back among the lost chances, pushing it down with time back to the cellar——

"I'm going to faint."

"You'll let me make love to you? Love to you?"

"Please stop."

On the verge, trodden with two feet to a stop, with dead engine and lights, grabbing a stuffed doll, plundering a doll that came to life under the summer lightning, knees clapped together over the hoarded virginity, one hand pushing down the same tweed skirt, one to ward off, finding with her voice a protection for the half-naked breast——

"I shall scream!"

"Scream away."

"You filthy, beastly——"

Then the summer lightning over a white face with two staring eyes only a few inches away, eyes of the artificial woman, confounded in her pretences and evasion, forced to admit her own crude, human body—eyes staring now in deep and implacable hate.

Nothing out of the top drawer now. Vowels with the burr of the country on them.

"Don't you understand, you swine? You can't——"

The last chance. I must.

"I'll marry you then."

More summer lightning.

"Christ. Stop laughing. D'you hear? Stop it! I said stop it!"

"I *loathe* you. I never want to see you or hear of you as long as I live."

Peter was riding behind him and they were flat out. It

152

was his new bike under him but it was not as good as Peter's new one. If Peter got past with that new gear of his he'd be uncatchable. Peter's front wheel was overlapping his back one in a perfect position. He'd never have done that if he weren't deadly excited. The road curves here to the right, here by the pile of dressing. They are built up like rock—a great pile of stones for mending the road down to Hodson's Farm. Don't turn, go straight on, keep going for the fraction of a second longer than he expects. Let him turn, with his overlapping wheel. Oh clever, clever, clever. My leg, Chris, my leg—I daren't look at my leg. Oh Christ.

The cash-box. Japanned tin, gilt lines. Open empty. What are you going to do about it, there was nothing written down. Have a drink with me some time.

She's the producer's wife, old boy.

Oh clever, clever, clever power, then you can bloody well walk home; oh clever, real tears break down triumph, clever, clever, clever.

Up stage. Up stage. Up stage. I'm a bigger maggot than you are. You can't get any further up stage because of the table, but I can go all the way up to the french window.

"No, old man. I'm sorry, but you're not essential."
"But George—we've worked together! You know me——"
"I do, old man. Definitely."

"I should be wasted in the Forces. You've seen my work."

"I have, old man."

"Well then——"

The look up under the eyebrows. The suppressed smile. The smile allowed to spread until the white teeth were reflected in the top of the desk.

"I've been waiting for something like this. That's why I didn't kick you out before. I hope they mar your profile, old man. The good one."

There were ten thousand ways of killing a man. You could poison him and watch the smile turn into a rictus. You could hold his throat until it was like a hard bar.

She was putting on a coat.

"Helen——"

"My sweet."

The move up, vulpine, passionate.

"It's been so long."

Deep, shuddering breath.

"Don't be corny, dear."

Fright.

"Help me, Helen, I must have your help."

Black maggot eyes in a white face. Distance. Calculation. Death.

"Anything my sweet, but of course."

"After all you're Pete's wife."

"So crude, Chris."

"You could persuade him."

Down close on the settee, near.

"Helen——"

"Why don't you ask Margot, my sweet, or that little thing you took out driving?"

154

Panic. Black eyes in a white face with no more expression than hard, black stones.

Eaten.

Nathaniel bubbling over in a quiet way—not a bubble over, a simmer, almost a glow.

"I have wonderful news for you, Chris."

"You've met an aeon, at last."

Nat considered this, looking up at the reference library. He identified the remark as a joke and answered it with the too profound tones he reserved for humour.

"I have been introduced to one by proxy."

"Tell me your news. Is the war over? I can't wait."

Nathaniel sat down in the opposite armchair but found it too low. He perched himself on the arm, then got up and rearranged the books on the table. He looked into the street between the drab black-out curtains.

"I think finally, I shall go into the Navy."

"You!"

Nodding, still looking out of the window:

"If they'd have me, that is. I couldn't fly and I shouldn't be any use in the Army."

"But you clot! You don't have to go, do you?"

"Not—legally."

"I thought you objected to war."

"So I do."

"Conchie."

"I don't know. I really don't know. One thinks this and that—but in the end, you know, the responsibility of deciding is too much for one man. I ought to go."

"You've made your mind up?"

155

"Mary agrees with me."

"Mary Lovell? What's she got to do with it?"

"That's my news."

Nathaniel turned with a forgotten book in his hands. He came towards the fire, looked at the armchair, remembered the book and put it on the table. He took a chair, drew it forward and perched on the edge.

"I was telling you after the show last night. You remember? About how our lives must reach right back to the roots of time, be a trail through history?"

"I said you were probably Cleopatra."

Nat considered this gravely.

"No, I don't think so. Nothing so famous."

"Henry the Eighth, then. Is that your news?"

"One constantly comes across clues. One has—flashes of insight—things given. One is——" The hands began to spread sideways by the shoulders as though they were feeling an expansion of the head—"One is conscious when meeting people that they are woven in with one's secret history. Don't you think? You and I, for example. You remember?"

"You used to talk an awful lot of cock."

Nathaniel nodded.

"I still do. But we are still interwoven and the same things hold good. Then when you introduced me to Mary —you remember? You see how we three act and re-act. There came that sudden flash, that—stab of knowledge and certainty that said, 'I have known you before.'"

"What on earth are you talking about?"

"She felt it too. She said so. She's so—wise, you know! And now we are both quite certain. These things are

156

written in the stars, of course, but under them, Chris, we have to thank you for bringing us together."

"You and Mary Lovell?"

"Of course these things are never simple and we've meditated apart from each other and together——"

An enchantment was filling the room. Nat's head seemed to grow large and small with it.

"And I should be awfully pleased, Chris, if you'd be best man for me."

"You're going to marry! You and——"

"That was the joyous news."

"You can't!"

He heard how anguished his voice was, found he was standing up.

Nat looked past him into the fire.

"I know it's sudden but we've meditated. And you see, I shall be going into the Navy. She's so good and brave. And you, Chris—I knew you would bring your whole being to such a decision."

He stood still, looking down at the tousled black hair, the length of limb. He felt the bleak recognition rising in him of the ineffable strength of these circumstances and this decision. Not where he eats but where he is eaten. Blood rose with the recognition, burning in the face, power to break. Pictures of her fell through his mind like a dropped sheaf of snapshots—Mary in the boat, carefully arranging her skirt; Mary walking to church, reeking of it, the very placing of her feet and carriage of her little bum an insolence; Mary struggling, knees clapped together over the hoarded virginity, trying with one hand to pull down her skirt, with the other to ward off,

157

the voice finding the only protection for her half-naked breast——

"I shall scream!"

Nat looked up, his mouth open.

"I'm not being a fool this time you know. You needn't worry."

The snapshots vanished.

"I was—I don't know what I was saying, Nat—quoting from some play or other."

Nat spread his hands and smiled diffidently.

"The stars can't be thwarted."

"Especially if they happen to agree with what you want."

Nat considered this. He reddened a little and nodded gravely.

"There is that danger."

"Be careful, Nat, for God's sake."

But not known, not understood—what is he to be careful of? Of staying near me? Of standing with her in the lighted centre of my darkness?

"You'll be here to look after her, Chris, when I've gone."

There is something in the stars. Or what is this obscure impulse that sets my words at variance with my heart?

"Only be careful. Of me."

"Chris!"

Because I like you, you fool and hate you. And now I hate you.

"All right, Nat, forget it."

"There's something the matter."

An impulse gone, trodden down, kicked aside.

"I shall be in the Navy, too."

"But the theatre!"

Gone down under calculation and hate.

"One has one's better feelings."

"My dear man!" Nat was standing and beaming. "Perhaps we can be in the same ship."

Drearily and with the foreknowledge of a chosen road.

"I'm sure we shall be. That's in our stars."

Nat nodded.

"We are connected in the elements. We are men for water."

"Water. Water."

The clothes bound him like a soggy bundle. He hauled himself out into the sun. He lay there feeling that he spread like seaweed. He got his hands up and plucked at the toggles of his duffle while the snapshots whirled and flew like a pack of cards. He got the toggles free and plucked at the rest of his clothing. When he had only vest and pants on he crawled away, yards over the rock to the water-hole. He crawled up the High Street and lay down by the Dwarf.

"If I am not delirious this is steam rising from my clothes. Sweat."

He propped his back against the Dwarf.

"Be intelligent."

His legs before him were covered with white blotches. There were more on his stomach when he lifted his vest, on his arms and legs. They were deformations at the edge of the eye-sockets.

"Stay alive!"

Something fierce pushed out of his mind.

"I'll live if I have to eat everything else on this bloody box!"

159

He looked down at his legs.

"I know the name for you bloody blotches. Urticaria. Food poisoning."

He lay quiet for a time. The steam rose and wavered. The blotches were well-defined and of a dead whiteness. They were raised so that even swollen fingers could feel their outline.

"I said I should be ill and I am."

He peered hazily round the horizon but it had nothing to give. He looked back at his legs and decided that they were very thin for all the blotches. Under his vest he could feel the trickle of water that found its way down from blotch to blotch.

The pressure of the sky and air was right inside his head.

11

A thought was forming like a piece of sculpture behind the eyes but in front of the unexamined centre. He watched the thought for a timeless interim while the drops of sweat trickled down from blotch to blotch. But he knew that the thought was an enemy and so although he saw it he did not consent or allow it to become attached to him in realization. If the slow centre had any activity now it brooded on its identity while the thought stayed there like an ignored monument in a park. Christopher and Hadley and Martin were separate fragments and the centre was smouldering with a dull resentment that they should have broken away and not be sealed on the centre. The window was filled with a pattern of colour but in this curious state the centre did not think of the pattern as exterior. It was the only visible thing in a dark room, like a lighted picture on the wall. Below it was the sensation of water trickling and discomfort of a hard surface. The centre for a time was sufficient. The centre knew self existed, though Christopher and Hadley and Martin were fragments far off.

A curtain of hair and flesh fell over the picture on the wall and there was nothing to be examined but the thought.

It became known. The terror that swept in with the thought shocked him into the use of his body. There was a flashing of nerves, tensing of muscles, heaves, blows, vibration; and the thought became words that tumbled out of his mouth.

"I shall never get away from this rock."

The terror did more. It straightened the hinged bones and stood him up, sent him reeling round the Look-out in the pressure of the sky till he was clinging to the Dwarf and the stone head was rocking gently, rocking gently, and the sun was swinging to and fro, up and down in the silver face.

"Get me off this rock!"

The Dwarf nodded its silver head, gently, kindly.

He crouched down by a whitish trench and the pattern of colour was sight again.

Christopher and Hadley and Martin came part way back. He forced the pattern to fit everywhere over the rock and the sea and the sky.

"Know your enemy."

There was illness of the body, effect of exposure. There was food-poisoning that made the world a mad place. There was solitude and hope deferred. There was the thought; there were the other thoughts, unspoken and unadmitted.

"Get them out. Look at them."

Water, the only supply, hung by a hair, held back by the slimy tamping; food that grew daily less; pressure, indescribable pressure on the body and the mind; battle with the film-trailers for sleep. There was——

"There was and is——"

He crouched on the rock.

"Take it out and look at it.

"There is a pattern emerging. I do not know what the pattern is but even my dim guess at it makes my reason falter."

The lower half of his face moved round the mouth till the teeth were bare.

"Weapons. I have things that I can use."

Intelligence. Will like a last ditch. Will like a monolith. Survival. Education, a key to all patterns, itself able to impose them, to create. Consciousness in a world asleep. The dark, invulnerable centre that was certain of its own sufficiency.

He began to speak against the flat air, the blotting-paper.

"Sanity is the ability to appreciate reality. What is the reality of my position? I am alone on a rock in the middle of the Atlantic. There are vast distances of swinging water round me. But the rock is solid. It goes down and joins the floor of the sea and that is joined to the floors I have known, to the coasts and cities. I must remember that the rock is solid and immovable. If the rock were to move then I should be mad."

A flying lizard flapped overhead, and dropped down out of sight.

"I must hang on. First to my life and then to my sanity. I must take steps."

He dropped the curtains over the window again.

"I am poisoned. I am in servitude to a coiled tube the length of a cricket pitch. All the terrors of hell can come down to nothing more than a stoppage. Why drag in good and evil when the serpent lies coiled in my own body?"

163

And he pictured his bowels deliberately, the slow, choked peristaltic movement, change of the soft food to a plug of poison.

"I am Atlas. I am Prometheus."

He felt himself loom, gigantic on the rock. His jaws clenched, his chin sank. He became a hero for whom the impossible was an achievement. He knelt and crawled remorselessly down the rock. He found the lifebelt in the crevice, took his knife and sawed the metal tit away from the tube. He crawled on down towards the Red Lion and now there was background music, snatches of Tchaikovsky, Wagner,˙Holst. It was not really necessary to crawl but the background music underlined the heroism of a slow, undefeated advance against odds. The empty mussel shells cracked under his bones like potsherds. The music swelled and was torn apart by brass.

He came to the pool on the rock with the one weedy limpet and three prudish anemones. The tiny fish still lay in the water but on a different part of the rock. He pushed the lifebelt under the surface of the water so that the fish flicked desperately from side to side. A string of bubbles came out of the tube. He collapsed the long bladder and then began to pull it open again. Little spits of water entered the tit and worked down between more bubbles. Strings only, now, deep. He lifted the whole lifebelt out and hefted the bag. There was a washing sound from the bladder. He sank it in the pool again and went on working. The strings were working too, and woodwind was added and a note or two of brass. Presently, and soon there would come the suspended chord that would stand the whole orchestra aside for the cadenza. The weedy top of the limpet was above the surface. The tiny fish, tricked by this unnatural ebb was lying on wet rock in the sun and trying to wriggle against the surface tension. The anemones had shut their mouths even tighter. The bladder of the life-belt was two-thirds full.

He hutched himself back against a rock with his legs sprawled apart. The music rose, the sea played and the sun. The universe held its breath. Grunting and groaning he began to work the rubber tube into his backside. He folded the two halves of the long bladder together and sat on it. He began to work at the bladder with both hands, squeezing and massaging. He felt the cold trickle of the sea water in his bowels. He pumped and squeezed until the bladder was squashily flat. He extracted the tube and crept carefully to the edge of the rock while the orchestra thundered to a pause.

And the cadenza was coming—did come. It performed with explosive and triumphant completeness of technique into the sea. It was like the bursting of a dam, the smashing of all hindrance. Spasm after spasm with massive chords and sparkling arpeggios, the cadenza took of his strength till he lay straining and empty on the rock and the orchestra had gone.

He turned his face on the rock and grunted at the antagonist.

"Are you beaten yet? I'm not."

The hand of the sky fell on him. He got up and knelt among the mussel shells.

"Now I shall be sane and no longer such a slave to my body."

He looked down at the dead fish. He pushed the body

165

with his finger to the mouth of an anemone. Petals emerged and tried to take hold.

"Stings. Poison. Anemones poisoned me. Perhaps mussels are all right after all."

He felt a little stronger and no longer so heroic that he need crawl. He went slowly back to the Look-out.

"Everything is predictable. I knew I shouldn't drown and I didn't. There was a rock. I knew I could live on it and I have. I have defeated the serpent in my body. I knew I should suffer and I have. But I am winning. There is a certain sense in which life begins anew now, for all the blotting-paper and the pressure."

He sat down by the Dwarf and drew up his knees. His sight was right on the outside and he lived in the world.

"I believe I'm hungry."

And why not, when life begins again?

"Food on a plate. Rich food in comfort. Food in shops, butchers' shops, food, not swimming, shutting like a fist and vanishing into a crevice but dead on a slab, heaped up, all the sea's harvest——"

He examined the sea. The tide was running and glossy streaks were tailing away from the three rocks.

"Optical illusion."

For of course the rock was fixed. If it seemed to move slowly forward in the tide that was because the eye had nothing else as a point of reference. But over the horizon was a coast and that remained at a constant distance while the water flowed. He smiled grimly.

"That wasn't a bad trick. It might have caught most people."

Like the train that seems to move backwards when the

other one steams away from beside it. Like hatched lines with one across.

"For of course the rock is still and the water moves. Let me work it out. The tide is a great wave that sweeps round the world—or rather the world turns inside the tide, so I and the rock are— —"

Hastily he looked down at the rock between his feet.

"So the rock is still."

Food. Heaped on a slab, not swimming free but piled up, all the spoils of the sea, a lobster, not shutting like a fist and shooting back into a crevice but——

He was on his feet. He was glaring down at the place where the weed grew under water by the three rocks. He cried out.

"Whoever saw a lobster like that swimming in the sea? A red lobster?"

Something was taken away. For an instant he felt himself falling; and then there came a gap of darkness in which there was no one.

Something was coming up to the surface. It was uncertain of its identity because it had forgotten its name. It was disorganized in pieces. It struggled to get these pieces together because then it would know what it was. There was a rhythmical noise and disconnection. The pieces came shakily together and he was lying sideways on the rock and a snoring noise was coming from his mouth. There was a feeling of deep sickness further down the tunnel. There was a separation between now, whenever now was, and the instant of terror. The separation enabled him to forget what had caused that terror. The darkness

167

of separation was deeper than that of sleep. It was deeper than any living darkness because time had stopped or come to an end. It was a gap of not-being, a well opening out of the world and now the effort of mere being was so exhausting that he could only lie sideways and live.

Presently he thought.

"Then I was dead. That was death. I have been frightened to death. Now the pieces of me have come together and I am just alive."

The view was different too. The three rocks were nearer and there were sharp things—mussel shells, he thought, brilliantly—cutting his cheek.

"Who carried me down here?"

There came a little pain with the words which he traced to his tongue. The tip was swollen, and aching, and there was salt in his mouth. He could see a pair of empty trousers lying near him and curious marks on the rock. These marks were white and parallel. There was blood in them and traces of froth.

He attended to the rest of his body. He identified a hard, bar-like object as his right arm, twisted back. That led him to the pain in the joints. He eased over so that his arm was free and gazed at the hand on the end.

Now he saw that he was not wearing his pants because they were out there in his right hand. They were torn and there was blood on them.

"I've been in a fight."

He lay, considering things dully.

"There is someone else on the rock with me. He crept out and slugged me."

The face twisted.

168

"Don't be a fool. You're all alone. You've had a fit."

He felt for his left hand and found it with a grunt of pain. The fingers were bitten.

"How long was I? Is it today or yesterday?"

He heaved himself up on hands and knees.

"Just when I was myself again and victorious, there came a sort of something. A Terror. There was a pattern emerging from circumstances."

Then the gap of not-being.

"This side of the gap is different from the other. It's like when you've finished a lights rehearsal and they cut. Then where there was bright, solid scenery is now only painted stuff, grey under the pilot light. It's like chess. You've got an exultant attack moving but overlooked a check and now the game is a fight. And you're tied down."

Bright rock and sea, hope, though deferred, heroics. Then in the moment of achievement, the knowledge, the terror like a hand falling.

"It was something I remembered. I'd better not remember it again. Remember to forget. Madness?"

Worse than madness. Sanity.

He heaved himself on hands and knees and laboured to trace his fit, by the scattered clothing and the marks on the rock, back to where he had begun. He stopped by the Dwarf, looking down at rock with a pattern scratched on it—a pattern now crossed by the gritted mark of teeth.

"That was to be expected. Everything is to be expected. The world runs true to form. Remember that."

He looked thoughtfully down at the streaks that the rock was leaving behind in the sea.

"I must not look at the sea. Or must I? Is it better to be

sane or mad? It is better to be sane. I did not see what I thought I saw. I remembered wrongly."

Then he had an important idea. It set him at once searching the rock, not in a casual way but inch by inch. Only after an eternity of searching, of cracks and bumps and roughnesses did he remember that he was foolish to search for a piece of wood to touch because there was none.

His pants were still trailing from his hand and he had a sudden thought that he could put them on. When he had done this his head cleared of all the mists except the pain. He put his hand up to the pain and found that there was a lump under the hair and the hair was stuck with blood. He examined his legs. The white blotches were smaller and no longer important. He remembered a custom and clambered into the water-hole. When he was in there he noticed a sudden, bright light in the opening over the far end and some deep seat of rationality drove him back to the Lookout; and he knew what the light and the noise that had come after it portended.

The sun was still shining but there was a change over a part of the horizon. He knelt to look at this change and it was divided again by a vertical jab of light. This light left a token in each eye that made seeing a divided business. He peered round the green streak that the light left and saw that the darkness made a definite line on the surface of the sea. It was coming nearer. Instantly he was in his body and knew where he was.

"Rain!"

Of course.

"I said there would be rain!"

170

Let there be rain and there was rain.

He scrambled down the High Street, got his sou'wester and arranged it in the lay-back under the end of the Claudian. He pulled off what clothes he was wearing and thrust them into the crevice. He was aware of bright lights and noise. He put his oilskin in a trench and rucked the body into a basin. He went almost upright to the Look-out and heard the hiss of the rain as the edge of the curtain fell on the Safety Rock. It hit him in the face, sprang in foot-high leaps from the Dwarf and the surface of the look-out. He glistened and streamed from head to foot in a second.

There was a merciless flash-bang from the curtain and then he was stumbling down to the crevice and burrowing in head first while the thunder trampled overhead. Even in the depth of the crevice he saw a livid light that hurt his ears; and then there was the cessation of all noises but a high, singing note. This was so intimate to the head that it took the place of the thunder. His feet were being bastina-doed. His mouth said things but he could not hear them so did not know what they were. There was water running in the crevice, under his face, dripping from the rock, water running round his loins, water. He made his body back out of the crevice and was under a waterfall. He stumbled into a trench and found his sou'wester full and spilling. There was a tap of water running from the end of the Claudian and he took up the heavy sou'wester and poured water into his mouth. He put the sou'wester back and went to his oilskin. There was a bath ready for him but the rain was washing over him like a shower. He went back to the sou'wester, watched it fill and took it to the

171

water-hole. He could hear the running click and trickle under the rock now—water running down, seaping through in unguessed crannies, falling with a multitudinous chattering into the hollow. Already the stretch of red clay was narrower.

"I said it would rain, and it has."

He waited, shivering in the chilly cave, waited for the satisfaction that ought to come with the fulfilled prediction. But it would not come.

He crouched there, no longer listening to the water but frowning down at his shadow.

"What piece have I lost in my game? I had an attack, I was doing well, and then——" And then, the gap of dark, dividing that brighter time from this. On the other side of the gap was something that had happened. It was something that must not be remembered; but how could you control if you deliberately forgot? It was something about a pattern that was emerging.

"Inimical."

He considered the word that his mouth had spoken. The word sounded harmless unless the implications were attached. To avoid that, he deliberately bent the process of thought and made his mouth do as he bid.

"How can a rock be inimical?"

He crawled away quickly into a rain that fell more lightly. The storm had hurried away over the three rocks and dulled the motion of the water. The clouds had dulled everything. They had left a grey, drizzly sea over which the air moved, pushed at the rock in a perceptible wind.

"That was a subsidiary thunder-storm on the edge of a cyclone. Cyclones revolve anti-clockwise in the northern

172

hemisphere. The wind is southerly. Therefore we are on the eastern edge of a cyclone that is moving east. Since I can foretell the weather I can be armed against it. The problem will be now to cope with too much water, not too little."

He paid only half-attention to his mouth. It lectured on reassuring nothing but itself. But the centre of the globe was moving and flinching from isolated outcrops of knowledge. It averted attention from one only to discover another. It attempted to obliterate each separate outcrop when it found that they could not be ignored.

"The whole problem of insanity is so complex that a satisfactory definition, a norm, has never been established."

Far out from the centre, the mouth quacked on.

"Where, for example, shall we draw the line between the man whom we consider to be moody or excitable, and the genuine psychopathic manic-depressive?"

The centre was thinking, with an eye lifted for the return of the storm of terror, about how difficult it was to distinguish between sleeping and waking when all one experienced was a series of trailers.

"A recurrent dream, a neurosis? But surely the normal child in its cot goes through all the symptoms of the neurotic?"

If one went step by step—ignoring the gap of dark and the terror on the lip—back from the rock, through the Navy, the stage, the writing, the university, the school, back to bed under the silent eaves, one went down to the cellar. And the path led back from the cellar to the rock.

"The solution lies in intelligence. That is what distinguishes us from the helpless animals that are caught in their patterns of behaviour, both mental and physical."

But the dark centre was examining a thought like a monument that had replaced the other in the dreary park.

Guano is insoluble.

If guano is insoluble, then the water in the upper trench could not be a slimy wetness, the touch of which made a flaming needle nag at the corner of an eye.

His tongue felt along the barrier of his teeth—round to the side where the big ones were and the gap. He brought his hands together and held his breath. He stared at the sea and saw nothing. His tongue was remembering. It pried into the gap between the teeth and re-created the old, aching shape. It touched the rough edge of the cliff, traced the slope down, trench after aching trench, down towards the smooth surface where the Red Lion was, just above the gum—understood what was so hauntingly familiar and painful about an isolated and decaying rock in the middle of the sea.

12

Now there was nothing to do but protect normality. There was the centre wielding the exterior body as by strings. He made the body go down from the Look-out to the crevice. He found damp clothes and put them on until he could see extensions of clothing and seaboot stockings like piles of waste. The body and the clothing were ungainly as a diving dress. He went to Food Cliff and gathered mussels, made his mouth receive them. He did not look outwards but down where the water danced alongside the rock. The sea was ruffled and there were wavelets each carrying smaller wavelets on its back so that the depth was obscured and the water grave and chilly. As his jaws worked he sat still with two lobsters lying on the rock beside him. The meal went on under pricking rain, a stirring of wind and scuds of dimples across the surface of the water. He took morsels of food with one lobster and brought them to his face. The lobsters wore armour to protect them from the enormous pressure of the sky.

Between mouthfuls his voice quacked, veering in towards reason and truth and then skating away.

"I have no armour and that is why I am being squeezed

thin. It has marred my profile too. My mouth sticks out such a long way and I have two noses."

But the centre thought of other things.

"I must be careful when I look round at the wind. I don't want to die again."

Meanwhile there were many mussels and one could make the mouth perform and obliterate the other possibilities.

"I was always two things, mind and body. Nothing has altered. Only I did not realize it before so clearly."

The centre thought of the next move. The world could be held together by rivets driven in. Flesh could be mended by the claws of ants as in Africa. The will could resist.

And then there were no more mussels within reach. He made the lobster mime eating but the sensations in the mouth were not the same.

"Have to do it."

He turned himself on all fours. He held his breath and looked up and there was the old woman from the corner of the cellar standing on the skyline.

"She is the Dwarf. I gave her a silver head."

Wind pushed in his face and a touch of rain. The old woman nodded with her face of dulled silver.

"It is lucky I put a silver mask over the other face. She is the Dwarf. That is not the next move."

He worked his way back towards the Look-out, carried his body near the Dwarf and made it kneel down. Above him the Dwarf nodded gently with a face of dulled silver.

There was something in the topmost trench that was different. Immediately he flinched back and looked warily. The white stuff in the bottom was broken up and scattered because a chunk of rockleaf had fallen from the side of the trench. He crept forward and examined the chunk. On one edge the leaves were worn and ancient but on the other three they were white as muck and freshly broken. The chunk was about a yard each way and six inches thick. It was a considerable book and there was a strange engraving in the white cover. For a while his eye liked the engraving because it made a pattern and was not words, which would have killed him immediately. His eye followed the indented and gouged lines again and again as his mouth had eaten mussels. By the edge of the book was the recess from which it had come.

There was an engraving in the recess too. It was like a tree upside down and growing down from the old edge where the leaves were weathered by wind and rain. The trunk was a deep, perpendicular groove with flaky edges. Lower down, the trunk divided into three branches and these again into a complication of twigs like the ramifications of bookworm. The trunk and the branches and the twigs were terrible black. Round the twigs was an apple blossom of grey and silver stain. As he watched, drops of water dulled the stain and lay in the branches like tasteless fruit.

His mouth quacked.

"Lightning!"

But the dark centre was shrunk and dreadful and knowing. The knowing was so dreadful that the centre made the mouth work deliberately.

"Black lightning."

There was still a part that could be played—there was
177

the Bedlamite, Poor Tom, protected from knowledge of the sign of the black lightning.

He grabbed the old woman with her nodding, silver head.

"Help me, my sweet, I must have your help!"

The mouth took over.

"If you let him go on doing that, my sweet, he'll knock the whole bloody rock apart and we shall be left swimming."

Swimming in what?

The mouth went frantic.

"There was that rock round by Prospect Cliff, my sweet, that one moved, the water moved it. I wouldn't ask anyone but you because the rock is fixed and if he'll only let it alone it'll last for ever. After all, my sweet, you're his wife."

Out of bed on the carpet with no shoes. Creep through the dark room not because you want to but because you've got to. Pass the door. The landing, huge, the grandfather clock. No safety behind me. Round the corner now to the stairs. Down, pad. Down, pad. The hall, but grown. Darkness sitting in every corner. The banisters high up, can just reach them with my hand. Not for sliding down now. Different banisters, everything different, a pattern emerging, forced to go down to meet the thing I turned my back on. Tick, tock, shadows pressing. Past the kitchen door. Draw back the bolt of the vault. Well of darkness. Down pad, down. Coffin ends crushed in the wall. Under the churchyard back through the death door to meet the master. Down, pad, down. Black lumps piled, smell damp. Shavings from coffins.

178

"A man must be mad when he sees a red lobster swimming in the sea. And guano is insoluble. A madman would see the gulls as flying lizards, he would connect the two things out of a book and it would come back to him when his brain turned no matter how long ago and forgotten the time when he read that—wouldn't he, my sweet? Say he would! Say he would!"

The silver face nodded on gently and the rain spattered.

Kindling from coffins, coal dust, black as black lightning. Block with the axe by it, not worn for firewood but by executions.

"Seals aren't inimical and a madman wouldn't sleep properly. He would feel the rock was too hard, too real; he would superimpose a reality, especially if he had too much imagination. He would be capable of seeing the engraving as a split into the whole nature of things—wouldn't he?"

And then fettered in the darkness by the feet, trying to lift one and finding a glue, finding a weakness where there should be strength now needed because by nature there was nothing to do but scream and try to escape. Darkness in the corner doubly dark, thing looming, feet tied, near, an unknown looming, an opening darkness, the heart and being of all imaginable terror. Pattern repeated from the beginning of time, approach of the unknown thing, a dark centre that turned its back on the thing that created it and struggled to escape.

"Wouldn't he? Say he would!"

There was a noise by his left arm and water scattered across the look-out. He made the exterior face turn into the wind and the air pushed against the cheeks. The water

179

on the dwarf now was not rain but spray. He crept to the edge of the cliff and looked down the funnel. The water was white round Safety Rock and as he looked a dull sound in the funnel was followed by a plume of spray.

"This weather has been investigated before but from a lower level. He climbed there and the limpets held on."

There was a gathering rhythm in the sea. The Safety Rock tripped the waves and shot them at the cleft below the funnel. Nine times out of ten these waves would meet a reflection coming back and spurt up a line of spray like a fuse burning—a fast fuse that whipped over the water. But the tenth time the wave would find the way clear because the ninth wave had been a very small one. So the tenth wave would come wheeling in, the cleft would squeeze the water so that it speeded up and hit the back of the angle—bung! and a feather of spray would flicker in the funnel. If the tenth wave was big the feather would become a plume and the wind would catch a handful from the top and sling shot across the Dwarf to go scattering down the High Street.

To watch the waves was like eating mussels. The sea was a point of an attention that could be prolonged even more than eating. The centre concentrated and left the mouth to itself.

"Of course a storm has to come after a time. That was to be expected. And who could invent all that complication of water, running true to form, obeying the laws of nature to the last drop? And of course a human brain must turn in time and the universe be muddled. But beyond the muddle there will still be actuality and a poor mad creature clinging to a rock in the middle of the sea."

There is no centre of sanity in madness. Nothing like this "I" sitting in here, staving off the time that must come. The last repeat of the pattern. Then the black lightning.

The centre cried out.

"I'm so alone! Christ! I'm so alone!"

Black. A familiar feeling, a heaviness round the heart, a reservoir which any moment might flood the eyes now and for so long, strangers to weeping. Black, like the winter evening through which the centre made its body walk—a young body. The window was diversified only by a perspective of lighted lamps on the top of the street lampposts. The centre was thinking—I am alone; so alone! The reservoir overflowed, the lights all the way along to Carfax under Big Tom broke up, put out rainbow wings. The centre felt the gulping of its throat, sent eyesight on ahead to cling desperately to the next light and then the next—anything to fasten the attention away from the interior blackness.

Because of what I did I am an outsider and alone.

The centre endured a progress through an alley, across another road, a quadrangle, climbed bare wooden stairs. It sat by a fire and all the bells of Oxford tolled for the reservoir that overflowed and the sea roared in the room.

The centre twisted the unmanliness out of its face but the ungovernable water ran and dripped down the cheeks.

"I am so alone. I am *so* alone!"

Slowly, the water dried. Time stretched out, like the passage of time on a rock in the middle of the sea.

The centre formulated a thought.

Now there is no hope. There is nothing. If they would

only look at me, or speak—if I could only be a part of something——

Time stretched on, indifferently.

There was the sound of feet on the stairs, two stories down. The centre waited without hope, to hear which room they would visit. But they came on, they climbed, were louder, almost as loud as the heart-beats so that when they stopped outside the door he was standing up and his hands were by his chest. The door opened a few inches and a shock of black curls poked round by the very top.

"Nathaniel!"

Nathaniel bowed and beamed his way into the room and stood looking down at the window.

"I thought I might catch you. I'm back for the week-end." Then as an afterthought: "Can I come in?"

"My dear man!"

Nathaniel operated on his great-coat, peered round solemnly as though the question of where to put it was a major one.

"Here. Let me take that for you—sit down—I'm—my dear man!"

Nathaniel was grinning too.

"It's good to see you, Christopher."

"And you can stay? You don't have to rush away?"

"I've come up to give a lecture to the——"

"But not this evening?"

"No. I can stay this evening."

The centre sat opposite, right on the outside of its window—right out in the world.

"We'll talk. Let's talk, Nat."

"How's the social whirl?"

182

"How's London?"

"Doesn't like lectures on heaven.'

"Heaven?"

Then the body was laughing, louder and louder and the water was flowing again. Nat was grinning and blushing too.

"I know. But you don't have to make it worse."

He smeared away the water and hiccupped.

"Why heaven?"

"The sort of heaven we invent for ourselves after death, if we aren't ready for the real one."

"You would—you curious creature!"

Nathaniel became serious. He peered upwards, raised an index finger and consulted a reference book beyond the ceiling.

"Take us as we are now and heaven would be sheer negation. Without form and void. You see? A sort of black lightning, destroying everything that we call life——"

The laughter came back.

"I don't see and I don't much care but I'll come to your lecture. My dear Nat—you've no idea how glad I am to see you!"

The burning fuse whipped through Nathaniel's face and he was gone. The centre remained looking down into the funnel. His mouth was open in astonishment and terror.

"And I liked him as much as that!"

Black and feeling one's way to the smooth steel ladder that glinted only faintly in the cloud light. The centre tried to resist, like a child trying to resist a descent into the midnight cellar but its legs bore it on. Up and up, from the waist to the level of the fo'c'sle, up past B gun. Shall I meet him? Will he stand there to-night?

And there, sketched against the clouds in Indian ink, random in limb and gesture, an old binder by a rick, was Nathaniel, swaying and grabbing at a midnight salute. Wotcher, Nat, rose in his throat and he swallowed it. Pretend not to see. Be as little connected as possible. Fire a fuse from the bridge that will blow him away from her body and clear the way for me. We are all past the first course, we have eaten the fish.

And it may not work. He may not bother to lay aft and pray to his aeons. Good-bye, Nat, I loved you and it is not in my nature to love much. But what can the last maggot but one do? Lose his identity?

Nathaniel stood swaying and spread-eagled in the dark, understanding obediently that he had not been seen. Instead he stood away from the officer's approach and fumbled on down the ladder.

Everything set, the time, the place, the loved one.

"You're early for once, thank God. Course o-four-five, speed twenty-eight knots. Nothing in sight and we press on for another hour."

"Anything new?"

"Same as was. We're thirty miles north of the convoy, all on our own, going to send off the signal in an hour's time. The old man'll be up for that. There you are. No zigzag. Dead easy. Oh—the moon'll be up in ten minutes' time and we'd make quite a target if we tripped over a U-boat. Pass it on. Nighty night."

"Sweet dreams."

He heard the steps descending. He crossed to the starboard side of the bridge and looked aft. There was engine-noise, outline of the funnel. The wake spread out dull white astern and a secondary wave fanned out from midships. The starboard side of the quarter-deck was just visible in outline but the surface was dark by contrast and all the complications of the throwers, the depth-charges, the sweeps and lifted gun made it very difficult to see whether there was a figure leaning on the rail among them. He stared down and wondered whether he saw or created in his mind, the mantis shape with forelegs lifted to the face.

It is not Nathaniel leaning there, it is Mary.

I must. I must. Don't you understand, you bloody bitch?

"Messenger!"

"Sir."

"Get me a cup of cocoa."

"Aye aye, sir!"

"And messenger—never mind."

Feet descending the ladder. Darkness and the wind of speed. Glow over to starboard like a distant fire from a raided city. Moonrise.

"Port look-out!"

"Sir?"

"Nip down to the wheel-house and get me the other pair of night-glasses. I think these need overhauling. You'll find them in the rack over the chart table."

"Aye aye, sir!"

"I'll take over your sector while you're gone."

"Aye aye, sir!"

Feet descending the ladder.

Now.

185

Ham it a bit. Casual saunter to the port side. Pause.
Now. Now. Now.

Scramble to the binnacle, fling yourself at the voice pipe,
voice urgent, high, sharp, frightened——

"Hard a-starboard for Christ's sake!"

A destroying concussion that had no part in the play.
Whiteness rising like a cloud, universe spinning. The shock
of a fall somewhere, shattering, mouth filled—and he was
fighting in all directions with black impervious water.

His mouth screamed in rage at the whiteness that rose
out of the funnel.

"And it was the right bloody order!"

Eaten.

He was no longer able to look at the waves, for every
few minutes they were hidden by the rising whiteness. He
made his sight creep out and look at his clothed body. The
clothes were wringing wet and the seaboot stockings
smeared like mops. His mouth said something mechanical.

"I wish I hadn't kicked off my seaboots when I was in
the water."

The centre told itself to pretend and keep on pretending.

The mouth had its own wisdom.

"There is always madness, a refuge like a crevice in the
rock. A man who has no more defence can always creep
into madness like one of those armoured things that
scuttle among weed down where the mussels are."

Find something to look at.

"Madness would account for everything, wouldn't it,
my sweet?"

186

Do, if not look.

He got up and staggered in the wind with the rain and spray pelting him. He went down the High Street and there was his oilskin made into a basin and full of water. He took his sou'wester and began to bail out the oilskin and take the water to the water-hole. He concentrated on the laws of water, how it fell or lay, how predictable it was and manageable. Every now and then the rock shook, a white cloud rose past the look-out and there were rivulets of foam in the upper trenches. When he had emptied his oilskin he held it up, drained it and put it on. Fooling with buttons the centre could turn away from what was to come. While he did this he was facing the Claudian where the foam now hung in gobs and the oilskin thrust him against the cut. As he stood pinned, he was struck a blow in the back and bucketfuls of water fell in the trench. It washed round then settled scummily in the bottom. He felt his way along the Claudian to the crevice and backed himself in. He put on his sou'wester and laid his forehead on his arms. The world turned black and came to him through sound.

"If a madman heard it he would think it was thunder and of course it would be. There is no need to listen like that. It will only be thunder over the horizon where the ships are passing to and fro. Listen to the storm instead. It is going to flail on this rock. It is going to beat a poor wretch into madness. He does not want to go mad only he will have to. Think of it! All you people in warm beds, a British sailor isolated on a rock and going mad not because he wants to but because the sea is a terror—the worst terror there is, the worst imaginable."

The centre co-operated but with an ear cocked. It concentrated now on the words that spilt out of the mouth because with the fringes of flesh and hair lowered over the window the words could be examined as the thoughts had been. It provided background music.

"Oh help, help! I am dying of exposure. I am starving, dying of thirst. I lie like driftwood caught in a cleft. I have done my duty for you and this is my reward. If you could only see me you would be wrung with pity. I was young and strong and handsome with an eagle profile and wavy hair; I was brilliantly clever and I went out to fight your enemies. I endured in the water, I fought the whole sea. I have fought a rock, and gulls and lobsters and seals and a storm. Now I am thin and weak. My joints are like knobs and my limbs like sticks. My face is fallen in with age and my hair is white with salt and suffering. My eyes are dull stones——"

The centre quivered and dwindled. There was another noise beyond the storm and background music and sobbed words from the mouth.

"——my chest is like the ribs of a derelict boat and every breath is an effort——"

The noise was so faint in comparison with the uproar of the wind and rain and waves that it caught and glued attention. The mouth knew this too and tried harder.

"I am going mad. There is lightning playing on the skirts of a wild sea. I am strong again——"

And the mouth sang.

The centre still attended through the singing, the background music, the uproar from outside. The noise came again. The centre could confuse it for a while with thunder.

"Hoé, hoé! Thor's lightning challenges me! Flash after

188

flash, rippling spurts of white fire, bolts flung at Prometheus, blinding white, white, white, searing, the aim of the sky at the man on the rock——"

The noise, if one attended as the centre was forced to attend was dull and distant. It might have been thunder or gun-fire. It might have been the sound of a drum and the mouth seized on that.

"Rata tat tat tat! The soldiers come, my Emperor is taken! Rat a tat!"

It might have been the shifting of furniture in an upper room and the mouth panicked after that thought with the automatic flick of an insect.

"Put it down here. Roll back that corner of the carpet and then you can get the table out. Shall we have it next to the radiogram? Take that record off and put on something rocklike and heroic——"

It might have been flour-sacks slid down an iron ladder to resound on the steel deck.

"Hard a-starboard! Hard a-starboard!"

It might have been the shaking of the copper sheet in the wings.

"I must have the lead or I shall leave the coal flat——"

The cellar door swinging to behind a small child who must go down, down in his sleep to meet the thing he turned from when he was created.

"Off with his head! Down on the block among the kindling and coal-dust!"

But the centre knew. It recognized with a certainty that made the quacking of the mouth no more help than hiccups. The noise was the grating and thump of a spade against an enormous tin box that had been buried.

189

13

"Mad," said the mouth, "raving mad. I can account for everything, lobsters, maggots, hardness, brilliant reality, the laws of nature, film-trailers, snapshots of sight and sound, flying lizards, enmity—how should a man not be mad? I will tell you what a man is. He goes on four legs till Necessity bends the front end upright and makes a hybrid of him. The finger-prints of those hands are about his spine and just above the rump for proof if you want it. He is a freak, an ejected foetus robbed of his natural development, thrown out in the world with a naked covering of parchment, with too little room for his teeth and a soft bulging skull like a bubble. But nature stirs a pudding there and sets a thunderstorm flickering inside the hardening globe, white, lambent lightning, a constant flash and tremble. All your lobsters and film-trailers are nothing but the random intersections of instant bushes of lightning. The sane life of your belly and your cock are on a simple circuit, but how can the stirred pudding keep constant? Tugged at by the pull of the earth, infected by the white stroke that engraved the book, furrowed, lines burned through it by hardship and torment and terror-unbalanced, brain-sick, at your last gasp on a rock in the sea, the pudding has boiled over and you are no worse than raving mad."

Sensations. Coffee. Hock. Gin. Wood. Velvet. Nylon. Mouth. Warm, wet nakedness. Caves, slack like a crevice or tight like the mouth of a red anemone. Full of stings. Domination, identity.

"You are the intersections of all the currents. You do not exist apart from me. If I have gone mad then you have gone mad. You are speaking, in there, you and I are one and mad."

The rock shook and shook again. A sudden coldness struck his face and washed under him.

To be expected.

"Nathaniel!"

Black centre, trying to stir itself like a pudding.

The darkness was shredded by white. He tumbled over among the sensations of the crevice. There was water everywhere and noise and his mouth welcomed both. It spat and coughed. He heaved himself out amid water that swirled to his knees and the wind knocked him down. The trench was like a little sea, like the known and now remembered extravagances of a returning tide among rocks. What had been a dry trench was half-full of moving water on which streaks of foam were circling and interlacing. The wind was like an express in a tunnel and everywhere there was a trickling and washing and pouring. He scrambled up in the trench, without hearing what his mouth said and suddenly he and his mouth were one.

"You bloody great bully!"

He got his face above the level of the wall and the wind

191

pulled the cheeks in like an airman's. Bird-shot slashed. Then the sky above the old woman jumped. It went white. An instant later the light was switched off and the sky fell on him. He collapsed under the enormous pressure and went down in the water of the trench. The weight withdrew and left him struggling. He got up and the sky fell on him again. This time he was able to lurch along the trench because the weight of water was just not sufficient to break him and the sea in the trench was no higher than his knees. The world came back, storm-grey and torn with flying streamers, and he gave it storm-music, crash of timpany, brass blare and a dazzle of strings. He fought a hero's way from trench to trench through water and music, his clothes shaking and plucked, tattered like the end of a windsock, hands clawing. He and his mouth shouted through the uproar.

"Ajax! Prometheus!"

The old woman was looking down at him as he struggled through bouts of white and dark. Then her head with its silver mask was taken by a whiteness and she hunched against the sky with her headless shoulders. He fell in the white trench over the book with his face against the engraving and the insoluble muck filled his mouth. There came a sudden pressure and silence. He was lifted up and thrown down again, struck against rock. For a moment as the water passed away he saw the look-out against the sky now empty of the old woman but changed in outline by scattered stones.

"She is loose on the rock. Now she is out of the cellar and in daylight. Hunt her down!"

And the knife was there among all the other sensations,

192

jammed against his ribs. He got it in his hands and pulled the blade open. He began to crawl and hunt and swim from trench to trench. She was leaning over the rail but vanished and he stole after her into the green room. But she was out by the footlights and when he crouched in the wings he saw that he was not dressed properly for the part. His mouth and he were one.

"Change your clothes! Be a naked madman on a rock in the middle of a storm!"

His claws plucked at the tatters and pulled them away. He saw a glimpse of gold braid and an empty seaboot stocking floating away like a handful of waste. He saw a leg, scarred, scaly and stick thin and the music mourned for it.

He remembered the old woman and crawled after her down the High Street to the Red Lion. The back wash of the waves was making a welcome confusion round the three rocks and the confusion hid the place where the red lobster had been. He shouted at the rocks but the old woman would not appear among them. She had slipped away down to the cellar. Then he glimpsed her lying huddled in the crevice and he struggled up to her. He fell on her and began to slash with his knife while his mouth went on shouting.

"That'll teach you to chase me! That'll teach you to chase me out of the cellar through cars and beds and pubs, you at the back and me running, running after my identity disc all the days of my life! Bleed and die."

But he and his voice were one. They knew the blood was sea water and the cold, crumpling flesh that was ripped and torn nothing but oilskin.

Now the voice became a babble, sang, swore, made

meaningless syllables, coughed and spat. It filled every tick of time with noise, jammed the sound so that it choked; but the centre began to know itself as other because every instant was not occupied by noise. The mouth spat and deviated into part sense.

"And last of all, hallucination, vision, dream, delusion will haunt you. What else can a madman expect? They will appear to you on the solid rock, the real rock, they will fetter your attention to them and you will be nothing worse than mad."

And immediately the hallucination was there. He knew this before he saw it because there was an awe in the trench, framed by the silent spray that flew over. The hallucination sat on the rock at the end of the trench and at last he faced it through his blurred window. He saw the rest of the trench and crawled along through water that was gravely still unless a gust struck down with a long twitch and shudder of the foamy scum. When he was near, he looked up from the boots, past the knees, to the face and engaged himself to the mouth.

"You are a projection of my mind. But you are a point of attention for me. Stay there."

The lips hardly moved in answer.

"You are a projection of my mind."

He made a snorting sound.

"Infinite regression or better still, round and round the mulberry bush. We could go on like that for ever."

"Have you had enough, Christopher?"

He looked at the lips. They were clear as the words. A tiny shred of spittle joined them near the right corner.

"I could never have invented that."

The eye nearest the look-out was bloodshot at the outer corner. Behind it or beside it a red strip of sunset ran down out of sight behind the rock. The spray still flew over. You could look at the sunset or the eye but you could not do both. You could not look at the eye and the mouth together. He saw the nose was shiny and leathery brown and full of pores. The left cheek would need a shave soon, for he could see the individual bristles. But he could not look at the whole face together. It was a face that perhaps could be remembered later. It did not move. It merely had this quality of refusing overall inspection. One feature at a time.

"Enough of what?"

"Surviving. Hanging on."

The clothing was difficult to pin down too so that he had to examine each piece. There was an oilskin—belted, because the buttons had fetched away. There was a woollen pullover inside it, with a roll-neck. The sou'wester was back a little. The hands were resting one on either knee, above the seaboot stockings. Then there were seaboots, good and shiny and wet and solid. They made the rock behind them seem like cardboard, like a painted flat. He bent forward until his bleared window was just above the right instep. There was no background music now and no wind, nothing but black, shiny rubber.

"I hadn't considered."

"Consider now."

"What's the good? I'm mad."

"Even that crevice will crumble."

He tried to laugh up at the bloodshot eye but heard barking noises. He threw words in the face.

"On the sixth day he created God. Therefore I permit you to use nothing but my own vocabulary. In his own image created he Him."

"Consider now."

He saw the eye and the sunset merge. He brought his arms across his face.

"I won't. I can't."

"What do you believe in?"

Down to the black boot, coal black, darkness of the cellar, but now down to a forced answer.

"The thread of my life."

"At all costs."

Repeat after me:

"At all costs."

"So you survived."

"That was luck."

"Inevitability."

"Didn't the others want to live then?"

"There are degrees."

He dropped the curtains of flesh and hair and blotted out the boots. He snarled.

"I have a right to live if I can!"

"Where is that written?"

"Then nothing is written."

"Consider."

He raged on the cardboard rock before the immovable, black feet.

"I will not consider! I have created you and I can create my own heaven."

"You have created it."

He glanced sideways along the twitching water, down

at his skeleton legs and knees, felt the rain and spray and the savage cold on his flesh.

He began to mutter.

"I prefer it. You gave me the power to choose and all my life you led me carefully to this suffering because my choice was my own. Oh yes! I understand the pattern. All my life, whatever I had done I should have found myself in the end on that same bridge, at that same time, giving that same order—the right order, the wrong order. Yet, suppose I climbed away from the cellar over the bodies of used and defeated people, broke them to make steps on the road away from you, why should you torture me? If I ate them, who gave me a mouth?"

"There is no answer in your vocabulary."

He squatted back and glared up at the face. He shouted.

"I have considered. I prefer it, pain and all."

"To what?"

He began to rage weakly and strike out at the boots.

"To the black lightning! Go back! Go back!"

He was bruising skin off his hands against the streaming rock. His mouth quacked and he went with it into the last crevice of all.

"Poor mad sailor on a rock!"

He clambered up the High Street.

> *Rage, roar, spout!*
> *Let us have wind, rain, hail, gouts of blood,*
> *Storms and tornadoes . . .*

He ran about on the look-out, stumbling over scattered stones.

> *. . . hurricanes and typhoons. . . .*

197

There was a half-light, a storm-light. The light was ruled in lines and the sea in ridges and valleys. The monstrous waves were making their way from east to west in an interminable procession and the rock was a trifle among them. But it was charging forward, searing a white way through them, careless of sinking, it was thrusting the Safety Rock forward to burst the ridges like the prow of a ship. It would strike a ridge with the stone prow and burst water into a smother that washed over the fo'c'sle and struck beneath the bridge. Then a storm of shot would sweep over the bridge and strike sense and breath away from his body. He flung himself on a square stone that lay where the old woman had stood with her masked head. He rode it astride, facing into the wind and waves. And again there was background music and a mouth quacking.

"Faster! Faster!"

His rock bored on. He beat it with his heels as if he wore spurs.

"Faster!"

The waves were each an event in itself. A wave would come weltering and swinging in with a storm-light running and flickering along the top like the flicker in a brain. The shallow water beyond the safety rock would occur, so that the nearer part of the wave would rise up, tripped and angry, would roar, swell forward. The Safety Rock would become a pock in a whirlpool of water that spun itself into foam and chewed like a mouth. The whole top of the wave for a hundred yards would move forward and fall into acres of lathering uproar that was launched like an army at the rock.

"Faster!"

His hand found the identity disc and held it out.

The mouth screamed out away from the centre.

"I spit on your compassion!"

There was a recognizable noise away beyond the waves and in the clouds. The noise was not as loud as the sea or the music or the voice but the centre understood. The centre took the body off the slab of rock and bundled it into a trench. As it fell the eye glimpsed a black tendril of lightning that lay across the western sky and the centre screwed down the flaps of flesh and hair. Again there came the sound of the spade against the tin box.

"Hard a-starboard! I'll kill us both, I'll hit the tree with that side and you'll be burst and bitched! There was nothing in writing!"

The centre knew what to do. It was wiser than the mouth. It sent the body scrambling over the rock to the water-hole. It burrowed in among the slime and circling scum. It thrust the hands forward, tore at the water and fell flat in the pool. It wriggled like a seal on a rock with the fresh water streaming out of its mouth. It got at the tamping at the farther end and heaved at the stones. There was a scraping and breaking sound and then the cascade of falling stones and water. There was a wide space of storm-light, waves. There was a body lying in the slimy hollow where the fresh water had been.

"Mad! Proof of madness!"

It made the body wriggle back out of the hole, sent it up to the place where the Look-out had been.

There were branches of the black lightning over the sky, there were noises. One branch ran down into the sea, through the great waves, petered out. It remained there.

The sea stopped moving, froze, became paper, painted paper that was torn by a black line. The rock was painted on the same paper. The whole of the painted sea was tilted but nothing ran downhill into the black crack which had opened in it. The crack was utter, was absolute, was three times real.

The centre did not know if it had flung the body down or if it had turned the world over. There was rock before its face and it struck with lobster claws that sank in. It watched the rock between the claws.

The absolute lightning spread. There was no noise now because noise had become irrelevant. There was no music, no sound from the tilted, motionless sea.

The mouth quacked on for a while then dribbled into silence.

There was no mouth.

Still the centre resisted. It made the lightning do its work according to the laws of this heaven. It perceived in some mode of sight without eyes that pieces of the sky between the branches of black lightning were replaced by pits of nothing. This made the fear of the centre, the rage of the centre vomit in a mode that required no mouth. It screamed into the pit of nothing voicelessly, wordlessly.

"I shit on your heaven!"

The lines and tendrils felt forward through the sea. A segment of storm dropped out like a dead leaf and there was a gap that joined sea and sky through the horizon. Now the lightning found reptiles floating and flying motionlessly and a tendril ran to each. The reptiles resisted, changing shape a little, then they too, dropped out and were gone. A valley of nothing opened up through Safety Rock.

200

The centre attended to the rock between its claws. The rock was harder than rock, brighter, firmer. It hurt the serrations of the claws that gripped.

The sea twisted and disappeared. The fragments were not visible going away, they went into themselves, dried up, destroyed, erased like an error.

The lines of absolute blackness felt forward into the rock and it was proved to be as insubstantial as the painted water. Pieces went and there was no more than an island of papery stuff round the claws and everywhere else there was the mode that the centre knew as nothing.

The rock between the claws was solid. It was square and there was an engraving on the surface. The black lines sank in, went through and joined.

The rock between the claws was gone.

There was nothing but the centre and the claws. They were huge and strong and inflamed to red. They closed on each other. They contracted. They were outlined like a night sign against the absolute nothingness and they gripped their whole strength into each other. The serrations of the claws broke. They were lambent and real and locked.

The lightning crept in. The centre was unaware of anything but the claws and the threat. It focused its awareness on the crumbled serrations and the blazing red. The lightning came forward. Some of the lines pointed to the centre, waiting for the moment when they could pierce it. Others lay against the claws, playing over them, prying for a weakness, wearing them away in a compassion that was timeless and without mercy.

14

The jetty, if the word would do for a long pile of boulders, was almost under the tide at the full. The drifter came in towards it, engine stopped, with the last of her way and the urging of the west wind. There was a wintry sunset behind her so that to the eyes on the beach she seemed soon a black shape from which the colour had all run away and been stirred into the low clouds that hung just above the horizon. There was a leaden tinge to the water except in the path of the drifter—a brighter valley of red and rose and black that led back to the dazzling horizon under the sun.

The watcher on the beach did not move. He stood, his seaboots set in the troughs of dry sand that his last steps had made, and waited. There was a cottage at his back and then the slow slope of the island.

The telegraph rang astern in the drifter and she checked her way with a sudden swirl of brighter water from the screws. A fender groaned against stone. Two men jumped on to the jetty and sought about them for the bollards that were not there. An arm gesticulated from the wheel-house. The men caught their ropes round boulders and stood, holding on.

An officer stepped on to the jetty, came quickly towards the beach and jumped down to the dry sand. The wind ruffled papers that he held in his hand so that they chattered like the dusty leaves of late summer. But here they were the only leaves. There was sand, a cottage, rocks and the sea. The officer laboured along in the dry sand with his papers clattering and came to a halt a yard from the watcher.

"Mr. Campbell?"

"Aye. You'll be from the mainland about the——?"

"That's right."

Mr. Campbell removed his cloth cap and put it back again.

"You've not been over-quick."

The officer looked at him solemnly.

"My name's Davidson, by the way. Over-quick. Do you know, Mr. Campbell, that I do this job, seven days a week?"

Mr. Campbell moved his seaboots suddenly. He peered forward into Davidson's grey and lined face. There was a faint, sweet smell on the breath and the eyes that did not blink were just a fraction too wide open.

Mr. Campbell took off his cap and put it on again.

"Well now. Fancy that!"

The lower part of Davidson's face altered to the beginnings of a grin without humour.

"It's quite a widespread war, you know."

Mr. Campbell nodded slowly.

"I'm sorry that I spoke. A sad harvest for you, Captain. I do not know how you can endure it."

The grin disappeared.

"I wouldn't change."

Mr. Campbell tilted his head sideways and peered into Davidson's face.

"No? I beg your pardon, sir. Come now and see where we found it."

He turned and laboured away along the sand. He stopped and pointed down to where an arm of water was confined by a shingly spit.

"It was there, still held by the lifebelt. You'll see, of course. There was a broken orange-box and a tin. And the lineweed. When we have a nor'wester the lineweed gets caught there—and anything else that's floating."

Davidson looked sideways at him.

"It seems important to you, Mr. Campbell, but what I really want is the identity disc. Did you remove that from the body?"

"No. No. I touched—as little as possible."

"A brown disc about the size of a penny, probably worn round the neck?"

"No. I touched nothing."

Davidson's face set grim again.

"One can always hope, I suppose."

Mr. Campbell clasped his hands, rubbed them restlessly, cleared his throat.

"You'll take it away to-night?"

Now Davidson peered in his turn.

"Dreams?"

Mr. Campbell looked away at the water. He muttered.

"The wife——"

He glanced up at the too-wide eyes, the face that seemed to know more than it could bear. He no longer evaded the

204

meeting but shrank a little and answered with sudden humility.

"Aye."

Davidson nodded, slowly.

Now two ratings were standing on the beach before the cottage. They bore a stretcher.

· Mr. Campbell pointed.

"It is in the lean-to by the house, sir. I hope there is as little to offend you as possible. We used paraffin."

"Thank you."

Davidson toiled back along the beach and Mr. Campbell followed him. Presently they stopped. Davidson turned and looked down.

"Well——"

He put his hand to the breast pocket of his battledress and brought out a flat bottle. He looked Mr. Campbell in the eye, grinned with the lower part of his face, pulled out the cork and swigged, head back. The ratings watched him without comment.

"Here goes, then."

Davidson went to the lean-to, taking a torch from his trouser pocket. He ducked through the broken door and disappeared.

The ratings stood without movement. Mr. Campbell waited, silently, and contemplated the lean-to as though he were seeing it for the first time. He surveyed the mossed stones, the caved-in and lichenous roof as though they were a profound and natural language that men were privileged to read only on a unique occasion.

There was no noise from inside.

Even on the drifter there was no conversation. The only

noises were the sounds of the water falling over on the little beach.

Hush. Hush.

The sun was a half-circle in a bed of crimson and slate.

Davidson came out again. He carried a small disc, swinging from a double string. His right hand went to the breast pocket. He nodded to the ratings.

"Go on, then."

Mr. Campbell watched Davidson fumble among his papers. He saw him examining the disc, peering close, transferring details carefully to a file. He saw him put the disc away, crouch, rub his hands backwards and forwards in the dry, clean sand. Mr. Campbell spread his arms wide in a gesture of impotence and dropped them.

"I do not know, sir. I am older than you but I do not know."

Davidson said nothing. He stood up again and took out his bottle.

"Don't you have second sight up here?"

Mr. Campbell looked unhappily at the lean-to.

"Don't joke, sir. That was unworthy of you."

Davidson came down from his swig. Two faces approached each other. Campbell read the face line by line as he had read the lean-to. He flinched from it again and looked away at the place where the sun was going down—seemingly for ever.

The ratings came out of the lean-to. They carried a stretcher between them that was no longer empty.

"All right, lads. There's a tot waiting for you. Carry on."

The two sailors went cautiously away through the sand towards the jetty. Davidson turned to Mr. Campbell.

"I have to thank you, Mr. Campbell, in the name of this poor officer."

Mr. Campbell took his eyes away from the stretcher.

"They are wicked things, those lifebelts. They give a man hope when there is no longer any call for it. They are cruel. You do not have to thank me, Mr. Davidson."

He looked at Davidson in the gloom, carefully, eye to eye. Davidson nodded.

"Maybe. But I thank you."

"I did nothing."

The two men turned and watched the ratings lifting the stretcher to the low jetty.

"And you do this every day."

"Every day."

"Mr. Davidson——'

Mr. Campbell paused so that Davidson turned towards him again. Mr. Campbell did not immediately meet his eye.

"—we are the type of human intercourse. We meet here, apparently by chance, a meeting unpredictable and never to be repeated. Therefore I should like to ask you a question with perhaps a brutal answer."

Davidson pushed his cap back on his head and frowned. Mr. Campbell looked at the lean-to.

"Broken, defiled. Returning to the earth, the rafters rotted, the roof fallen in—a wreck. Would you believe that anything ever lived there?"

Now the frown was bewildered.

"I simply don't follow you, I'm afraid."

"All those poor people——"

"The men I——?"

"The harvest. The sad harvest. You know nothing of my—shall I say—official beliefs, Mr. Davidson; but living for all these days next to that poor derelict—Mr. Davidson. Would you say there was any—surviving? Or is that all? Like the lean-to?"

"If you're worried about Martin—whether he suffered or not——"

They paused for a while. Beyond the drifter the sun sank like a burning ship, went down, left nothing for a reminder but clouds like smoke.

Mr. Campbell sighed.

"Aye," he said, "I meant just that."

"Then don't worry about him. You saw the body. He didn't even have time to kick off his seaboots."

FREE
FALL

I have walked by stalls in the market-place where books, dog-eared and faded from their purple, have burst with a white hosanna. I have seen people crowned with a double crown, holding in either hand the crook and flail, the power and the glory. I have understood how the scar becomes a star, I have felt the flake of fire fall, miraculous and pentecostal. My yesterdays walk with me. They keep step, they are grey faces that peer over my shoulder. I live on Paradise Hill, ten minutes from the station, thirty seconds from the shops and the local. Yet I am a burning amateur, torn by the irrational and incoherent, violently searching and self-condemned.

When did I lose my freedom? For once, I was free. I had power to choose. The mechanics of cause and effect is statistical probability yet surely sometimes we operate below or beyond that threshold. Free-will cannot be debated but only experienced, like a colour or the taste of potatoes. I remember one such experience. I was very small and I was sitting on the stone surround of the pool and fountain in the centre of the park. There was bright sunlight, banks of red and blue flowers, green lawn. There was no guilt but only the plash and splatter of the fountain at the centre. I had bathed and drunk and now I was sitting on the warm stone edge placidly considering what I should do next. The gravelled paths of the park radiated from me: and all at once I was overcome by a new knowledge. I could take whichever I would of these paths.

There was nothing to draw me down one more than the other. I danced down one for joy in the taste of potatoes. I was free. I had chosen.

How did I lose my freedom? I must go back and tell the story over. It is a curious story, not so much in the external events which are common enough, but in the way it presents itself to me, the only teller. For time is not to be laid out endlessly like a row of bricks. That straight line from the first hiccup to the last gasp is a dead thing. Time is two modes. The one is an effortless perception native to us as water to the mackerel. The other is a memory, a sense of shuffle fold and coil, of that day nearer than that because more important, of that event mirroring this, or those three set apart, exceptional and out of the straight line altogether. I put the day in the park first in my story, not because I was young, a baby almost; but because freedom has become more and more precious to me as I taste the potato less and less often.

I have hung all systems on the wall like a row of useless hats. They do not fit. They come in from outside, they are suggested patterns, some dull and some of great beauty. But I have lived enough of my life to require a pattern that fits over everything I know; and where shall I find that? Then why do I write this down? Is it a pattern I am looking for? That Marxist hat in the middle of the row, did I ever think it would last me a lifetime? What is wrong with the Christian biretta that I hardly wore at all? Nick's rationalist hat kept the rain out, seemed impregnable plate-armour, dull and decent. It looks small now and rather silly, a bowler like all bowlers, very formal, very complete, very ignorant. There is a school cap, too. I had no more than hung it there, not knowing of the other hats

6

I should hang by it when I think the thing happened—the decision made freely that cost me my freedom.

Why should I bother about hats? I am an artist. I can wear what hat I like. You know of me, Samuel Mountjoy, I hang in the Tate. You would forgive me any hat. I could be a cannibal. But I want to wear a hat in private. I want to understand. The grey faces peer over my shoulder. Nothing can expunge or exorcise them. My art is not enough for me. To hell with my art. The fit takes me out of a deep well as does the compulsion of sex and other people like my pictures more than I do, think them more important than I do. At heart I am a dull dog. I would sooner be good than clever.

Then why am I writing this down? Why do I not walk round and round the lawn, reorganizing my memories until they make sense, unravelling and knitting up the flexible time stream? I could bring this and that event together, I could make leaps. I should find a system for that round of the lawn and then another one the next day. But thinking round and round the lawn is no longer enough. For one thing it is like the rectangle of canvas, a limited area however ingeniously you paint. The mind cannot hold more than so much; but understanding requires a sweep that takes in the whole of remembered time and then can pause. Perhaps if I write my story as it appears to me, I shall be able to go back and select. Living is like nothing because it is everything—is too subtle and copious for unassisted thought. Painting is like a single attitude, a selected thing.

There is another reason. We are dumb and blind yet we must see and speak. Not the stubbled face of Sammy Mountjoy, the full lips that open to let his hand take out

7

a fag, not the smooth, wet muscles inside round teeth, not the gullet, the lung, the heart—those you could see and touch if you took a knife to him on the table. It is the unnameable, unfathomable and invisible darkness that sits at the centre of him, always awake, always different from what you believe it to be, always thinking and feeling what you can never know it thinks and feels, that hopes hopelessly to understand and to be understood. Our loneliness is the loneliness not of the cell or the castaway; it is the loneliness of that dark thing that sees as at the atom furnace by reflection, feels by remote control and hears only words phoned to it in a foreign tongue. To communicate is our passion and our despair.

With whom then?

You?

My darkness reaches out and fumbles at a typewriter with its tongs. Your darkness reaches out with your tongs and grasps a book. There are twenty modes of change, filter and translation between us. What an extravagant coincidence it would be if the exact quality, the translucent sweetness of her cheek, the very living curve of bone between the eyebrow and hair should survive the passage! How can you share the quality of my terror in the blacked-out cell when I can only remember it and not re-create it for myself? No. Not with you. Or only with you, in part. For you were not there.

And who are you anyway? Are you on the inside, have you a proof-copy? Am I a job to do? Do I exasperate you by translating incoherence into incoherence? Perhaps you found this book on a stall fifty years hence which is another now. The star's light reaches us millions of years after the star is gone, or so they say, and perhaps it is true.

What sort of universe is that for our central darkness to keep its balance in?

There is this hope. I may communicate in part; and that surely is better than utter blind and dumb; and I may find something like a hat to wear of my own. Not that I aspire to complete coherence. Our mistake is to confuse our limitations with the bounds of possibility and clap the universe into a rationalist hat or some other. But I may find the indications of a pattern that will include me, even if the outer edges tail off into ignorance. As for communication, to understand all they say is to pardon all. Yet who but the injured can forgive an injury? And how if the lines at that particular exchange are dead?

I have no responsibility for some of the pictures. I can remember myself as I was when I was a child. But even if I had committed murder then, I should no longer feel responsible for it. There is a threshold here, too, beyond which what we did was done by someone else. Yet I was there. Perhaps, to understand, must include pictures from those early days also. Perhaps reading my story through again I shall see the connection between the little boy, clear as spring water, and the man like a stagnant pool. Somehow, the one became the other.

I never knew my father and I think my mother never knew him either. I cannot be sure, of course, but I incline to believe she never knew him—not socially at any rate unless we restrict the word out of all useful meaning. Half my immediate ancestry is so inscrutable that I seldom find it worth bothering about. I exist. These tobacco-stained fingers poised over the typewriter, this weight in the chair assures me that two people met; and one of them was Ma. What would the other think of me, I wonder? What celebration do I commemorate? In 1917 there were victories and defeats, there was a revolution. In face of all that, what is one little bastard more or less? Was he a soldier, that other, blown to pieces later, or does he survive and walk, evolve, forget? He might well be proud of me and my flowering reputation if he knew. I may even have met him, face to inscrutable face. But there would be no recognition. I should know as little of him as the wind knows, turning the leaves of a book on an orchard wall, the ignorant wind that cannot decipher the rows of black rivets any more than we strangers can decipher the faces of strangers.

Yet I was wound up. I tick. I exist. I am poised eighteen inches over the black rivets you are reading, I am in your place, I am shut in a bone box and trying to fasten myself on the white paper. The rivets join us together and yet for all the passion we share nothing but our sense of division. Why think of my dad then? What does he matter?

But Ma was different. She had some secret, known to the cows, perhaps, or the cat on the rug, some quality that rendered her independent of understanding. She was content with contact. It was her life. My success would not impress her. She would be indifferent. In my private album of pictures, she is complete and final as a full stop.

At odd moments when the thought occurred to me I asked her about my dad but my curiosity was not urgent. Perhaps if I had insisted, she might have been precise— but what was the need? The living space round her apron was sufficient. There were boys who knew their fathers just as there were boys who habitually wore boots. There were shining toys, cars, places where people ate with grace;

but these pictures on my wall, this out-thereness amounted to a Martian world. A real father would have been an unthinkable addition. So my inquiries were made in the evening before the "Sun" opened, or much later in the evening when it shut again and Ma was mellow. I might have asked as indifferently for a story and believed it as little.

"What was my dad, Ma?"

Out of our common indifference to mere physical fact, came answers that varied as her current daydream varied. These were influenced by the "Sun" and the flickering stories at the Regal. I knew they were daydreams and accepted them as such because I daydreamed too. Only the coldest attitude to the truth would have condemned them as lies, though once or twice, Ma's rudimentary moral sense made her disclaim them almost immediately. The result was that my father was sometimes a soldier, he was a lovely man, an officer; though I suspect Ma was past the officer and gentleman stage by the time I was conceived. One night when she came back from the Regal and pictures of battleships being bombed off the shores of America, he was in the Royal Air Force. Later still in our joint life—and what was the celebration this time? What prancing horses, plumed helmets and roaring crowds? Later still, he was none other than the Prince of Wales.

This was such tremendous news to me, though of course I did not believe it, that the red glow behind the bars of the grate has remained on my retina like an afterimage. We neither believed it but the glittering myth lay in the middle of the dirty floor, accepted with gratitude as beyond my own timid efforts at invention. Yet almost before she threw the thing there, she was prepared to snatch it back. The story was too enormous, or perhaps the daydream too private to be shared. I saw her eyes shift in the glow, the faint, parchment colour of her lighted face move and alter. She sniffed, scratched her nose, wept an easy gin-tear or two and spoke to the grate where there could well have been more fire.

"You know I'm a sodding liar, dear, don't you?"

Yes. I knew, without condemnation, but I was disappointed all the same. I felt that Christmas had disappeared and there was no more tinsel. I recognized that we should return to Ma's fictitious steady. The Prince of Wales, a soldier, an airman—but whores claim to be the daughters of clergymen; and despite all the glitter of court life, the church won.

"What was my dad, Ma?"

"A parson. I keep telling you."

On the whole, that has been my steady, too. There would be nothing in common between us but our division yet we should at least recognize it: and I should know behind the other face, the drag, the devil, the despair, the wry and desperate perceptions, conforming hourly to a creed until they are warped as Chinese feet. In my bitter moments I have thought of myself as connected thereby to good works. I like to think then that my father was not doing something for which he had either an excuse or moral indifference. My self-esteem would prefer him to have wrestled desperately with the flesh. Soldiers traditionally love them and leave them; but the clergy, either abstemious or celibate, the pastors, ministers, elders and priests—I should be an old anguish once thought forgiven now seen to be scarlet. I should blow up in some manse or parsonage or presbytery or close, I should blow up like a forgotten abscess. They are men as I am,

12

acquainted with sin. There would be some point to me.

Which branch, I wonder? Only a day or two ago I walked down a side street, past the various chapels, the oratory, round the corner by the old church and the vast rectory. Of what denomination shall I declare my fictitious steady to be? The church of England, the curator's church? Would not my father have been a gentleman first and a priest afterwards, an amateur like me? Even the friars walk round with trousers showing under their well-cut habits. They remind me of the druids on Brown Willie, or somewhere, coming in cars and spectacles. Shall I choose a Roman Catholic to my father? There is a professional church even when you hate her guts. Would a bastard tug one of them by the heart as well as the sleeve? As for the ranks of nonconformity so drearily conforming, the half-baked, the splinter parties, the tables, and tabernacles and temples—I'm like Ma; indifferent. He might as soon be an Odd Fellow or an Elk.

"What was my dad, Ma?"

I lie. I deceive myself as well as you. Their world is mine, the world of sin and redemption, of showings and conviction, of love in the mud. You deal daily in the very blood of my life. I am one of you, a haunted man—haunted by what or whom? And this is my cry; that I have walked among you in intellectual freedom and you never tried to seduce me from it, since a century has seduced you to it and you believe in fair play, in not presuming, in being after all not a saint. You have conceded freedom to those who cannot use freedom and left the dust and the dirt clustered over the jewel. I speak your hidden language which is not the language of the other men. I am your brother in both senses and since freedom was my curse I throw the dirt at you as I might pick at a sore which will not break out and kill.

"What was my dad, Ma?"

Let him never know. I am acquainted with the warm throb myself and think little enough of physical paternity compared with the slow growth that comes after. We do not own children. My father was not a man. He was a speck shaped like a tadpole invisible to the naked eye. He had no head and no heart. He was as specialized and soulless as a guided missile.

Ma was never a professional any more than I am. Like mother, like son. We are amateurs at heart. Ma had not the business ability nor the desire to make a career and a success. Neither was she immoral for that implies some sort of standard from which she could decline. Was Ma above morals or below them or outside them? Today she would be classed as subnormal, and given the protection she did not want. In those days, if she had not clad herself in such impervious indifference she would have been called simple. She staked small but vital sums on horses in the "Sun", she drank and went to the pictures. For work, she took whatever was available. She charred for chars, she—we—picked hops, she washed and swept and imperfectly polished in such public buildings as were within easy reach of our alley. She did not have sexual connection for that implies an aseptic intercourse, a loveless, joyless refinement of pleasure with the prospect of conception inhibited by the rubber cup from the bathroom. She did not make love, for I take that to be a passionate attempt to confirm that the wall which parted them is down. She did none of these things. If she had, she would have told me in her slurred, rambling monologues, with their vast pauses, their acceptance that we are inescapably here. No. She was a creature. She shared pleasure round like a wet-nurse's teat, absorbed, gustily laughing and sighing. Her casual intercourse must have been to her what his works are to a real artist—themselves and nothing more. They had no implication. They were meetings in back streets or fields, on boxes, or gateposts and buttresses. They were like most human sex in history, a natural thing without benefit of psychology, romance or religion.

Ma was enormous. She must have been a buxom girl in the bud but appetite and a baby blew her up into an elephantine woman. I deduce that she was attractive once, for her eyes, sunk into a face bloated like a brown bun, were still large and mild. There was a gloss on them that must have lain all over her when she was young. Some women cannot say no; but my ma was more than those simple creatures, else how can she so fill the backward tunnel? These last few months I have been trying to catch her in two handfuls of clay—not, I mean, her appearance; but more accurately, my sense of her hugeness and reality, her matter-of-fact blocking of the view. Beyond her there is nothing, nothing. She is the warm darkness between me and the cold light. She is the end of the tunnel, she.

And now something happens in my head. Let me catch the picture before the perception vanishes. Ma spreads as I remember her, she blots out the room and the house, her wide belly expands, she is seated in her certainty and indifference more firmly than in a throne. She is the unquestionable, the not good, not bad, not kind, not bitter. She looms down the passage I have made in time.

She terrifies but she does not frighten.

She neglects but she does not warp or exploit.

She is violent without malice or cruelty.

She is adult without patronage or condescension.

She is warm without possessiveness.

But, above all, she is there.

So of course I can remember her only in clay, the common earth, the ground, I cannot stick the slick commercial colours on stretched canvas for her or outline her in words that are ten thousand years younger than her darkness and warmth. How can you describe an age, a world, a dimension? As far as communication goes there are only the things that surrounded her to be pieced together and displayed with the gap that was Ma existing mutely in the middle. I fish up memory of a piece of material which is grey with a tinge of yellow. The one corner is frayed—or as I now think, rotted—into a fringe, a damp fringe. The rest is anchored up there somewhere about my ma and I swing along, fingers clutched up and in, stumbling sometimes, sometimes ungently removed without a word said, by a huge hand falling from above. I seem to remember searching for that corner of her apron and the pleasure of finding it again.

We must have been living in Rotten Row then for certain directions were already as settled as the points of the compass. Our bog was across worn bricks and a runnel, through a wooden door to a long wooden seat. There was an upthereness over our room, though surely not a lodger? Perhaps we were ever so slightly more prosperous then, or perhaps gin was cheaper, like cigarettes. We had a chest of drawers for a dresser and the grate was full of little iron cupboards and doors and things that pulled out. Ma never used these but only the little fire in the middle with the hot metal disc that closed the top. We had a rug, too, a chair, a small deal table and a bed. My end of the bed was near the door and when Ma got in the other end, I slid down. All but one of the houses in our row were the same, and the brick alley with a central gutter ran along in front of them. There were children of all sizes in that world, boys who stepped on me or gave me sweets, girls who picked me up when I had crawled too far and took me back. We must have been very dirty. I have a good and trained colour sense and my memory of those human faces is not so much in passages of pink and white as of grey and brown. Ma's face, her neck, her arms—all of Ma that showed was brown and grey. The apron which I visualize so clearly I now see to have been filthily dirty. Myself, I cannot see. There was no mirror within my reach and if Ma ever had one it had vanished by the time I was a conscious boy. What was there in a mirror for Ma to linger over? I remember blown washing on wire lines, soap suds, I remember the erratic patterns that must have been dirt on the wall, but like Ma I am a neutral point of observation, a gap in the middle. I crawled and tumbled in the narrow world of Rotten Row, empty as a soap bubble but with a rainbow of colour and excitement round me. We children were underfed and scantily clothed. I first went to school with my feet bare. We were noisy, screaming, tearful, animal. And yet I remember that time as with the flash and glitter, the warmth of a Christmas party. I have never disliked dirt. To me, the porcelain and chromium, the lotions, the deodorants, the whole complex of cleanness, which is to say, all soap, all hygiene, is inhuman and incomprehensible. Before this free gift of a universe, man is a constant. There is a sense in which when we emerged from our small slum and were washed, the happiness and security of life was washed away also.

I have two sorts of picture in my mind of our slum. The earlier are the interiors because I can remember a time when for me there was no other world at all. The brick path and gutter down the middle ran between the row of houses and the row of yards with each a bog. At one end and to our left was a wooden gate; at the other, a passage out to the unvisited street. At that end, the "Sun" was an old and complicated building and the back door was inside the alley. Here was the focus of adult life; and here the end house in the row extended across the passage and joined the pub overhead so it was in a position of some eminence and advantage. When I was old enough to notice such things I looked up, together with the rest of our alley, to the good lady who lived there. She had two rooms upstairs, she was mortared to the pub, she did for nice people and she had curtains. If I told you more of our geography and put us in the general scheme of things I should be false to my memories; for I first remember the alley as a world, bounded by the wooden gate at one end and the rectangular but forbidden exit to the main road at the other. Rain and sunshine descended on us between the shirts flapping or still. There were poles with cleats on and a variety of simple mechanisms for hoisting away the washing where it would catch the wind. There were cats and what seems to me like crowds of people. I remember Mrs. Donavan next door who was withered and Ma who was not. I remember the loudness of their voices, used straining from the throat with heads thrust forward when the ladies quarrelled. I remember the fag-end of one quarrel, both ladies moving slowly away from each other sideways, neither in this case victorious, each reduced to single syllables full of vague menace, indignation and resentment.

"Well then!"

"Yes!"

"Yes!"

"Ah——!"

This remains with me because of the puzzle that Ma had not won outright. She did, usually. Withered Mrs. Donavan with her three daughters and many troubles was not Ma's weight in any sense. There was one occasion of apocalyptic grandeur when Ma not only won but triumphed. Her voice seemed to bounce off the sky in brazen thunder. The scene is worth reconstructing.

Opposite each house across the brick alley with the gutter down the middle was a square of brick walls with an entry. The walls were about three feet high. In each square on the left-hand side was a standpipe and beyond it, at the back of the square, was a sentry-box closed by a wooden door which had a sort of wooden grating. Open the door by lifting the wooden latch and you faced a wooden box running the whole width between the walls and pierced by a round, worn orifice. There would be a scrap of newspaper lying on the box, or a whole sheet crumpled on the damp floor. Some dark, subterranean stream flowed slowly along below the row of boxes. If you closed the door and dropped the latch by means of a piece of string which dangled inside, you could enjoy your private, even in Rotten Row. If someone from your house entered the brick square—for you saw them through your grating—and lifted a hand to the latch, you did not move, but cried out, inarticulately avoiding names or set words so that the hand dropped again. For we had our standards. We had progressed from Eden—that is, provided the visitor came from your own house. If, on the other hand, they had loitered in the alley and made a mistake you might be as articulate as you pleased, be wildly Rabelaisian, suggest new combinations of our complex living patterns to include the visitor until the doorways were screaming with laughter and all the brats by the gutter screamed, too, and danced.

But there were exceptions. In the twenties progress had caught up with us and added a modern superstition to the rest so that we firmly believed a legend about lavatories. Rotten Row sometimes suffered from more than a cold in the head.

It must have been a day in April. What other month could give me such blue and white, such sun and wind? The clothing on the lines was horizontal and shuddering, the sharp, carved clouds hurried, the sun spattered from the soap suds in the gutter, the worn bricks were bright with a dashing of rain. It was the sort of wind that gives grown-ups headaches and children frantic exultation. It was a day of shouting and wrestling, a day aflame and unbearable without drama and adventure. Something must happen.

I was playing with a matchbox in the gutter. I was so small that to squat was natural but the wind even in the alley would sometimes give me a sidelong-push and I was as much in the soapy water as out. A grating was blocked so that the water spread across the bricks and made a convenient ocean. Yet my great, my apocalyptic memory is not of stretched-out time, but an instant. Mrs. Donavan's Maggie who smelt so sweet and showed round, silk knees was recoiled from the entrance to our brick square. She had retreated so fast and so far that one high heel was in my ocean. She was caught in act to turn away, her arms were raised to ward off. I cannot remember her face—for it is mesmerized in the other direction. Poor Mrs. Donavan, the dear withered creature, peeps out of her own bog with the air of someone unfairly caught, someone who could explain everything, given time—but knows, in that tremendous instant, that time is not to be given her. And from our bog, our own, private bog, with its warm, personal seat, comes my ma.

She has burst out for the door has banged against the wall and the latch hangs broken. My ma faces Maggie, one foot in front of the other for she has come out of the narrow box sideways. Her knees are bent, she is crouched in a position of dreadful menace. Her skirts are huddled up round her waist and she holds her vast grey bloomers in two purple hands just above her knees. I see her voice, a jagged shape of scarlet and bronze, shatter into the air till it hangs there under the sky, a deed of conquest and terror.

"You bloody whore! Keep your clap for your own bastards!"

I have no memory of majesty to match that one from Rotten Row. Even when the Twins Fred and Joe, who dealt so deviously in scrap at the other end of the alley near the wooden gate, were fetched away by two giraffe-like policemen the drama dwindled down into defeat. We watched one of the coppers walking, rolling up the alley and we muttered, I not knowing why. We watched Fred and Joe dash out of their house and bundle themselves through the wooden gate; but of course the second copper was standing on the other side. They ran right into him, small men, easily grabbed in either hand. They were brought down the alley handcuffed between two dark blue pillars surmounted by silver spikes, the van was waiting for them. We shouted and muttered and made the dull tearing sound that was Rotten Row's equivalent of booing. Fred and Joe were pale but perky. The coppers came, took, went, unstoppable as birth and death, the three cases in which Rotten Row accepted unconditional defeat. Whether the extra mouth was coming, or the policeman's van, or the long hearse that would draw up at the end of the passage, made no difference. A hand of some sort was thrust through the Row to take what it would and no one could stop it.

We were a world inside a world and I was a man before I achieved the intellectual revolution of thinking of us as a slum. Though we were only forty yards long and the fields lapped against us we were a slum. Most people think of slums as miles of muck in the East End of London or the jerry-built lean-to's of the Black Country. But we lived right in the heart of the Garden of England and the hop gardens glowed round us. Though on the one side were brick villas, schools, warehouses, shops, churches, on the other were the spiced valleys through which I followed my ma and reached for the sticky buds. Yet that takes me out of our home and I want to stay in it for a while. I will put back the picture postcards of dancing, flame-lit men, and creep back under the lid. True there were bonfires, rivers of beer, singing, gipsies and a pub set secretly among trees, wearing its thatch like a straw hat pulled down over the eyes; but our slum was the point of return. We had a pub, too. We were a huddle. Now I am out in the cold world away from my crying shame in the face of heaven I am surprised to find what number of people will go to any length just to get themselves into a huddle. Perhaps then I was not deceived and we had something. We were a human proposition, a way of life, an entity.

We centred on the pub. There was a constant coming and going through the blistered brown door with its two panes of opaque glass. The brass knob of the door was worn uneven and gleamed with use. I suppose there were licensing laws and forbidden hours but I never noticed them. I saw the door from ground level and it is huge in my memory. Inside was a brick floor, some settles and two stools by a counter in the corner. This was the snug; a warm, noisy, mysterious, adult place. Later I went there if I wanted my ma urgently; and no one ever told me that my presence was illegal. I went there first, because of our lodger.

Our lodger had our upstairs, use of the stove, our tap and our bog. I suppose he was the tragedy about which so many sociologists and economists wrote so many books in the nineteenth and twentieth centuries. I can re-create him in my mind easily enough. To begin with, even from my ground level, he was small. I think he must have been, so to speak, the fag-end of a craftsman, for he was neat, and in a sense, distinguished. A plumber? A carpenter? But he was very old—always had been, for who could think of him as anything else? He was a tiny skeleton, held together by skin and a shiny blue suit. He wore a brown muffler tucked down inside the serge of his suit and I cannot remember his boots—perhaps because I was always looking up at him. He had interesting hands, complicated with knots and veins and brown patches. He always wore a trilby, whether he was sitting by the window in our upstairs, or shuffling down the alley or going into the bog, or sitting by the counter in the "Sun". One remarkable thing about him was his moustache, which faced downwards and seemed of the texture and whiteness of swan's feathers. It covered his mouth and was very beautiful. But even more remarkable, was his breathing, quick as a bird's and noisy, in out, in out, in out, all the time, tick tick tick, brittle as a clock with the same sense of urgency and no time to waste, no time for anything else. Over the moustache, under hanging brows on each side of his sharp nose, his eyes looked out, preoccupied and frightened. To me, he always seemed to be looking at something that was not there, something of profound interest and anxiety. Tick tick tick all the time all the time. Nobody cared. I didn't, Ma didn't; and he was our lodger, hanging on to the fag-end of his life. When I was going to sleep in the night or when I woke in the morning I could hear him up there, through the single deal boards, tick tick tick. If you asked him a question he answered like a man who has just run a four-minute mile with fuff and puff and inspiration of grasped breath, with panic need to stay alive like a man coming up for the third time in out in out in out. I asked him as he sat staring through the stove. I wanted to know. He fuffed the panel answer back at me—just got the words out and then caught up with the air again like a man who snatches a cup from his ankles an inch above shattering.

"Wart——" fuff gasp tick tick "in me——" tick tick tick—"chest". Fuff fuff and another desperate, lunging inspiration towards the end.

I never saw him eat; though I suppose he must have

eaten. But how? There was no time. What number of days must run before the body uses all the fat and flesh, all the stored fuel? How long then can the spirit hold itself up by its own bootstraps, focused as it seemed to be, in the eyes? Tick tick tick and though he went into the "Sun" with the others he could never drink much if anything and that was why the downward tufts that covered his mouth were like white swan's feathers. As I remember him and his breathing it occurs to me that what he had was lung cancer; and I notice with a certain wry amusement my instant effort to fit that uninformed guess into a pattern. But then I remember that all patterns have broken one after another, that life is random and evil unpunished. Why should I link that man, that child with this present head and heart and hands? I can call to mind a technical crime of this period, for I stole tuppence from the old man once—bought liquorice for which I still have a passion—and got clean away with it. But those were days of terrible and irresponsible innocence. I should be literary if I shaped my story to show how those two pennies have lain on the dead eyes of my spiritual sight for I am clear of them. Then why do I write? Do I still expect a pattern? What am I looking for?

Our bed downstairs was within an arm's reach of the chest of drawers and our alarm clock stood near the edge. It was an early make, round, on three short legs, and it held up a bell like an umbrella. It would shatter Ma into wakefulness when she had to go out charring in the early dark and my sleeping ears would note the noise and dream on. Sometimes if the night had been long and thick, Ma would take no notice or groan and bury herself. Then the clock woke me. All night it had ticked on, repressed, its madness held and bound in; but now the strain burst. The umbrella became a head, the clock beat its head in frenzy, trembling and jerking over the chest of drawers on three legs until it reached a point where the chest would begin to drum in sympathy, sheer madness and hysteria. Then I would wake Ma and feel very business-like and virtuous till she rose in the dark like a whale. But during the night if I woke myself or could not get to sleep the clock was always present and varied as I felt. Sometimes and most often it was friendly and placid; but if I had my seldom night terrors, then the clock had them, too. Time was inexorable then, hurrying on, driving irresistibly towards the point of madness and explosion.

Once, near midnight, I woke with a jolt because the clock had stopped so that I was menaced and defenceless. I was frightened and I had to find Ma. There was the same compulsion on me as there is now before this paper, a compulsion irrational and deep. I fell out of bed, went scrambling and crying through the door and into the alley, along and across the gutter to the back door of the pub. There was no light from the panes of glass. The pub was blind. I scrabbled and reached up for the brass handle and swung there.

"Ma! Ma!"

The brass turned under my hand and pulled me into the back snug, still half-swinging. I squatted on the floor and there were shadowy people looking down at me, shadows that moved a little in the dull light from the fire. Ma was sitting on most of a settle facing the door and she held a little glass buried in her hand. The place was larger than daylight. Now I know they were only a few neighbours drinking after hours—but then they presented the whole mystery of adult life in one shadowy picture.

"The clock's stopped, Ma."

I could not convey the impossibility of returning by myself to the dark silence; I was wholly dependent on their understanding and goodwill. They loomed and muttered. So the party broke up without much kindness but some noise so that for two or three minutes the alley rang with comfortable voices. Ma shoo'd me across the gutter and switched on our naked bulb. She took the alarm clock in one hand—it was hidden almost as the glass had been hidden—and held it to the side of her head. She set it down again with a bang and turned to me with a punitive hand lifted.

And stopped.

She looked slowly up at the ceiling where our lodger lay a few feet over my head and listened; listened in such silence that now I found that I had made a quite incomprehensible mistake, for I could hear clearly how the alarm clock was still hurrying on towards the hysterical explosion, hurrying on, brittle, trivially insistent, tick tick tick.

Did our lodger subscribe to some burial insurance? I remember the stately car that came for him so that his body was much more important to the Row dead than alive. Rotten Row believed in death as a ritual and spectacle, as a time to mourn and rejoice. Why then did I never see his body? Did the Row cheat me or is there some mystery here? Normally, the dead held higher court than the newly born. They were washed, straightened out, tidied; and received homage as if they were Pharaoh bandaged and with a belly full of spices. I cannot think of

27

death in Rotten Row without the word "royal" coming to mind. To the backward sight which hangs events in their symbolic colours, Rotten Row is draped for death in hatchments of black and violet and purple, is big with the enjoyment of booze and sorrow.

Why then did I not see his or any other body? Had those shadowy adults from the snug, some lore or theory of my nightmare knowledge? Did I know too much? I had a special reason for feeling cheated. I was told that under his trilby there was a thatch of that same swan's feather whiteness; and in my mind it became a precious thing, exquisite as the cap that fits the head of the Swan Maiden herself. Evie told me about the swan's feathers under the hat. She saw him in his box. She had touched him, too—been made to touch him by her mother. That way, went our belief, the child will never fear a dead body. So Evie touched him, reaching out her right forefinger to his sharp nose. She showed me the finger, I looked, I saw, I was awed and admired Evie. But I never saw or touched him. Death rolled by me in the high black car behind panes of chased and frosted glass. Then, as always, I stood, only partly comprehending, on the pavement. But Evie was always at the heart of things. She was a year or two older and she bossed me. How could I be jealous of Evie who knew so much? Even though he had been our own private lodger with use of our bog, not Evie's mum's, I could not grudge her the sharp nose of death. She was majestic. It was her right. But I could feel insufficient and I did. For me there was no thatch of white but only the frosted glass rolling away down the street. I made fantasies of myself daring the most awful and gruesome loneliness to know the very feel of death. But it was

28

too late. I can see that time in my mind's eye if I stoop to knee height. A doorstep is the size of an altar, I can lean on the sloping sign beneath the plate-glass of a shop window, to cross the gutter is a wild leap. Then the transparency which is myself floats through life like a bubble, empty of guilt, empty of anything but immediate and conscienceless emotions, generous, greedy, cruel, innocent. My twin towers were Ma and Evie. And the shape of life loomed that I was insufficient for our lodger's thatch, for that swan-white seal of ultimate knowing.

I wonder if he had a thatch at all? As I ponder the empty bubble from knee-height, I see for the first time that I only had Evie's word for it. But Evie was a liar. Or no. She was a fantasist. She was taller than I was, brown and thin, with a bob of lank brown hair. She wore brown stockings with wrinkles concertina'd under each knee. She had a variety of immense and brilliant hair-ribbons; and I adored these and desired them with hopeless cupidity. For what was the good of a hair-ribbon without the hair to tie it in? And what was the good of that symbol without the majesty and central authority of Ma and Evie? When she bent sideways to talk out of the world of what people ought really to be, her hair fell and leaned out and the pink bow flopped sideways, august and unattainable.

Yet I was in her hands and content to be so. For now I was to go to the infant school and she was to convoy me. In the morning I would be out first by the gutter waiting for her to come out of her door. She would appear and the world would fill with sunlight. She would call and I would rush into her collection. She cleaned me up at the tap, took me by the hand, talking all the time and led me out past the "Sun", past the window of the lady with the

29

leathery-green plant and into the street. The school was three hundred yards away or a little more, along, across round a corner, across the main road and along a pavement. We stopped to examine everything and Evie was much more interesting than school in her explanations. Most of all I remember the antique shop. What must have been the firm's name was displayed in huge gold letters on a sloping sill just below the window and my nose. I can only remember one golden W. Perhaps I had reached that letter in the alphabet.

There were some ornate candlesticks in that shop. They stood on a gold-gilded table and each one held up a dunce's cap as our alarm clock held up the umbrella. Evie explained that you had only to turn the dunce's cap over, pour in the melted wax and it would burn for ever. Evie had seen them doing so in her cousin's house in America —not a house exactly, a palace, rather. She elaborated the house all the way down the road and when I was set before a piece of paper with crayons at my side, I drew her house—her cousin's house, a huge downstairs and a huge upstairs; and the dunce's caps burning with flames of gold.

There was a little spoon among some litter, a spoon which was much longer than a spoon should be. Evie explained that they'd given a man poison with this by mistake, thinking it was medicine. He had bitten the spoon with his teeth and started to jerk about on the bed. Then they realized of course that they had given him poison instead of friar's balsam but it was too late. They had pulled and pulled but the spoon wouldn't come out. Three of them had held him down and three had pulled as hard as they could but the spoon only stretched and stretched—then Evie was running away down the pavement, knees hitting each other, heels kicking out; she was twitching and giggling and horrified, and I was running after her, crying Evie! Evie!

There was a suit of armour in the dim back of the shop. Evie said her uncle was inside the suit. Now this was demonstrably ridiculous. You could see through the suit where the pieces did not quite join. Yet I never questioned that he was there for my faith was perfect. I simply felt that he was an unusual creature with all those holes in him; and this may have been because he was a duke. Evie explained that he was waiting there until he could rescue her. She had been stolen by the people she lived with— she was really a princess and one day he would come out and take her away in his car. She described the car, with frosted and chased glass, and I recognized it. The people would cheer, said Evie; but I knew I should stand on the pavement and the hair-ribbon would vanish as the white cap of swan's feathers had vanished.

Evie must have watched my lifted and trusting eyes for a flicker of doubt; because soon her stories took wings to themselves. I know now that I was privileged to see a soul spread out before me; was introduced to one of our open secrets. But my innocent credulity was a condition of the sights so that I learned nothing. She was, she confided to me, she was sometimes a boy. She told me that, but first she swore me to a secrecy which I violate now for the first time. The change, she said, was sudden, painful, and complete. She never knew when, but then pop! out it came and she had to stand up in the bog—*had* to, she explained, she couldn't do anything else. She had to pee the way I did. What was more, when she changed she could pee higher up the wall than any of the boys in our

Row, see? I saw and was appalled. To think of Evie, putting off the majesty and beauty of her skirt and pulling on common trousers—to see her cut short the lank hair, abandon hair-ribbons! Passionately I implored her not to be a boy. But what could she do, she said? Hesitantly I grasped at the only comfort. Might I perhaps change into a girl, wear skirts and a hair-ribbon? No, she said. It only happened to her. So there I was, on the pavement again.

I adored Evie. I was grief-stricken and terrified. She nursed this terror as a tribute to the reality of the situation. Next time it happened, she said, she would show me. But that would mean that she would vanish out of my life; for I understood that no boy could possibly take me by the hand and lead me to school. How should I pass the long spoon and her uncle in safety without her? I begged her not to change—knowing all the while that we were powerless in the face of this awful thing yet preserving the faith that Evie of all people could control our world even if no one else could. I watched her closely for symptoms. In the playground, if she vanished into the girl's lavatory, I stood in anguish, wondering if she had gone to look. I hung about, I pestered her; and at last I bored her. Somehow, in some way that is not clear to me, she detached herself. So there I was, going to school unattended, crossing the road to keep away from the long spoon and her uncle, going in the gate to a different world.

This was my first break with Rotten Row, for Evie's stories had linked it to school and I was unaware of any transition. But now Rotten Row fell into a geographical context and was no longer the whole world. Yet when I see in popular magazines some excavated plan of dwellings and read the dry précis of conjectured life, I wonder how Rotten Row will fare under the spade, two thousand years after the V2 hit it. The foundations would tell a story of planned building and regimentation. They would be a bigger, if duller liar than Evie. For Rotten Row was roaring and warm, simple and complex, individual and strangely happy and a world unto itself. It gave me two relationships which were good and for which I am still grateful: one, for my mother, blocking out the backward darkness: two, for Evie, for the excitement of knowing her and for my trust in her. My mother was as near a whore as makes no matter and Evie was a congenital liar. Yet if they would only exist there was nothing more I wanted. I remember the quality of this relationship so vividly that I am almost tempted into an aphorism: love selflessly and you cannot come to harm. But then I remember some things that came after.

So I moved out of Evie's shadow and became the inhabitant of two linked worlds. I liked them both. The infants' school was a place of play and discovery in which the mistresses leaned down like trees. There were new things to do, a tall jangly box out of which one of the trees beat entrancing music. At the end of prayers while we were still standing in rows, the music changed and became marching music. If I heard a brass band in the street today, I should break step, refusing the shame of so simple a reaction; but in those days I stamped and stuck my chest out. I could keep step.

Minnie could never keep step and no one expected her to. She was lumpy. Her arms and legs were stuck on the corners of her square body and she had a large, rather old face which she carried slightly tilted to one side. She walked with an ungainly movement of the arms and legs.

33

She shared a table desk with me so that I noticed her more than the others. If Minnie wanted to pick up a crayon she would make perhaps three sideways movements at it with one hand while the other was held up in the air and jerked in sympathy. If she reached the crayon she made hard, crushing movements with her fingers until somehow they fastened round it. Sometimes the sharpened end of the crayon would be uppermost; and then Minnie would make scratches on the paper for a moment or two with the blunt end. Usually, a tree would lean down at this point and reverse the crayon; but then one day the crayons appeared on her side of the desk sharpened at both ends, so life was easier. I neither liked nor disliked Minnie. She was an appearance, to be accepted like everything else. Even her voice, with its few, blunted words, was just the way Minnie spoke and nothing more. Life was permanent and inevitable in this shape. The pictures on the wall of animals and people in strange clothes, the clay, the beads, the books, the jar on the window-sill with its branch of sticky chestnut buds—these and Johnny Spragg and Philip Arnold and Minnie and Mavis, these were an un-changing entity.

There came a time when we sensed that the trees were tossed by a high wind. There was to be an inspection and the trees whispered the news down to us. A taller tree was coming to find out if we were happy and good and learn-ing things. There was much turning out of cupboards and pinning up of especially good drawings. Mine were prominent which is perhaps one reason why I remember the occasion so vividly.

One morning there was a strange lady at prayers and by then we had been wrought to a state of some tension. We had our prayers and a rather tremulous hymn and waited for the marching music which would take us back to our room. But things were altered. While we stood in our rows the strange lady came along and bent down and asked each of us our names in turn. She was a nice lady and she made jokes so that the trees laughed. She was coming to Minnie. I could see that Minnie was very red.

She bent down to Minnie and asked her name.

No answer.

One of the trees bent down to help.

"My name is M——?"

The nice lady guessed. She was helping, too.

"Meggie? Marjorie? Millicent?"

We began to giggle at the idea of Minnie being called anything but Minnie.

"May? Mary?"

"Margaret? Mabel?"

Minnie pissed on the floor and the nice lady's shoes. She howled and pissed so that the nice lady jumped out of the way and the pool spread. The jangly box struck up, we turned right, marked time, then filed away to our room. But Minnie did not come with us. Neither did the trees for a time. We were impressed and delighted. We had our first scandal. Minnie had revealed herself. All the differences we had accepted as the natural order, drew together and we knew that she was not one of us. We were exalted to an eminence. She was an animal down there, and we were all up here. Later that morning Minnie was taken home by one of the trees for we watched them pass through the gate, hand in hand. We never saw her again.

2

The general has left his house along the road. The gate house is still there, projecting across the wide pavement from the high wall that surrounded his acres of shrub and garden. The house has been taken over by the health service and I cannot claim much social prestige from living almost next door. The slums are not what they were; or perhaps there are no slums. Rotten Row is a dusty plan outlined among rubble. The people who lived there and in similar huddles live now in an ordered housing estate that crawls up the hill on the other side of the valley. They have money, cars, telly. They still sometimes sleep four in a room but there are clean sheets on the bed. Here and there where the old, filthy cottages are left, either in the town or in the country, beams are blue or red. The sweet-shop with its two windows of bottle-glass, is yellow, picked out in duck's egg blue. There are the usual offices indoors now, and the dreamy couple who live there throw pottery in the shed. The town does not stand on its head for the head is gone. We are an amoeba, perhaps waiting to evolve—and then, perhaps not. Even the airfield that lay on the other hill is silent now. The three inches of soil are ploughed up and planted with wheat that sometimes grows as much as a foot high, reaching for the govern-ment grant. In winter you can see the soil smeared away from the chalk by the rain like the skin from a white skull. Is my sickness mine, or do we all suffer?

Once the airfield was a Mecca for children. I and Johnny

Spragg used to climb the escarpment towards the edge, our feet bent sideways by the slope as we tacked up to get our breath again. There was a grassy ditch at the top, one of those sprawling relics that are smoothed into the downs at every few miles from coast to coast. The wire ran along the farther lip and we could lie side by side, among the scabious, the yellow cowslips and purple thistles; we could watch all the tiny crawling and flying things in the tall grass and wait for the planes to buzz out over us. Johnny was a great sage in this. He had that capacity which many small boys have—but not I—of absorbing highly technical knowledge through the pores of his skin. He had no access to the appropriate publications but he knew every plane that came within sight. He knew how to fly almost, I think, before he could read properly. He understood how the planes sat in the air, had an instinctive, a loving grasp of the balanced, invisible forces that kept them where they were. He was dark, chunky, active and cheerful. He was absorbed. If the planes were high up, not just circling and landing, he liked us to lie on our backs to watch them. I think that gave him some sort of sense of being up there with them. I guess now, with my adult sympathy, that he felt he was turning his back on the immobile earth and sharing the lucid chasms, free heights of light and air.

"That's the old DH. They went all the way to—somewhere—in one like that."

"He's going into a cloud."

"No. Too low. There's that Moth again."

Johnny was an expert. He knew things that still astonish me. We were watching a little plane once that was hanging half a mile over the town in the valley when Johnny shouted.

"Look, he's going to spin!"

I made jeering noises but Johnny hit out sideways with his fist.

"Watch!"

The plane flicked over, nose down and spun, flick, flick, flick. It stopped turning, the nose came up, it flew sedately over us, the sequences of engine noises following each manœuvre a second or two later.

"That's an Avro Avian. They can't spin more than three times."

"Why?"

"Couldn't come out."

But for most of the time we watched the planes taking off and landing. If we followed the ditch and turned the corner at the shoulder of the hill we could see them from the side for the prevailing wind blew to the hill across the town. They were an enchantment to Johnny and the figures that climbed out of them, gods. I caught a little of his enthusiasm and became fairly knowledgeable. I knew that a plane should touch down with both wheels and the skid at the same time. This was fun, because very often the gods would err and the plane land twice in fifty yards. These occasions filled me with excitement but they hurt Johnny. He felt, I think, that each time a plane was strained, or a strut in the landing gear buckled, his chances of learning to fly when he was old enough were lessened. So part of our duty was to identify the planes and note when they were out of the hangars, serviced again, and flying. As far as I can remember, there was always at least one of the half a dozen off the air, being mended. I was not very interested but watched obediently; for in some ways I gave Johnny the devotion that I had once given Evie. He was very complete. If there was no flying we would be off along the downs, in the rain and wind, Johnny most of the time with his arms held out as wings.

One day it hardly seemed worth climbing the hill for we could only just see the top. But Johnny said to go and we went. That must have been in some Easter holiday. The early afternoon had not been so bad—windy but clear enough—but now the rain and mist were sweeping right through the valley. The wind pushed us up the hill and the rain searched us out. If we turned for a moment our cheeks bulged where the wind got in them. The windsock at the top was roaring and shorter than usual for the end was being frayed and torn away. They ought to have taken it down, we agreed, but there the windsock was, stays singing, the mast whipping in the rain. Johnny climbed through the wire.

I hung back.

"We better not."

"Come on."

We could not see more than fifty yards of the airfield at a time. I followed Johnny, running over the shuddering grass; for I knew what he wanted. We had argued about the marks that a plane would make on landing and we wanted to see—or at least Johnny did. We kept our eyes open because this was sacred and forbidden ground and children were not encouraged. We were well out from the wire, getting towards the patch where planes landed, when Johnny stopped.

"Down!"

There was a man, just visible in the rain ahead of us. But he was not looking our way. He had a square can at his feet, a stick in his hand and he had something huddled under his raincoat.

"We better go back, Johnny."

"I want to see."

The man shouted something and a voice answered out of the mist upwind of him. The airfield was crowded.

"Let's go home, Johnny."

"We'll get round the other side of him."

We retreated carefully into the rain and mist and ran downwind. But there was another man waiting by another can. We lay close, wet through, while Johnny bit his fingers.

"There's a whole row of 'em."

"Are they after us?"

"No."

We got round the last man and were between the line and the hangar. I was tired of this game, hungry, wet and rather frightened. But Johnny wanted to wait.

"They can't see us if we keep away from them."

A bell clanged and rang by the hangar, a bell familiar to me and yet not to me in these surroundings.

"What's that?"

Johnny smeared his nose with the back of his hand.

"Nambulance."

The wind was not so strong but the air was darker now. The low clouds were bringing down the evening.

Johnny tensed.

"Listen!"

The man just visible by his can had heard something too, for we could see him waving. The DH appeared over us, hanging in the air, misted to a ghost, her antique profile slipping away into invisibility. We heard the engine of the ambulance start up by the hangar and someone shouted. The man was jabbing fiercely at his can. A light flickered upwind of him in the mist and a stream of black smoke swept past him. He had a bundle of cloth on a stick and suddenly it was ablaze. Downwind we could just see another fire. There was a line of them. The DH droned past again.

The mist was driving thick now so that the man and his flare were nothing but a vague patch of light. The DH droned round, now coming near, now receding. Suddenly she was near us in the mist, a dark patch crawling over us and on over the hangar. Her engine snarled, rose to a roar. There was a great sound of rending and tearing wood, then a dull boom like the report of a big gun. The line of flares broke formation and began to hurry past us in the mist.

Johnny whispered to me as if we might have been overheard, whispered with cupped hands.

"We better get out by the hangar and into the lane."

We ran away in the lee of the hangar, silent and awed. Smoke was drifting past the dark end and there was a smell in the wet air. A big fire was glowing and pulsing on the windward side of the hangar. As we rounded the end and made a bolt for the road a man appeared from nowhere. He was tall and hatless and smeared with black. He shouted:

"You kids shove off! If I catch you here again I'll put the police on you."

So then, for a time, Johnny avoided the airfield.

The other hill where I live now had the general's house on it. He was one of the Planks, he shot big game and his

41

wife opened bazaars. His family owned the brewery by the canal and you could not tell where the gasworks began and the brewery ended. But this was an entrancing piece of canal, dirty and coloured and enlivened by the pipes of hot water that discharged there continually. Sometimes barges lay up under the greasy wall and once we even got aboard one and hid under the tarpaulin. But we were chased out of there, too, and that was the first time we ever climbed the streets to the other hill. We ran all the way because the bargee was a giant and disliked children. We were excited by the exploit and trapped into another one by our exhilaration. We reached the wall of the general's garden in the late evening. As soon as we got our breath back Johnny danced on the pavement. No one could catch us. We were too quick for them. Not even the general could catch us.

"You wouldn't go in!"

Johnny would.

Now this was not so daring a vaunt as it appeared. Nobody could get into the general's garden because there was a very high wall all round; and this combined with his reputation for shooting lions had started the rumour that wild animals roamed those secluded acres—a rumour which we believed, in order to make life a little more exciting.

Johnny would. What was more—secure in the knowledge of the unclimbable wall—he would look for a way in. So off we padded along the road, excited by our daring, to look for a hole which was not there. We went along by the gatehouse to the corner, passed down the southeast side and round to the back. Everywhere the brick wall was impenetrable and the trees looked over. But then we stopped, without saying anything. There was really nothing to say. Thirty yards of the wall was down, fallen inward among the trees, the gap darkling and shaped like a lower lip. Someone knew about the gap. There was a gesture of chicken wire along the lower edge, but nothing that could keep determined climbers out.

Now it was my turn to be excited.

"You said you would, Johnny——"

"And you're coming, too."

"I didn't say I would!"

We could hardly see each other under the trees. I followed him and near the wall, shrubs and creepers grew thick and apparently unvisited.

I smelt lion. I said so to Johnny so that we held our breath and listened to our hearts beating until we heard something else. The something was far worse than a lion. When we looked back we could see him in the gap, his dome-shaped helmet, the top half of his dark uniform as he bent to examine the disarranged netting. Without a word spoken we made our choice. Noiselessly as rabbits in a hedge we stole forward away from the policeman and towards the lions.

That was a jungle and the land inside the walls was a whole country. We came to a part where there were furrows and small glass boxes in rows on the ground and there we saw another man, working in the door of a shed; so we nipped away again into shrubs.

A dog barked.

We peered at each other in the dull light. This was far more than an adventure.

Johnny muttered:

"How we going to get out, Sam?"

In a moment or two we were recriminating and crying

43

together. Coppers, men, dogs—we were surrounded.

There was a wide lawn in front of us with the back of the house running along the other side. Some of the windows were lighted. There was a terrace below the windows because as we watched we saw a dark figure pace along by them in ritual solemnity, and carrying a tray. Somehow this dignity was even more terrifying than the thought of lions.

"How we going to get out? I want to go home!"

"Keep quiet, Sam, and follow me."

We crept away round the edge of the lawn. The tall windows let long swathes of light lie across the grass and each time we came to one of these we had to duck into the bushes again. Our nerve began to come back. Neither the lions nor the policeman had spotted us. We found a dark corner by a white statue and lay still.

Slowly the noises of people died down and our tremors died away with them so that the lions were forgotten. The high parapet of the house began to shine, a full moon lugged herself over the top and immediately the gardens were translated. There was a silver wink from a pool nearer the house, cypresses, tall and hugely still, turned one frosted side to her light. I looked at Johnny and his face was visible and bland. Nothing could hurt us or would hurt us. We stood up and began to wander without saying anything. Sometimes we were waist-deep in darkness and then again drowned and then out in full light. Statues meditated against black deepnesses of evergreen and corners of the garden were swept by dashes of flowering trees that at that month were flowering nowhere else. There was a walk with stone railings on our right and a succession of stone jars with stone flowers draped round

44

them. This was better than the park because forbidden and dangerous; better than the park because of the moon and the silence; better because of the magic house, the lighted windows and the figure pacing by them. This was a sort of home.

There was a burst of laughter from the house and the dog howled. I spoke again mechanically.

"I want to go home."

What was the secret of the strange peace and security we felt? Now if I invent I can see us from outside, starry-eyed ragamuffins, I with nothing but shirt and trousers, Johnny with not much more, wandering together through the gardens of the great house. But I never saw us from outside. To me, then, we remain these two points of perception, wandering in paradise. I can only guess our innocence, not experience it. If I feel a kindly goodwill towards the ragamuffins, it is towards two unknown people. We went slowly towards the trees where the wall had broken down. I think we had a kind of faith that the policeman would be gone and that nothing would embarrass us. Once, we came to a white path and found too late that it was new, unset concrete where we slid; but we broke nothing else in the whole garden—we took nothing, almost we touched nothing. We were eyes.

Before we buried ourselves in undergrowth again, I turned to look back. I can remember this. We were in the upper part of the garden, looking back and down. The moon was flowering. She had a kind of sanctuary of light round her, sapphire. All the garden was black and white. There was one tree between me and the lawns, the stillest tree that ever grew, a tree that grew when no one was looking. The trunk was huge and each branch

45

splayed up to a given level; and there, the black leaves floated out like a level of oil on water. Level after horizontal level these leaves cut across the splaying branches and there was a crumpled, silver-paper depth, an ivory quiet beyond them. Later, I should have called the tree a cedar and passed on, but then, it was an apocalypse.

"Sammy! He's gone."

Johnny had undone the chicken wire and poked out his heroic head. The road was deserted. We became small savages again. We nipped through and dropped down on the pavement. We left the wall to be rebuilt and the tree to grow, unseen of us, in the garden.

I see now what I am looking for and why these pictures are not altogether random. I describe them because they seem to be important. They contributed very little to the straight line of my story. If we had been caught—as later I was indeed caught—and taken by the ear to the general, he might have set in motion some act that changed my whole life or Johnny's. But they are not important in that way. They are important simply because they emerge. I am the sum of them. I carry round with me this load of memories. Man is not an instantaneous creature, nothing but a physical body and the reaction of the moment. He is an incredible bundle of miscellaneous memories and feelings, of fossils and coral growths. I am not a man who was a boy looking at a tree. I am a man who remembers being a boy looking at a tree. It is the difference between time, the endless row of dead bricks, and time, the retake and coil. And there is something even more simple. I can love the child in the garden, on the airfield, in Rotten Row, the tough little boy at school because he is not I. He is another person. If he had murdered, I should feel no

46

guilt, not even responsibility. But then what am I looking for? I am looking for the beginning of responsibility, the beginning of darkness, the point where I began.

Philip Arnold was the other side of our masculine triangle. How shall I describe Philip? We had moved on from the infants' school. We were boys in a boys' school, elementary school, windy and asphalt. I was tough, sturdy, hard, full of zest. There is a gap between the pictures of Sammy Mountjoy with Evie and Sam Mountjoy with Johnny and Philip. One was a baby and the other a boy; but the steps have vanished. They are two different people. Philip was from outside, from the villas. He was pale, physically an extreme coward and he seemed to us to have a mind like a damp box of matches. Yet neither the general nor the god on the airfield, nor Johnny Spragg, nor Evie nor even Ma, altered my life as Philip altered it.

We thought him wet and violence petrified him. That made him a natural target for if you wanted something to hurt, Philip was always to hand. This was sufficient for the odd kick, or scragging; but anything more elaborate required careful preparation and Philip found a simple way of avoiding this. To begin with, he could run very fast; and when he was frightened he could run faster than anyone else. Sometimes, of course, we cornered him; and he evolved a technique for dealing with this, too. He would cower without fighting back. Perhaps it was an instinct rather than an invention, but a very effective one. If you find no resistance you do not become suddenly one with your victim; but after a time you become bored. Philip crouched like a rabbit under a hawk. He looked like a rabbit. Then, as he said nothing, but jerked about under

47

the blows that fell on him, the savour went out of the game. The scurrying victim had become a sack, dull and uninteresting. Without knowing that he was a political philosopher, Philip achieved the end to be desired. He turned the other cheek and we wandered away to find a sport with more savour.

I am anxious that you should not make too simple, too sympathetic a figure out of Philip. Perhaps he sounds like the hero of one of those books which kept turning up in the twenties. Those heroes were bad at games, unhappy and misunderstood at school—tragic, in fact, until they reached eighteen or nineteen and published a stunning book of poems or took to interior decoration. Not so. We were the bullies but Philip was not a simple hero. He loved fighting when anyone else was being hurt. If Johnny and I were fighting, Philip would come running and dance about, flapping his hands. When there was a heaving pile in the playground, our pale, timid Philip would be moving round the outside, giggling and kicking the tenderest piece he could reach. He liked to inflict pain and a catastrophe was his orgasm. There was a dangerous corner leading to the high street; and in a freeze-up, Philip would spend all his spare time on the pavement there, hoping to see a crash. When you see two or three young men on a street corner, or at a country cross-road, at least one of them is waiting for just this. We are a sporting nation.

Philip was—is—not a type. He is a most curious and complicated person. We said he was wet and we held him in contempt; but he was far more dangerous than any of us. I was a prince and Johnny was a prince. We had rival gangs and the issue of battle always hung in doubt be-

48

tween us. I think with rueful amusement of those two barbaric chieftains, so innocent and simple, who dismissed Philip as a wet. Philip is a living example of natural selection. He was as fitted to survive in this modern world as a tapeworm in an intestine. I was a prince and so was Johnny. Philip debated with himself and chose me. I thought he had become my henchman but really he was my Machiavelli. With infinite care and a hysterical providence for his own safety, Philip became my shadow. Living near the toughest of the lot he was protected. Since he was so close, I could not run after him and my hunting reflexes were not triggered off. Timorous, cruel, needing company yet fearing it, weak of flesh yet fleet of fear, clever, complex, never a child—he was my burden, my ape, my flatterer. He was, perhaps, to me, something of what I had been to Evie. He listened and pretended to believe. I was not quite the fantasist that Evie was; my stories were excess of life, not compensation. Secret societies, exploration, detectives, Sexton Blake—"with a roar the huge car leapt forward"—he pretended to believe them all and wove himself nearer and round me. The fists and the glory were mine; but I was his fool, his clay. He might be bad at fighting but he knew something that none of the rest of us knew. He knew about people.

There was the business of the fagcards. We all collected them as a matter of course. I had no dad to pass them on to me and Ma smoked some awful cheap brand that relied on the poverty of its clients rather than advertisement. No one who could have afforded anything better would have been content to smoke them. This is the only feeling of inferiority I can trace right back to the Row but it was strictly limited; not that I had no dad, but just that I had no fagcards. I should have felt the same if my parents had been married non-smokers. I had to rely on pestering men in the streets.

"Got a fagcard, mister?"

I liked fagcards; and for some reason or other my favourites were a series of the kings of Egypt. The austere and proud faces were what I felt people should be. Or do I elaborate out of my adult hind-sight? The most I can be certain of is that I liked the kings of Egypt, they satisfied me. Anything more is surely an adult interpretation. But those fagcards were very precious to me. I begged for them, bargained for them, fought for them—thus combining business with pleasure. But soon no one with any sense would fight me for fagcards because I always won.

Philip commiserated, rubbed in my poverty; pointed out the agony of my choice—never to have any more kings of Egypt or else exchange those I had for others and thus lose the first ones for good. I toughed Philip up mechanically for insolence but knew he was right. The kings of Egypt were out of my reach.

Now Philip took the second step. Some of the smaller boys had fagcards which were wasted on them. What a shame it was to see them crumpling kings of Egypt they were unable to appreciate!

I remember Philip pausing and my sudden sense of privacy and furtive quiet. I cut right through his other steps.

"How we going to get 'em?"

Philip went with me. Immediately I had jumped to the crux, he adapted himself to my position without further comment. He was elastic in such matters. All we—he said we, I remember that clearly—all we had to do was to waylay them in some quiet spot. We should then remove the more precious cards which were of no use to them. We needed a quiet place. The lavatory before school or after school—not in break time, he explained. Then the place would be crowded. He himself would stand in the middle of the playground and give me warning if the master or mistress on duty came too near. As for the treasure, for now the cards had become treasure, and we, pirates, the treasure should be divided. I could keep all the kings of Egypt and he would take the rest.

This scheme brought me one king of Egypt and Philip about twenty assorted cards. It did not operate long and was never really satisfactory. I waited in the smelly shed, idly looking at the graffiti of our more literate members, graffiti rendered more conspicuous by their careful deletion. I would wait in the creosoted quiet as the cisterns filled automatically and discharged—filled and discharged all day and night, whether they had customers or not. If a small victim appeared, I did not mind twisting his arm, but I disliked taking his fagcards. And Philip had miscalculated, though I am sure he profited by the lesson. The situation was never as simple as we had envisaged. Some of the older boys got to know and wanted to share the loot, which gave me more but unprofitable fights and some of them actually objected to the whole business. Then the supply of small boys dried up and only a day or two went by before I found myself being interviewed by the head teacher. A small boy had been found being excused behind a brick buttress by the boiler-shed. Another had wetted himself handsomely in class, burst into tears and sobbed that he was frightened to be excused because of the big boy. The ordinary course of their instruction was immediately interrupted. Soon there was a file of little boys outside the head teacher's room all waiting to give evidence. The fingers pointed straight at Sammy Mountjoy.

This was a humane and enlightened school. Why punish a boy if you can make him conscious of his guilt? The head teacher explained carefully the cruelty and dishonesty of my actions. He did not ask me whether I had done it or no, for he would not give me a chance to lie. He traced the connection between my passion for the kings of Egypt and the size of the temptation that had overcome me. He knew nothing about Philip and found out nothing.

"It's really because you like pictures, eh, Sammy? Only you mustn't get them that way. Draw them. You'd better give back as many as you can. And—here. You can have these."

He gave me three kings of Egypt. I believe he had gone to great trouble over those fagcards. He was a kindly, careful and conscientious man who never came within a mile of understanding his children. He let the cane stay in the corner and my guilt stay on my back.

Is this the point I am looking for?
No.
Not here.

But that was not the profoundest thing that Philip achieved for me. His next was a masterpiece of passion. It was, I suppose, a clumsier exhibition, a botched job from his prentice hand. It reveals Philip to me as a person in three D, as more than a cutout. Like the appearing ice, a point above water, it gives evidence of great depths in Philip. He has always had much in common with an iceberg. He is still pale, still involved and subtle, still dangerous to shipping. He avoided me for a time after the fag-card case. As for me, I fought more than ever; and I do not think it an adult wisdom to say that now I fought with a more furious desire to compel and hurt. At this time I had my greatest hour with Johnny. Out of an obscure and ungovernable rage against something indefinable, I went for the only thing I knew would not flinch at a battering—Johnny's face. But when I hit his nose he tripped and cut his head open on the corner of the school building. So then his ma came and saw the head teacher—Johnny was most anxious that I should understand he had asked her not to—and I was in trouble again. I can still sense my feelings of defiance and isolation; a man against society. For the first, but not the last time I was avoided. The head teacher thought a period in Coventry would show me the value of social contact and persuade me to stop using people as a punchball.

During this period Philip slid alongside again. He assured me of his friendship and we quickly became intimate because he was the only friend I had. Johnny always had a great respect for authority. If the head teacher said no talk, then Johnny was mum. Johnny was adventurous but dared an authority he respected. Philip had no respect for authority, but caution rather. So he quickly slid alongside again. Perhaps among the teachers he may even have built up a little credit as a faithful friend. Who knows? Certainly I was grateful.

As I piece together and judge our relationship during those few weeks I am overcome with astonishment. Can it be possible? Was he so clever so early? Was he even then so cowardly, so dangerous, so elaborate?

When he had got me fast to him Philip led the conversation round to religion. This was unbroken ground for me. If I were baptized now the baptism would have to be conditional. I slipped through the net. But Philip was C. of E.; and what was unusual in those days, his parents were strict and devout. I explored the fringes of this incredible situation by report, understanding very little. We had prayers and a hymn at school, but all I remember of them is the march which got us back to our rooms and the occasion when Minnie showed us the difference between a human being and an animal. We were visited once or twice by a parson but nothing happened. True; I liked what we heard of the Bible. I accepted everything within the limits of a lesson. I should have fallen into the hands of any denomination that made the gesture like a plum.

But Philip, even at that raw age, had begun to watch his parents objectively and had come to certain conclusions. He could not quite take the plunge but he hesitated on the verge of thinking the whole thing daft. Yet not quite. The trouble was the curate. Philip had to go to some class or other—were they confirmation classes or was he not far too young? The rector had nothing to do with this class. He was a strange, lonely old man. He was rumoured to be writing a book and he lived in the vast rectory with a housekeeper almost as old as he.

How had religion touched us so far? I was neutral and Philip tormented. Perhaps Johnny Spragg had the best of it with his unthinking acceptance and untroubled mind. He knew where he was with Miss Massey who ensured that we knew what we ought to know. And you knew where you were with her—scared out of your wits and struck by lightning if your attention wandered. She was fair but fierce. She was a thin, grey-haired woman, in complete control of everything. We were having a lesson with her one day on a fine afternoon with piles of white clouds and blue sky outside the window. We were watching Miss Massey because no one dared to do anything else—all of us except Johnny. His ruling passion had caught up with him. The Moth had appeared among the clouds, climbing, looping, spinning and threading the high valleys over Kent. Johnny was up there, too. He was flying. I knew what was going to happen and I made cautious attempts to warn him; but the whistle of the wind in the wires and the smooth roar of the engine drowned out my whisper. We knew that Miss Massey had noticed because of an additional awe in the atmosphere. She went on speaking as if nothing out of the way was happening. Johnny spun.

She finished her story.

"Now do you remember why I told you those three little stories? What do they show us, children? Could you tell us, Philip Arnold?"

"Yes, miss."

"Jenny?"

"Yes, miss."

"Sammy Mountjoy? Susan? Margaret? Ronald Wakes?"

"Miss. Miss. Miss. Miss."

But Johnny was diving for a loop. He was sitting, building up under his seat the power that would swing him into his sky. He was helmeted, assured, delicate at the rudder-bar and joystick in the fish-'n-chip smell of the engine oil and great wind. He pulled the joystick back slowly, a huge hand thrust him up and he rolled off the top of the loop while the irrelevant dark earth reeled sideways as easy as a shadow.

"Johnny Spragg!"

Johnny made a crash landing.

"Come here."

He clattered out of his desk for the pay off. Flying was always expensive—three pounds dual and thirty shillings solo, for an hour of it.

"Why did I tell you those three stories?"

Johnny's hands were behind his back, his chin on his chest.

"Look at me when I speak to you."

The chin lifted, ever so slightly.

"Why did I tell you those three stories?"

We could just hear his muttered answer. The Moth had flown away.

"Idunnomiss."

Miss Massey hit him on both sides of the head, precisely with either hand, a word and a blow.

"God——"

Smack!

"—is——"

Smack!

"—love!"

Smack! Smack! Smack!

You knew where you were with Miss Massey.

So religion, if disorganized, had entered our several lives. I think Johnny and I accepted it as an inevitable part of an enigmatic situation which was quite beyond our control. But we had not met Philip's curate.

He was pale, intense, sincere and holy. The rector had withdrawn from a multitude of fears and disappointments into secluded eccentricity; and more and more of the church work fell into the hands of Father Anselm. He enthralled and frightened his little pitchers. He adjusted his discourse to their level. He got Philip. He slipped past his guard and menaced his knowledge of people, his selfishness. He took them to the high altar and made them kneel. He was not emotional, no Welsh hwyll for him. He made everything concrete. He showed them the cup. He talked about the *Queen Mary* or some other great work then a-building. He talked about wealth. He held out the silver cup. Have you a sixpence, children, a silver sixpence?

He bowed the cup towards them. Look, children; that is what they think, the kings of Egypt. The cup is lined with pure gold.

Philip was torn down to the soles of his feet. So there was something in it after all. They treated the reality of this subject with the same practical reverence as they treated anything else. They gave it gold. In his clever, tortuous mind, religion swam up out of deceit and gooseberry bush into awful power. The curate would not let him be. Having knocked him down with the cup he finished him off with the altar.

You cannot see it, dear children; but the Power that made the universe and holds you up, lives there. Mercifully you cannot see it as Moses could not see though he asked to. If the veils were lifted from your eyes you would be blasted and destroyed. Let us pray, meekly kneeling on our knees.

You may go now, dear children. Take with you the thought of that Power, uplifting, comforting, loving and punishing, a care for you that will not falter, an eye that never sleeps.

Philip walked away on riven feet. He could not tell me what the matter was but I know now. If what they said was true, and not just another bit of parental guff then what future was there for Philip? What of the schemes, the diplomacy? What of the careful manipulations of other people? Suppose there was indeed another scale of values in which the means were not wholly justified by the results? Philip could not express this. But he could convey his urgent, his desperate desire to know. Gold has never been a metal to me but a symbol. I picked it delightedly out of school, myrrh and fine gold, a golden calf—what a pity they had to grind it to powder!—golden fleece, Goldilocks, Goldilocks let down, golden apple O golden apple, they irradiated my mind's eye and I saw nothing in Philip's cup but another bit of myths and legend. But I was isolated now and in Coventry. It was for this reason that Philip had slid alongside again. With that dreadful perspicacity of his he had assessed my loneliness and resentment, my braggadocio. He knew, even then, the right man and the right moment for a job.

Because how could you test the truth of what Father Anselm said? The only way, surely, was the method used with an unlighted house. I was to ring the bell and run away. Philip would be stationed where he could watch and judge by the ensuing reaction whether anyone was at home or not. I was to be manœuvred into that position, using as a lever my isolation and the excesses of my character. He got me grateful first. Here we were, walking together by the canal. He had talked to me in break when the master on duty was not looking. He was my only true friend. Not that I cared about them of course, did I? No. I cared for nobody like the Miller and I would break the head teacher's window as like as not, just to show.

"Bet you wouldn't."

"Would."

"Wouldn't."

I'd break a policeman's window, see?

Philip introduced the subject of the church. It was autumn and growing dusky. It was the right hour for a desperate deed.

No, not the window, said Philip; but he bet and he bet. So we moved by dare and vaunt and dare and vaunt until I was where he wanted me. Before the light had drained down and the dusk turned to darkness—I might lick every boy in the school but not this, I wouldn't, I wouldn't dare—honest, Sammy, you better not! and giggling, appalled and flapping his hands at awed promise of an accident——

"I would, then, see? I'd piss on it."

Giggle flap tremor, heart-thud.

And so by dare upon dare in the autumn streets I found myself at last engaged to defile the high altar. O streets, cold with copper smoke and brazen noise, with brown profile of warehouse and gasworks glory be for you under the eternal sky. Glory be for the biggest warehouse of all, huddled away from the shining canal among trees and bones.

Philip led the way with his dance and flap and I followed in the net. I was not cold particularly but my teeth had a tendency to shake in my mouth if I did not clench them. I had to cry to Philip to wait a bit under the bridge over the canal and I made concentric, spreading circles in the water and a speck of foam. He ran ahead and came back like a puppy, for all the world as if I were the master.

As we went, I found that something seemed to be wrong with my guts and I had to stop again in a dark alley. But Philip danced round me, his white knees gleaming in the dusk. I wouldn't, he bet.

We came to the stone wall, the lych-gate, the glooming yews. I stopped again and used the wall that the dogs used and then Philip clicked the latch and we were through. He went on tiptoe and I followed with strange shapes of darkness expanding before my eyes. The stones were tall about us and when Philip lifted a longer latch in the yawning porch it sounded like a castle gate. I crouched in after him, hand out to feel him in this thicker darkness but still we were not inside. There was another door, soft-covered; and when Philip pushed, it spoke to us.

Wuff.

I followed still, Philip let me through. I did not know the drill and the released door spoke again behind us.

Wubb wuff!

There were miles of church—first a sense of a world of hollowed stone, all shadow, all guessed-at glossy rect-angles dim as an after-image, sudden, startling figures near at hand. I was nothing but singing teeth and jumping skin and hair that crawled without orders. Philip was as bad. His need must have been deep indeed. I could see nothing of him but hands and face and knees. His face was close to mine. We had a fierce and insane argument under the shadow of the inner door with Prayer Books piled on a table at shoulder height.

"It's too dark, I tell you! I can't see!"

"You're a coward then, you can just talk that's all——"

"It's too dark!"

We even struggled there, unhandily, I made impotent

60

by his unpredictable female strength. And then it was not too dark. The distances were visible. I cannoned into something wooden with green lights revolving round me; then saw a path stretching and guessed rather than knew that this was the way on. Blasts of hot air blew up my legs from metal grilles in the ground. At the end of the path a clutch of dully shining rectangles went careering away up into the sky and below them there was a great shape. There was a light by the altar jazzing as if a maniac were holding it. Silence began to sound, to fill with a high, nightmare note. There were steps to mount and then a blankness of cloth with a line of white at the top. I ran back to Philip, pattering through the blasts of hot air from the grilles in the floor. We argued and tussled again. The awe of the place was on me; even on my speech.

"But I been three times, Phil—don't you see? I can't pee any more!"

Philip raged at me out of the darkness, raged weakly, vilely, cleverly—my brother.

"All right then. I can't pee. But I can spit."

I went back through the hot air and a brass eagle ignored me. Though evening had come on there was more light rather than less—enough to show high fences of carved oak on either hand, a carpet, a pattern of black and grey in the stone floor. I stood as near as I dared to the bottom step; but now my mouth was dry, too. I was involutely thankful for that dry mouth. I snatched wildly and legalistically at the hope of another misfire.

Leaning forward, the green lights swimming round me, I made my motions loud so that Philip should hear them.

"Ptah! Ptah! Ptah!"

The universe exploded from the right-hand side. My

right ear roared. There were rockets, cascades of light, catherine-wheels; and I was fumbling round on stone. A bright light shone down on me from a single eye.

"You little devil!"

I tried mechanically to get my body on its feet but they slithered under me and I fell down again before the angry eye. Through the singing and roaring I heard only one natural noise.

Wubb. Wuff.

I was being hauled across the stone floor and the eye was dancing a beam of light over carved wood, books and glittering cloth. The verger held me all the way and as soon as he had me in the vestry he switched on a light. It was a fair cop. But I could manage neither the insolence nor the stoicism of Black Hand when unmasked by Sexton Blake and Tinker. The floor and the ceiling could not decide between them on up and down. The verger had me cornered literally in an angle and when he let me go I slid all the way down the wall and was a boneless heap. Life had suddenly rearranged itself. On one side of my head life was bigger and more portentous than on the other. The sky, with stars of infinite velocity and remote noise that patterned their travel had opened into me on the right. Infinity, darkness and space had invaded my island. What remained of normal inspected a light, a wooden box, white cloaks hanging up and a brass cross—looked through an arch, and saw that it was lighted now. This world of terror and lightning was only a church being prepared for an evening service. I did not look at the verger, cannot remember at that time what sort of face he had, saw only black trousers and shiny shoes—for at any moment I might have dropped off the floor and broken my bones on the ceiling by the single electric light. A lady appeared in the arch, a grey lady carrying a sheaf of flowers and the verger talked a lot, calling her madam. They talked about me and by that time I was sitting on a low stool, inspecting the lady in one direction and the universe in the other through the hole that had been blown in the side of my head. The verger said I was another of them. What was he going to do? He had to have help, that was what it had come to and the church must be kept locked. The grey lady looked down at me across whole continents and oceans and told him that the rector must decide. So the verger opened another door and led me through into darkness on gravel. He was talking down to me, I deserved the birch and if he had his way I should get it—boys! They were young devils and getting worse every day, like the world and where it would end he didn't know and no one else seemed to, either. The gravel felt as if it had been ploughed and my feet were unclever. I said nothing but tried to get along without tumbling over. Then I found the verger was holding my hand instead of my ear and soon after that he was bending sideways with his hand under my elbow and the other somewhere round my waist. He talked all the time. We came to another door and another grey lady who opened it but carried no flowers and the verger was still talking. We went up some stairs and crossed a landing to a big door. This was a bog because I could hear someone straining inside.

"Ooh! Aah-ooh!"

The verger tapped on the door and inside someone scrambled to his feet.

"Come in then, come in! What is it?"

We went through into a dark room over limitless carpet. There was a parson standing in the middle. He was so tall that he seemed to me to ascend into the shadows that surrounded and roofed everything. I looked at what I could with a strange lack of fear or interest. The nearest thing to me was a section of the parson's trousers. They were sharply creased except at the knees just below my face where the cloth was rounded and shone like black glass. Once more two people argued above me and my attention, in terms which meant nothing to me and which I have forgotten. I was more concerned with and puzzled by my tendency to lurch sideways; and I thought I would like to kneel down, not because of the parson but because if I rolled into a ball there might be no need to wonder so absurdly about which way was up. All I knew was that the parson was refusing to do something and that the verger was pleading with him.

Then the parson spoke loudly and as I now think, with a kind of despair.

"Very well, Jenner. Very well. If I must be invaded—"

I was alone with him. He moved away, sat down in a mother-shaped chair by the dead fire.

"Come here."

I moved my feet carefully over the carpet and stood by the arm of the chair. He bent his head, beyond the length of black thigh, looked searchingly into my face, examined me carefully from head to foot. He came back at last to my face.

He spoke slowly, absently.

"You'd be a pretty child if you kept yourself clean."

He gripped the arms of the chair deep and a goose walked over his grave. I saw that he was straining away

64

from me and I looked down in sudden shame for the girl's word "pretty" and for my so obviously distasteful dirt. We fell into a long silence while I saw that his narrow shoes were turned in towards each other. And on the right-hand side the universe was still roaring and full of stars.

"Who told you to do it?"

That was Philip, of course.

"A little boy like you couldn't have an idea like that without someone suggesting it."

Poor man. I glanced up and then down again, I inspected the enormous explanation, saw it was beyond me and gave up.

"Now tell me the name of the man who told you to do it and I'll let you go."

But there was no man. There was only Philip Arnold and Sammy Mountjoy.

"Why did you do it then?"

Because. Because.

"But you *must* know!"

Of course I knew. I had a picture in my mind of the whole transaction that had led me into this position—I saw it in elaborate detail. I did it because that other parson who talked to Philip had made it seem possible that the church contained more excitement and adventure than the pictures; because I was an outcast and needed something to hurt and break just to show them; because a boy who has hit Johnny Spragg so hard that his mum complained to the head teacher has a position to keep up; because, finally, among the singing stars, I'd been, three times and couldn't pee any more. I knew so many things. I knew I should be interrogated with terrible, adult patience. I knew I should never grow up to be as tall and majestic, knew that he had never been a child, knew we were different creations each in our appointed and changeless place. I knew that the questions would be right and pointless and unanswerable because asked out of the wrong world. They would be righteous and kingly and impossible from behind the high wall. Intuitively I knew this, that the questions would be like trying to lift water in a sieve or catch a shadow by the hand: and this intuition is one of the utter sorrows of childhood.

"Now then. Who told you to do it?"

For of course, when the glamour is gone, the phantom enemies, the pirates and highwaymen, robbers, cowboys, good men and bad, we are faced by the brute thing; the adult voice and four real walls. That is where the policemen and probation officers, teachers and parents achieve the breakdown of our integrated simplicity. The hero is overthrown, remains whimpering and defenceless, a nothing.

How long should I have lasted? Should I have lived up to Tinker? He was frequently threatened with some elaborate form of extinction if he refused to tell. But I was saved at that time from any suspicion of my own inadequacy; for suddenly I wanted to go home and lie down; and then even going home seemed an impossible exertion. The universe bored into my head, the milky way swam past, the green lights of the singing stars expanded and were everything that was.

My memories of that time are confused as mountainous country in misty weather. Did I walk home? How could I? But if I was carried, what arms held me? I must have reached Rotten Row somehow. I went to school next day as usual, I remember that clearly. Perhaps I was not quite as usual. I seem to remember feeling as if I had been drizzled on for a long time and had reached the crisis of whimpering; but there was no rain. There was warmth instead on my right side and a deep throbbing in my right ear. How many days? How many hours? Then, at the end, I was sitting in a classroom and it must have been late afternoon because both the naked lights on their long flexes were switched on. I was tired of the throbbing, tired of school, tired of everything, wanted to lie down. I looked at the paper in front of me and I could not think what I had to write. I heard whispering and knew without understanding, that I was the centre of excitement and awe. A boy in front of me and to the left had his coat pulled and looked round. There was more whispering so that the master moved at his desk. Then Johnny Spragg who was sitting to the right of me got out of his seat and put up his hand.

"Please, sir! Sammy's crying."

Ma and Mrs. Donavan knew about earache. There were rituals to be performed. For a while I was an object of interest to all the women in the row. They would gather and nod and look down at me. It comes to me now with faint surprise that we never used our upstairs after the lodger died in it. Perhaps Ma was hoping for another lodger; or perhaps her neglect of the bare room was a symptom of her decline. We had lived and slept downstairs, just as if he were still ticking and fuffing above the whitewashed boards; so I had my earache near the stove which was as comfortable a place as any. Ma kept up a good fire in the centre hole. The lady with the green leathery plant brought in a bucket of coal and some advice. They gave me bitter white pills to swallow, aspirin perhaps; but the universe kept boring in, bringing the earache with it. Things became more than lifesize. I kept trying to get away from the pain but it went with me. Ma and Mrs. Donavan took council with the plant lady and they decided to iron me. Mrs. Donavan brought an iron —perhaps Ma always borrowed?—and it was black, with a piece of brown cloth round the handle. It was really iron too, deeply pitted with rust, and only shiny on the bottom part. The plant lady put a piece of cloth over the side of my head while Ma set the iron on the fire. When she took it off she spat on the shiny side and I saw the little balls of spit dance, dwindle and vanish. She sat by me and ironed the side of my head through the cloth and the plant lady held my hand. Then while I was still accepting the warmth with good faith and hoping the pain would go away, the door opened and the tall parson bowed himself through. Ma took away the cloth and the iron and got up. The pain was worse if anything so that I began to turn on this side and then on that and then lie on my face; and every time I happened to see the tall parson he was still standing in the door with his mouth open. Perhaps they moved and spoke, but I have no memory of it. To my hindsight they seem motionless as a ring of stones. Just then the pain began to knock on the door where I was, my own private, inviolable centre so that I made noises and flung myself about. The parson disappeared and at some remove, over gulfs of fire and oceans of blackness under wild green stars there was a big man in the room who was fighting me, binding me, getting my arms in a hold, fastening me down with terrible strength and saying the same thing over and over again.

"Just the tiniest little prick."

Behind my right ear there is a new moon of scar and a pucker. They are so old that they feel natural and right. I got them that same day, or at least, before the next morning. There was no penicillin, no wonder-drug to control and reduce infection in those days. If the doctor had any doubt at all he operated for mastoid straight away. I came round in a new place, a new world. I was lying over a bowl, too sick and faint to notice anything else but the bowl, whiteness and a brown, polished floor. The pain was reduced to the same dull throbbing that had made me cry at school; but now even crying was too much effort. I lay, drugged and miserable with a turban of gauze and cotton-wool and bandages round my head. Ma appeared at some time or other in that period. I saw her then for the first and last time, not as the broad figure blotting out the darkness but as a person. There is a wan sanity about the drugged eye sometimes that the healthy one does not have. In my misery I saw her as a stranger might see her, a massive, sagging creature, mottled and dirty. Her hair was in wisps over her brown forehead, her face was a square-ish, drawn-down mass with a minute fag sticking in one corner of her mouth. I see now the sausage hands, brown, with discolorations of red and blue, clutching the string-bag into her lap. She sat as she always sat, in majestic indifference; but the gas was escaping from the balloon. She had little enough to bring me, for what has a woman to spare who even borrows an iron? Yet she had taken thought and found what she could. There was a pedestal by the head of the bed and she had placed there a handful of rather dirty fagcards—my cherished kings of Egypt.

And still I ask myself: "Well. There?" and myself answers: "No. Not there." He is no more a part of me than any other child. I simply have better access to him. I cannot remember what he looked like. I doubt if I ever knew. He is still this bubble floating, filled with happiness or pain which I can no longer feel. In my mind those feelings are represented by colours; they are as exterior to what I feel, as the child itself. His insufficiency and guilt were not mine. I have my own which sprang out of my life somewhere like weeds. I cannot find the root. However I try I can bring up nothing which is part of me.

The ward was a fine place to be when my head stopped hurting. I got complications, had ups and downs. I was a lifetime in that ward, so that I can switch my mind from the world of Rotten Row to the world of the ward as from planet to planet. I have a sense of timelessness in both places. I cannot remember the doctors or nurses or even the other children at all clearly. Survival in this mode must surely be random or why can I not remember who had the beds to right and left? But there was a little girl who had the bed opposite me. She was tiny and black with tight curls and a round, shining, laughing face. Nobody understood the language she spoke. Now I remember that she had a cot instead of a bed like the older children, because when she stood up at the foot she could hold the top rail and swing up and down. She talked all the time. She laughed and sang, she talked to anyone within reach in her babbling, meaningless talk, talked to doctors, nurses, visitors, matron, children, happily and irrepressibly. She was entirely without fear or sorrow and everybody who saw her loved her. I deduce from the line of bricks that she came, had her graph of sickness, recovered and went. But to me, if I think of the ward, she is always there, a small figure in a white nightdress with two jet black hands and a black, flashing face, swinging and laughing.

I remember the matron, too, because I had a little more to do with her than most of the patients. She was tall and thin. She must have been handsome, in a severe sort of way. Her uniform was dark blue with wings on her head of blinding white. She had stiff, glossy cuffs, small at the wrist but expanding a little up the forearm. When she came into the ward the world stopped turning. We gave the nurses a terrible time; but not matron. She was surrounded by awe. Perhaps the deference of the nurses had something to do with that but as far as I was concerned awe came from her as naturally as comfort from a mother.

She did a job for me.

One of the nurses told me that Ma had been taken poorly which was why she did not come to see me. I accepted this without thought for I was entirely taken up in the endless world of the ward. Somehow my pedestal was as full as the others and the visitors did not seem to belong too particularly to other children. I shared the visitors and everything. Things were so different, so ample, so ordered. One day matron came and sat on my bed instead of standing by it or in front of it. She told me that Ma had died— gone to heaven and was very happy. And then she produced the thing I had been wanting without ever believing it could belong to me; a stamp album and some envelopes of assorted stamps. There were transparent windows in each envelope so that you could see the coloured squares inside. There was a packet of transparent hinges, one side dull, the other shiny with gum. She made me open one of the packets and showed me how to put the hinges on and search through the album for the right country. She must have stayed there a long time because I remember putting in a lot of stamps with great concentration. I am unable to report on sorrow. I cannot even see a colour. All I remember is one vast, vertical sniff because it spilt the bitter liquid in a little glass that matron was holding and she had to send a nurse for another one. So at last I dozed off over my album and when I woke up the ward was the same as it had always been only with another fact added to life—and it seems to me now—already accepted out of a limitless well of acceptance.

I was not entirely without visitors either. The tall parson came to see me and stood, looking down at me helplessly. He brought me a cake from his housekeeper and wandered off, gazing at the ceiling and finding the way out of the door with his shambling feet. The verger came to see me too. He sat anxiously by the bed and tried to talk; but it was so long since he had done anything to children but chase them out of the church if they were noisy that he didn't know how. He was a crumpled little man in daylight, wearing the black clothes of his profession and carrying a black bowler hat. This worried him in the ward and he would put it on the bed and then take it off and try the pedestal and then take the hat back again as if certain that sooner or later he would find the exact spot that was right and proper for a black bowler hat in a hospital. He was used to ritual, perhaps, to an exact science of symbols. He had a high, bald forehead, no eyebrows, and a moustache very like our lodger's in everything but colour. You could see the last wisps of his hair smeared black across the top of his baldness. I was shy of him because he was shy of me and worried. He talked to me as if I were another grown-up so his complicated story eluded me. I could not make out what he meant and only picked up odd bits here and there; and most of these were misunderstandings. There had been trouble with a society, he said, and I inferred a secret society at once. They had had people standing up in the back of the church and shouting during the service. That was bad enough; but the society had gone even further. People—he wouldn't like to name them either, seeing he had no proof and couldn't swear to a single one in a court of law—people had sneaked in during the dark evenings and spoiled ornaments, torn down curtains all because they thought the church was too high. I remembered the sheaf of rectangles soaring dizzily above the altar and thought I understood. The verger said the rector had always been high but in the last few years he had seemed to be getting higher and higher. Then when Father Anselm came, the curate he was, of course, he was just as high as the rector was or even a bit higher—in fact, said the verger, he wouldn't be a bit surprised if one of these days——

But there he broke off, leaving me to wonder mildly how high you could get and what happened when you reached the top. If the curate was as high as the rector then he, too, had his head in shadows when he stood in the middle of the carpet. I ceased to listen when the verger went on. His talk of aumbries, chasubles, images, apparels

73

and thurifers went right over my head. My mind's eye was occupied with a dim church full of elongated clergymen.

Then I realized that he was talking of the time he had heard Philip and me in the church. He never turned the lights on until the last possible minute; if Lady Crosby was waiting for confession, he never turned the lights on until she left. Father Anselm had told him not to. But most evenings he wouldn't anyway. It was the only way he could hope to catch the people from the society. When he heard us he made sure. He got his torch and crept out from the vestry and along the choir stalls. He saw it was only a kid and it made him angry.

I was interested. He was kind to tell me exactly how he had done it, creeping along the choir stalls and then tiptoeing out. He had done a nice bit of work and he had caught me nicely.

He took his bowler hat off the bed and put it on the pedestal. He began to talk urgently. Of course the ear must have been giving trouble but he hadn't known, you see, and they'd had such a time with the society . . .

He paused. He was red. Sallow red. He held out his right hand.

"If I'd known what was going to happen I'd sooner have cut that hand off. I'm sorry, lad, sorrier than I can say."

Something to forgive is a purer joy than geometry. I've found that out since, as a bit of the natural history of living. It is a positive act of healing, a burst of light. It is real and precise as aesthetic enjoyment, not weak or soft but crystalline and strong. It is the sign and seal of adult stature, like that man who reached out both arms and gathered the spears into his own body. But innocence does not recognize an injury and that is why the terrible sayings are true. An injury to the innocent cannot be forgiven because the innocent cannot forgive what they do not understand as an injury. This, too, I understand as a bit of natural history. I guess the nature of our universe is such that the strong and crystalline adult action heals a wound and takes away a scar not out of today but out of the future. The wound that might have gone on bleeding and suppurating becomes healthy flesh; the act is as if it had never been. But how can the innocent understand that?

What was the verger talking to me about then? Was he sorry about the whole story, starting when I and Philip had concocted our plan? But he did not know that story or so I hoped. Was he sorry that little boys are devils, that their brash and violent world would knock down the high walls of authority if it could? As I saw the truth the adult world had hit me good and proper for a deed that I knew consciously was daring and wrong. Hazily and in pictures more than in thought I saw my punishment to have been nicely graded. I had spat though rather drily and inadequately on the high altar. But I had meant to pee on it. My mind flinched away from the possibilities of what might have happened if I had not been three times before we reached the church. Men were hanged but boys got nothing worse than the birch. I saw with a sane and apprecia·tive eye the exact parallel between the deed and the result. Why should I think of forgiveness? There was nothing to forgive.

The verger's hand was still held out. I examined it and him and waited.

At last he sighed, took his bowler off the pedestal and stood up. He cleared his throat.

"Well——"

He turned his hat round and round in his hands, sucked his moustache, blinked. Then he was away, walking quickly and silently on his professional creepers down the centre of the ward and through the double door.

Wubb. Wuff.

When did I discover that the tall parson was now my guardian? I cannot dissect his motives because I never understood him. Was it perhaps the opening of the Bible that decided my fate? Was he touched by me more than I can think? Had the verger any hand in it? Was I an expiation, not of the one blow, but of numberless fossilized uneases and inadequacies, old sins and omissions that had hardened into impenetrable black stone? Or was I only a forbidden fruit, made accessible but still not eaten? Whatever it was, the result did not seem to do him much good, bring him much peace. Other people understood him no more than I did. They always laughed at him behind his back—might have laughed in his face if he had had less care to be solitary and hidden. Even his name was ridiculous. He was Father Watts-Watt. His choirboys used to think it very funny to ask each other: "Do you know what's what?" I wish now I could look back down his story as I can look down my own. He could never have been tough as I was tough. Things must have gone right through him.

So he came fairly often and hung about, trying to talk, trying to find out about me. He would stand, knit his jutting grey eyebrows and swoop a look up under them at the ceiling. All his movements were like that, writhings as though the only source of movement was a sudden pain. There was so much of him, such lengths that you could

76

see the motion travel outwards, bend his body sideways, stretch an arm out and end in the involuntary gesture of a clenched fist. Did I like school? Yes, I liked school. Good —bend, stretch, clench. It was like a nonsense story; talking with him was like a nightmare ride on a giraffe. Yes, bashfully, I liked drawing. Yes, I could swim a bit. Yes, I should like to go to the grammar school, ultimately, whenever that was. Yes, yes, yes, agreement but still no communication. Did I go to church? No, I didn't—at least—Wouldn't I like to go? Yes, I would like to go.

Well—balancing movement, bend stretch clench— good-bye, my dear child, for the time being.

And so the world of the ward must have come to an end.

I have searched like all men for a coherent picture of life and the world, but I cannot write the last word on that ward without giving it my adult testimony. The walls were held up by sheer, careful human compassion. I was on the receiving end and I know. When I make my black pictures, when I inspect chaos, I must remember that such places are as real as Belsen. They, too, exist, they are part of this enigma, this living. They are brick walls like any others, people like any others. But remembered, they shine.

That, then, is all the infant Samuel I can remember. He trailed no clouds of glory. He was spirit and beauty-proof. He was hard as nails and gave better than he got. Yet I should deceive myself if I refused to recognize something special about the period up to mastoid, up to the end of the ward-world. Let me think in pictures again. If I imagine heaven metaphorically dazzled into colours, the pure white light spread out in a cascade richer than a peacock's tail then I see that one of the colours lay over me. I was innocent of guilt, unconscious of innocence; happy, therefore, and unconscious of happiness. Perhaps the full sheaf of colours is never to be experienced by the human being since if he experiences these colours they must lie in the past or on someone else. Perhaps consciousness and the guilt which is unhappiness go together; and heaven is truly the Buddhist Nirvana.

That must be the end of a section. There is no root of infection to be discovered in those pictures. The smell of today, the grey faces that look over my shoulder have nothing to do with the infant Samuel. I acquit him. He is some other person in some other country to whom I have this objective and ghostly access. Why does his violence and wickedness stop there, islanded in pictures? Why should his lies and sensualities, his cruelty and selfishness have been forgiven him? For forgiven him they are. The scar is gone. The smell either inevitable or chosen came later. I am not he. I am a man who goes at will to that show of shadows, sits in judgment as over a strange being. I look for the point where this monstrous world of my present consciousness began and I acquit him in the ward.

Here?

Not here.

And even by the time I was on the bike by the traffic light, I was no longer free. There was a bridge over a skein of railway lines among the smoky huddles of South London and the traffic lights were a new thing there. They sorted the traffic which went north and south beside the lines from the dribble that tried to pick a way round London, east and west. They were so new a thing in those days that an art student like myself could not see them without thinking of ink and wash—ink line for the sudden punch-ball shape, wash for the smokes and glows and the spilt suds of autumn in the sky.

No. I was not entirely free. Almost but not quite. For this part of London was touched by Beatrice. She saw this grime-smothered and embossed bridge, the way buses heaved over its arch must be familiar. One of these streets must be hers, a room in one of these drab houses. I knew the name of the street, Squadron Street; knew, too, that sight of the name, on a metal plaque, or sign-posted might squeeze my heart small again, take away the strength of my knees, shorten my breath. I sat my bike on the downward slope of the bridge, waiting for a green light and the roll down round to the left; and already I had left my freedom behind me. I had allowed myself the unquiet pleasure of picturing her, taken the decisive step of moving toward. I sat, waiting, watching the red light.

There was a large chapel that rose among the houses perhaps a quarter of a mile off in the smoke and the feelings I had thought seared out of me, stirred as if seeds had burst their cases. Make an end and these feelings die at last. But I had not made an end. Sitting there, I could feel all the beginnings of my wide and wild jealousy; jealousy that she was a girl, the most obscure jealousy of all—that she could take lovers and bear children, was smooth, gentle and sweet, that the hair flowered on her head, that she wore silk and scent and powder; jealousy that her French was so good because she had that fortnight in Paris with the others and I was forbidden to go—jealousy of the chapel-deep inexplicable fury with her respectable devotion and that guessed-at sense of communion: jealousy, final and complete of the people who might penetrate her goodwill, her mind, the secret treasures of her body, getting where I if I turned back could never hope to be—I began to scan the men on the pavement, these anonymities who were privileged to live in this land touched by the feet of Beatrice. Any one of them might be he, could be he, might be her landlady's husband or son; landlady's son!

Still the traffic lights said stop. I became aware that the roads were filled with a jam of traffic—so the lights could break down then. We were held up. There was still time to turn round and go away again. A few days and the feelings would sear themselves out. But even as that possibility presented itself I knew that I should not go back; felt myself get off the bike, lift it on the pavement and wheel it under the red light.

Courage. Your clothes are clean if cheap; your hair is cut and combed; your mug if ugly is carefully shaved and slightly scented with a manly scent as in the advertisements. You have even cleaned your shoes.

"I didn't ask to fall in love!"

I found I was fifty yards on, still pushing my bike along the pavement though here the road was free. I was under a huge hoarding which was flourishing beans and red cheeks ten feet in the air. My heart was beating quickly and loud, not because I had seen her or even thought of her, but because in the walk along the pavement I had understood at last the truth of my position. I was lost. I was caught. I could not push my bike back again over the bridge; there was nothing physical to stop me and only the off-chance of seeing Beatrice to push me on. I had cried out aloud, cried out of all the feelings that were bursting their seed-cases. I was trapped again. I had trapped myself.

For to go back is—what? Not only all that has gone before, but also this added: that I had seen her pavements and people, invented an addition in the landlady's son, was far worse off than when I started. Going back would end somewhere—in Australia perhaps, or South Africa— but somewhere it would end in one way only. Somewhere a man would accost me casually.

"Did you ever know a girl called Beatrice Ifor?"

Myself, with reeling heart and straight, painful face:

"A bit. At school——"

"She's——"

She's what? Become a Member of Parliament. Been canonized by the Catholic Church. Is on the hanging committee.

"She's married a chap——"

A chap. She could marry the Prince of Wales. Be queen. Oh God, myself on the pavement. Queen Beatrice, her secret plumbed and known, but not by me——

I was addressing the beans.

81

"Does everyone fall in love like this? Is so much of their love a desperation? Then love is nothing but madness."

And I do not want to hate her. Part of me could kneel down, could say as of Ma and Evie, that if she would only be meward and if she would be by me and for me and for nothing else, I wanted to do nothing but adore her.

Pull yourself together. You know what you want. You decided. Now move towards that consummation step by step.

They were coming out of the training college already, I could see them, fair heads and mousy ones, giggling and laughing in flocks, tinkling their good-byes and waving, so girlish and free, the thin ones, tall ones, dumpy ones, humpy ones, inky ones, slinky ones, gamesy ones and stern ones with glasses on. I was in the gutter, sitting my bike, willing them to die, be raped, bombed or otherwise obliterated because this demanded split-second timing. And, of course, she might not come out at all—might be —what the hell did you do in a girls' training college at half-past four on an autumn afternoon? The crowd was thinning out. If she saw me first so obviously sitting my saddle in the gutter and waiting, the game would be up. Had to be accident, I had to be riding when she saw me; so I pushed off and balanced along with circus slowness, half-hoping now that the crisis was at hand that she would not come out and my misbehaving heart would be able to settle again, wobble wobble heart and bike and she appeared with two others, turned and walked away without seeing me. But I had rehearsed this too often in my bed for my heart and swelling hands to let me down. The whole thing was mechanical, fruit of terrible concentrated thought and repetition. I rode casually, one hand in my pocket and the other on my hip, look no hands, swaying thisway and that. She was past and behind me. Startled I looked back, grabbed the handle-bars, braked and skidded to a stop by the pavement, looked back brazenly as she approached, grinned brazenly in immense surprise——

"Why, if it isn't Beatrice Ifor!"

So they stopped all three while my rehearsed prattle left her no chance of moving off without being rude; and those other two, those blessed damozels, they were in the freemasonry of this sort of meeting and moved on almost immediately, waving back and giggling.

"—was just cycling past—never dreamed—so this is the training college, is it? I come along this road a lot or shall do in the future. Yes a course. I prefer cycling between the other place and the other place—no buses for me. Can't stand 'em. Course in lithography. Were you going back to your digs? No. I'll walk. Can I carry? Are you enjoying it here? Is the work hard? You seem to be thriving on—yes. Look. I was going to have a cup of tea before I ride the rest—how—oh, but you must! One doesn't meet—and after all these months, too! Lyons. Yes. I can leave the bike——"

There was a small round table of imitation marble on three iron legs. She was sitting on the other side. I had her now for whole minutes, islanded out of all the complexities of living. By sheer hard work and calculation I had brought this about. There was much to be achieved in those minutes, things noted down and decided, steps to be taken; she was to be brought—oh, irony! a little nearer to a complete loss of freedom. I heard my voice babbling on, saying its lines, making the suggestions that were too general to be refused, the delicately adjusted assumptions that were to build up into an obligation; I heard my voice consolidating this renewed acquaintance and edging diplomatically a trifle further; but I watched her unpaintable, indescribable face and I wanted to say—you are the most mysterious and beautiful thing in the universe, I want you and your altar and your friends and your thoughts and your world. I am so jealousy-maddened I could kill the air for touching you. Help me. I have gone mad. Have mercy. I want to be you.

The clever, unscrupulous, ridiculous voice murmured on.

When she got up to go, I went with her, talking all the time, talking an attentive, amusing—oh, the calculated stories! pleasant young man into the picture; erasing the other Sammy, so incalculable, insolent and namelessly vicious. When she stopped dismissively on the pavement I accepted this as if the sky was not reeling round me. I allowed her to go, attached to me by a line no thicker than a hair, but at least, if one could not say that she had swallowed the fly, it was still there, dancing over the water; and she, she was still there—she had not flicked her tail and vanished under weed or rock. I watched her go and turned to my bike with something accomplished—a meeting with Beatrice in the privacy of a crowd, a contact re-established. I rode home, my heart molten with delight, goodness and gratitude. For it was good. She was nineteen and I was nineteen; we were male and female, we would marry though she did not know that yet—must not know that yet, lest she vanish under weed or rock. Moreover there was peace. For she would be working at her books tonight. Nothing could touch her. Until the next afternoon—for who knew what she would do that evening? Dance? Cinema? With whom? Nevertheless the jealousy was to-morrow's jealousy and for twenty-four hours she was safe. I surrounded her with gratitude and love that came out strongly as a sense of blessing, un-sexual and generous. Those who have nothing are made wild with delight by very little. Once again as at school I yearned not to exploit but protect.

So my tiny thread was attached to her and I did not see that with every additional thread I myself was bound with another cable. Of course I went back next day, against my better judgment but with a desperate impulse to move on, to hurry things up; and she was not there, did not come. Then I spent an evening of misery and hung about the next day all the afternoon.

"Hullo, Beatrice! It looks as if we are going to meet quite often!"

But she had to hurry, she said, was going out that even-ing. I left her on the pavement with Lyons like an un-visited heaven and agonized as she vanished into the in-finite possibilities of going out. Now I had ample time to consider the problems of attachment. I began to appre-ciate dimly that a thread must be tied at both ends before it can restrain anything.

Facetious.

"Hullo, Beatrice! Here we are again!"

When we were sitting at the marble-topped table my plans began to come apart.

"Did you enjoy yourself last night?"

"Yes, thank you."

Then, out of the unendurable compulsion to know; with heart beat and damp hand with plea and anger——

"What were you doing?"

She was wearing, I remember, a suit, grey, some sort of smoothed flannel with a vertical stripe, alternately green and white. She had a blouse on beneath it with some throat and chest showing. Two fine gold chains fell down the glossy skin and vanished into the treasury. What was there at the end, between the Hesperides? A cross? A locket with a curl of hair? An aquamarine to shake and glimmer there, a perfection secret and unattainable?

"What were you doing?"

The contrast between the formal suit, the masculinity of the lapels, the neatness of the waist—and the soft body that sat in it—don't you know what you do to me? But there were changes, too, a faint hint of pink now over each cheekbone and under the long lashes a level look. Suddenly the air between us was filled with comprehension—understanding on the small-change level. This was not worded, did not need to be. She knew and I knew; but still I could not keep the fatal word back. It vibrated in my head, was unstoppable as a sneeze, came out with fury and contempt and pain.

"Dancing?"

The hints of pink were definite now. The round chin lifted. The thread stretched and broke.

"Well, really——"

She lifted off the chair, took her books.

"I'm late. I must go."

"Beatrice!"

I had to run after her as she walked along the pavement. I hung by her, walking sideways.

"I'm sorry. Only I—*hate* dancing—hate it! And the thought of you——"

We were stopped and half turned to each other.

"*Were* you dancing?"

There were three steps up to the front door, curved iron railings descending them on either side. Neither of us had the right vocabulary. She wanted to tell me, that assuming what she sensed was correct then I still had no right to insist on knowing. I wanted to cry—look how I burn! There are flames shooting out of my head and my loins and my heart! She wanted to say: however I may have half unconsciously appraised you as a mate—and of course you seemed impossible, only slightly amended by your recent behaviour—however much I have exercised my normal function of female living and allowed you to approach thus far; nevertheless, the rules of the game should have been observed; whereas you have broken them and affronted my dignity.

So we stood, she on the lower step, I, hand on the rails, red tie blown by my own violence over my right shoulder.

"Beatrice! Were you——?"

She had such clear eyes, such untroubled eyes, grey, honest because the price of dishonesty had never been offered to her. I looked into them, sensed their merciless and remote purity. She was contained in herself. Nothing had ever come to trouble her pool. If I held out my hand, desperate and pleading, inarticulate and hot out of raw youth and all the tides that bundled me along, what could she do but examine it and me and wait and wonder what I wanted?

"Were you?"

Indignation and hauteur; but both scaled down because the thread had been after all so hair-thin and to make much of the offence would imply that I had threatened her freedom.

"Maybe."

And so she took herself away wonderfully into the house.

How big is a feeling? Where is the dial that registers in degrees? I found my way back across South London, trying to come up out of my mind. I said that there was no need to exaggerate; you are not an adult, I said—there will be far worse things than this. There will be times when you will say—did I ever think I was in love? All that long ago? He was in love. Romeo was. Lear died of a broken heart. But where is the means of comparison? Where in the long scale did Sammy come? For now there were rough ropes on my wrists and ankles and round my neck. They led through the streets, they lay at her feet and she could pick them up or not as she chose. It was torture to me as I rode away with the miles of rope trailing, that she did not choose. She was perhaps tied herself in another direction? But I did not believe it. At my fever heat, processes went on more than apace. I was a local and specialized psychologist. I had seen her eyes, knew them and her untroubled. What fool was it insisted that he should know where she had been when at the same time he knew how thin that thread was in the beginning? There had been no risk. Her quality was untouched and the only risk was that somewhere and somehow she might meet the inscrutable chance and be set on fire. I walked in my room, beating my hands together.

The party was a relief. Robert Alsopp was in the chair and the air was thick with smoke and importance. The others were standing or sitting or lying, full of excitement and contempt. Everything was bloody, comrades. But passion, we know where we are going if no one else does. Sammy, you're next. Now keep quiet, comrades, for Comrade Mountjoy.

Comrade Mountjoy made a very small report. In fact he had not worked out any report from the Y.C.L. at all. He vamped. But the smoke and the technicalities the urgency and passion were a place hollowed out. So when I came to my lame conclusion I was disciplined and directed to undertake some self-examination. I began it there and it is still going on; but I remember my first decision; namely, to write to Beatrice that very night and be honest. I remember my second decision, too, and that was that I would never bring Beatrice into this home from home because she would have first to go to bed with Comrade Alsopp. He had a wife who didn't understand him just as though he were a bourgeois school teacher instead of a progressive one; but what with the war only a week or two off, the decay and break-up, the excitement, nobody noticed that this was not Marxism but the oldest routine in the world. Nevertheless, it provided our more personable females with a kind of graduation and, as it were, softened them up.

Comrade Wimbury was speaking. He was very tall and vague, and he was another teacher. I remember how we were ruled by Alsopp and Wimbury because they were, if I could only have seen it at the time, an act of low comedy. Alsopp had an immense bald head, a ruined face with a wet lecherous mouth scrawled across it. He was broad and most impressive at the table; but then you found he was not sitting down but standing up. He had the stumpiest legs of any man I have ever seen. He did not sit on a chair. He leaned his seat against it. Wimbury, on the other hand, had a tiny body so that when he sat by Alsopp his narrow chin and rabbit face only just appeared over the table. But if he stood up, this doll's body was elevated on two stilt-like legs that pushed him right up towards the ceiling. That evening, he was giving us our political lecture and he was proving with a wealth of reference and initials that there would be no war. It was all a capitalist plot to do something, I forget what. We listened and nodded wisely. We were on the inside. We knew that in a few years the world would be communist: and of course we were right. I tried to sink myself in listening; but the ropes were still there.

That night I wrote Beatrice a letter. The Christmas card had taught me that words are our only communication, so it was a long letter. I wish I could read it now. I begged her to read the letter carefully—not knowing how common this opening was in such a letter—not knowing that there were thousands of young men in London that night writing just such letters to just such altars. I explained about school, about the rumoured aphrodisiac. I went back to the first day when I had sat by Philip and tried to draw her. I explained what I had seen or thought I had seen. I told her that I was a helpless victim, that pride had prevented me from making this clear to her, but she was the sun and moon for me, that without her I should die, that I did not expect much—only that she should agree to some special relationship between us that would give me more standing than these acquaintances so casually blessed. For she might come to care for me, I said, in my bourgeois pamphlet, she might even—for I have loved you from the first day and I always shall.

Two o'clock in the morning and autumn mist, London

fog about. I sneaked out of the house for the family I lived with were supposed to report my movements to the authorities. I rode off, through the night, not daring to lose a post. First one policeman stopped me and took my name and address and then two stopped me. The third time I was tired enough to be honest and I told the statue in the blue coat that I was in love so he waved me on and wished me luck. At last I came to her door, pushed the package through and heard it fall. I was saying to myself as I nodded on the bike: at least I have been honest, been honest, I don't know what to do.

How do they react in themselves, these soft, cloven creatures? Where is the dial that marks their degrees of feeling? I had had my sex already. The party had seen to that, Sheila, dark and dirty. We had given each other a little furtive pleasure like handing round a bag of toffees. It was also our absurd declaration of independence, a declaration made by behaving as much like Alsopp as possible. It was freedom. But these other contained, untouched girls—how do they feel and think? Or are they like Sammy in Rotten Row, a clear bubble blown about, vulnerable but unwounded? Surely she must have known! But how did the situation present itself? Granted the whole physical process appears horrible and unmentionable—for so it did, I know that—what then does love appear to be? Is it an abstract thing with as little humanity as the dancing advertisements of Piccadilly? Or does love immediately imply a white wedding, a house? She had dressed and undressed herself, tended her delicate body year in year out. Did she never think with faster pulse and breath—he is in love, he wants to do—that—to me? Perhaps now with the spread of enlightenment virginity has lost sacred caste and girls go eager to swim. It was, after all, a social habit. She was lower middle class where the instinct or habit was to keep what you had intact. It was a class in those days of great power and stability, ignoble and ungenerous. I cannot tell what flutter if any I made in her dovecote, could not, cannot, knew and know nothing about her. But she read the letter.

This time I did not pretend to be riding by. I sat my saddle, one hand on the handle-bars one foot on the pavement. I watched them tumble out of the double doors and she came with them. The blessed damozels had been tipped off because they marched away without a giggle. I looked her in the eye and burned with the shame of my confession.

"You read my letter?"

They were not terms on which she blushed. Without a word we went to Lyons and sat in silence.

"Well?"

She did pinken a bit then, she spoke softly and gently as to an invalid.

"I don't know what to say, Sammy."

"I meant every word of it. You've"—spread hands—"got me. I'm defeated."

"How?"

"It's a kind of competition."

But I saw that her eyes were still empty of understanding.

"Forget it, Beatrice. If you can't understand—look. Have goodwill. You see? Give me a chance to—*am* I so awful? I know I'm nothing to look at, but I do"—deep breath—"I do—you know how I feel."

Silence.

"Well?"

"Your course. It won't last for ever. Then you won't come this way."

"My course? What? Oh—that! I mean I thought if you and I—we could go walking in the country and then you could—I'm quite harmless really."

"Your course!"

"So you guessed, did you? I'm cutting the Art School at this moment. There are some things that are more important."

"Sammy!"

Now the untroubled pools began to fill. There was wonder and awe and a trace of speculation. Did she think to herself; it is true, he is in love, he has done a real thing for me? I am that, after all, which can be loved. I am not entirely empty. I have a stature like the others. I am human?

"You'll come? Say you'll come, Beatrice!"

She was commendably virtuous on every level. She would come; but I must promise—not in exchange, for that would be bargaining—must promise I would not cut the art school any more. I think she began to see herself as a centre of power, as an influence for good; but her interest in my future gave me such delight that I did not analyse it.

Not on Sunday. On Saturday. She couldn't come on Sunday, she said, with a kind of mild surprise that anyone should expect her to. And so I met my first, indeed, my only rival. That surprised me then and surprises me now; first, that I should rage so at this invisible rival, second, that I had none physical. She was so sweet, so unique, so beautiful—or did I invent her beauty? Had all young men been as I, the ways where she went would have been crowded. Did no other man have as I this unquenchable desire to know, to be someone else, to understand; was mine the only mixture near her of worship and jealousy and musky tumescence? Were there others, is it the common experience to be granted a favour, and at once to be a tumult of delight and gratitude for the granting and wild rage because the favour had to be asked for?

We walked on the downs in grey weather and I shook out my talent before her. I impressed myself. When I described the inner compulsion that drove me to paint I felt full of my own genius. But to Beatrice, of course, I was describing a disease which stood between me and a respectable, prosperous life. Or so I think; for all these are guesses. Part of the reality of my life is that I do not understand it. Moreover she did not make things easy for she hardly spoke at all. All I know is that I must have succeeded in giving her a picture of a stormy interior, an object of some awe and pity. Yet the truth was on a smaller scale altogether, the wound less tragic and paradoxically less easily healed.

"Well? What do you think?"

Silence; averted profile. We were coming down from the ridge, about to plunge into wet woods. We stopped where they began and I took her hand. The rags of my self-respect fell from me. Nothing venture, nothing win.

"Aren't you sorry for me?"

She let her hand lie in mine. It was the first time in my life I had touched her. I heard the little word float away, carried by the wind.

"Maybe."

Her head turned, her face was only a few inches from

94

mine. I leaned forward and gently and chastely kissed her on the lips.

We must have gone on and I must have talked yet the words are gone. All I remember is my astonishment.

Not quite all. For I remember the substance of my discovery. I was, by that mutely invited salute admitted to the status of boy friend. The perquisites of this position were two. First, I had a claim on her time and she would not go out with any other male. Second, I was entitled to a similar strictly chaste salute on rare occasions and also on saying good night. I am nearly sure that at that moment Beatrice meant her gesture as prophylactic. Boy friends were nice boys and therefore—so her reasoning may have gone—if Sammy is a boy friend it will make him nice. It will make him normal. Dear Beatrice!

I kept my communism to myself. It would not have suited my rival. He was apparently as jealous as I, holding that they that touch pitch shall be defiled. But to tell the truth, if it had not been for Nick and his socialism I should never have bothered with politics at all. I shouted and nodded with the rest; but went along with them because at least they were going somewhere. If it had not been for Miss Pringle's nephew who now was high up in the blackshirts I might as well have been a blackshirt myself. But there was something special about that time. Though Wimbury convinced himself and us that there would be no war, our bones knew better. The world around us was sliding on and down through an arch into a stormy welter where morals and families and private obligations had no place. There was a Norse sense of no future in the air. Perhaps that was why we could sleep around with such a deep irresponsibility; only the sleeping had to be among the people who felt the same headlong rush. Beatrice was outside it. Workers of the world—unite!

We had a worker. The rest of our branch were teachers and a parson or two, some librarians, a chemist, assorted students like myself and our jewel—Dai Reece. Dai worked in the gas works, trimming coal or something. I believe that Dai had social aspirations and looked on our branch as gentry. He never came within a mile of showing any of the textbook reactions. Our army, in fact, was all generals. Dai did what he was told for a time obediently and did not even guess what it was all about. Then he rebelled and got disciplined. Wimbury and Alsopp and the rest were all closed communists. The only people who could do anything publicly for the party were students like myself and of course our worker, Dai. He got so much that he broke out into a tirade at a branch meeting. "You sit on your fat ass in your 'ouse all the week, Comrade and I 'ave to go out in the cold to sell the bloody *Worker* every night, man!"

So he got disciplined and I got disciplined because it was the night I had let Philip into the branch meeting without authority. I wanted to keep him with me because we could have talked about Beatrice and Johnny. Otherwise be would have gone back and vanished into central London. What astonished me most was the anxiety in Philip's pale face. Almost, one could have fancied him in love; and it was symptomatic of my state that I should begin to wonder whether he, too, had been throwing away his career to move closer to Beatrice. But Philip watched faces and went close to Dai. When the meeting broke up he insisted that we should all three go off for a drink. He cross-examined Dai who treated him with great respect. I began to answer for Dai who was being appallingly bourgeois and not acting like the white hope of the future at all. I became warm and moved on Philip with conviction and heart-throb. But he was elusive and worried. He treated Dai, too, with an authority I could not yet recognize. At last he dismissed him.

"One more half, Dai, and then you must go home. I have some things to discuss with Mr. Mountjoy."

When we were alone, he bought me a drink but would have no more himself.

"Well, Sammy. So you know where you're going."

Helter-skelter, rush down to the dark arch.

"Does anyone?"

"That chap—Wimbury. Does he? How old is he?"

"I don't know."

"Teacher?"

"Of course."

"What's he up to?"

I drank up and ordered another.

"He's working for the revolution."

Philip was following the movements of my drinking with careful eyes.

"Where does he go from here?"

I must have thought for a long time because Philip went on speaking.

"I mean—he's an ordinary teacher? An assistant?"

"That's right."

"Being a communist won't make him a head teacher."

"You are the most bloody awful ungenerous——"

"Listen, Sammy. What does he get out of it? What can he become?"

"Well!"

But what could Comrade Wimbury become?

"Don't you understand, Philip? We aren't in this for ourselves. We've——"

"Seen the light."

"If you like."

"So have the blackshirts. Now look—don't start a fight."

"Fascist bastards!"

"I'm trying to find things out. I've been to their meetings too. Now don't make a fuss, Sammy. I'm—as you would say—uncommitted."

"You're too damned middle-class that's your trouble."

Drink warmed me, gave me virtue and self-righteousness. I began a rambling and laboured exposition. Philip watched me, always watched me. Finally he straightened his tie and smoothed down his hair.

"Sammy. When the war comes——"

"What war?"

"Next week's war."

"There won't be a war."

"Why not?"

"You heard Wimbury."

Philip began to laugh. I had never seen him so genuinely merry. At last he wiped his eyes and looked at me solemnly again.

"Do something for me, Sammy."

"Paint your portrait?"

"Keep me informed. No. Not just about politics. I can read the *Worker* as well as you. Just let me know what it's like in the branch. The feeling. That other chap with the bald head——"

"Alsopp?"

"What does he get out of it?"

I knew what Alsopp got out of it, but I was not going to say. After all, love was free and private life irrelevant— all except your own.

"How should I know? He's an older man than I am."

"You don't know much, do you, Sammy?"

"Have 'nother drink."

"And you respect your elders."

"Hell with my elders."

Beer in those days was cold and flabby for two half-pints and then took off, had golden wings with the third. I peered for Philip.

"What you up to, Philip? You come here—blackshirts and communists——"

Philip was looking back through my haze with an air of clinical detachment. He was tapping his long teeth with one white finger.

"Know Diogenes?"

"Never heard of 'im."

"Went round with a lamp. Wanted to find an honest man."

"You being bloody rude? I'm honest. So's comrades. Bloody blackshirts."

Philip was forward and peering into my face.

"Dai wants booze more than anything. What do you want more than anything, Sammy?"

I mumbled.

Philip was very near and very loud.

"Beetroots? You want beetroots?"

"What do you want then?"

The reeling eye is sometimes as percipient as the drugged one. Essentials only. Philip was isolated in bright

99

light. Feeling my own uncertainties, my lopsided and illogical life, now lugged into a semblance of upright by bass, I could see why he was not drinking. For Philip, pale, freckled Philip who was skimped in every line of his body by a cosmic meanness was keeping himself intact. What I have I hold. Therefore the bony hands and the cut-price face, the brow pushed in on either side as though supplies had run out, were defended against giving, were incapable by nature of natural generosity, were tight and aware.

Let me describe him as I saw him at that instant. His clothes were better than mine, cleaner and neater. His shirt was white, his tie subdued and central. He sat, not hunched, but precisely, on a vertical spine. His hands were in his lap, his knees together. His hair was of a curious indefinable texture—growing all ways, but so weak that it still lay close to his skull like a used doormat. It was so indeterminate that the large, light freckles blurred the hair line on his sloping forehead. His eyes were pale blue and seemed curiously raw in that electric light for he had neither eyebrows nor eyelashes. No, madam, I'm sorry, we don't supply them at that price. This is a utility model. His nose was generous enough but melted, and the sphincter muscles round his mouth, only just sufficient to get it shut. And the man inside, the boy inside? I had schemed with him for fagcards, wrestled with him in the dark church—I had been cheated by him and beaten by him—I had accepted his friendship at a time when friendship was very dear to me.

The man inside?

It could smile. Was doing so now, with a localized convulsion of the sphincter.

"What do *you* want, Philip?"

"I told you."

He got up and began to put on his raincoat. I was about to suggest he should escort me home for I began to feel uncertain of getting there; but while the suggestion was rising to my lips he cut it off.

"Don't bother to come with me to the station. I shall have to hurry. Here's an envelope with my address on it. Remember. Just every now and then—let me know how things go on in the branch. What people are feeling."

"What the hell are you trying to do?"

Philip pulled the door open.

"Do? I'm—I'm inspecting the political racket."

"An honest man. And you haven't found one."

"No. Of course not."

"What if you find one?"

Philip paused with the door open. There was darkness and a glint of rain. He looked back at me out of his raw eyes from a long, long way away.

"I shall be disappointed."

I kept my drinking from Beatrice because she thought of pubs as only one degree less damned than the Church of England. In her little village, three miles beyond Rotten Row, all the boozers were Church of England and all the boys in broad cloth, chapel. Church of England was top and bottom; chapel was middle, was the class grimly keeping its feet out of the mud. I kept an awful lot of things from Beatrice. I see myself haunted and hurrying, dishevelled, my shoes uncleaned, grey shirt unbuttoned, blue jacket bulging on either side with oddments till the pockets looked like panniers. I had a lot of hair and I shaved when

I was going to see Beatrice. I was thankful for the party's red tie; it settled one item of wardrobe for me. As for my hands, the cigarette stain was creeping towards my wrists. I had neither Johnny's sunny simplicity, nor Philip's sense of direction; and yet I was for something. I was intended. When I did as I was told; when I drew and painted in obedience I was praised judiciously. I would make a good teacher, perhaps, a man who knew all the ropes and understood why each thing must be done. Set a problem, and I could produce the straight, the safe academic answer. Yet sometimes I would feel myself connected to the well inside me and then I broke loose. There would come into my whole body a feeling of passionate certainty. Not that—but this! Then I would stand the world of appearances on its head, would reach in and down, would destroy savagely and re-create—not for painting or precisely for Art with a capital A, but for this very concrete creation itself. If, like Philip and Diogenes I had been looking for an honest man in my own particular racket I should have found him then and he would have been myself. Art is partly communication but only partly. The rest is discovery. I have always been the creature of discovery.

I do not say this to excuse myself—or do I? You cannot have two moral standards one for artists and one for the rest. That is a mistaken view on both sides. Whoever judges me must judge me as if I had been a grocer addicted to chapel. If I have painted some good pictures—brought people slap up against another view of the world —on the other hand I have sold them no sugar nor left the early milk on their doorsteps. I say it rather, perhaps to explain what sort of young man I was—explain it to myself. I can think of no other audience. I am here as well as on canvas, a creature of discovery rather than communication. And all the time, oscillating between resentment and gratitude I was straining towards Beatrice as I have seen a moored boat tugged by the tide. You cannot blame the boat if it breaks loose at last and goes where the water carries it. This young man, sucking first pleasure then drug then nothing out of fags until they became as he smoked them no more than a gesture—drinking first for the phosphorescence and reality it brought to a wall or a lintel, then drinking to escape from a world of nonsense into one of apocalyptic meaning—throwing himself into the party because there people knew where the world was going—this young man, wild and ignorant, asking for help and refusing it, proud, loving, passionate and obsessed: how can I blame him for his actions since clearly at that time he was beyond the taste or the hope of freedom?

But Beatrice hoped to do me good. We walked again. We wrote each other little letters. I became familiar with her vocabulary, found out less and less about her. She stood by a tree and I put my arm round her and vibrated, but she never noticed. I was determined to be good, to move on the highest level, to settle once and for all the hauntings. I bent and put my cheek against hers. I was looking where she looked.

"Beatrice."

"Mm?"

"What is it like to be you?"

A sensible question; and asked out of my admiration for Evie and Ma, out of my adolescent fantasies, out of my painful obsession with discovery and identification. An impossible question.

"Just ordinary."

What is it like to hold the centre of someone's universe, to be soft and fair and sweet, to be neat and clean by nature, to be desired to distraction, to live under this hair, behind these huge, unutterable eyes, to feel the lift of these guarded twins, the valley, the plunge down to the tiny waist, to be vulnerable and invulnerable? What is it like in the bath and the lavatory and walking the pavement with shorter steps and high heels; what is it like to know your body breathes this faint perfume which makes my heart burst and my senses swim?

"No. Tell me."

And can you feel them all the way out to the rounded points? Do you know and feel how hollow your belly is? What is it like to be frightened of mice? What is it like to be wary and serene, protected and peaceful? How does a man seem to you? Is he clothed, always, jacketed and trousered, is he castrated like the plaster casts in the art room?

Beatrice made a slight movement as though she would move away from the tree. We were both leaning against it, she against me, too; and my arm was round her waist. I would not let her go.

Above all else, even beyond the musky treasures of your white body, this body so close to me and unattainable, above all else: what is your mystery? This is not a question I can ask you because I can hardly frame it to myself. But as freedom of the will is to be experienced like the taste of potatoes, as I once saw in and round your face what I cannot draw and hardly remember—as I am unable to make a picture of you that remotely resembles the breathing Beatrice; for mercy's sake admit me to the secret. I have capitulated to you. I go with the tide. Even if you do not know what you are at least admit me.

"Where do you live, Beatrice?"

She stirred again suddenly.

"Don't move. No, silly girl, not your address. Inside. The side of my head is against the side of yours. Do you live in there? We can't be an inch apart. I live near the back of my head, right inside—nearer the back than the front. Are you like that? Do you live—just in here? If I put my fingers there on the nape of your neck and move them up am I close? Closer?"

She pulled away.

"You're—don't, Sammy!"

How far do you extend? Are you the black, central patch which cannot examine itself? Or do you live in another mode, not thought, stretching out in serenity and certainty?

But the musk won.

"Sammy!"

"I said I loved you. Oh God, don't you know what that means? I want you, I want all of you, not just cold kisses and walks—I want to be with you and in you and on you and round you—I want fusion and identity—I want to understand and be understood—oh God, Beatrice, Beatrice, I love you—I want to be you!"

It was the moment when she might have got away, got far enough away to write me a letter and avoid me. It was, in fact, her last chance; but she did not know that. And perhaps even to her contained skin there was some warmth and excitement of the body in my stronger arms.

"Say you love me or I shall go mad!"

"Sammy—be sensible. Someone might——"

"To hell with someone. Turn your face round."

"I thought——"

"Thought we were friends? Well, we aren't, are we?"

"I thought——"

"You are wrong. We aren't friends, can't ever be friends. Don't you feel it? We are more—must be more. Kiss me."

"I don't want to. Look, Sammy—please! Let me think."

"Don't think. Feel. Can't you?"

"I don't know."

"Marry me."

"We couldn't. We're both at college—we haven't any money."

"But say you will. Some time. When we can. Will you?"

"There's someone coming."

"If you don't marry me I shall——"

"They'll see us."

"I shall kill you."

The man and woman came up the track, hand in hand, some of their problems settled. They looked everywhere but at us. They passed out of sight.

"Well?"

And rain was beginning to flick and trickle among the naked branches. Killing is one thing, rain another. We moved on, I hanging a little behind her shoulder.

"Well?"

Her face was pink and wet and shiny. Tiny pearls and diamonds hung clustering in her hair.

"We'd better hurry, Sammy. If we miss that bus there won't be another for ages."

I seized her wrist and swung her round on the path.

"I meant it."

They were still clear eyes, still untroubled. But they were brighter, brighter with mutiny or triumph.

"You said you cared for me."

"Oh, my God!"

I looked at her slight body, sensed the thin bone of the skull, the round and defenceless neck.

"We couldn't get married for ages."

"Beatrice!"

She moved a little closer and looked at me squarely with bright, pleased eyes. She put herself in the position for a permitted kiss.

"You will? Say you will!"

She smiled and uttered the nearest she ever knew to saying yes.

"Maybe."

For maybe was sign of all our times. We were certain of
nothing. I should have said "Maybe" not Beatrice. The
louder I cried out in the wake of the party the more an inner voice told me not to be silly, that no one could be certain of anything. Life waded knee-deep in shadows,
floundered, was relative. So I could take "maybe" from
Beatrice for "yes".

A young man certain of nothing but salt sex; certain
that if there was a positive value in living it was this un-
deniable pleasure. Be frightened of the pleasure, condemn
it, exalt it—but no one could deny that the pleasure was
there. As for Art—did they not say—and youth with the
resources of all human knowledge at its disposal lacks
nothing but time to know everything—did they not say in
the thick and unread textbooks that the root of art was
sex? And was this not certain to be so since so many clever
people said so and what was more to the point, behaved
so? Therefore the tickling pleasure, the little death shared
or self-inflicted was neither irrelevant nor sinful but the
altar of whatever shoddy temple was left to us. But there
remained deep as an assessment of experience itself the
knowledge that if this was everything it was a poor return
for birth, for the shames and frustrations of growing up.
Nevertheless I had now brought Beatrice into the sexual
orbit. Even she must know that marriage and the sexual
act are not unconnected. My thighs weakened, my lungs
tripped over a hot breath at the thought of it.

"Sammy! No!"

For, of course, there was only one answer to that "maybe" and I tried for a clinch—she unco-operating. Then I was trembling, I remember distinctly, as if love and sex and passion were a disease. I was trembling regularly from head to foot as if my button had been pressed. There in the winter sunlight, among the raindrops and rusted foliage I stood and trembled regularly as if I should never stop and a sadness reached out of me that did not know what it wanted; for it is a part of my nature that I should need to worship, and this was not in the textbooks, not in the behaviour of those I had chosen and so without knowing I had thrown it away. This sadness had no point therefore, and came out at the eyes of that ridiculous, unmanly, trembling creature so that Beatrice was frightened by it. What accepted suitor in a book ever started to tremble and weep? Her better nature or her commonsense would have taken back that binding maybe there and then if I had not turned away and made a dramatic effort to master my emotion. That was a cliché of behaviour and therefore not frightening. The trembling passed and suddenly I was overwhelmed by realization that here was the beginning of the end of that long path. One day, yes, one real day and not in fantasy I should achieve her sweet body. She would be safely mine beyond doubt or jealousy.

I turned again and began to chatter out of my unbearable excitement. So I led her away down the path, chattering and laughing, she silent and astonished. I see now how extraordinary these reactions must have seemed to her; but at the time I felt them as natural to me. It was an instability that I feel now should have ended in madness and perhaps at the time she felt that too. But for me, old scars were vanishing. The pursuer's hate was swallowed up in gratitude. The burns seared into me by overheated emotion were swealed away, I was unfolding, luxuriating in peace of deep heart over which delight danced, wildly invisible.

I don't think for a moment that she loved me then. If it comes to that I have asked myself how many people know at all the complete preoccupation and dependence? She was much more taken up with custom and precedent. She was now engaged and perhaps I was necessary as a shadowy adjunct in the life of the training college; an adjunct which she could accept more easily as she felt how she did me good. If marriage entered her head at all it was far off after college, was so to speak at the end of the film, was a golden glow near enough the end. But I had definite thoughts and purpose.

I am amazed now at my shyness and ignorance. After all the imagined passion of bed, at first I hardly dared kiss her and made the most tentative advances. Of course she warded them off and they served to bring up the central affair and impossibility of years of waiting.

"Girls don't feel like that."

"I'm not a girl!"

Indeed I was not. I have never felt more severely heterosexual. But she was a girl, her emotions and physical reactions enclosed as a nun. She herself was hidden. All the time I knocked and then hammered at the door she remained shut up within. We continued to see each other, to kiss, to plan marriage in several years' time. I got her a ring and she felt achieved and adult. I could place one hand gently on her left breast provided my hand remained outside her clothes. Beyond that point she became very positive. I have never been able to follow the precise train of thought that guided her reactions. Perhaps there was no thought at all and merely reactions. It is better to marry than burn. How I agreed with Saint Paul! But we could not marry. So I kissed the cold edge of her lips, laid one hand on her hidden pap and blazed like a haystack.

I got myself a bed-sitting-room, moving out of the care which a landlady was supposed to give me. If it had not been for Beatrice that room would have been very bleak; but I designed it as a place to seduce her in.

I had no precedents outside the cinema and these I was not in a position to imitate. I could not surround Beatrice with luxury, had no gipsy violinist to shudder his way into her ear. That room with its couch bed, narrow for two unless they were glued together or superimposed, with its brown dado and pink lamp shade gave me no help. The Van Gogh sunflowers of course were prominent—was there a single bed-sitter in London without them? But there was nothing to draw Beatrice there except our poverty. It was cheaper to sit on the couch than drink coffee in a little shop; it was cheaper, even, than walking in the country, because you had to break out of the smoke by train or bus. So when I finally got her there, though I knew why, she herself may very well have believed it was from laudable motives of economy.

She came; and there were huge, desert areas of silence. For this was so unlike my fevered fantasies that she had no immediate attraction for me. She maddened me by being there; yet I could not cross the gulf of her silence. She would sit on the couch, her elbows on her knees and her chin between her two palms and look placidly at nothing.

Sometimes I would squat in front of her and intercept her gaze.

"What are you thinking of?"

She would smile slightly and shake her head. If I stayed there, she would sit up and look past me again. It seemed like boredom; but it was a strange and untouched content with the process of living. She was at peace. The chapel with its assurances was behind her and for the rest she enjoyed sitting in her pretty body. Nobody told her this was a sin, this calm and selfish enjoyment of her own delicate warmth and smoothness; they told her it was virtue rather and respectability. I see now that her nun-like innocence was an obedient avoidance of the deep and muddy pool where others lived. Where I lived. I gesticulated to her from the pool and she was sorry for me. But all that was taken care of, was it not? For she was to marry me; and that was what nice boys wanted, the dual vanish into a golden haze, all folly smoothed away.

"What are you thinking of?"

"This and that."

"About us?"

"Maybe."

Outside the window the long winter road would darken. A sky-sign would become visible, a square of red words with a yellow line chasing round them; a whole mile of street lights would start and quiver into dull yellow as though they suddenly awoke. There would not be many minutes left.

"What are you thinking about?"

The time would come, she would stand up, allow me my careful embrace and then balance away, feminine and untouched.

I wonder what she was thinking of? She baffles me still, she is opaque. Even though she enjoyed being herself innocently as a young cat before the fire, yet surely there must have been some way to her for someone—for some girl, perhaps, if not for me? Would she have seemed accessible to her own children? Would a lifetime with her bring up a transparency first and then reveal in it the complex outlines of the soul in itself?

Yet she was accustomed to my room—to our room as I began to call it. I worked hard at lines of approach, subtle or logical. I did violence to our physical shyness, hid my face in her hair and begged her—unconscious perhaps of the humour of the narrow couch—begged her to sleep with me. She would not, of course; and I played another card. She must marry me immediately. Let it be secret——

Beatrice would not. What was she up to? What did she want? Was she doing nothing but giving me stability? Did she ever intend to marry me?

"Marry me. Now!"

"But we can't!"

"Why not?"

We had no money. She was not supposed to marry, had signed some sort of agreement. It wouldn't be honest——

The poor girl had delivered herself into my hand.

"Then come to bed with me——"

"No."

"Yes. Why not?"

"It wouldn't be——"

"It wouldn't be what? I'm supposed to suffer because you—I've got to wait—you know what a man is—all because you signed some damned agreement to turn you into a sour school marm——"

113

"Please, Sammy——"

"I love you."

"Let me go."

"Don't you understand? I love you. You love me. You ought to be coming gladly to me, we to each other, all your beauty given, shared—why do you keep me out? Don't you love me? I thought you loved me!"

"So I do."

"Say it then."

"I love you."

But still she would not. We would be sitting and wrestling ridiculously on the edge of the narrow bed; there was nothing but foolishness. After a time even desire would tire of this and we would sit, side by side, I suddenly conversational about an exhibition or the picture I happened to be painting. Sometimes I would take up the conversation if such a monologue was conversation—where I had dropped it a quarter of an hour before.

Beatrice belonged to my only rival. Her body, therefore, was not hers to give. This she thought, this she acted upon. And we could not get married yet. So she came, time after time to my room and sat with me on the edge of the bed. Why did she do it? Was there the taste of salt curiosity in her mouth, was she going as near the edge of excitement as she dared? Or what?

"I shall go mad."

She had a most wonderfully mobile body that seemed to yield wherever you touched it; but when I threw off that obscene remark her body stiffened between my arms.

"You mustn't ever say such a thing, Sammy."

"I shall go mad, I tell you!"

"Don't say it!"

114

Madness was not quite so fashionable in those days. People did not so cheerfully claim to be unbalanced or schizo. I may claim to have been before my time in this as in many other things. So where today a girl would be sympathetic, in those days Beatrice was frightened. She gave me the lever I wanted.

"I think I *am* mad, a bit———"

Once a human being has lost freedom there is no end to the coils of cruelty. I must I must I must. They said the damned in hell were forced to torture the innocent live people with disease. But I know now that life is perhaps more terrible than that innocent medieval misconception. We are forced here and now to torture each other. We can watch ourselves becoming automata; feel only terror as our alienated arms lift the instruments of their passion towards those we love. Those who lose freedom can watch themselves forced helplessly to do this in daylight until who is torturing who is? The obsession drove me at her.

But, of course, once she had got over her fear and we were bound so closely together by lovemaking, there would be no end to the brightness of the sunlight future.

My madness was Wagnerian. It drove me forth on dark nights forsooth striding round the downs. I should have worn a cloak.

I sent a message in by the porter. Mr. Mountjoy wishes to speak to Miss Ifor.

"Sammy!"

It was a quarter to eight in the morning.

"I had to come and look at you. To make sure you were real."

"But how did you get here at this time?"

"I wanted to see you."

"But how——"

"I wanted—oh that? I've been walking all night, keeping ahead of it."

"But——"

"You are my sanity, Beatrice. I had to come and see you. Now everything is all right."

"You'll be late, Sammy, you must go. Are you all right?"

Compunction in compulsion, almost weeping. What is madness after all? Can a man who pretends to be mad claim to be sane?

Compulsion, weeping.

"I have to do it. I don't know why. I have to."

"Oh look, Sammy—here I'm not supposed to—I'll see you to the bus stop. Come on. You know the number? You're to go straight to bed."

"You won't leave me?"

"Look—dear!"

"As soon as you can then—the very first moment——"

"I promise."

The bus top was among branches part of the way. I was shaking and shuddering by myself with no need to act. I was muttering like a drunk man.

"I don't understand. I don't know anything. I'm on rails. I have to. Have to. There is too much life. I could kick myself or kill myself. Is my living to be nothing but moving like an insect? Scuttering, crawling? I could go away. Could I? Could I go away? Across the sea where the painted walls wait for me, I might. I am tied by this must."

The muscles of the chest get tautened, the sinews stand out in the wrists, the heart beats faster till the air is eaten up with red shapes expanding; and then you understand that you ought to breathe again; for even if compulsion is a pitiless thing a man does not have to let it take charge of his physical reflexes, no, he can suffer emotionally without starving himself of air—there, I thought, I have breathed the load off my back.

She came to me malleable, and at the same time authoritative, for she was very firm about eating regularly and so on. She was very sweet. She only put up a token fight. She was my sanity. I would take any consequences that ensued would I not, who was so breathlessly assuring her that there would be no consequences. And then Beatrice of four years' fever lay back obediently, closed her eyes and placed one clenched fist bravely on her forehead as though she were about to be injected for T.A.B.

And what of Sammy?

There could be no consequences because there was no cause.

What precisely was he after? Why should it be that at this most triumphant or at least enjoyable moment of his career, the sight of the victim displayed humble, acquiescent and frightened should not only be less stimulating than the least of his sexual inventions but should even be damping and impossible? No, said his body, no not this at all. That was not the thing I meant, thing I wanted. How far was I right to think myself obsessed with sex when that potency which is assumed in all literature was not mine to use at the drop of a knicker? It seemed then that some co-operation was essential. If she were to make of herself a victim I could not be her executioner. If she were to be frightened, then I was ashamed in my very flesh that she should be frightened of me. This did not seem to me to tally with the accepted version of a man who was either wholly incapable or heroically ready, aye ready. There were gradations. But neither I nor Beatrice were prepared to admit them. On the other hand my feelings about her were without doubt obsessive if not pathological. Should they not then make my achievement of her easy? But she, out of my suggested madness and her own religious taboos was incapable of thinking about this moment, this pre-marital deed, without a sense that was at once one of sin, one of fear, one of love and consequently one of drama. Unconsciously we were both setting ourselves to music. The gesture with which she opened her knees was, so to speak, operatic, heroic, dramatic and daunting. I could not accompany her. My instrument was flat.

But of course there were other occasions. I was not wise enough to know that a sexual sharing was no way of bringing us together. So instead of abandoning the game then and there—and of course my own opinion of my masculinity was at stake—I persevered. We began to accept that she should submit to caresses and as all old wives know these things come right in the end. I had my warm, inscrutable Beatrice, triumphed in a sort of sorrow and pity; and Beatrice cried and did not want to go away but, of course, she had to, that was the penalty of jumping the gun. She took her secret back to the training college and endured the faces that might guess, then came back, went to chapel, did there whatever she did, came to what arrangement—and went to bed with me again. I was full of love and gratitude and delight, but I never seemed to get near Beatrice, never shared anything with her. She remained the victim on the rack, even a rack of some enjoyment. But there was nothing in this that we could share; for poor Beatrice was impotent. She never really knew what we were doing, never knew what it was about.

"Don't you feel anything?"

"I don't know. Maybe."

Her silences were if anything longer. She wasn't the boss any more. Instead of my searching her face for a clue, wondering what was inside, I found myself being watched. After our one-sided lovemaking, I would wander up and down the room, thinking to myself that if this was all, there was nothing that would give us a unity and substantial identity. She would lie still on the narrow bed and her eyes would follow me, back and forward as long as I liked to walk. She was not unhappy. If, in the time that followed, I think of and visualize Beatrice below me, it is not entirely a sexual image. She was adjusting herself to a conceived place in life. She was beginning to look up, to belong, to depend, to cling, to be an inferior in fact, however the marriage service may gloss it. Instinctively she was becoming what she believed to be a wedded wife. Her contribution, after the heroic sacrifice, was negative. Death of a maidenhead pays for all.

I loved her and was grateful. When you are young, you cannot believe that a human relationship is as pointless as it seems. You always think that tomorrow there will come the revelation. But in fact we had had our revelation of each other. There was nothing else to know.

Sometimes when I was alone I would think of the future. What sort of life would it be? I should paint, of course, and Beatrice would always be around, making tea. She would have children, probably, be a very good mother. I began to think desperately, not of abandoning her but of some way to force myself towards that wonderful person who must be hidden somewhere in her body. Such grace of body could surely not be its own temple, must enshrine something——

"I'm going to paint you, paint your body. Naked. Like this, all slack and given up."

"No. You mustn't."

"I shall. Lie there. Let me pull the curtain back——"

"No! Sammy!"

"They can't see in across the road. Now lie still."

"Please!"

"Look, Beatrice—didn't you admit that the Rokeby Venus is beautiful?"

She turned her face away. She was being injected for T.A.B. again.

"I shan't paint your face at all. I just want your body. No. Don't rearrange it. Just lie still."

Beatrice lay still and I began to draw.

When the drawing was finished I made love to her again. Or rather, I repeated what my pencil had done, finished what my pencil had begun. The lovemaking accepted that she was unable to take part. The lovemaking was becoming an exploitation. I see now that she could not enjoy or welcome our commerce because she was brought up not to. All the little books and the occasional talks, all the surface stuff were powerless against the dead weight of her half-baked sectarianism. All her upbringing ensured that she should be impotent.

It is difficult for a man to know anything about a woman. But how, when he is passionate can he reach her through her obedient stillness? Does she feel nothing but a kind of innocent lubricity? Can she share nothing?

"What are you thinking of——?"

Her body was a perpetual delight. Moving or still she was finished in colour and texture. And yet she was not there.

"What are you thinking about——?"

Nevertheless from the moment that she let me take her virginity the change began between us. Her clear absence of being leaned in towards me, lay against me, clung. As though from conception she had waited for this, now she bowed against me. She watched me with doggie eyes, she put the lead in my hand.

"What shall we talk about?"

I became angry. I tried to force some response. But we could not even row and fight face to face. Always there was to be a difference of levels. As soon as she detected the touch of hardness in my voice she would grab me and hold me tight, she would hide her face against me.

I would try to explain.

"I'm trying to find out about you. After all if we're going to spend our lives together—where are you? What are you? What is it like to be you?"

Her arms would shake—those arms that bent in at the elbows, were so delicate they seemed for receiving only—her breasts and her face would push against me, be hidden.

Impatient and angry. Continue the catechism.

"Aren't you human, then? Aren't you a person at all?"

And with shudders of her wrists and shaking of the long, fair hair she would whisper against me:

"Maybe."

It comes into my memory now that at this time we never met face to face. Either she is a white body, the head hidden in her hair; or she holds me round the waist and looks up at me with big, faithful eyes, her chin against my stomach. She liked to look up. She had found her tower and was clinging to it. She had become my ivy.

There were days of content—there must have been. I must remember that "last time" was never love but only "infatuation". Therefore we went on for nearly two years until the ripples and then waves of war washed round us. We corresponded when we could not meet. I was full of wit and protestations; she full of simplicity and small change. She would buy a dress. Did I think green suited her? The lecturer in hygiene was very nice. She hoped we should be able to afford a little house some time. When we were married she would have to think of making her own clothes. On some of her letters, in the top left-hand corner, was a little cross-sign that for another few weeks we were safe from having children, though by then the risk was small enough. Her work was going badly and she was getting into hot water over it, but she didn't seem to care any more, except about hygiene! The lecturer in hygiene was very nice. Insensibly I drifted rather than went deliberately into the last cruel effort to reach her.

I must be careful. How much was conscious cruelty on my part? How much was her fault? She had never in her life made one movement towards me until I roared over her like a torrent. She was utterly passive in life. Then was that long history of my agony over her, my hell—real as anything in life could be real—was that self-created? Was it my doing? Did I put the remembered light in her face? Did I? I saw her on the platform in the art room with the bridge behind her, and she did not see me. Yet the descent we were now to embark upon and at my hands was one I was powerless to control or stop. What had been love on my part, passionate and reverent, what was to be a triumphant sharing, a fusion, the penetration of a secret, raising of my life to the enigmatic and holy level of hers became a desperately shoddy and cruel attempt to force a response from her somehow. Step by step we descended the path of sexual exploitation until the projected sharing had become an infliction.

Yet even here, in the sewers of my memory, nothing is sure. How did that good girl that uninscribed tablet receive these violations? What did she think of them if she thought of them at all? They made her as far as I could see, more devoted, more dog-like, more secure. They are memories of my own failure, my own degradation, not hers. Those fantasies of adolescence now brought to half realization on my side were sad, dreary and angry. They reinforced the reality of physical life and they destroyed the possibility of anything else; and they made physical life not only three times real but contemptible. And under everything else, deep, was an anguish of helplessness and loss.

These advances in lubricity then, bound her arms more closely round my waist. I could not paint her face; but her body I painted. I painted her as a body and they are good and terrible paintings, dreadful in their story of fury and submission. They made me my first real money—except for the mayor's portrait, of course—and one of them is hung publicly so that I can go back and see that time, my room—our room—and try to understand, without apology or pity. There hangs the finished perfection of her sweet, cleft flesh. The light from the window strikes gold from her hair and scatters it over her breasts, her belly and her thighs. It was after the last and particularly degrading step of her exploitation; and in my self-contempt I added the electric light-shades of Guernica to catch the terror, but there was no terror to catch. There ought to have been but there was not. The electric light that ought to sear like a public prostitution seems an irrelevance. There is gold, rather, scattered from the window. There was dog faith and big eyes and submission. I look at the picture and I remember what the hidden face looked like; how after my act and my self-contempt she lay, looking out of the window as though she had been blessed.

Those were the great days of the Communist Party in England. There was a certain generosity in being a communist; a sense of martyrdom and a sense of purpose. I began to hide from Beatrice in the uproar of streets and halls. There was a meeting at the Town Hall in which a local councillor was going to give his reasons for joining the party. The decision has come down from above. He was a business man, so by remaining "closed" he could never hope to be in a better position, that is, one of governmental trust. There was no reason why his faith should not be capitalized there and then. That was in autumn, a chill autumn of blackout and phoney war. "Why I am joining the Communist Party" said the bills and hoardings, and the hall was crowded. He never got a chance to speak really; there were storms of cheering and counter-cheering, chairs overturned, local swirls in the thick blue cigarette smoke, cheers, shouts, boos. Someone went down at the back of the hall and there was a scuffle while paper arched up and glass smashed. I was looking at the councillor and his silent film mouthing so I saw when a bottle hit him over the right eye and he went down behind the green baize table. So I made to help him as someone turned out the lights and a police whistle blew. We huddled his limp body off the platform, through a side door and into his car, I and his daughter, while the police stood guard because after all he was a councillor. There was still much noise and darkness, and out of that uproar

I can remember the first words her unseen mouth said to me.

"Did you see the bastard who threw that bloody bottle?"

I had never met Taffy before, but as my eyes got used to the blackout I could hardly believe what I saw. She was dark and vivid. She had the kind of face that always looks made-up, even in the bath—such black eyebrows, such a big, red mouth. She was the prettiest girl I ever saw, neat in profile, with soft cheeks and two dimples that were in stunning contrast with her tenor voice and scarifying language. She was dabbing her father's head with a scrap of a handkerchief and muttering over and over again:

"I could kill that bloody sod!"

We took him to hospital and waited. Then there came a moment when we both looked at each other, were face to face; and a dozen things were obvious at once to both of us. We took him home and I waited again, below in the hall while he was put to bed—waited though not a word had been said. She came down the stairs and stood and there was nothing to do but look, nothing needing to be said. She took a scarf—her father's, I think—and we went out together. We went to a blacked-out pub and sat hand in hand, both stunned by this overwhelming sense of recognition. We kissed then and there in public without shame or bravado because although people stood within a yard of us, we were alone. We were both deeply committed elsewhere and we both recognized without a moment's doubt that we should never let each other go. I cannot remember how much we said of this or how much we felt. That very night she came to my spartan room and we made love, wildly and mutually. After all, we were communists and our private life was our own concern. The world was exploding. None of us would live long. Then she went home and left me to think of her next coming; and to think of Beatrice. What was I to do about her? What could I do? Give Taffy up? Presumably that would be the standard reply of the moralist. But was I now to live the rest of my life with Beatrice, knowing all the time that I was in love with Taffy?

In the end I did nothing. I merely ensured that they should not meet. But poor Beatrice bored me. The old magic, the familiar nerve was deadened or burned out. I no longer desired to understand her, no longer believed that she had some secret. I was sorry for her and exasperated by her. I tried to hide this; hoping that time would produce some solution but I was just not callous enough to get away with it. Beatrice noticed. She knew that I was colder and more distant. Her grip on me tightened, her face, her breasts bored in at my stomach. Perhaps if I had had the courage then to look her down in the eye I should have seen all the terror and fear that did not get into my pictures of her; but I never met her eye for I was ashamed to. Beatrice clung to me in tears and fear saying nothing.

She was the image of a betrayed woman, of outraged and helpless innocence. At this distance in time I find myself cynical enough or detached enough to question the tilt of her chin. Was she being operatic again? I cannot think that she had the emotional resources. She was sincere. She was helpless and terrified. The grip of her arms had a pitiful strength as though she could hold physically what was escaping her emotionally. Now I became acquainted with tears, now if I had been brutal enough I might have cried quits for the distraught bed of my school days; now I saw the very water of sorrow hanging honey-thick in eyelashes or dashed down a cheek like an exclamation mark at the beginning of a Spanish sentence. In between her visits to my room and when the requirements of her course made it impossible for her to see me, she took a leaf out of my old book. She began to write me letters. They were elaborate in their queries. What was the matter? What had she done? What could she do? Didn't I love her any more?

One day I was walking in a country lane and came out on the high road. I could see then what was making the noise. A car had caught a cat and taken away about five of its nine lives, and the poor, horrible thing was dragging away and screaming and demanding to be killed; and I ran away, my fingers in my ears until I had put the writhing thing out of mind and could play supposing again, or when the ship comes home. For, after all, in this bounded universe, I said, where nothing is certain but my own existence, what has to be cared for is the quiet and the pleasure of this sultan. Therefore the exposed nerve of the monocular homunculus the rack is all, is the point of my hunting Beatrice. In the curious and half-forgotten image of Beatrice on the platform before the Palladian bridge I saw nothing now but the power of the mind's self-deception. Certainly there was no light in her face. There were blemishes under the skin if one looked for them, and beneath the corner of each eye a little triangle of darkness that told of long nights. Her only power now was that of the accuser, the skeleton in the cupboard; and in this bounded universe we can easily put paid to that.

So Taffy and I went our way regardless. She was a lady by my low standards. She was fastidious except when she remembered that we were the spearhead of the proletariat. She also had a little money—not enough to support a husband or a lover but enough to help. So I left my room and address—gave no notice and paid no rent; and where in the bomb-broken basement, the square of blasted concrete, the crazy leaning brickwork that flowers are bursting should I post the money—but sneaked back to take the letter out of the box after a day or two; the letter that Beatrice wrote to me when she could not find out where I was. It was full of upbraiding, weak, gentle, frightened upbraiding. I saw Taffy and we were estranged for a while. She knew something and she sulked. We had one of those interminable, reasonable conversations about the relationship between men and women. One would not be jealous, one would understand enjoyment taken with a third person. Nothing was permanent, nothing was more than relative. Sex was a private business. Sex was a clinical matter and contraception had removed the need for orthodox family life. And then suddenly we were clinging to each other as though we were the only stable thing in an earthquake. I was muttering into the back of her neck.

"Marry me, Taffy, for Pete's sake marry me."

And Taffy was sniffing under my chin, cursing hoarsely, grabbing and rubbing her face against my jersey.

"You cock an eye at another woman and I'll have your guts for a girdle."

I left my temporary bed at the Y.M.C.A. and we shifted into a studio on Taffy's money. We got married at a registry office as an afterthought and the ceremony meant nothing to us except that we were free now to go back to the studio. I got a letter from Beatrice by way of Nick Shales who was still teaching at school then; and I did not know whether to open it or not. Nick wrote too, a wounded letter. Beatrice had been to every common acquaintance, looking for me. I saw her in my mind's eye standing on doorsteps, crimsoning with the shame of it all yet forced to go on.

"Do you know where Sammy Mountjoy is? I seem to have mislaid his address——"

I opened the letter and the first lines were a plea for forgiveness; but I read no further because the sight of the first page stabbed me with a knife. In the top left-hand corner she had drawn a little cross. We were out of danger.

I have one more memory of her, memory of a dream so vivid that it has taken a place in my history. I am receding along a suburban road that is infinitely long and the houses on either side are mean, unpainted, but drearily respectable. Beatrice is running after me, crying out with a shrill bird cry. It is evening in that horrible country and the shadows are closing round her. And the water is rising from the basements and gutters so that her feet trip and splash: but I have avoided the water somehow. It rises round her, always rises.

But as for Taffy and I, we made ourselves a place between four walls and we faded out of the party as the bombs began to fall and the time of my soldiering drew nearer. We explored our histories, mine edited a bit, and perhaps hers, too. We achieved that extraordinary level of security when we did not expect entire truth from each other, knowing it to be impossible and extending a *carte blanche* of forgiveness beforehand. Beatrice faded from me, like the party. I told Taffy about her and the small cross did it. Taffy had a baby.

What else could I have done but run away from Beatrice? I do not mean what ought I to have done or what someone else could have done. I simply mean that as I have described myself, as I see myself in my backward eye, I could do nothing but run away. I could not kill the cat to stop it suffering. I had lost my power to choose. I had given away my freedom. I cannot be blamed for the mechanical and helpless reaction of my nature. What I was, I had become. The young man who put her on the rack is different in every particular from the child who was towed along the street past the duke in the antique shop. Where was the division? What choice had he?

I saw Johnny about then—saw him for one perfect and definable instant that remains a measure in my mind of the difference between us. I was walking away from myself one afternoon in the country—coming to the top of Counter's Hill where the road seems to leap over. Johnny leapt over towards me on his motor-bike and I had to jump out of the way. He must have come up the other side at about a hundred miles an hour so that when he reached the top and appeared to me he seemed to go straight on in the air and fly past. I remember him against the sky, six inches clear of the road. His left hand is on the handle-bars. He leans back and turns his helmeted head round and back as far as he can to the right. The girl has her head over his shoulder, her right arm reaching round him and her mop flies in the wind. Johnny's right arm is round her head with his hand prone on top and they are kissing there at that speed on a blind hill-top, careless of what has been and what is to come; because what is to come might be nothing.

I welcomed the destruction that war entails, the deaths and terror. Let the world fall. There was anarchy in the mind where I lived and anarchy in the world at large, two states so similar that the one might have produced the other. The shattered houses, the refugees, the deaths and torture—accept them as a pattern of the world and one's own behaviour is little enough disease. Why bother to murder in a private capacity when you can shoot men publicly and be congratulated publicly for it? Why bother about one savaged girl when girls are blown to pieces by the thousand? There is no peace for the wicked but war with its waste and lust and irresponsibility is a very good substitute. I made poor use of destruction because I was already well enough known to be a war artist.

No gun for Sammy. He became a recording angel instead.

"Here, then?"

"No. Not here."

Then where? I am wise in some ways, can see unusually far through a brick wall and therefore I ought to be able to answer my own question. At least I can tell when I acquired or was given the capacity to see. Dr. Halde attended to that. In freedom I should never have acquired any capacity. Then was loss of freedom the price exacted, a necessary preliminary to a new mode of knowing? But the result of my helplessness out of which came the new mode was also the desperate misery of Beatrice and the good joys of Taffy. I cannot convince myself that my mental capacities are important enough to justify either the good or the harm they started. Yet the capacity to see through the brick wall rose directly and inevitably at Halde's hands out of my sow's ear. I have an over-clear picture of the room in which he started the process. The Gestapo whipped the coverings off yesterday and unveiled the grey faces.

The room was real and matter of fact and sordid.

The main bit of furniture was an enormous table that occupied one-third of the floor area. The table was old, polished and had legs like the bulbous legs of a grand piano. There were papers piled at each end, leaving the centre for the commandant's blotting-pad. We faced him across the pad, man to man, except that he sat and we stood. There were filing cabinets behind him and the card slips on each drawer were lettered in careful gothic script. Behind and above the commandant's chair was a large photograph of the Fuehrer. It was a harmless room, dull and comfortless. Some of the piles of paper had been on the table for a long time because you could see what the dust was doing to them.

March in, right turn, salute.

"Captain Mountjoy, sir."

But the commandant was not sitting in his chair neither was his fat little deputy. This man was a civilian. He wore a dark lounge suit and he sat back in the swivel chair, elbow on each arm, finger-tips together. Left and behind him was the commandant's deputy and three soldiers. There were also two anonymous figures in the uniform of the Gestapo. We were a full house; but I could look nowhere but straight at the man in front of me. Is it hindsight to say that already I liked him, was drawn to him, could have spent as much time with him as with Ralph and Nobby? I was fearful, too, my heart was beginning to run away with me. We did not know for certain in those days how bad the Gestapo were, but we heard rumours and made guesses. And he was a civilian—too high up to wear uniform unless he felt like it.

"Good morning, Captain Mountjoy. Shall we say mister or even Samuel or Sammy? Would you like a chair?"

He turned and spoke rapidly in German to a soldier on my left who placed a metal chair with a fabric seat for me. The man leaned forward.

"My name is Halde. Dr. Halde. Let us get to know each other."

He could smile, too, not a wintry smile but a genuine one of joy and friendliness, so that the blue eyes danced and the flesh lifted to his cheek-bones. And now I heard how perfect his English was. The commandant spoke to us mostly through an interpreter or briefly in throaty German-English. But Dr. Halde spoke better English than I did. Mine was the raw, inaccurate stuff of common use, but his had the same ascetic perfection as his face. His enunciation had the purity that goes with a clear and logical mind. My enunciation was slurred and hurried, voice of a man who had never stilled his brain, never thought, never been certain of anything. Yet still his was the foreign voice, nationless, voice of the divorced idea, a voice that might be conveyed better by the symbols of mathematics than printed words. And though his P's and B's were clearly differentiated they were a little too sharp, just a fraction too sharp as though his nose were pinched inside.

"Better?"

Doctor of what? The whole shape of his head was exquisitely delicate. At first it looked roundish, because your eye was caught by the polished bald top where the black hair streaked across; but then as you came down from there you saw that round was the wrong word because the whole face and head were included in an oval, wide at the top, pointed at the chin. He had a great deal of forehead, the widest part of the oval and his hair had receded. His nose was long and the hollows of his eye shallow. The eyes themselves were an astonishing cornflower blue.

Philosophy?

But what was most striking about his face was not the fineness of the bone structure but the firmness of the flesh over it. There are many things that can be learned from the general condition of such tissue. If it is wasted away solely by disease the general effects of suffering cannot be concealed. The eyes are dull and the flesh bags under them. But this flesh was healthy, was pale and the least amount compatible with decent human covering of the front of the head. Any less and the skull would start through. The lines were not necessarily the lines of suffering but of thought and good-humour. Taken with the fine hands, the almost translucent fingers and the answer was asceticism. The man had the body of a saint.

Psychology?

Psychology!

Suddenly I remembered that I should have refused the chair. Thank you, I prefer to stand. That was what a Buchan hero would do. But I had this engrossing face before me, this assured and superior English. I had sat down already in a chair that rocked slightly on an uneven floor. All at once I was vulnerable, a man trapped in a mountain of flesh, a man wielding a club against a foil fencer. The chair tipped again and I heard my voice, high and absurdly social.

":Thanks."

"Cigarette?"

This ought to be refused, should be waved away—but then I caught sight of my fingers, stained to the second knuckle.

"Thanks."

Dr. Halde reached behind the right-hand pile of papers, produced a silver cigarette-box and flicked it open. I leaned forward, groping in the box and saw what was behind the pile of papers. Nobby and Ralph had been at great pains to find out how to avoid the archaic smile of the seventh century; but those papier mâché heads of hair with the clownish ill-made faces would not have deceived a child. They would have done better after all to let me help, or relied on hair and the blankets pulled right up.

Dr. Halde was holding out a silver cigarette lighter with a quiet flame. I put half an inch of cigarette in the flame and drew back, puffing out smoke.

Nonchalant.

Dr. Halde began to laugh so that the flesh of his cheeks rolled up into a neat sausage under either eye. He remained pale mostly; but there was the faintest suggestion of rose under each sausage. His eyes danced, his teeth shone. A little V of wrinkles creased the skin outside each eye. He turned and included the deputy in his delighted laughter. He came back to me, put his fingers together and composed himself. He was an inch or two higher than I. He looked down at me therefore, friendly and amused.

"We are neither of us ordinary men, Mr. Mountjoy. There is already a certain indefinable sympathy between us."

He spread his hands out.

"I should be in my university. You should be in that studio to which it is my sincere wish you may return."

The nationless words had in them an awful quality of maturity as though the next sentence might well be all the answers. He was looking me in the eye, inviting me to lift this affair above the vulgar brawl into an atmosphere where civilized men might come to some arrangement. All at once I dreaded that he should find me uncivilized, dreaded so many indefinable things.

Suddenly I was fumbling with my cigarette.

"Did you burn yourself, Mr. Mountjoy? No? Good."

He was holding out a china ashtray with a Rhineland

137

river scene on it. I took the ashtray carefully and set it near me on the table.

"You're wasting your time. I don't know how they got away or where they were going."

He watched me for a moment in silence. He nodded gravely.

"That may well be."

I scraped back my chair and put a hand on either side of the seat to get up. I began to play unbelievingly with the fiction that the interview was over.

"Well, then——"

I was rising; but a heavy hand fell on my left shoulder and clamped me down. I recognized the colour of the fabric at the wrist, and the physical touch of what ought to be feared made me angry instead so that I could feel the blood in my neck. But Dr. Halde was frowning past my shoulder and making quietening gestures with both hands, palms down. The heaviness left my shoulder. Dr. Halde took out a white cloud of lawn and blew his nose precisely. So he was suffering from catarrh then, his nose really was pinched and his English really perfect.

He folded away the lawn and smiled at me.

"That may well be. But we must make certain."

My hands were too big and clumsy. I shoved them into the pockets of my tunic where they felt unnatural. I took them out and worked them into my trouser pockets instead. I said the phrases in one mechanical movement as I had learnt them. Even as I spoke I knew they were nothing but a nervous reflex.

"I am a commissioned officer and a prisoner-of-war. I demand to be treated in accordance with the Geneva Convention."

Dr. Halde made a sound that was half a laugh and half a sigh. His smile was sad and expostulatory as if I were a child again, making a mistake in my classwork.

"Of course you are. Yes indeed."

The deputy commandant spoke to him and there was a sudden quick exchange. The deputy was looking at me and back at Halde and arguing fiercely. But Halde had the best of it. The deputy clicked his heels, shouted an order and left the room with the soldiers. I was alone with Halde and the Gestapo.

Dr. Halde turned back to me.

"We know all about you."

I answered him instantly.

"That's a lie."

He laughed genuinely and ruefully.

"I see that our conversation will always jump from level to level. Of course we can't know all about you, can't know all about anybody. We can't know all about ourselves. Wasn't that what you meant?"

I said nothing.

"But then you see, Mr. Mountjoy, what I meant was something on a much lower level a level at which certain powers are operative, at which certain deductions may be made. We know, for example, that you would find asceticism, particularly when it was forced on you, very difficult. I, on the other hand—you see? And so on."

"Well?"

"You were a communist. So was I, once. It is a generous fault in the young."

"I don't understand what you're saying."

"I shall be honest with you though I cannot say whether

you will be honest with me. War is fundamentally immoral. Do you agree?"

"Perhaps it is."

"One must be for or against. I made my choice with much difficulty but I have made it. Perhaps it was the last choice I shall ever make. Accept such international immorality, Mr. Mountjoy, and all unpleasantnesses are possible to man. You and I, we know what wartime morality amounts to. We have been communists after all. The end justifies the means."

I ground the cigarette out in the ashtray.

"What's all that got to do with me?"

He made a circling gesture with the cigarette-box before holding it out again.

"For you and me, reality is this room. We have given ourselves over to a kind of social machine. I am in the power of my machine; and you are in my power absolutely. We are both degraded by this, Mr. Mountjoy, but there it is."

"Why pick on me? I tell you I know nothing!"

I had the cigarette in my fingers and was fumbling for a match. He exclaimed and reached out the lighter.

"Oh, please!"

I got the cigarette into the flame with both hands and sucked at the white teat. There were the shapes of two men standing at ease, but I had not seen their faces, could not see any face but the worried, donnish face behind the lighter. He put the lighter down, set his hands on the blotter and leaned towards me.

"If only you could see the situation as I see it! You would be willing, so willing, I might say anxious"—the hands gripped—"Mr. Mountjoy, believe me, I—Mr.

Mountjoy. Four days ago over fifty officers escaped from another camp."

"And you want me to—you want me——"

"Wait. They are—well, they are still at liberty, at large, they are not back in the camp."

"Good for them, then!"

"At any moment a similar escape may be made from this camp. Two officers, your friends, Mr. Mountjoy, have done that already. Our information is that morale makes a large-scale escape from this camp unlikely, but not impossible. It must not happen—if you only knew how much it must not happen!"

"I can't help you. Escape is the prisoner's business."

"Sammy—I beg your pardon, Mr. Mountjoy—how well you have responded to your conditioning! Am I wrong after all? Are you really nothing but a loyal, chuckle-headed British soldier of the king?"

He sighed, leant back.

"Why did you call me Sammy?"

He smiled with me and at me and the winter of his face turned to spring.

"I've been studying you. Putting myself in your place. An unpardonable liberty of course, but war is war."

"I didn't know I was all that important."

He stopped smiling, reached down and fumbled papers out of a briefcase.

"This is how important you are, Mr. Mountjoy."

He threw two small folders across the blotter. They were drab and worn. I opened them and examined the paragraphs of incomprehensible gothic print, the scribbled initials and names, the circular stamps. Nobby looked up at me from the photograph in one and Ralph from the other—Ralph posing for the photograph, being deliberately half-witted and deadpan.

"You got them then."

Dr. Halde did not reply; and something about the silence, some tension perhaps, made me look up quickly and turn my statement into a question.

"You caught them?"

Dr. Halde still said nothing. Then he took out the cloud of white lawn and blew his nose on it again.

"I'm sorry to tell you that your friends are dead. They were shot while trying to escape."

For a long time I looked at the dim photographs; but they meant nothing. I tried to stir myself, said silently and experimentally in my mind: their chests have been beaten in by a handful of lead, they have come to the end both of them, those indefatigable cricketers, have seen and recognized the end of the game. They were my friends and their familiar bodies are rotting away.

Do you feel nothing then?

Maybe.

Halde was speaking softly.

"Now do you understand, Mr. Mountjoy? It is vitally necessary that not another man should get outside the wire—necessary for their sakes, for our sakes, for the sake of humanity, for the sake of the future——"

"Bloody swine."

"Oh, yes, of course. That goes without saying, et cetera."

"I tell you I know nothing."

"And then when I am given, or if it comes to that, take the task of preventing a recurrence of this—where else should I look? Of all the men in this camp, who has a record so accessible, who has talked about painting and pigments, about lithography? And besides"—he was peering at me closely with those enormous cornflower eyes —"who among all these men is so likely to be reasonable? Should I chose as my lever Major Witlow-Brownrigg, that stiff gentleman and bend him till he breaks, or shall I choose material more pliable?"

"I tell you——"

"It is essential that I should be able to raid the camp swiftly and suddenly and with absolute certainty of what I am going to find, and where. Please, please listen to me. I must break up the printing press, confiscate the tools, the uniform, the civilian clothes, I must smash the radio, I must go straight to the tunnel and fill it in——"

"But I——"

"Please listen. I choose you not only because you must be part of the organization but because you are an artist and therefore objective and set apart from your fellows; a man who would know when betrayal was not betrayal and when one must break a rule, an oath, to serve a higher truth——"

"For the last time, I know nothing!"

He spread his hands palm uppermost on the table.

"Does that seem reasonable, Mr. Mountjoy? Consider all the indications that could point to the opposite conclusion—your various skills, your friendship with the two officers—even your past membership of a party famous for underground activities—oh, believe me, I have a great respect for you and a great distaste for my own work. I also understand you as far as one man may understand another——"

"You can't. I don't understand myself."

"But I am objective because although I can get inside

your skin I can leave it at will, can get out before the pain starts——"

"Pain?"

"And so I know, objectively, surely, serenely, that at one level or other of our alas, unfortunate association you will, how shall I put it——?"

"I won't talk. I know nothing."

"Talk. Yes, that is the word. At some point, Mr. Mountjoy, you will talk."

"I know nothing. Nothing!"

"Wait. Let us begin by giving you something of great value. I shall explain you to yourself. No one, not a lover, a father, a schoolmaster, could do that for you. They are all inhibited by conventions and human kindness. It is only in such conditions as these, electric furnace conditions, in which the molten, blinding truth may be uttered from one human face to another."

"Well?"

"What embryo if it could choose, would go through the sufferings of birth to achieve your daily consciousness? There is no health in you, Mr. Mountjoy. You do not believe in anything enough to suffer for it or be glad. There is no point at which something has knocked on your door and taken possession of you. You possess yourself. Intellectual ideas, even the idea of loyalty to your country sits on you loosely. You wait in a dusty waiting-room on no particular line for no particular train. And between the poles of belief, I mean the belief in material things and the belief in a world made and supported by a supreme being, you oscillate jerkily from day to day, from hour to hour. Only the things you cannot avoid, the sear of sex or pain, avoidance of the one suffering repetition and prolongation of the other, this constitutes what your daily consciousness would not admit, but experiences as life. Oh, yes, you are capable of a certain degree of friendship and a certain degree of love, but nothing to mark you out from the ants or the sparrows."

"Then you'd better have nothing to do with me."

"Have you not yet appreciated the tragicomedy of our situation? If what I have described were all, Mr. Mountjoy, I should point a gun at your head and give you ten seconds to start talking. But there is a mystery in you which is opaque to both of us. Therefore, even when I am almost certain that you would speak if you had anything to tell I must go on to the next step, the infliction of more suffering because of the gap between 'almost' and 'certain'. Oh, yes! I shall loathe myself, but how will that help you?"

"Can't you see I couldn't stand a threat?"

"And therefore I must go through the motions as though I knew nothing about you at all. I will pretend you can neither be bribed nor swayed by fear. I offer you nothing, then, but a chance to save lives. Tell me everything you know about the escape organization and you shall be what you were before, neither more nor less. You shall be taken from this camp to another camp neither more nor less comfortable. The source of our information shall be concealed."

"Why don't you talk to the senior officer?"

Blue cornflowers.

"Who would confide in a senior officer?"

"Why won't you believe me?"

"Who would believe you, Mr. Mountjoy, if he had any sense?"

145

"What's the good of asking me for the truth then?"

A sad, wry, reasonable face. Hands spread.

"Even if that is true, Mr. Mountjoy, I must go on. Surely you realize that? Oh, I agree, we're in the sewer together—both of us up to the neck."

"Well, then!"

"What do you want most in the world? To go home? That could be arranged—a mental breakdown—just a month or two in a pleasant sanatorium, a few papers signed and there you are—home, Mr. Mountjoy. I implore you."

"I'm feeling a bit dizzy."

The inside of my hands slipped on my face. I could feel the oily stuff running.

"Or if home does not seem so immediately attractive— how about an interim period of entertainment? I try to phrase this as delicately as one not born to the use of your ample language can manage; but do you not sometimes feel the deprivation of the companionship of either sex? The resources of Europe are at your disposal, I am told they are, are——"

His voice went right away into the distance. I opened my eyes and saw that I was holding on to the edge of the table, saw that where my fingers had slipped they left wet marks. Just the tiniest little prick. A kind of sobbing rage swelled up in my throat.

"You bloody fool! Do you think I wouldn't tell you if I knew? I tell you I know nothing—nothing!"

His face was white, shining with perspiration and compassionate.

"Poor boy. How beastly the whole thing is, Sammy. I may call you Sammy? Of course, you care nothing for the resources of Europe. Forgive me. Money? No. I think not. Well there. I have taken you up to a pinnacle of the temple and shown you the whole earth. And you have refused it."

"I haven't refused it. Can't you see, you, you—I don't know anything——"

"You have bidden me get behind you. Or perhaps you are right and you really know nothing. Are you a hero or not, Sammy?"

"I'm no hero. Let me go."

"Believe me, I wish I could. But if anyone else escapes they will be shot. I can't take any risks at all. No stone unturned, Sammy, no avenue unexplored."

"I'm going to be sick."

He fell silent. I swayed back in the dentist's chair which unbalanced incongruously as though it were metal and fabric on an uneven floor. The Fuehrer in his awful power slid apart and then closed like the hands of a hypnotist.

"Let me go. Can't you see? They wouldn't trust me. Nobby and Ralph—they tossed up perhaps, but even if they had not, nothing would have induced them to put me in the picture—I know now what they wanted with me; but all the time they must have had a reservation. Can't trust him. He'd squeal. Curious contorted chap—something missing in the middle——"

"Sammy. Sammy! Can you hear me? Wake up, Sammy!'

I came back out of chaos, was collected together mercilessly from those unnameable places. For the first time I had a pause in which I could have willingly remained for ever. Not to look, not to know or anticipate, not to feel, but only to be conscious of identity is the next best thing to complete unconsciousness. Inside me I neither stood nor sat or lay down, I was suspended in the void.

"Well, Sammy?"

Memory of the cornflowers tugged at me. I opened my eyes and he was still there opposite. I spoke to his understanding out of our naked souls.

"Can't you be merciful?"

"It is the karma of our two nations that we should torture each other."

With my hands on the edge of the table I spoke to him carefully.

"Isn't it obvious to you? You know me. Be reasonable. Do you think I'm the kind of man who can keep anything back when I am threatened?"

He did not answer immediately and as the silence stretched out I began to know what was inevitable. I even looked away from him, unable now to influence the event. The Fuehrer was there, both transparent pictures now slid exactly into one. The plaster round the photograph was institutional buff and needed redecorating. One of the Gestapo was standing easy and as my eyes swung to his face I saw him put one hand to his mouth and hide a yawn. The interminable argument in a foreign language was keeping him from his grey coffee and sticky bun. Dr. Halde waited till my eye came back to his face.

"And you can see, Sammy, that I have to make certain."

"I told you I know nothing!"

"Think."

"I won't think. I can't think."

"Think."

"What's the good? Please!"

"Think."

And the generalized sense of position, of a war on, of prison, of men shut in——

"I can't——"

—men who lay in their bunks, rotting away, men with bright faces who went in and out of chapel, incomprehensible as bees weaving their passes before a grassy bank——

"I tell you I can't!"

—the men going round the bend, wire-happy, running wildly as the guns tucked them in——

"I tell you——"

The men.

For, of course, I knew something. I had known something for more than a year. It was the standard of knowledge required that I did not know. But I could have said at any time that out of the hundreds of us there were perhaps twenty-five who might actually try to escape. Only the information had not been required. What we know is not what we see or learn but what we realize. Day after day a complex of tiny indications had added up and now presented me with a picture. I was an expert. Who else had lived as visually and professionally with these faces and taken knowledge of them in through his pores? Who else had that puzzled curiosity about man, that photographic apprehension, that worried faith in the kings of Egypt?

"I tell you——"

I could say to him quite simply; I do not know when or where the escape organization operates or how—but take these twenty men into your trawl and there will be no escapes.

"Well, Sammy? You tell me what?"

And he was right of course. I was not an ordinary man. I was at once more than most and less. I could see this war as the ghastly and ferocious play of children who having made a wrong choice or a whole series of them were now helplessly tormenting each other because a wrong use of freedom had lost them their freedom. Everything was relative, nothing absolute. Then who was most likely to know best what is best to do? I, abashed before the kingship of the human face, or Halde behind the master's desk, in the judge's throne, Halde, at once human and superior?

He was still there; but I had to focus again to bring my eyes back from the map of Europe and the locked armies. His eyes were not dancing but intent. I saw he was holding his breath because he let it out with a little gasp before he spoke:

"Well?"

"I don't know."

"Tell me."

"I've just told you!"

"Sammy. Are you being an exceptional man or are you tying yourself to the little code? Are you not displaying nothing more creditable than a schoolboy's sense of honour when he refuses to tell on his naughty comrades? The organization will steal sweets, Sammy; but the sweets they steal are poisoned——"

"I've had enough of this. I demand that you send for the senior officer——"

As the hands fell on either shoulder Halde made his placatory gesture again.

"Now I shall be plain with you. I will even give you some trumps. I dislike hurting people, I loathe my job and everything that goes with it. But what rights have you?

Rights still apply to your prisoners *en masse*, but they bend and break before necessity. You are too intelligent not to know that. We can transfer you from this room to another camp. Why should you not be killed by your own R.A.F. on the way? But to kill you now would benefit nobody. We want information, Sammy, not corpses. You saw the door to your left because you came through it. There is another one to your right. Don't look round. Choose, Sammy. Which door is going to be your exit?"

And, of course, I might be deceiving myself, might be building up a whole façade of knowledge which would collapse when tested by fact—I could feel something stinging in my eyes.

"I don't know anything!"

"You know, Sammy, history will be quite unable to unravel the tangle of circumstances between you and me. Which of us is right? Either of us, neither? The problem is insoluble, even if they could understand our reservations, our snatched judgments, our sense of truth being nothing but an infinite regression, a shifting island in the middle of chaos——"

I must have cried out because I heard my voice rise against the palate.

"But look. You want the truth. All right I'll tell you the truth. I don't know whether I know anything or not!"

I could see the moulding of his face more clearly now for the top of every fold shone with perspiration.

"Are you telling the truth, Sammy, or must I admire you, foolishly and jealously? Yes, Sammy. I admire you because I dare not believe you. Your exit is a better one than mine."

"You can't do anything to me. I'm a prisoner of war!"

His face shone. His eyes were like bright blue stones. The general light on his forehead increased as it ran together. It became a star that moved down the long line of his nose and fell on the blotter with an audible tap.

"I loathe myself, Sammy, and I admire you. If necessary I will kill you."

There is a heard beating of the heart when each beat is like the blow of a stick on concrete. There is also the soggy beat, in the indulged life of the chain smoker, a confusion in the breathing that struggles with phlegm and that centre in there—in here—dumping sacks of wet vegetables on a wooden floor and shaking the building to pieces. There was heat, too, that rose to the ears so that the chin lifted and the mouth opened, swallowing on hard nothing.

Halde swam.

"Go!"

There was a strange obedience about my two hands that grasped the sides of the seat and helped to lift me. I did not like to see the new door for the first time so I turned back to Halde, but he would not meet my eye and he was swallowing on nothing as I had done. So at last in this awful trance of obedience I turned away towards the ordinary wooden door and beyond it there was a corridor of concrete with a strip of coconut matting down the centre. My mind was reeling along, trying to say inside; now this is happening, this is the moment! But my mind could not take it. Therefore the feet trod obediently one in front of the other, there was no rebellion from the body, only astonishment and doom in the mind. And the flesh that quivered and jumped had a sense of occasion. My eyes went on with their own life, presented to me as precious trophies, the stains on the floor—one in the likeness of a brain. And there was another one, a long mark on the scrubbed concrete that might have been the crack in the bedroom ceiling, the raw material out of which imagination had constructed so many faces.

Tie. Belt. Shoelaces.

I stood there with neither belt nor braces and my one conscious thought was that I needed both hands to hold my trousers up. Some soft, opaque material was folded over my eyes from behind and this seemed a matter for expostulation because without light how can a man see and be ready for the approaching feet of the last terror? He may be ambushed, cannot assess the future, cannot tell when to give up his precious scrap of information if he indeed has a scrap and it is indeed precious——

But I was walking, propelled not ungently from behind. Another door was opened, for I heard the handle scrape. Hands pushed me and pressed down. I fell on my knees, head down, hands out protectively. I was kneeling on cold concrete and a door was shut roughly behind me. The key turned and feet went away.

How did I come to be so frightened of the dark?

Once there was a way of seeing which was a part of innocence. Far back on the very edge of memory—or further perhaps, because the episode is outside time—I saw a creature four inches high, paper-white, changing shape and strutting along a top edge of the open window like a cock. Then later, when I saw her first there was perhaps still time; but no one told me, no one knew what we might see and how easily we might lose the faculty.

The verger stepped in, opened me up with one blow of his hand. Now for the first time I was awash in a sea where I might drown, was defenceless against attack from any quarter. I wore vest and pants, grey shirt and tie, socks up to the knee, gartered and turned down. I wore half-shoes and a jacket; and presently I wore a bright blue cap. Father Watts-Watt fitted me out and threw me into a new life. He directed his housekeeper to see to me; and I was seen to. I was taken from the ward to the vast rectory and Mrs. Pascoe made me bathe at once as though all those weeks in the ward had not cleansed me of Rotten Row. But though the ward had accustomed me to baths, this bathroom was very different. Mrs. Pascoe went with me along a corridor then up two steps to the door. Inside the bathroom she showed me the new things I had to do. There was a box of matches tied to—but what was it tied to? What did I think that structure was? A man in copper armour? That would have gone with the whole structure of the room; for it was taller than long, with one high, glazed window, that looked at nothing; and a single naked bulb. But the copper, brass-bound idol dominated everything, even dominated the huge bath on its four splayed tiger feet, dominated me, with a blank look over my head from two dark caverns and an intimidation of pipes. Mrs. Pascoe turned on the water, struck a match and the idol roared and flamed. Later, when I read about Talus, the man of brass, in my mind's eye he had just such a voice, such flames, just such a copper, brass-bound body. But that first time I was so plainly terrified that Mrs. Pascoe stayed with me while the bath filled and the electric light was haloed in steam that bulged down from the ceiling and the yellow walls looked as though they were sweating in the heat. Then, when there was water enough in the bath—less than I would have liked—for in the womb we are immersed completely—she turned off the gas and the water, showed me the bolt on the door and left me. I bolted the door, put my new clothes on the chair and hurried to the bath with one eye on Talus. I squatted over the water, running cold and inspecting the long yellow smear on the white enamel so far away from me.

The bathroom door rattled and shook. Father Watts-Watt spoke softly outside.

"Sam. Sam."

I said nothing at all, before the idol, in that defence-less place.

"Sam! Why have you bolted the door?"

Before I could answer I heard him walking away along the corridor.

"Mrs. Pascoe!"

She said something and for a moment or two they muttered.

"But the child might have a fit!"

I could not hear her answer but Father Watts-Watt cried out jerkily.

"He must never bolt the bathroom door—*never*!"

I squatted there in the hot water and shivered with cold while the argument, if such it was, faded away downstairs. A door shut somewhere. After that bath when I had dressed and crept downstairs, it was an astonishment to find Mrs. Pascoe sitting so quietly in the kitchen and mending his socks. I had my supper with her and she shooed me off to bed. I had two lights for myself. One hung from a bulb in the middle of the ceiling and one was hidden in a little pink shade on a table by the bed. But Mrs. Pascoe saw me into bed and then, just when she was leaving, she took the bulb out of the bedside lamp.

"You won't want that one, Sam. Little boys should go to bed to sleep."

She hovered for a moment and paused by the door.

"Good night, Sam."

She turned out the other light and shut the door.

This was my first meeting with the generalized and irrational fear which attacks some children. They cannot localize it at first; and when at last they succeed, it becomes more unbearable still. I went down in that bed, hunched up and shivering, taking up a foetal shape first that only unfolded a little because I had to breathe. In Rotten Row I had never seemed to be so alone—there was always the brass knob of the pub's back door; and, of course, in the ward we were legion we little devils— but here, in this wholly not-understood milieu, among these strange, powerful people—and at that the church clock struck with a sound that seemed to make the rectory shake—here I was utterly and helplessly alone for the first time in darkness and a whirl of ignorance. Fear was spasms, any of which might have made me faint clean away if I had known of that refuge; and when, gasping for air, the disarranged clothes allowed me a glimpse of the glimmering window, the church tower looked in like an awful head. But there must have been in me still some of the prince whom Philip used, for I determined then and there that I would have a light at any cost. So I got out of bed into a white flame of danger that burnt and gave no light. I put a chair under the single bulb in the middle of the room because I planned to transfer the bulb to the lamp by my bed and put it back in the morning. But if you are undefended in bed, you are helpless out of it and utterly the sport of whatever dark thing waits for you when you stand on a chair in the middle of the room. I stood on that chair in the middle of the room with my back twitching. I was reaching up, I was holding the bulb when both my hands burst into cherry red and the light- ning flashed at me from between them. I dropped from the chair and bounded into bed with a dactylic rush dum- tydy umtydy and huddled there sitting knees up and bed- clothes drawn to my ears.

Father Watts-Watt stood in the open door, his hand on the switch. The light shone at me from his knees and his eyes and the swinging bulb moved all the shadows of the room in little circles. For a time we looked at each other through this movement. Then he seemed to pull his eyes away from me and look for something in the air over my bed.

"Did you call out, Sam?"

I shook my head without saying anything. He moved

away from the door, watching me now, trailing his right hand behind him on the switch and then letting it go consciously, like a swimmer who takes his feet off the sand and knows now he is out of depth. He struck out into the room where I was. He went first to the chair and examined my clothes, rubbing them between his fingers; and then he looked down past me.

"You must not play with the light, Sam. If you touch the bulb I shall have to take it away."

Still I said nothing. He came to the bed and very slowly sat himself down sideways near the foot. He could sit anywhere there without touching me. I did not stretch down so far. He began to tap with his fingers on the counterpane. He watched his fingers carefully as though what they did was very difficult and very important. He tapped slowly. He stopped tapping. His fingers had so occupied me that I was startled when I looked up to see that he was watching me sideways and that his mouth was open. When I looked up, he looked down and began to tap again, quickly.

He coughed and spoke.

"Did you say your prayers tonight?"

Before I could answer him he had hastened on. He talked fast about how necessary prayer was before sleeping as a protection from wicked thoughts which all people had no matter how good they were, no matter how hard they tried and so one must pray—pray in the morning and at midday and at night so that one could put away the thoughts and sleep quietly.

Did I know how to pray? No? Then he would teach me—but not tonight. Tonight he would pray for us both. There was no need for me to get out of bed. He prayed there, writhing his bony hands together, moving them and his head up and down so that the black patches of his eye-hollows changed shape. He prayed long, it seemed to me, sometimes in broken sentences of English and sometimes in another language. Then he stopped and put his hands down on either side of him so that they rested on the ribbed pattern of the counterpane. His two black patches, still moving a little as the hanging bulb settled deeper into the spiral, regarded me opaquely. Each was topped with a tangle of white and black hairs, as though youth and extreme age contended in that body without hope of compromise; and the lowish forehead shone and the bridge of the sharp nose. Then as I watched, the bedclothes still drawn up to my mouth, I saw the whole lower part of his face shorten and broaden, move upward. Lighted skin appeared under each patch. Father Watts-Watt was smiling at me, moving the set flesh of his face, rearranging the muscles of the cheek, showing folds and creases and bumps and teeth. I could hear him breathing, fast and shallow—and once he reared up with a curious jerk of the neck just as on that first evening, a shudder from feet to head, a goose walking over his grave. At last he moved six inches nearer on the counterpane. I could see his eyes now in the patches. They were peering at me closely.

"I suppose your mother used to kiss you good night, Sam?"

Dumbly I shook my head. Then for a long time there was silence again and no motion but the tiny dying circles of the shadows on the floor, no sound but breathing.

Suddenly he jerked off the bed. He strode to the window and then to the door. He turned with his hand on the switch and he seemed to me to be twice the height of a man.

"Don't let me catch you signalling again, Sam, or I shall take away this light, too."

He switched off the light and banged the door behind him. I dived into the bedclothes again, shielding myself from the church tower that looked in through the window with its black, concealing patches. Now there was not only the threat of the darkness but a complete mystery added to it.

Yet here, if I look for the moment of change I cannot find it; I was still the child from Rotten Row and if I had no freedom it was taken away physically not mentally. For Father Watts-Watt never repeated his advances, if that is what they were. Instead, he wrapped me in an occasional mystery of signals to the unnamed foes who surrounded him. He had a developing persecution mania; and presently the world saw him less and less. He watched me from far off to see if I would communicate with these enemies; or perhaps he wrapped me into his fantasies because that was a way of concealing his true motives from himself. On some involved level he pretended to be mad in order to evade the responsibility for his own frightening desires and compulsions and therefore in a sense he was not mad at all—yet is a man who pretends to be mad completely sane? This, for Father Watts-Watt and Samuel Mountjoy is another of those infinite regressions, an insoluble relativity. Thus when Father Watts-Watt stopped me on the gravel path outside the rectory side door, neither he nor I could have analysed his motives now or then.

"If anyone appears at your window, Sam, in the middle

of the night and tries to make you believe things about me, you are to come to my room at once."

"Sir."

And then it was such a long, writhing look across the garden, round and up the wall of the church, back above my head, his hands together—Father Watts-Watt moving with vast improbability like the caterpillar in Alice, then hands clasped up by his left cheek and looking past my own:

"I could tell you such things! They will go to any expense, Sam, any length——"

This was an example, I thought, of the elongating clergymen mentioned by the verger, here was one in fact before me on the daylight gravel now writhing sideways, winding up, flinging his arms wide with a gasp and smile:

"Back to work, eh, Sam? Back to my study——"

He moved away and then stopped, looking back in the door.

"You won't forget, Sam? Anything unusual—anything in the middle of the night——"

He went away and left me unfrightened. The curious intuition of childhood sensed his lies and did not mind them. He added nothing to the terror of the dark, the terror generalized and mindless that had to be endured nightlong and night after night. Once or twice more, I remember, he covered up that first passionate movement towards me by hinting at mysteries so that now I can piece them together.

His delusion or pretence, whichever it was, was basically that people were trying to take away his reputation. They were, I suppose, accusing him, trying to pin on him publicly all the acts of his fantasies. There was a complex system of lights employed as signals so that each of them should know where he was and what he was doing. The Russians—still in those days, *Punch* Bolshies—were at the back of it. Father Watts-Watt brought into his mania all the features of existence as it appeared to him, just as Evie had brought in hers. The only difference was that Evie told me everything whereas Father Watts-Watt only gave me hints. I did not believe Father Watts-Watt because I had known Evie. There had come a time and I cannot remember when or where, when I had realized that Evie's uncle did not live in the suit of armour because a duke would not do such a thing. I knew that Evie was telling stories—that childish, far more accurate description of half our talking—and now I knew that Father Watts-Watt was telling stories, too.

I knew that no lights would flash, no messages be passed; that no one would sidle up to me with a whispered condemnation of my guardian. There were laws which I knew as applying to this play. At the bottom of it all, of course, stood Ma's fantasy of my birth and her fictitious steady. As I progressed from person to person the fantasy changed in character but remained substantially the same in its relation to the teller. They were all trying to adjust the brute blow of the fist that daily existence dealt them till it became a caress. He and I at various crises in our lives, pretended to others that we were mad or going mad. He at least, ended by convincing himself.

I should be disingenuous if I pretended to be uncertain about what these frightening desires of my guardian's were. And yet I must be very careful in the impression I convey because although he teetered on the edge he never went further towards me than I have said, never went near

anyone as far as I know. There was, to account for his
shining knees and his complex lies of persecution, there
was an awful battle that raged year in year out in his study
where I could sometimes hear him groaning. There was
nothing ludicrous in this, either then, or in memory. He
was incapable of approaching a child straight because of
the ingrown and festering desires that poisoned him. He
must have had pictures of lucid and blameless academes
where youth and experience could walk and make love.
But the thing itself in this vineless and unolived landscape
was nothing but furtive dirt. He might have kissed me
and welcome if it would have done him any good. For
what was the harm? Why should he not want to stroke
and caress and kiss the enchanting, the more than vellum
warmth and roundness of childhood? Why should he in
his dry, wrinkled skin, his hair falling and his body becoming every day less comely and masterful, why should
he not want to drink at that fountain renewed so miraculously generation after generation? And if he had more
savage wishes why they have been common enough in the
world and done less harm than a dogma or a political
absolute. Then I could have comforted myself in these
later days, saying: I was of some use and comfort to such
a one.

The more I have thought over his action in adopting
me, the more I have seen that there is what I might call
one and a half explanations. First, of course, he would tell
himself and perhaps believe that I must be suffered to
come, that the shame of my reception at the altar must be
atoned for, that it were better for a millstone and except ye
do it to one of these little ones and so on. That is what I
call the half explanation. The whole one is nastier if you

have the conventional view of things, but if not, heroic. I was like the full bottle of gin that the repentant cobbler stood on his bench so as to have the devil always in full view. He must have thought that to know a child properly, to have as it were, a son, might exorcise the demon; but he had not the art of getting to know. We remained strangers. He became, if anything, more eccentric. He would be walking in the street shaking his head, striding along, knees bent, arms gesticulating—and then he would cry out from the heart of his awful battle.

"Why? Why on me?"

Sometimes half-way through his cry he would recognize a face and turn his voice down into the social gesture:

"Why—how do you do?"

Then he would writhe away, muttering. As he got older he got higher and higher in this attempt to get away from himself; and finally I think he came right out at the top to find himself a man who has missed all the sweetness of life and got nothing in exchange, a derelict, old, exhausted, indifferent. I cannot see then that we did each other much harm but little good either. He fed me, clothed me, sent me to a dame school and then the local grammar school. He was well able to afford this and I do not make the mistake of confusing his signatures on cheques with human charity. He effectually lifted me from the roaring squalor and happiness of Rotten Row to the luxury of more than one room to a person.

But where does the fear of darkness come in? The rectory itself was more daunting than he, full of unexpected levels and cupboards with one storey of vast rooms and two others of shadows and holes and corners. There were religious pictures everywhere and I liked the bad ones much better than the few that had any aesthetic merit. My favourite Madonna was terribly saccharine, coming right out of the picture at me with power and love, buckets of it. Her colours were lovely, like the piled merchandise in Woolworth's, so that she eclipsed that other lady floating impossibly with her child in Raphael's air. The house itself was cold with more than lovelessness. It was supposed to have central heating from some arrangement of gas tubes in a cellar like the engine-room of a ship. Mrs. Pascoe told me that if the arrangement was turned on it ate money; a vivid phrase which combined with the dark house and the rector's eccentricity to give me much thought. But whether the machinery ate money or not, what could a few puffs of lukewarm air do against those twisting stairs and corridors, those doors that never met the floor, those dormer windows, those attics where the warmth poured up and away through the warped boards? I have sat in the great drawing-room at the rectory, warming my hands at my Madonna before going up to bed and I have heard the slow tapping as a picture beat against the brown panelling though all the doors and windows were closed. I got little warmth in that house to take up to bed with me. And bed meant darkness and darkness the generalized and irrational terror. Now I have been back in these pages to find out why I am frightened of the dark and I cannot tell. Once upon a time I was not frightened of the dark and later on I was.

9

After the sound of the feet died away I did not know how to react or what to feel. My pictures of torment were unformed and generalized. Somewhere there was a bench in my mind, a wooden bench with clamps and a furrowed surface; but Nick Shales stood behind that bench and demonstrated the relativity of sense impressions. So I began to wonder on which side of my confusion the bench was and where my tormentors were. All that I felt or surmised was conditioned by the immediacy of extreme peril. I could not know how much warning I should have before they hurt me. I could not know whether they would speak or not or whether theirs was only the more bitter business of dealing with excruciated flesh. So I knelt in the thick darkness, holding my trousers up with both hands and flinched and listened for breathing. But an outside breathing to be heard must have been gusty indeed to penetrate that riotous duet of my lungs and heart. Also the composition of experience was disconcerting and unpredictable. Who could have told me, for example, that the darkness before my blindfolded eyes would take on the likeness of a wall so that I would keep lifting my chin in order to look over it? And I held up my trousers not for decency but protection. My flesh, though it crawled, cared nothing for the recent brain nor the important, social face. It cared only to protect my privates, our privates, the whole race. So at last in the riot of air and pulse, one hand still down at my trousers, I put up the other and tore the soft bandage away.

Nothing happened at all. The darkness stayed with me. It was not only trapped under the folds of cloth, it wrapped me round, lay close against the ball of the eye. I lifted my chin again to see over the wall which rose with me. A kind of soup or stew of all the dungeon stories flew through my head, oubliettes, walls that moved, the little ease. Suddenly, with pricking hairs, I remembered rats.

If necessary, I will kill you.

"Who's there?"

My voice was close to my mouth as the darkness was to the balls of my eyes. I made a sweeping movement out into the air with my right hand, then down, and felt smooth stone or concrete. I had a sudden panic fear for my back and scrabbled round in the darkness and then round again. Now I could no longer remember where the door was, and cursed suddenly as I felt the first thrust of Halde's ingenuity. He wanted me to move myself towards whatever there was here of torment and deception, would play with me, not to increase any suffering but solely to prove conclusively that he could call any reaction out of me he wanted—I let my trousers slide down and moved cautiously back on hands and knees. I found the back of my neck was hurting with the strain of my rigidity, I saw flashes of unreal light that obstructed my absence of view. I told myself fiercely that there was no view to be seen and I loosed the strain in my neck, bowing my head down towards my hand so that the pain and the lights passed away. My fingers found the bottom of a wall and instantly I doubted that it was a wall, was prepared to agree that it might be one but was too clever to be trapped by an assumption, and began to feel up, inch by inch. But Halde was cleverer than I after all, inevitably cleverer, for I crouched up, squatted, stood, then stretched on tiptoe with one hand up; and still the wallness of the wall went with me and derided my refusal to be caught, went beyond my reach, up to where there might be a ceiling or might not according to some insoluble equation of guess and probability and me and Halde. I squatted, then crouched and worked my way to the right, I found an angle and then wood. All the time I was trying to hold a new diagram in my head without displacing the old conjectural, instinctive one of a bench and a judge. Yet the new diagram was so rudimentary that it furnished at least a place for my back. Here was a corner which was a concrete wall coming to the wood of a door. I was so glad to be guarded at my back that I forgot my trousers and huddled down, huddled into the corner, tried to squeeze my backbone into the right-angle. I got my knees up against my chin and put my crossed arms before my face. I was defended. The attack from no matter where would find me with flimsy bulwarks of flesh to ward it off.

Eyes that see nothing soon tire of nothing. They invent their own shapes that swim about under the lids. Shut eyes are undefended. How then, what to do? They opened against my will and once more the darkness lay right on the jellies. My mouth was open and dry.

I began to touch my face with my hands for company. I felt bristles where I should have shaved. I felt two lines from nose down, cheekbones under the skin and flesh.

I began to mutter.

"Do something. Keep still or move. Be unpredictable. Move to the right. Follow the wall along or is that what you want? Do you want me to fall on thorns? Don't move then. I won't move; I shall stay defended."

168

I began to hutch myself to the right out of the angle. I pictured a corridor leading away and this picture had definition and was restful therefore; but then I guessed that at the far end would lie some warped thing that would seize on the shrieking flesh so though I was not more than a yard from my corner I yearned for its safety and flurried back like an insect.

"Don't move at all."

I began again, moving right, along the wall, a yard, five feet, hutch after hutch of the body; and then a wall struck my right shoulder and forehead, cold but a shock so white sparks spun. I came hutching back, knowing that I was returning to a right-angle next to a wooden door. I began to think of the diagram as a corridor leading sideways, a concrete corridor with a stain like a face.

"Yes."

Hutch and crawl. My trousers got under my knees and I allowed myself enough freedom from the wall to pull them up again. Then, on knees and not hutching, I crawled sideways along this wall and hutched along that one.

Another wall.

I had a whirling glimpse in my head of mazy walls in which without my thread and with my trousers always falling down I should crawl for ever. But trousers can only fall to the feet. I tried to work out in my head how many walls would be sufficient to strip me completely. I lay in my right angle, eyes shut, hearing the various sentences of my meeting with Halde and watching the amoeboid shapes that swam through my blood. I spoke aloud and my voice was hoarse.

"Took it out of me."

I? I? Too many I's, but what else was there in this

thick, impenetrable cosmos? What else? A wooden door and how many shapes of walls? One wall, two walls, three walls, how many more? I visualized a curious shape and an opening leading to a corridor—with many angles, a bench and an oubliette? Who was to say that the floor was level? Might this very concrete beneath me slope down, gently at first then turning more steeply till it became a footless skitter into the ant-lion's funnel, ant-lion not in the children's encyclopaedia, but here with harrow-high jaws of steel? I hutched and cowered my flesh over my slack pants into my angle. No one to see. A solo performance, look no eyes. No one to see a man turning into a jelly by the threat of the darkness.

Walls.

This wall and that wall and that wall and a wooden door——

But then I knew and had to confirm, even though until I could touch proof with my finger-tips I should not let the knowing loose in me. Busily I hutched along the walls, knees down, hands against concrete, fingers searching; and I came round four walls to the same wooden door, back to the same angle.

I scrambled up, trousers down, arms stretched against the wood.

"Let me out! Let me out!"

But then the thought of the Nazis outside the door hit me and a sense of the terrible ways in which steps might go down, many steps to the ultimate whatever that was, but at least worse off, worse even than uncompanioned darkness. So with instant appreciation I choked off that cry before it could bring them in. I whispered instead against wood.

"You Nazi bastards!"

Even this defiance was terrible. There were microphones which would pick up a whisper at half a mile. My bare knees ground down the floor to the concrete, I knelt among the concertina'd folds of my trousers, face crushed against wood. All at once defeat became physical and movement therefore too much effort. To flex a muscle was more than a man could do. The only life was to lie huddled, every fibre let lie as it would.

Not a corridor. A cell. This was a cell then, with concrete walls and floor and a wooden door. Perhaps the most terrible thing was the woodenness of the door, the sense that they did not need steel in their power but kept me there by sheer will of Halde. Perhaps even the lock was a fake, the door yielding to a touch—but what good was that? The old prisoner fooled by such a ruse, the man who had wasted twenty years, lived in a plain time when an open door was synonym for exit. Christian and Faithful pushing the door were escapers as soon as they found a way out. But the Nazis mirrored the dilemma of my spirit in which not the unlocking of the door was the problem but the will to step across the threshold since outside was only Halde, no noble drop from a battlement but immured in dust behind barbed wire, was prison inside prison. And this, I saw clearly as a demonstrated proposition when I lay huddled, this view of life blighted my will, blighted man's will and was self-perpetuating. So I lay on the concrete, having discovered that the place was a cell: examined dully the view of total defeat.

And then the arithmetic of Halde's intentions stood up before me. I was accepting something as final which was only the first step. There were many steps to follow so that the whole flight would be an accurate picture of his learning and genius. On which step would a man at last give up his scrap of information? If a man had a scrap of information to give up?

Because—and the strength of a nervous spasm came into my muscles—how could a man even be sure that he knew anything? If he had not been told where the radio was, but nevertheless could plot back through the months how the news had reached him, till all the plots pointed to one group of three men and still he had nothing but that plot to go on, did he know anything? How good is a guess? What use is an expert?

I began to mutter against the concrete, like Midas among the reeds.

"There are two men in that hut—I can't remember the number and I don't know the names. I might be able to point them out to you on parade—but what would be the good? They would deny everything and they might well be right. If they are like me then they know nothing; but if I am right and they know where the radio is hidden, do you think white hot hooks would tear the place out of them? For they would have something to protect, some simple knowledge, some certainty to die for. They could say no because they could say yes. But what can I say who have no knowledge, no certainty, no will? I could point out to you the men like myself rather who are to be ignored, the grey and hapless helpless over whom time rolls bringing them nothing but devaluation and dust——"

But there was no answer. Nothing communicated with nothing.

How large a cell? I began to move and break up the granite of my immobility, stretched myself carefully along my own wall; but before my knees were straight my feet came against the concrete of the other wall; and hutching round through what might be ninety degrees until my body lay along by the door I found the same. The cell was too small for me to stretch myself out.

"What did you expect? A bed-sitting room?"

Of course I could lie slantwise across the cell and then my feet would be in the unvisited far corner and my head in my own angle. But who could sleep with only the level floor as a contact? What dreams and phantoms might visit one unprotected at his back and not rolled up in cloth? And for that matter who could push his feet forward across the open space in the middle of this cell and not care what they might meet? Halde was clever, knew what he was at; they were all clever, far cleverer than one rotting prisoner whose hours were beginning to drip on him one by one. The centre was the secret—might be the secret. Of course they were psychologists of suffering, apportioning to each man what was most helpful and necessary to his case.

Unless, of course, they are cleverer even than you think. Why should they not sit back and wait for you to take the next step for yourself? Why should they rely on chance, and let you discover it in the middle there by accident? He was a student of Samuel Mountjoy, knew that Mountjoy would stay by the wall, would deduce the thing there in the middle, would endure all torment guessing and wondering and inventing—and would be forced in the end by the same insane twitch that avoids all the cracks between paving stones or touches and touches wood, would be forced, screaming but forced, forced by himself, himself forcing himself, compelled helplessly deprived of will, sterile, wounded, diseased, sick of his nature, pierced, would have to stretch out his hand——

They knew you would explore. He knew you would not be British you would be downhearted. They knew you would find this not-impossible confinement and go further, you might have sat slumped against the door, but *they* knew you would add a torment to the discovery of the confinement, would add the torture of the centre—and therefore would do. Would do what? Would put nothing there? Would let the whole thing be a joke? Would put there.

Would put there what is most helpful in your case, sum of all terror.

Accept what you have found and no more. Huddle into your corner, knees up to the chin, hand over the eyes to ward off the visible thing that never appears. The centre of the cell is a secret only a few inches away. The impalpable dark conceals it palpably. Be intelligent. Leave the centre alone.

The darkness was full of shapes. They moved and were self-supplying. They came, came and swam before the face of primordial chaos. The concrete ceased to be a material visualized because felt and became nothing but a cold feeling. The wood of the door was warm and soft by comparison; but not a female warmth and softness— only an absence of cold and immediate wounding. The darkness was full of shapes.

Was not the size of the cell adjusted to the exact dimension so that the impossibility of stretching out would become little by little more than the feeble will could bear?

I wiped my face with my hands, I gaped with blindness. The first step was an absence of light, light taken from the visual artist. He is an artist, they must have said and smiled at each other. If he had been a musician we would have plugged his ears with wool. We will plug his eyes with cotton-wool. That is the first step. Then he will find that the cell is small and that will be the second step. When the discomfort of not being able to stretch out at full length becomes more than he can bear, they said, he will stretch out diagonally and find what we have put there for him; find what he expects to find. He is a timid, a morbid and sensitive creature and he will crush himself against the wall until discomfort drives him into telling us what he knows, or drives him to stretch out on the diagonal——

"I don't know whether I know anything or not!"

Now more than the generalized dark, the centre of the cell boiled with shapes of conjecture. A well. Do you not feel that the floor of the cell slopes downward? You will begin to roll inward if you move, down to the well and the ant-lion at the bottom. If you are worn out with the fears of conjecture you will fall asleep and roll——

We want information, not corpses.

We want you to feel forward, inch by inch, line by line over the concrete, with one ungloved hand. We want you to find a curious half-moon of hardness, polished, at the edge polished, but in the centre rough. We want you to feel forward over the slope and spread your fingers till you have found the sole of a shoe. Will you go on then, pull gently and find that the sole resists? Will you, under the erected hair in the blindness, deduce without more effort the rigor, the body curled there like a frozen foetus? How long will you wait? Or will you stretch out your fingers and find our surprise curled there not eighteen inches from your own? It has a moustache of white swan's feathers. You never touched his sharp nose then. Touch his nose now. All those dark roads of grue were unnecessary. The test is here.

We want you to take the third step. We know you will because we are never wrong. We have beaten the world. We have hung in a row the violated bodies of Abyssinia, Spain, Norway, Poland, Czecho-Slovakia, France, Holland, Belgium. Who do you think we are? Our Fuehrer's photograph hangs on the wall behind us. We are the experts. We do not torture you. We let you torture yourself. You need not take the third step towards the centre; but your nature compels you. We know you will.

The darkness was tumbling and roaring. I lost the door.

Don't let them know you've lost it. Find it again. Ignore those green, roaring seas, ignore the mouth agape, the hair erected, the eyes now streaming with wetness down both cheeks. And then I was back in my corner again after that frantic scramble round the wall, was back in a recognized corner with the wood of the door pressing against me. The patch in the middle was perhaps three feet across or even less. Then the body could not be lying there, must be standing up, balanced on the frozen feet like a statue. They had stood him up to wait for me. If I touched him he would sway forward.

I came out of the storm. I was saying nonsense, nonsense, nonsense to myself without remembering clearly what the nonsense was. I began to talk aloud in a croaking and jerky voice.

"If they stood a body there it could not be our lodger because he died and was buried in England thirty years ago. Thirty years ago. Thirty years ago. He was buried in

England. The huge car came for him with frosted and chased glass. He was buried there. This could not be his body——"

Then I lifted my face away from the wall and spoke in great anger.

"What is all this about bodies?"

Up there is up and down there is down. There where the concrete is getting harder every moment is down. Don't forget which is which or you will be seasick.

Whatever else you do don't take the third step.

They know what they are about. They have you on the fork. One way you take the next step and suffer for it. The other way, you do not take it but suffer on your own rack trying not to think what the next step is. They are past-masters.

A square not three feet each way. No, not so much. Not much room. And, of course, nothing could be standing there. Whatever held the centre must be small. Curled up.

Snake.

I was standing up, pressed back against the wall, trying not to breathe. I got there in the one movement my body made. My body had many hairs on legs and belly and chest and head, and each had its own life; each inherited a hundred thousand years of loathing and fear for things that scuttle or slide or crawl. I gasped a breath and then listened through all the working machinery of my body for the hiss or rattle, for the slow, scaly sound of a slither, except that in the zoo they made no sound but oozed like oil. In the desert they would vanish with hardly a furrow and a trickle of sand. They could move towards me, finding me by the warmth of my body, the sound of the blood in

177

my neck. Theirs was the wisdom and if one of them had been left at the centre there was no telling where it would be next.

My knees had their automatic fear, too, but my body was weakened by it, lost all sense of gravity, fell clumsily into my corner. I lay there huddled, pulling my hands back to my face. I stared blindly at the place where the thing might be. Of course he would not have a snake or a tarantula on tap and if he had he would not leave it about in a cell as cold as the inside of a coffin. Nothing lived in the cell but me. Whatever lay out there at the third step could not be living and could not be a body because a body could not stand up.

I began to creep round the wall again. I forced myself challengingly into each corner and I kept my eyes shut because that way they did not water so and I could imagine daylight outside them.

Four corners, all empty.

I knelt in my own corner, muttering to myself.

"Well? Well then?"

Let me find out before my mind invents anything worse, anything still unimaginable.

I crept along the wall again, making my eighteen inches into twenty-four. There was a space in the centre no bigger than a big book. Perhaps that was what was there, a book waiting for me to read all the answers.

I let my fingers creep out of my corner. They ate away part of the unknown patch, they went line by line and as they went they chilled and prickled. The space that might be a large book, minutely decreased.

Fingers ate away another line of concrete.

The feeling changed at the tips. They were in some

other mode, now. Or no. The concrete was changing, was not the same, was smoother.

Smooth. Wet. Liquid.

My hand snatched itself back as though the snake had been coiled there, whipped back without my volition, a hand highly trained by the tragedies of a million years.

My eye stung where a flung-back nail had grazed the ball, one deep physical automatism outsmarted by another.

Be reasonable. Did you weep there in the centre, or did you wipe the tears of strain from your cheeks?

Another hand crept forward, found the liquid, even rubbed a tiny distance backwards and forwards, found the liquid smooth like oil.

Acid?

"Nothing has happened to you yet. Be reasonable. All the torments he implied have not yet begun. Though the steps of approach are as real as the steps of a town hall, yet still you need not climb them. Even if they had spilt poison there in the centre I need not lick it up. They want information not corpses. Cannot be acid because fingertips are still smooth and cold, not burning and blistered. Cannot be lye because as with acid, no pain. Only cold, cold as the air, as the concrete where I can hear the stridulation of fabric under my hip. Nothing has happened to you yet. Don't be tricked into selling cheap."

Selling what? What was the information that I was so uncertain I really had? What could I have said? What was it, my last bargaining token, last scrap of value, only chock between me and a sliding descent of infinite length and cleverness, torment after torment? He said it was for my own good, for all our goods—so the last of human

179

faces had said, that delicately adjusted face, so delicate over the delicate, fragile bones.

But now there began to build up in me the conviction that even if I wanted to I could not remember, would never remember. I could see a layer of concrete build up in my mind over the forgotten thing, the thing down there that I had meant to say. But when that concrete forms in the mind, no internal road drill can break it up.

"Wait a minute. Let me remember——"

For, of course, you can only remember such a thing by forgetting to remember and then glancing back at it quickly before the concrete has a chance to form; but Halde would use a road drill, he would know of one. Yet no pain will break that concrete; hammer and you leave no mark——

"I tell you I've forgotten—I'd remember if I could! You must give me a moment——"

But there would be no moment of mercy. I knew now that I had forgotten and that I should never remember. The ladder of pain would stretch away from this stone pillow to an unknown height, I forced to climb. Let the road drill dance on the nerves savagely, on the flesh, spill the blood. What is your name? Muriel Millicent Mollie? Mary Mabel Margaret? Minnie Marcia Moron?

Oil, acid, lye. None of them.

No.

I could feel my cheekbone against wood; and a voice was talking loudly and hysterically through the cotton-wool.

"I tell you I can't remember! I would if I could—why don't you let me alone? If you only gave me a time not to think but a time to lie down under the sky without steps or pain then the concrete would slip away and the information come blurting out if there is any information and then we could start fair——"

There was that harvest picture yearned for, a harvest under one star and the moon. The light lay heavy on the heads of corn and he was going down through the light, leaning on his stick, a man soon to be harvested, too, creeping towards peace. There was the blue girl leaning back, a quiet river under her shoulder, the meal having crept on towards the shared siesta time.

But I was standing up again, shuffling through my trousers round the wall, facing it with hands feeling. But the wall was still there, right round. I reached up again as high as I could and still there was no ceiling—only darkness weighing heavy, smothering like a feather bed.

Oil. Acid. Lye.

No.

My body slid down and its right hand crept out, touched smoothness. Its fingers slipped on with tiny steps in smoothness that nibbled away the unknown space.

He knew they would nibble, he is the master.

Something, not touched yet or not with the sensitive tips, something touched, lying against the nail of the third finger, the weak one. Something touched my nail about a third of the way from the pared edge, cold as the smoothness. Mercilessly the fingers lifted in the darkness and explored, sending back their messages from the sensitive tips.

The thing was cold. The thing was soft. The thing was slimy. The thing was like an enormous dead slug—dead because where the softness gave way under the searching tips it did not come back again.

I could see everything now except the slug-thing because there was almost no darkness left. There was light falling away in a torrent, there were shouts and screams visible as shapes, long curves that shone and vibrated. But the shape of the thing on the floor was communicated to me through one enslaved finger that would not let go, that rendered the outline phosphorescent in my head, a strange, wandering haphazard shape with here a tail drawn out in slimy thinness and there the cold, wet bulk of a body. But this was no complete body of any animal or man. I knew now why this was the shape of no animal, knew what the wetness was. I knew too much. I should have touched his sharp nose and been armoured. Their cleverness was to shatter all the taboos of humanity, to crash through with an exhibition so brutal, a warning so unequivocal that the third step was like standing on a step of sheer horror above the others. They had laid there this fragment of human flesh, collapsed in its own cold blood. So the lights fell and spun and blood that was pumped out of the heart was visible too, like a sun's corona, was part noise, part feeling, part light.

A darkness ate everything away.

When I came together again, moaning, sick, huddled there was no intermission of knowledge. As soon as I remembered who I was I knew where I was and what thing lay there in the darkness, flung down from what misused body? And how long, my mind thought busily to itself, how long had that fragment been lying there? But they were not infallible then, for this morgue-like coldness gave me some protection. Yet even so, my nose now noticed in the air, noticed and tried to reject, certain elements other than the fetor of confinement. Or perhaps they were infallible indeed, when dealing *ex cathedra* with a matter of faith and morals such as this one and even the rate of decomposition was nicely calculated to increase. I recognized and miserably applauded the virtuosity of their torture for torture it was. This third step, they said, is unbearable, becomes unbearable, yet he must continue to bear it because the fourth step is worse. Do you think the cliff of loathing on which you are now huddled is our highest point? It is nothing but a preparatory ledge on our Everest. Base camp. Climb now. Try.

I felt upwards for the ceiling and in that moment the fourth step revealed itself. There was a whirlpool which had once been my mind but which now was slipping round, faster and faster; and a story leapt into the centre of it, a story completely remembered, vividly visualized—story of the small cell and the ceiling that came down slowly with all the weight of the world. I was scrabbling at the high wall, but the ceiling was still out of reach and I could not tell. But I knew that there were crushed things hanging from it that stank as the cold scrap in the centre was stinking; and presently I should hear the sound of its descent as it made unbearably small what was too small already, and came mercilessly down. So I was crouched in my fetid corner, gasping, sweating, talking.

"Why do you torment yourself? Why do you do their work for them? Nothing has touched you physically yet——"

For of course he knew. That fine, intellectual head was dedicated. What had I with my feelings, my gross sensuality, my skipping brain to put against a man who taught in a German university? Reason and common sense told me there was no body hanging crushed from which other

183

pieces might fall and yet I believed in the body because Halde wanted me to.

I started to cry out.

"Help me! Help me!"

Let me be accurate now if ever. These pages I have written have taught me much; not least that no man can tell the whole truth, language is clumsier in my hands than paint. And yet my life has remained centred round the fact of the next few minutes I spent alone and panic-stricken in the dark. My cry for help was the cry of the rat when the terrier shakes it, a hopeless sound, the raw signature of one savage act. My cry meant no more, was instinctive, said here is flesh of which the nature is to suffer and do thus. I cried out not with hope of an ear but as accepting a shut door, darkness and a shut sky.

But the very act of crying out changed the thing that cried. Does the rat expect help? When a man cries out instinctively he begins to search for a place where help may be found; and so the thing that cried out, struggling in the fetor, the sea of nightmare, with burning breath and racing heart, that thing as it was drowning looked with starting and not physical eyes on every place, against every wall, in every corner of the interior world.

"Help me!"

But there was no help in the concrete of the cell or the slime, no help in the delicate, the refined and compassionate face of Halde, no help in those uniformed shapes. There was no file for prison bars, no rope ladder, no dummy to be left in the pallet bed. Here the thing that cried came up against an absolute of helplessness. It struck with the frantic writhing and viciousness of a captive snake against glass and bars. But in the physical world there was neither help nor hope of weakness that might be attacked and overcome. The bars were steel, were reinforcements of this surrounding concrete. There was no escape from the place, and the snake, the rat struck again from the place away from now into time. It struck with full force backwards into time past, saw with the urgency of present need that time past held only balm for a quieter moment; turned therefore and lunged, uncoiled, struck at the future. The future was the flight of steps from terror to terror, a mounting experiment that ignorance of what might be a bribe, made inevitable. The thing that cried fled forward over those steps because there was no other way to go, was shot forward screaming as into a furnace, as over unimaginable steps that were all that might be borne, were more, were too searing for the refuge of madness were destructive of the centre. The thing that screamed left all living behind and came to the entry where death is close as darkness against eyeballs.

And burst that door.

10

Therefore when the commandant let me out of the darkness he came late and as a second string, giving me the liberty of the camp when perhaps I no longer needed it. I walked between the huts, a man resurrected but not by him. I saw the huts as one who had little to do with them, was indifferent to them and the temporal succession of days that they implied. So they shone with the innocent light of their own created nature. I understood them perfectly, boxes of thin wood as they were, and now transparent, letting be seen inside their quotas of sceptred kings. I lifted my arms, saw them too, and was overwhelmed by their unendurable richness as possessions, either arm ten thousand fortunes poured out for me. Huge tears were dropping from my face into dust; and this dust was a universe of brilliant and fantastic crystals, that miracles instantly supported in their being. I looked up beyond the huts and the wire, I raised my dead eyes, desiring nothing, accepting all things and giving all created things away. The paper wrappings of use and language dropped from me. Those crowded shapes extending up into the air and down into the rich earth, those deeds of far space and deep earth were aflame at the surface and daunting by right of their own natures though a day before I should have disguised them as trees. Beyond them the mountains were not only clear all through like purple glass, but living. They sang and were conjubilant. They were not all that sang. Everything is related to every-

186

thing else and all relationship is either discord or harmony. The power of gravity, dimension and space, the movement of the earth and sun and unseen stars, these made what might be called music and I heard it.

And now came what is harder to confess than cruelty. It happened as the first of my fellows left our hut and moved along the path towards me. He was a being of great glory on whom a whole body had been lavished, a lieutenant, his wonderful brain floating in its own sea, the fuel of the world working down transmuted through his belly. I saw him coming, and the marvel of him and these undisguised trees and mountains and this dust and music wrung a silent cry from me. This cry travelled away and along a fourth dimension at right-angles to the other three. The cry was directed to a place I did not know existed, but which I had forgotten merely; and once found, the place was always there, sometimes open and sometimes shut, the business of the universe proceeding there in its own mode, different, indescribable.

The awesome and advancing creature so arranged his flesh that sounds came visibly out of his mouth.

"Have you heard?"

But then he noticed the water on my face and was embarrassed by the sight of a crying Englishman.

"Sorry, Sammy. They're a lot of bloody murderers."

He looked away because he would have found it very easy to cry himself. But I was surrounded by a universe like a burst casket of jewels and I was dead anyway myself, knowing how little it mattered. So he wandered off, thinking I was round the bend, not comprehending my complete and luminous sanity. I returned to my fourth dimension and found that love flows along it until the heart, the physical heart, this pump or alleged pump makes love as easy as a bee makes honey. This seemed to me at that time the only worth-while occupation; and while I was so engaged the pace became so hot that a flake of fire, a brightness, flicked out of the hidden invisible and settled on the physical heart for all the world as though the heart is what poetry thinks it to be and not just a bit of clever machinery. Standing between the understood huts, among jewels and music, I was visited by a flake of fire, miraculous and pentecostal; and fire transmuted me, once and for ever.

How can a man listen and speak at the same time? There was so much to learn, so many adjustments to make that prison life became extremely busy and happy. For now the world was reorientated. What had been important dropped away. What had been ludicrous became common sense. What had had the ugliness of frustration and dirt, I now saw to have a curious reversed beauty—a beauty that could only be seen, out of the corner of the eye, a beauty which often only became apparent when it was remembered. All these things, of course, were explicable in two ways; the one explained them away, the other accepted them as data relevant to the nature of the cosmos. There was no argument possible between people holding either view. I knew that, because at different times of my life I had been either kind in turn. It seemed natural to me that this added perception in my dead eyes should flow over into work, into portraiture. That is why those secret, smuggled sketches of the haggard, unshaven kings of Egypt in their glory are the glory of my right hand and likely to remain so. My sketches of the transfigured camp, the prison which is no longer a prison are not so good, I think, but they have their merit. One or two of them see the place with the eye of innocence or death, see the dust and the wood and the concrete and the wire as though they had just been created. But the world of miracle I could not paint then or now.

For as time went on and I became accustomed to the rhythm of silence I began to learn about the new world. To be part of it was not just an ambition, but was a necessity. Therefore the thing in here, the dead thing that looked out must adapt its nature to conform. What was the nature of the new world outside and what was the nature of the dead thing inside?

Gradually I came to see that all this wonder formed an order of things and that the order depended on pillars. But the substance of these pillars when I understood what it was, confounded me utterly. We had thrown it away in the world, it was a joke. The brilliance of our political vision and the profundity of our scientific knowledge had enabled us to dispense with this substance. It had not been perceptible in the laboratory test-tube when we performed our simple qualitative analysis. It had caught no votes, it had not been suggested as a remedy for war, it was accounted for, if any account was needed as a byproduct of the class system, the same way as you get aniline dyes from the distillation of coal—an accident, almost. This substance was a kind of vital morality, not the relationship of a man to remote posterity nor even to a social system, but the relationship of individual man to individual man— once an irrelevance but now seen to be the forge in which all change, all value, all life is beaten out into a good or a bad shape. This live morality was, to change the metaphor, if not the gold, at least the silver of the new world.

Now at last, the eyes of Sammy turned and looked where Halde had directed them. To die is easy enough in the forcing chamber of a cell and to see the world with dead or innocent eyes is easy enough, too, if you can find the trick. But when the eyes of Sammy were turned in on myself with that same stripped and dead objectivity, what they saw was not beautiful but fearsome. Dying, after all, then was not one tenth complete—for must not complete death be to get out of the way of that shining, singing cosmos and let it shine and sing? And here was a point, a single point which was my own interior identity, without shape or size but only position. Yet this position was miraculous as everything else since it continually defied the law of conservation of energy, rule one as it were, and created shapes that fled away outwards along the radii of a globe. These shapes could be likened to nothing but the most loathsome substances that man knows of, or perhaps the most loathsome and abject creatures, continuously created, radiating swiftly out and disappearing from my sight; and this was the human nature I found inhabiting the centre of my own awareness. The light that showed up this point and these creatures came from the newly perceived world in all its glory. Otherwise I might have been a man who lived contentedly enough with his own nature.

But now to live with such a thing was unendurable. Nothing that Halde could do seemed half so terrible as what I knew myself. Was this thing common? Did I underestimate the privacies of the kings, would they too make such a showing? I did not think so then and I do not think so now. I knew one of them, Johnny Spragg, and I understood how there had been in him what had been missing in me; namely a natural goodness and generosity so that even his sins were peccadilloes because all the time the root of the matter was in him. But either I had been born without this natural generosity or I had lost it somewhere. The small boy trotting by Evie was nothing to do with me: but the young man waiting on the bike for the traffic lights to change from red—he and I dwelt in one skin. We were responsible the one for the other. So that when I thought back and came on the memory of Beatrice the beauty of her simplicity struck me a blow in the face. That negative personality, that clear absence of being, that vacuum which I had finally deduced from her silences, I now saw to have been full. Just as the substance of the living cell comes shining into focus as you turn the screw by the microscope, so I now saw that being of Beatrice which had once shone out of her face. She was simple and loving and generous and humble; qualities which have no political importance and do not commonly bring their owners much success. Like the ward for children, remembered, they shine. And yet as I remembered myself as well as Beatrice I could find no moment when I was free to do as I would. In all that lamentable story of seduction I could not remember one moment when being what I was I could do other than I did.

Oh, the continent of a man, the peninsulas, capes, deep bays, jungles and grasslands, the deserts, the lakes, the mountains and high hills! How shall I be rid of the kingdom, how shall I give it away?

If I could say with Nick Shales that the word freedom is a pious hope for an illusion I might accept the drag of all those half-dead days and not mind them. If I could say with Rowena Pringle only believe, might I not subside into some calming system of reward and punishment, profit and loss? But I know the taste of potatoes and I do not believe merely—I see. Or if I could only take the mud as mud, if I could only see people as ciphers and be bored by the average impact of a day! If I could only take this world for granted!

Somewhere, some time, I made a choice in freedom and lost my freedom. I lost nothing before the verger knocked me down; or perhaps that blow was like death and paid all debts. Between there, then and the boy on the bike, the young man—that was the whole time of the other school. There, somewhere there? Back among the flowers and smell of cloakrooms, among the exercise-books and savage emotions, back among the rewards and penalties, back with the sense of life going on like that for ever?

That school catered for both sexes. Mixed, officially, I can think of no other institution so rigidly divided. This division, however, was not forced on us. We created it ourselves from the very first day. In the first hours of awe, we sat by instinct, girls on the left-hand side of the classroom, boys on the right. A line was drawn then, and by our common consent was never broken. No boy, not even I, who still remembered the majesty of Evie's hairribbons, could have sat among the girls. Had I done so the sky would have broken apart and fallen on us. We did our best to pretend that we went to a boys' school; we understood that the pattern of education for us in our little country grammar school was dictated not by theoretic pedagogy but by economics. We were being done on the cheap and ought to be thankful for being done at all. So our gang warfare that rioted by the stream at the bottom of the playground was for boys only. Here, my anomalous position in the rectory gave me a rootless background so that I boasted in compensation—boasted with rudimentary feeling for the shape of our social pyramid that I was the rector's son, sort of—and became unpopular. It was in the shadows of this unpopularity that I moved slowly into adolescence, when the skin is flayed off and a feather weighs like lead and pricks like a pin. I was at home nowhere. There was bed, but bed with the irrational fear of ghosts and horrors; so that at this time I discovered how to huddle up and pull out of the body that comfort which the world could not give. Gradually I learned to short-circuit my own current and be sufficient, running myself down like a battery in one incandescent flash.

Under what sign in the sky did Sammy develop then? There were two of them. They loom now in my memory, the virgin and the water-carrier. They form an arch, not of triumph but of defeat, they are supporters to my shield, if anyone made me, they made me, spiritual parents, but not in the flesh.

She was the one who taught Scripture and various form subjects. She was the form mistress over us for a year, she was a middle-aged spinster with sandy hair and the beginnings of a sandy moustache and beard, she was Miss Rowena Pringle and she hated me partly because I was hateful and partly because she was hateful and partly because she had a crush on Father Watts-Watt—who had adopted me instead of marrying her—and who was slowly going mad. She had an exquisite niminy-piminy lady-like air. To see her find that she had a blot of ink on her finger—hand up, fingers tapping in a bunch at each other like a tiny, lily-white octopus—was to appreciate how hysterically clean a lady can be. She withdrew from anything that was soiled—not dirty, soiled—and her religious instruction was just like that. Her clothes were usually in tones of brown. In rainy weather she would come to school in a brown macintosh neatly belted, she would wear goloshes and gloves, and be protected over all by a brown umbrella with scallops and silk tassels. She would vanish into the women's staffroom and presently appear in class, picking her way to her high desk, as delicately neat and clean as a chestnut. She wore pince-nez, gold rimmed with a fairy gold chain of almost invisible gold links that descended to the frilly lace on her bosom and was pinned there with a teeny-weeny gold pin. Near the pin there was the watery-gold glimmer of a cut topaz. She had sandy hair, a freckled, slightly fattened face that usually wore a smile of professional benevolence, as arranged and external as her clothes.

Miss Pringle never touched anyone. A good, solid clout such as the verger gave me, was not in her repertoire. You knew that for Miss Pringle to touch human flesh would be a defilement. Those white fingers, with the gold ring on the right hand, were private and set apart. She ruled, not by love but by fear. Her weapons were no cane, they were different, subtle and cruel, unfair and vicious. They were teeny, arch sarcasms that made the other children giggle and tore the flesh. She was a past-master of crowd psychology and momentum. She could give our giggles a touch at the right moment, wait, touch again, like a man with a pendulum, wait, touch, wait, touch until her victim was savaged by the storm of derision, was gasping for breath in the wretched flayed flesh—was on the hooks. And all the time she would be smiling her professional smile while the gold chain of her pince-nez flicked and twinkled; for, after all, it is a joy to practise one's religion and be paid for it.

She need not have disliked me so much for I was with her. I was still innocent of the major good and evil; I thought no evil, I believed when she made me suffer that the fault was mine. I condemn her out of my adult stature. The flayed child that I was in her hands did not understand that truth is useless and pernicious when it proceeds from nothing but the mouth.

For I was with her. To me, these stories of good and

wicked men, these stories where the scale is good and evil seemed the hub of life, the essential business. Agincourt was a great victory; but Jacob laid his head on a stone—I saw how hard it was and uncomfortable—and dreamed of a ladder of gold that reached into heaven. Watt invented the steam-engine; but a voice spoke to Moses out of a bush that burned and was not consumed away. Yes. I was with her.

For in that way she was a good teacher. She told her stories with the vivid detail you sometimes get from people who are frustrated mentally and sexually. It was years before I saw the stories of the Old Testament in any way but through her eyes. It was years before I saw how she had achieved the apparently impossible by bowdlerizing the stories and yet keeping their moral implications clear to us. My hand was always the first up with an earnest question, my maps of the Holy Land were the most detailed, my illustrations of lightning flashing from Mount Sinai the most vividly realized. All would not do. My question was sure to turn into nothing but a dolly service to Miss Pringle who could ace me with a return as vivid as my own lightning; as for my maps, they were marked in such a way that her red ink contrived to ruin them.

I pry round my memories of this relationship. Did she perhaps know that I had spat, however dryly, on the altar? Did she resent my presence as a piece of slum-land that was in process of reclamation? Did she resent my living in the rectory? Did she perhaps divine intuitively what was unusual about Father Watts-Watt and credit me with his affection? Were we simply incompatible temperaments, the involved, frustrated spinster and the boy, tough—but now not so tough—simple and incredibly still innocent? What did I do that I should always be her target? Or can I place my hand on my heart and claim for once to be a blameless victim? Is there something that is not my fault? Certainly she was not always in such ordered control of herself. She was not invulnerable. She bore the curse of Eve like all women and with less stoicism than most. As time went on we found that she had occasional days when teaching was too much for her altogether. She would sit at her high desk, lolling back, eyes closed, rolling her head from side to side and sighing. Then, such was the force of her cruelty and discipline that we would not dare to sympathize or exploit—we were mouse-still all the period until the heavenly bell. It was almost a relief to return to her a day or so later and find her in control again, smiling and dangerous.

I see her with my fatal eye, I span the gulf. Her mouth is flapping open and shut. Is the electric light on? If only I could hear as well as see!

There is a chalk triangle on the board behind her, an irrelevant triangle. The lace is light brown, extends halfway up her neck. If I drove my elbow sideways I should hit Johnny Spragg in the ribs. Philip is in front of me and to the right. But this is not that sort of lesson, this is important, can be breath-taking. Moses.

I am deeply interested in Moses. He is more important than the composition of water. I am willing to be told about water when we get to Mr. Shales's lesson but Moses is far more important. I want to know all about Moses that can be known. I know the story from infant school days, have had it here and there, till the plagues and all that are etched in me. But they—Miss Massey, pugilistic

Miss Massey—they stop just where you want to know. His story turns into the story of the Israelites, that wearisome bunch who can be relied on to do the wrong thing. Perhaps Miss Pringle—I recognize her expertise—will not make this mistake, if it is a mistake. Perhaps she can fill in the gaps for me. I know that the Bible contains many laws that Moses is alleged to have ordained; but these, too, are irrelevant. What was that rock in which he was hidden, where the Lord passed by and covered Moses meanwhile with one hand? There should be as full an account of that end of his life as there is of the beginning. Perhaps—I think as the class settles itself—perhaps Miss Pringle who knows so much will let us into that secret. This, then, will be a real step up, a step forward; to be old enough for her to lift the curtains from that end of his life——

For she could lift curtains, could Miss Pringle. She told us why the veil of the temple was torn at the crucifixion, told us directly and explicitly why it was torn not transversely nor destroyed but torn from the top to the bottom. This was deeply satisfactory; and sometimes she did the same for Moses. We understood the relationship between the speaker Aaron and the seer Moses by the time she had finished with us. Yet she would mix this profound exegesis with matter that was useless and even distressing. I would sit in my desk, and wonder why when she could speak so deeply to us, she could also say such cheap and silly things, like the Red Sea sometimes being parted—the waters driven back—by the wind; or snakes being cataleptic like lobsters when you stroke them or chicken at a chalk line; and therefore the rods thrown down were not a plain and lovely miracle but explicable, if you leant over backwards.

And Moses came to the mountain, even to Horeb.

Flap, flap, twinkle from the spectacles, watery glimmer of topaz——

I cannot hear her.

You did these things to me. In some ways you were wise; but you were cruel. Why can I not hear you? You did these things, you said the words that have vanished. They did not go into the air and die; they sank into me deep, they have become me, they are so close to me I cannot hear them. You said them and passed on, you were preoccupied with your own affairs. Will you not stand to them? Is the world truly what the world looks like to the outward eye, a place where anything goes if you can get away with it?

Flap, flap, twinkle.

There were three ways she might have taken. She might have explained that there is a kind of bush in the desert which burns for a very long time and sometimes catches fire in the sun.

No.

Flap flap.

She might have told us that Moses saw this with the eyes of the spirit. There was no bush to the outward eye; and only to dwell on this bush—for bush will do as well as any other word—only to dwell, is to find it expanding, filling all space and being, taking fire with colours like the rainbow.

Flap——

"I am sure you have all heard this part of the Bible before. So I shall ask you some questions about it. After all you are supposed to be a little wiser now than you were a year ago. Mount Horeb. What did Moses see on Mount Horeb?"

"A bush, miss, a burning bush'n the Angel of the Lord spoke out of the bush 'n——"

"That will do. Yes. Was there anyone in the bush?"

"Miss! Miss! Miss!"

"Wilmot? Yes. Did Moses ever meet him again?"

"Miss! Miss!"

"Jennifer? Yes. On Mount Sinai. Did he see clearly?"

"Miss!"

"Of course not. Even Moses had to be content with 'I am that I am'."

"Miss! Miss!"

"What is it, Mountjoy?"

"Please, miss, 'e knew more'n that!"

"Ah——"

I knew then what a fool I was; I knew that if explaining myself to Father Watts-Watt was impossible it was dangerous with Miss Pringle. How could I say—of course you know, too, I am only reminding you or perhaps you were only pretending so that one of us would please you by giving more than a dull agreement—but I was too late.

Miss Pringle spread a delighted beam over the class and invited them to share with her the enjoyment of this captive.

"Mountjoy is going to tell us something we do not know, children."

There was, as she knew, a little ripple at that. She took the ripple just before it had died away.

"Mountjoy knows the Bible better than we do, of course. After all, he lives very near the church."

The pendulum began to swing.

"Silence for Mr. Mountjoy, children. He is going to explain the Bible to us."

I could see how red my nose was getting.

"Well, Mountjoy? Aren't you going to give us the—scholarly results of your researches?"

"It was later on, miss, after 'e'd——"

"He'd, Mountjoy, not 'e'd. I'm sure the rector wants you to improve your accent as quickly as possible. Well?"

" 'E—He wanted to see, miss, but it would 've been too much for—him."

"What are you talking about, Mountjoy?"

"Miss, Moses, miss."

Now the laughter flailed. There were cries of Miss Moses that Miss Pringle allowed to increase just this side of riot.

"It was after, miss."

"After?"

"It would 've been too much. So he was hid in a crack in the rock 'n 'e—he saw 'is backparts it says, miss, an' I was going to ask you——"

"What did you say?"

Now I was conscious of the silence, shocked off short.

"It says 'e saw——"

"When did you read that?"

"It was when you told us to learn the, learn the——"

"That was the New Testament lesson, Mountjoy. Why were you looking at the Old?"

"I'd finished, miss, 'n I thought——"

"So you'd finished? You didn't say so. You didn't think to tell me and ask my permission for this, this——"

The topaz shook and glittered.

"Very well, Mountjoy, so you'd finished your verses. Say them."

But next to my mind as I stood, blinded and dumb in

the desk was the picture of this event as a journey on the wrong track, a huge misunderstanding.

"It was jus' that I wanted to know, miss, the way you said about the veil and all that——"

"Say them!"

The blackness of torment turned red. There were no words on my tongue.

"Say them, Mountjoy. 'Blessed are the——' "

Don't you understand? I'm on your side, really. I know that the openings are more important to you than the silly plausibilities of explaining away. I know that the book is full of wonder and importance. I am not like Johnny on my left who will take it as read, or Philip in front who is looking at you and wondering how he can learn to use you. My delight is your delight.

Miss Pringle shifted her hand forward to another manual. Here was *vox humana*. We heard this voice sometimes, her wounded voice, voice of Rachel weeping for her children, always the prelude to savagery.

"——thought I could trust you. And so I can, most of you. But there is one boy who cannot be trusted. He uses a lesson—not even an ordinary lesson——"

"But, miss! Please, miss——"

Miss Pringle had me standing up where she wanted me. If I did not understand the enormity of my offence, if I was still acquainted with innocence and held the belief that there was room for me somewhere in the scheme of things, nevertheless Miss Pringle felt herself able to undermine me and dedicated herself to that end.

"Come out here in front of the class."

There was a strange obedience about my two hands that grasped the sides of the seat and helped to lift me. My feet trod obediently and deeper into the dark. She had implied so much in one sentence. By an inflection, a quiver of the topaz she had lifted this episode now above laughing so that the rest of the class had to readjust to seriousness. Miss Pringle had enough showmanship to know that she must not run away from her audience. She gave them time to settle into the new mood by looking so long and searchingly into my face that my blush burned and their silence began to fill with excitement.

"That's what you think the Bible is for then. Oh, no, Mountjoy, don't start to deny it. Do you suppose that I really don't know what you're like? We all know where you come from, Mountjoy, and we were willing to regard it as your misfortune."

I saw her brown leather shoes that were polished like chestnuts take a little step back.

"But you have brought the place with you. Money has been spent on you, Mountjoy. You have been given a great opportunity. But instead of profiting by it, instead of being grateful, you use your time here, searching through the Bible with a snigger, searching for—for——"

She paused and the silence was deeper still. They all knew what little boys searched the Bible for, because most of them did it. Perhaps that was why my crime—but what was it, I thought?—my crime seemed monstrous to them, too. I thought then, that the trouble was my lack of ability to explain myself. I had a hazy feeling that if only I could find the right words, Miss Pringle would understand and the whole business be disposed of. But I know now that she would not have accepted even the most elaborately accurate explanation. She would have dodged it with furious agility and put me back in the wrong.

She was clever and perceptive and compelled and cruel.

"Look at me. I said, 'Look at me!' "

"Miss."

"And then—then! To have the insolence—there is no other word for it—to have the insolence to throw your nastiness in my face!"

She had both white hands up and away. They were cleaning their own fingers as if they would never be clean. The cascade of lace was moving quickly in and out. Now the class understood that this was to be execution in form, public and long drawn out.

Miss Pringle proceeded to the next step. Justice must not only be done, must be seen to be done. She required evidence of misdoing more than my unfortunate slip in theology. Of course there was one sure way of getting that. Most of the masters and mistresses in that school did not care enough about us to be cruel. They even recognized our right to separate existence and this recognition took a pleasant shape. We were made to keep our exercise-books very clean and neat; but we had rough work books, too; and by custom, unspoken, undefined, these books were private. So long as you did not defile them too openly or be outrageously wasteful, they were as private to us as his study to the scholar.

Had she convinced herself? Did she believe by now that I regularly searched the Bible for smut? Did she not understand that we were two of a kind, the earnest meta-physical boy and the tormented spinster, or did she know that and get an added kick from hatred of her own image? Did she really think she would find smut in my rough book; or was she willing to take anything legally wrong if she could find it?

"Get your rough work book."

I went back to my desk underground. The silence vibrated and Johnny would not meet my eye. One of my stockings was down round my ankle. My right ankle. There was no cover on the rough work book. The first four pages were crumpled and then the pages got flatter and cleaner. Since the first page now did duty for the cover most of my drawing there had worn away.

"Ugh!"

Miss Pringle refused my offer.

"I am not going to touch it, Mountjoy. Put it on the desk. Now. Turn over the pages. Well? What do you say?"

"Miss."

I began to turn the pages and the class watched eagerly.

Arithmetic and a horse pulling the roller over the town cricket pitch. Some wrongly spelt French verbs, repeated. A cart on the weighing machine outside the town hall. Lines. I must not pass notes in class. I must not—the old DH coming round a tower of clouds. Answers to grammar questions. Arithmetic. Latin. Some profiles. A landscape, not drawn, so much as noted down and then elaborated in my own private notation. For how could a pencil convey the peculiar attraction of a white chalk road seen from miles away as it wound up the side of the downs? In the middle distance was a complication of trees and hillocks into which the eye was drawn and into which the troubled spectator could vanish. This was not sketched but put down meticulously. This was so much my own private property that I turned a page hurriedly.

"Wait! Turn back."

Miss Pringle looked from me to the landscape, then back again.

"Why do you hurry over that page, Mountjoy? Is there something there that you don't want me to see?"

Silence.

Miss Pringle examined my landscape inch by inch. I could feel the excitement of my fellows, now transformed to bloodhounds on the trail and hot on the back of my neck.

Miss Pringle extended a white finger and began to give the edge of the rough work book little taps so that it moved round and presented my hillocks, my scalloped downs and deep woodlands to her, upright. Her hand clenched and whipped away. She drew a shuddering breath. She spoke and her voice was deep with awe and passionate anger, with outrage and condemnation.

"Now, I see!"

She turned to the class.

"I had a little garden, children, full of lovely flowers. I was glad to work in my little garden because the flowers were so gay and lovely. But I did not know that there were weeds and slugs and snails and hideous slimy, crawling things——"

Then she turned on me and tore a vivid gash through my soul with the raw edge of a suddenly savage voice.

"I shall see that the rector knows about this, Mountjoy, and I'm going to take you to the headmaster now!"

I waited outside the door with my book while she went into the headmaster's study. I heard their voices and the interview was short. She came out and swept past me and then the headmaster told me sternly, to come in.

"Give me the book."

He was angry, there was no doubt about that. I suppose she had pointed out what was unnecessary—that we were a mixed school and this sort of thing must be stamped on immediately. I think perhaps he was resigned to having an expulsion on his hands.

He thumbed through the whole book, paused and then thumbed through it again. When he spoke next, the gruffness had gone from his voice—or rather was modified as though he knew that he must retain some outrage for the sake of appearances.

"Well, Mountjoy. Which page does Miss Pringle object to?"

She seemed to object to all of them. I was confused by events and unable to answer.

He thumbed through again. His voice became testy.

"Now listen, Mountjoy. Which page is it? Did you tear it out while you were waiting outside?"

I shook my head. He examined the sewn centre of the book, saw that there was no odd page. He looked back at me.

"Well?"

I found my voice.

"It was that one, sir, there."

The headmaster bent over the book. He examined my landscape. I saw that the complex centre trapped his sight, too. His eye went forward, plunged through the paper among hillocks and trees. He withdrew from it and his forehead was puzzled. He glanced down at me, then back at the paper. Suddenly he did what Miss Pringle had done —turned the book so that my lovely curved downs were upright, the patch of intricate woodland projecting from them.

We entered a place then which I should now call chaos. I did not know what was the matter, I felt nothing but pain and astonishment. But he, the adult, the headmaster, he did not know anything either. He had taken a pace forward and the ground had disappeared. He had realized something in a flash and the knowledge had presented him at once with a number of insoluble problems. But he was a wise man and he did what is always best in such circumstances; that is, nothing. He allowed me to watch his face on which so much became visible. I saw the results of his knowledge even though I could not share it. I saw an appalled realization, I saw impotence to cope, I saw even the beginning of wild laughter.

Then he went and looked out of the window for a little.

"You know, Mountjoy, we don't give you a rough work book to draw in, do we?"

"Sir."

"Miss Pringle objects to your wasting so much time with a pencil."

There was nothing to be said to this. I waited.

"These pages——"

He turned round then and opened the book to show me, but caught sight of something. It was a page where I had drawn as many of the form as I could. Some of them had defeated me; but for one or two I had drawn face after face, elaborating then simplifying so that the final result gave me a deep satisfaction as I sent the passionate message down the pencil. He pushed his spectacles up on his forehead and held the page close.

"That's young Spragg!"

At that the chaos came out of my eyes. It was wet and warm and I could not stop.

"Oh, now, look here!"

I felt round me for a handkerchief but, of course, I had

none. I took out my bright school cap and used it instead. When I could see again the headmaster was stroking his moustache and looking defeated. He gave himself another breather out of the window. Gradually I dried up.

"Well, there you are then. Keep your drawing within bounds. I think perhaps I'd better keep this rough work book. And try to——"

He paused for a long time.

"Try to understand that Miss Pringle cares deeply about you all. See if you can please her. Well?"

"Sir."

"And tell Miss Pringle that I—should be glad to have a word with her in break. Right?"

"Sir."

"You'd better go and—no. Go now. Straight back to the class as you are. I'll see that you get a new rough work book."

I went back to the class with my stained face and gave her the headmaster's message. She ignored me save for one imperious sweep of the hand and a pointing finger. I saw why. In my absence she had had my desk moved out of the body of the class. It rested now against the wall right out in front where I should not contaminate the others by my presence. I sank into the seat and was alone. Here I was, with the waves of public disapprobation beating on the back of my neck. I have never minded them since. There I remained for the rest of that term. Sitting alone, I was introduced to the Stuarts. Sitting alone I followed Miss Pringle forward from Gethsemane.

Nowadays I can understand a great deal about Miss Pringle. The male priest at the altar might have taken a comely and pious woman to his bosom; but he chose to withdraw into the fortress of his rectory and have to live with him a slum child, a child whose mother was hardly human. I understand how I must have taxed her, first with my presence, then with my innocence and finally with my talent. But how could she crucify a small boy, tell him that he sat out away from the others because he was not fit to be with them and then tell the story of that other crucifixion with every evidence in her voice of sorrow for human cruelty and wickedness? I can understand how she hated, but not how she kept on such apparent terms of intimacy with heaven.

But now, on that first ignorant and chaotic day we were still with Moses. The harrow had been over my soul and I cared a little less about him.

"And so as a sign to Moses that the Lord was present, the bush burned with fire but was not consumed away."

High in the belfry, relief sounded. We piled out of the room, I uncertain of my reception after my crucifixion and went straight into the lecture-room for general elementary science.

Mr. Shales, Nick Shales, Old Nick was there, waiting for us. He was impatient to begin. The light shone from his enormous bald head and his thick glasses. He had cleaned the board with the tail of his gown and a pillar of white dust hung in the air round him. There was bent glass on the demonstration bench and he stood, leaning his weight on his knuckles, and watching us as we clambered up the steps between the ranged forms.

Nick was the best teacher I ever knew. He had no particular method and he gave no particular picture of brilliance; it was just that he had a vision of nature and a passionate desire to communicate it. He respected children too. This was not a verbal respect for children's rights because it never occurred to Nick that they had any. They were just human beings and he treated each one with serious attention indistinguishable from courtesy. He kept discipline by ignoring the need to enforce it. See him now, waiting impatiently for us all, he included, to examine some fascination of fact, some absorbing reality which never could fail to astonish——

"Better take this down in your books because we are going to try and disprove it. Ready? Here you are then. 'Matter can neither be destroyed nor created'."

Obediently we wrote. Nick began to talk. He was imploring us to find a case where matter was either destroyed or created.

"In a shell."

"A candle burning——"

"Eating."

"When a chicken comes out——"

Eagerly we gave him examples. Sagely he nodded and disposed of each.

Yet not one of us thought of Miss Pringle next door and her lessons. We might have shouted together that a burning bush that burned and was not consumed away surely violated the scheme of Nick's rational universe as he unfolded it to us. But no one said a word about her. We crossed from one universe into another when we came out of her door and went into his. We held both universes in our heads effortlessly because by the nature of the human being, neither of them was real. Both systems were coherent—was it some deep instinct that told us the universe does not come so readily to heel and kept us from inhabiting either? For all Miss Pringle's vivid descriptions that world existed over there, not here.

Neither was this world of Nick's a real thing. It was not enveloping; each small experimental result was not multiplied out to fill the universe. If he did the multiplication we watched and marvelled. Nick would paint a picture of the stars in their courses as a consequence of his demonstrations of captive gravity. Then not science but poetry filled him and us. His deductions stood on tiptoe reaching out to the great arithmetical and stellar dance; but neither he nor we looked at the sky. A generation was to pass before I myself saw the difference between the imaginary concept and the spread picture overhead. Nick thought he spoke of real things.

A candle burnt under a bell-jar. Water rose and filled the space once occupied by oxygen. The candle went out but not before it had lighted up a universe of such orderliness and sanity that one must perforce cry; the solution to all problems is here! If there were problems, nevertheless they must contain their own solution. It would not be a rational universe in which problems were insoluble.

What men believe is a function of what they are; and what they are is in part what has happened to them. And yet here and there in all that riot of compulsion comes the clear taste of potatoes, element so rare the isotope of uranium is abundant by comparison. Surely Nick was familiar with that taste for he was a selfless man. He was born of poor parents and had nearly killed himself working his way up. Knowledge, therefore, was most precious to him. He had no money for apparatus and made things work from tin and bent glass and vulcanite. His mirror galvanometer was a wonder of delicacy; and once he pro-

duced the aurora borealis for us, captive like a rare butter-
fly, in a length of glass tubing. He did not care to make
technicians of us, he wanted us to understand the world
around us. There was no place for spirit in his cosmos and
consequently the cosmos played a huge practical joke on
him. It gave Nick a love of people, a selflessness, a kindness and justice that made him a homeland for all people;
and at the same time it allowed him to preach the gospel
of a most drearily rationalistic universe that the children
hardly noticed at all. At the beginning of break he could
not get away to the staffroom for the crowd of children
round his dirty gown who were questioning, watching, or
just illogically and irrationally wanting to be near. He
would answer patiently, would say when he did not know
the answer, would receive the creature before him openly
as of equal stature and importance. Nick had come out of
a slum as I had, but by his own brains and will. He was not
lifted; he lifted himself and his short body was the legacy
of semi-starvation and years of overwork. He was a
socialist and had been one in the heat of the day; but his
socialism was like his natural philosophy; logical and kind
and of astonishing beauty. He saw a new earth, not one
in which he himself would have more money and do less
work for it, but one in which we country children would
have schools as good as Eton. He wanted the whole
bounty of the earth for us and for all people. Sometimes
now that the British Empire has been dissolved and I meet
natives of one hot land or another who are triumphant in
their claims to have freed themselves, I think of Nick;
Nick who would have freed them sixty years ago to his
own cost. Yet he had no possessions himself; he neither
drank nor smoked nor had a car. He had nothing that I

saw except an old blue serge suit and a black gown gnawed into a net by acid. He denied the spirit behind creation; for what is nearest the eye is hardest to see.

These two people, Nick Shales and Rowena Pringle, loom larger behind me as I get older. Mine is the responsibility but they are part reasons for my shape, they had and have a finger in my pie. I cannot understand myself without understanding them. Because I have pondered them both so deeply I know now things about them which I did not know then. I always knew that Miss Pringle hated Nick Shales; and now, because I am so much like her, I know why. She hated him because he found it easy to be good. The so-respectable school marm with her clean fingers was eaten up with secret desires and passions. No matter how she built up the dam on this and that, the unruly and bilious flood of her nature burst forth. May she not have tortured herself in despair and self-loathing, every time she tortured me? And how she must have writhed, to see Nick, the rationalist, followed by children as if he were a saint! No one liked her, except a succession of dim and sycophantic girls, a line of acolytes not worth having. Perhaps she half understood how flimsy a virtue her accidental virginity was, perhaps sometimes in a grey light before the first bird she saw herself as in a mirror and knew she was powerless to alter. But to Nick the rationalist, the atheist, all things were possible.

I needed Nick that lesson, not to teach but be there. I think he noticed my stained face and this led him into his usual error of exercising charity for the wrong reason. He fancied, I believe, that the contrast between my position at the rectory and my known, my almost brandished bastardy had been flung at my head. So he took pains to keep me back after the class had gone, to help him put the apparatus away.

But I said nothing. I was incapable of explaining what had happened. So Nick talked instead. He cleaned the board again with his filthy gown and put his notes away in the desk.

"Have you got any more drawings to show me, young Mountjoy?"

"Sir."

"What I like about your drawings is that they look like the things they're meant to be."

"Yes, sir."

"Faces. Now how do you manage to draw faces? I can see that a landscape might need rearranging; but faces have to look like somebody. Wouldn't a photograph be better?"

"I s'pose it would, sir."

"Well then!"

"Haven't got a camera, sir."

"No. Of course not."

We had finished putting away the apparatus. Nick turned and sat perched on his high stool and I stood near him, one hand on the demonstration bench. He said nothing at all; but there was in his silence a placid acceptance of me and all my ways. He took off his spectacles, polished them, put them on and looked up out of the window. There were rich bulges of cloud unfolding above the horizon and he began to tell me about them. They were thunderheads, anvil-shaped spaces in which power was building up. This time he went from the particular to the general for my benefit. The weather from the Arctic down became a gorgeous dance in slow, tremendous time. When

he finished, we were side by side, contemplating this together and as equals.

"You wouldn't think people could be cruel. You
wouldn't think they would have the time, not in a world
like this. Wars, persecutions, exploitations—I mean,
Sammy, there's so much to look at, for me to examine and
for you to paint—put it this way. If you took all this away
from a, a millionaire, he'd give all his money for no more
than a glimpse of the sky or the sea——"

I was laughing and nodding back at him; because it *was*
so obvious to us both and so astonishingly not obvious to
all the others.

"—I remember when I first learnt that a planet sweeps
out equal areas in equal times—it seemed to me that
armies would stop fighting—I mean—I must have been
about your age—that they would see how ridiculous a
waste of time——"

"Did they, sir? Did they really?"

"Did who?"

"The armies."

Slowly the difference between the adult and the child
re-established itself.

"No. They didn't. I'm afraid not. If you do that sort of
thing you become that sort of animal. The universe is
wonderfully exact, Sammy. You can't have your penny
and your bun. Conservation of energy holds good mentally as well as physically."

"But, sir——"

"What?"

Understanding came to me. His law spread. I saw it
holding good at all times and in all places. That cool allay-
ing rippled outward. The burning bush resisted and I un-

derstood instantly how we lived a contradiction. This was a moment of such importance to me that I must examine it completely. For an instant out of time, the two worlds existed side by side. The one I inhabited by nature, the world of miracle drew me strongly. To give up the burning bush, the water from the rock, the spittle on the eyes was to give up a portion of myself, a dark and inward and fruitful portion. Yet looking at me from the bush was the fat and freckled face of Miss Pringle. The other world, the cool and reasonable was home to the friendly face of Nick Shales. I do not believe that rational choice stood any chance of exercise. I believe that my child's mind was made up for me as a choice between good and wicked fairies. Miss Pringle vitiated her teaching. She failed to convince, not by what she said but by what she was. Nick persuaded me to his natural scientific universe by what he was not by what he said. I hung for an instant between two pictures of the universe; then the ripple passed over the burning bush and I ran towards my friend. In that moment a door closed behind me. I slammed it shut on Moses and Jehovah. I was not to knock on that door again, until in a Nazi prison camp I lay huddled against it half crazed with terror and despair.

Here?

Not here.

12

Yet the future was not wholly in her hands or his, for now there was wine spilt in our blood to emerge in pimples and fantasies of the wakeful bed and in sniggers, in sexual sniggers, the lore of the small town and the village. There were catchwords only mentioned to call forth the dirty laugh. There was a sense of inferiority because Self did not know why the guffaw, would like to be on the ball, know the inside story, the dirt, would like the social security of belonging to the tribe, to those who know. And, of course, here Nick's universe of cause and effect, his soulless universe fitted like a glove. I was more intelligent than Nick. I saw that if man is the highest, is his own creator, then good and evil is decided by majority vote. Conduct is not good or bad, but discovered or got away with. Self, then, emerging from his preoccupation with Moses and trying to find out why for two days cherries are so ludicrous and somehow to do with the silent country girl Selina. Self listening to Johnny and getting in on a bit of current dirt for the first time. Self hearing Mr. Carew use the crash word in history and laughing before anyone else and getting fifty lines but well, well worth it. Self right in, knowing all the dirt, inventing dirt, a leading muck raker in the warm sniggery world, home.

Self looking in the mirror.

I saw myself as a very ugly creature. The face that looked at mine was always solemn and shadowed. The black hair, the wiry black eyebrows were not luxuriant but coarse. The features set themselves sternly as I strove to draw them and find out what I really was. The ears stood out, the forehead and the jaw receded. I felt myself to be anthropoid and tough, in appearance, no lady's man but masculine.

But I would have liked to be a girl. This was in the fantasy world where their skirts and hair, their soft faces and the neatness of their bellies had always been. But now when the wine spilt, with added intensity came the scent of talcum, the difference of a breast, glitter of brooches in Woolworth's, round, silk knees, the black treacle of their celluloid mouths, their mouths like wounds. I wanted to be one of them and thought this unique as self-abuse and very shameful. But I was mistaken all round. Masturbation is universal. Our sex is always uncertain. I wanted not so much to become as to enjoy. Then when the mechanism of sex became clear to me I knew only too well what I wanted. In the pages of my rough book the girls' faces began to outnumber the others. The currents were running. Ambivalent and green we had sat for three years in the same room, neutral as anemones on the wet rock. The tide was stirring us. There was scent in the air and on the lips of the celluloid beauties. We looked across the room, searching among the live creatures for a trace of those lineaments that had launched a thousand films.

How if Miss Pringle had been as good and as attractive as Nick? Would prayer and meditation have cooled the fever? Would the beauty of holiness have triumphed over the cheap scent and the flickering, invented faces? Should I have drawn the nine orders of the angels?

Philip could not draw at all. He sat by me in Art and it was an understood thing that I would do his work quickly before I did my own. Miss Curtis, the spinster who taught us, was a sensible woman. She let sleeping dogs lie though she knew well enough what was going on. The morning I think of was no more outwardly noteworthy than she—yet she first encouraged me and I liked her well enough. We sat round in a hollow square; and sometimes the platform in the middle would have a cone or ball on it, sometimes a chair and a violin: sometimes a live model.

The girl who sat there that morning was known to me slightly. She sat usually across the room and to the back. She was a mouse. I proposed in my mind not to draw her, but to concentrate on little stick men besieging a castle instead. But Philip nudged me. I glanced at the girl and scrawled her in with about two lines and a couple of patches of offhand shading. Then I returned to my scaling ladders.

Miss Curtis moved round behind the desks. I began to make tokens of working at this model. Perhaps there was something unusual in my decision not to draw her. I may have—who knows? Seen with other eyes, or remembered the future. I may have been trying to avoid the life laid down for me.

"Philip Arnold! Why, Philip!"

Miss Curtis was behind and between us. We turned our shoulders together.

"That's very good indeed!"

She leaned forward, she seized the paper and walked quickly to the board with it. All the boys and girls leaned back and looked up. The model coughed and moved, Miss Curtis went over the drawing in detail. Philip sunned himself and I chewed up a pencil in my rage. She came back to the desk.

"Don't do any more work on it, Arnold. Just sign it."

Philip smirked and signed. Miss Curtis looked at me with creased cheeks and a glittering eye.

"If you could draw like that, Mountjoy, I would say that one day you might be an artist."

She went away, smiling a little and I examined my orphaned portrait. I was astonished. In carelessness and luck I had put the girl on paper in a way that my laborious portraitures could never come at. The line leapt, it was joyous, free, authoritative. It achieved little miracles of implication so that the viewer's eye created her small hands though my pencil had not touched them. That free line had raced past and created her face, had thinned and broken where no pencil could go, but only the imagination. Astonished and proud I looked back at the model.

There was a certain flamboyance in the pictures on the wall behind her, dancers by Degas, some rococo Italian architecture and a palladian bridge; and she took her place by appearance and cooled them. The egg and the sperm had decreed a girl and that difference was there in the bone. I could see that one of these fingers held against the light would be transparent; and possibly the palm also. I could assess the fragility of the skeleton, the hollows either side of the brow—like the reverse of a petal. I saw—let me be exact where exactitude is impossible—I saw in her face what I can neither describe or draw. Say she was beautiful to me. Say that her face summed up and expressed innocence without fatuity, bland femininity without the ache of sex. Say that as she sat there, hands in her lap, face lit from a high window she was contained and harmless, docile and sweet. Then know that nothing has been said to touch or describe the model set before us.

221

Only I now declare across a generation to the ghost of Nick Shales and to the senile shape of Rowena Pringle, I saw there in her face and around the openness of her brow, a metaphorical light that none the less seemed to me to be an objective phenomenon, a real thing. Instant by instant she became an astonishment, a question, a mountain standing in my path. I could tell myself before that first lesson ended that she was nothing but a girl with fair hair and a rather sweet expression; but even then I knew better.

How big is a feeling? Where does an ache start and end? We live from hand to mouth, presented with a situation before which and in which we execute our dance. I have said that our decisions are not logical but emotional. We have reason and are irrational. It is easy now to be wise about her. If I saw that light of heaven, why then it should have been a counterpoise to Nick's rationalism. But my model was flesh and blood. She was Beatrice Ifor; and besides that unearthly expression, that holy light, she had knees sometimes silk and young buds that lifted her blouse when she breathed. She was one of those rare girls who never have an awkward age, who are always neat, always a little smoother than their sisters. They become a blinding contradiction. Their untouched, bland faces are angels of the annunciation; and yet there is a tight-rope poise in their walk which is an invitation to what Father Watts-Watt would have called Bad Thoughts. She was demure but unconsciously so. She was like other girls in that she was a girl, but she was unique for me in being what I can only describe as a lot more so. She was untouched and unapproachable. She came from a home of respectable tradespeople and now that the barrier down the middle of the class was breaking, now that the currents were sorting us into types and groups and temporary pairs she remained remote and untroubled. No one could expect giggles or badinage from her. Her great eyes, light grey and lucent under the long lashes, looked at nothing, at a nothing hanging in the air. Now with passion I repeated her profile on the page but she eluded me. I never recaptured the inspired ease which came from luck and not caring. Yet my masterpiece lay there and Philip Arnold had written his name across the bottom right-hand corner. Miss Curtis extracted some amusement from the situation. When that stolen portrait, or if you like, when that freely given portrait was put up in pride of place at the prize-day exhibition she went out of her way to praise it. After I had resented Miss Curtis long enough she merely remarked to me that there was plenty more where that came from. But to my terror and continuing frustration I could not catch the being of Beatrice on paper no matter how I studied her. She was flattered by the portrait and gave Philip the beginnings of a smile that stabbed me to the heart. For now I was lost. She could not be avoided or walked round. The compulsion was on me. Somehow I must draw her again successfully; and this required careful study. But the careful study only blinded me. She was of fearful importance and yet when the door closed behind her I could not remember her face. I could not catch this particular signature of being which made her unique; I could not remember it. I could only suffer. Then when she appeared again my reeling heart recognized a beauty that is young as the beginning of the world. In my fantasy world the dreams were generous enough. I wanted to rescue her from something violent. She was lost in a forest and I found her. We slept in a hollow tree, she in my arms, close, her face on my shoulder. And there was the light round her brow of paradise.

Let us see if the outcome could have been different. To whom could I have gone and spoken of this? Nick would have dismissed that light. Miss Pringle would have had me expelled as a danger to her dim girls. As for Father Watts-Watt, by now everything about him was lack-lustre, including his knees. Because the whole situation had to remain inexplicable, suffering was at once inevitable and pointless. For Beatrice saw no light in my face. The tides of my passion and reverence beat on her averted cheek and she never looked round. I could not say I love you, or do you know there is a light in your face? In a desperate effort to make some contact I took to facetiousness. I heard myself being silly and rude and all the time I could have kissed her feet.

So she noticed me at last only to ignore me with point and I fell into the pit of hell. Calf-love is no worse or stronger than adult love; but no weaker. It is always hopeless since we come to it under the lee of economics. How old was Juliet?

Beatrice lived some miles out in the country and came to school by bus. That part of the landscape took on significance and any fact about it was relevant to me. With flayed off skin and a new knowledge of life I walked many miles spiralling in towards her village and flinching off again. What mysteries there were behind the white fence of her garden I could not tell but felt them. There was, in and around me, an emotional life strange as dinosaurs. I was jealous of her not only because someone else might take her. I was jealous of her because she was a girl. I was jealous of her very existence. Most terribly and exactly I felt that to kill her would only increase her power. She would go through a gate before me and know what I did not know. The tides of life became dark and stormy. The grey, failing man in the rectory thought of nothing but his book on Pelagianism. When I went near him now, no goose walked over his grave because he stood on the edge of it. What had we to do with each other? And those other adults that surrounded me, remote and august as images from Easter Island—how could I speak of my hell and let them in? Even today I can hardly speak of it to myself.

In this forcing bed I tried to come to decisions about the world. There was this terror that walked by day and night, referred to so casually by a four-letter Saxon word. There was the well in me from which occasionally came the need to express and the certainty of doing so. I could draw a face now in one swift line—any face but the one I could not remember—and the likeness leapt from the paper. I even tried indirect communication with Beatrice. I made a Christmas card for her. I painted it with desperate care, elaborating, tearing up and simplifying with such passionate intentness that I flashed through a whole history of art without knowing it. Those purples and reds became flying shapes in which the blue and white thing, once a star but now battered could scarcely survive. The black and jagged slash down the centre of my picture had been her profile, once drawn with literal, dead accuracy, but now acknowledged to be a symbol only. Behind that savage crack in daily life the torrential colours fought, an indescribable confusion. What did I think to achieve? Did I think that two continents could communicate on such a level? Did I not understand that none of my tide had come to trouble her quiet pool? Better if I had written two words on paper—help me! Then after all that I sent the card to her anonymously—strange, involved, proud contradiction! and of course nothing happened.

Sex, you say; and now we have said sex where are we? The beauty of Miss Pringle's cosmos was vitiated because she was a bitch. Nick's stunted universe was irradiated by his love of people. Sex thrust me strongly to choose and know. Yet I did not choose a materialistic belief, I chose Nick. For this reason truth seems unattainable. I know myself to be irrational because a rationalist belief dawned in me and I had no basis for it in logic or calm thought. People are the walls of our room, not philosophies.

My deductions from Nick's illogically adopted system were logical. There is no spirit, no absolute. Therefore right and wrong are a parliamentary decision like no betting slips or drinks after half-past ten. But why should Samuel Mountjoy, sitting by his well, go with a majority decision? Why should not Sammy's good be what Sammy decides? Nick had a saintly cobbler as his father and never knew that his own moral life was conditioned by it. There are no morals that can be deduced from natural science, there are only immorals. The supply of nineteenth-century optimism and goodness had run out before it reached me. I transformed Nick's innocent, paper world. Mine was an amoral, a savage place in which man was trapped without hope, to enjoy what he could while it was going. But since I record all this not so much to excuse myself as to understand myself I must add the complications which makes nonsense again. At the moment I was deciding that right and wrong were nominal and relative, I felt, I saw the beauty of holiness and tasted evil in my mouth like the taste of vomit.

In the year of manliness sex was demonstrated to us and because it involved those whom we admired in part, I at least thought that now I understood. Miss Manning taught us French. She was about twenty-five, a sleepy, creamy woman with gusty black hair and a splash of mouth. She taught; but all the time as if she were thinking of something else. Sometimes she would stretch, cat-like, and smile slowly as if she found us and the classroom and education amiable but ridiculous. She looked as if in some other place she could teach us something really worth knowing; and I have no doubt this was true. She excited us boys agreeably with the V of her bosom between blue lapels and with her round, silk knees, too; for this was the era of the knee if a woman sat down so that there was a little competition to get the strategic desks and our Miss Manning, I believe, was not unaware of it. She was never angry and never particularly helpful. She seemed to be thinking all the time: poor little green-stick girls and hopeful, pustular rowdies! Be patient—presently the gates will be unlocked and you will walk out of the nursery. Miss Manning, in fact, was altogether too attractive a woman to have her heart in her work.

Mr. Carew thought her attractive, too. We had believed him to exist for the twin purposes of rugby and Latin, but now we saw that he shared the common image with us. If he were coaching us on the field and Miss Manning appeared on the touchline not only we, but he, were driven to excesses of manly activity. How we hurled ourselves into a loose scrum! And taking up our positions for a kick-off, how loping, rangy and altogether unconscious of Miss Manning our strides became! But Mr. Carew would coach us twice as hard, would demonstrate that particular action with which he threw the ball like a torpedo far past the forwards in a line-out to where the threes might get it. Now all this activity was strange because Mr. Carew was married and had a small baby. He was a large, fair, red, sweaty man—or perhaps that was the rugby, but in my memory he always sweats. He had been to a minor public school and his rugby was much better than his Latin. He would not have found a job easy to get surely—but we had just changed over to rugby from soccer so we must have been his life's luck. But our Miss Manning took to appearing on the touchline very often, sensibly cautious of getting her feet muddy. With what laughter and care did Mr. Carew help her round a particularly dirty patch! Then the game would be delayed and he would hang round her, laughing very loud and sending up clouds of breath and steam into the November air. He displayed his club colours before her in male splendour and Miss Manning smiled her creamy smile.

Our school caretaker was a sodden old soldier who chased us off the grass when we were small and told us about life when our pimples were out. There was a pub handy to the school and when he returned after the dinner break, fumes went before him like a king's messenger. Then he would smooth out his grey, military moustache and tell us about being in action at two thousand yards against cavalry and show us the scar he got when he was serving on the north-west frontier. The more beer he had drunk the more military he became. This increase in martial ardour was paralleled by a rise in his moral temper. Normally he was opposed to puttees and lipstick; but when he had well drunken, short-skirted women in Parliament were unnatural. Bobbing, bingling, Eton crops—

but not apparently shaving—were flying in the face of providence and one of the reasons for the decadence of the modern army. He advocated the bayonet, Mr. Baldwin, and generally no nonsense.

At that time, a Novemberish time of short days and cold and mud, he was worried. He had something on his mind. Slurred by beer, fuming in our eager faces from veined nose, moustached mouth and eyes of yellow, he could only indicate that were he to tell us all, our mothers would remove us to a purer place. There were some things that young chaps had no business to know about, that's what. So don't you ask me no more, young Mountjoy. See?

He got so near letting on that we were wrought to a fever of conjecture and suspicion. We would not let him be. Our wings touched this honey and stuck there. Mr. Carew and Miss Manning were our Adam and Eve, were sex itself. This excitement was male, was kept from the green-stick girls, was knowledge, was glamour, was life. During the dinner-hour there was a master on duty for the boys and a mistress on duty for the girls; but who looks after the guardians? What more natural than that they should meet and that Benjie, going the round of the boiler-rooms or whatever he did, should see them, himself unseen? What was more, he now had a moral issue on his hands. What should he do? Should he tell the headmaster? This was what kept him awake and was turning him to drink. Where was his duty? Should he not, or should he tell?

There seemed to be only one way of pushing this crisis uphill. Yes, we cried, with a virtue even stronger than his, yes, of course he should. Roll on the crisis! After all, it was a bit thick if—so we delighted in our virtue and excitement. Miss Manning! Creamy, luscious Miss Manning! Mr. Carew, steaming and red!

Five of us sneaked after Benjie when he made up his mind. We hung about in a deserted corridor, watched as he tapped the study door and went in. After that we waited for nearly ten minutes with just too little courage to go and listen outside the door. Presently it opened and Benjie appeared backwards, cap in hand and talking. The headmaster came after trying to silence him. But Benjie was fuming and loud.

"I said it once, sir, and I'll say it again. It couldn't 'ave been worse if they was married!"

Then the headmaster saw us. I imagine it was perfectly obvious to him why we were there and why we were so interested. I, at least, expected a blast from him, but he said nothing to us. He only looked sad as if he had lost something. He was no fool, that headmaster. He knew when a story could be forgotten and when it had reached too many ears.

For the time of their stay Mr. Carew and Miss Manning were now most popular and admirable. They were not just teachers, they had reached the adult stature of those who sin. They were our film stars. We would have sat at Miss Manning's feet and listened to her with devoted attention if she had cared enough about us to tell us all the secrets of life. Whatever she said we should have believed her; and this is another contradiction. At her last lesson we examined our Miss Manning with bated breath for some sign of the experience that had been hers. But the gusty black hair, the V, the slow, creamy smile and the wide red mouth were the same. Her silk knees were the same. Once she caressed her leg, starting at the knee, running her hand down, stretching and drawing up the shin at the same time, running the silken snake through the palm of one hand, bending the instep back till you might have thought she could smooth the whole limb small and squeeze it through a ring. Then the end of the lesson came and as we stood in our desks she dismissed us with a strange phrase for someone who was about to disappear for ever.

"Eh bien, mes amis. Au revoir!"

Then they were gone, the two of them and the staff was grey and dingy again. Miss Pringle had a series of days when the world was too much for her—head lolling back, desperate sighing; but once when I presumed on her inattention she gave me a raving blast like a blowlamp. Nick reacted differently. He let me down for the first and last time in his life. I screwed up my courage and asked him a hesitant question about sex and all that, asked out of the fantasy life and our Miss Manning and Beatrice and having wanted to be a girl and wondering whether I was killing myself.

Nick shut me up violently. Then he spoke, flushing, his eyes watching water boiling in a flask.

"I don't believe in anything but what I can touch and see and weigh and measure. But if the Devil had invented man he couldn't have played him a dirtier, wickeder, a more shameful trick than when he gave him sex!"

So that was that. "It couldn't have been worse if they was married!" And though I scored a hit with my suggestion among the lads that what Benjie should have said was "It couldn't have been better——" nevertheless, I recognized the fallen angel. In my too susceptible mind sex dressed itself in gorgeous colours, brilliant and evil. I was in that glittering net, then, just as the silk moths were when they swerved and lashed their slim bodies and spurted the pink musk of their mating. Musk, shameful and heady, be thou my good. Musk on Beatrice who knows nothing of it, thinks nothing of it, is contained and cool, is years from mating if ever, and with another man. Musk if man is only an animal, must be my good because that is the standard of all animals. He is the great male who keeps the largest herd for himself. Do not tell us that we are highest animals and then expect from us only the fierce animal devotion to the young, the herd instinct and not the high, warring hooves of the stallion. As for that light round the brow, the radiance of the unending morning of paradise—that is an illusion, a side effect. Pay no attention to it. Forget it, if you can.

Therefore I moved forward to the world of the lads, where Mercutio was, where Valentine and Claudio and for this guilt found occasion to invent a crime that fitted the punishment. Guilty am I; therefore wicked I will be. If I cannot find the brilliant crimes to commit then at least I will claim to have committed them. Guilt comes before the crime and can cause it. My claims to evil were Byronic; and Beatrice looked the other way.

The time came for me to leave. Beatrice was going to a training college in South London where they would make a teacher of her. I was going to the Art School. I had no clear desire for success. I repeated the catch-phrases of the party because in that society one had the illusion of perpetual freedom, the monk's freedom in reverse. We had our blessings and farewells. Nick told me, in strangely religious phraseology, "Whatsoever thy hand findeth to do, do it with all thy might."

The headmaster took longer but said much the same.

"Going, Sam?"

"Yes, sir."

"Come to me for words of wisdom?"

"I've seen the others, sir."

"Trouble with advice is you might remember it."

"Sir?"

"Sit down, boy, for a minute and don't fidget. There. Cigarette?"

"I——"

"Look at your fingers and come off it. Throw the ash in that basket."

Sudden, inexplicable emotion.

"Want to thank you for all you've done, sir."

He waved his cigarette.

"What am I going to say to you? You'll go a long way from Rotten Row."

"That was Father Watts-Watt, sir."

"Partly."

Suddenly he swung round in the seat and faced me.

"Sam. I want your help. I want—to understand what you're after. Oh, yes, I know all about the party, it'll last you a year or two. But for yourself—you're an artist, a born artist, the Lord knows why or how. I've never seen anyone so clearly gifted. Yet these portraits—aren't they important to you?"

"I suppose so, sir."

"But surely—isn't anything important to you? No, wait! Never mind the party. I'll take that as read, Sammy, I'm a moderate man. But for yourself. Isn't anything important?"

"I don't know."

"You've got this gift and you haven't thought if it's important? Look, Sammy. We don't have to pretend any more, do we? You have an exceptional talent that makes you as distinct as if you had a sixth finger on each hand. You know that and I know it. I'm not flattering you. You're dishonest and selfish as well as being a—whatever you are. Right?"

"Sir."

"Your talent isn't important to you?"

"No, sir."

"You aren't happy."

"No, sir."

"Haven't been for some years now, have you?"

"No, sir."

"Happiness isn't your business. I tell you that. Leave happiness to the others, Sammy. It's a five-finger exercise."

He held up his right hand and twisted the fingers about.

"So your portraits aren't important in themselves. Are they a means to an end? No. Forget the dictatorship of the proletariat. What end?"

I don't know, sir."

"Aren't you looking forward to being famous and rich?"

Now it was my turn to think.

"Yes, sir. That would be very nice."

He gave a sudden jerk of laughter.

"Which is as much as to say you don't care a damn. And I'm supposed to advise you. Well, I won't. Good-bye."

He took my stub from me and shook me by the hand. But before I could close the door, the incorrigible schoolmaster in him had called me back.

234

"I'll tell you something which may be of value. I believe it to be true and powerful—therefore dangerous. If you want something enough, you can always get it provided you are willing to make the appropriate sacrifice. Something, anything. But what you get is never quite what you thought; and sooner or later the sacrifice is always regretted."

I went out of there and out of the school into high summer. It seemed to me, though in fact I was only exchanging one tutelage for another, that the world had opened to me. I would not go back to the rectory but walked out of the town instead and along beside the downs. There was the forest here, clinging to the downs between the escarpment and the river. I took my sudden excitement into them, I began to wade into the tall bracken as though somewhere in here was the secret.

Even the wood-pigeons co-operated for they sang the refrain of a dance tune over and over. "If you knew Susie" they sang from their green penthouses and all the forest, the bracken, the flies and uncatalogued small moths, the thumping rabbits, the butterflies, brown, blue and white, they murmured sexily for musk was the greatest good of the greatest number. As for the heavy sky, the blue to purple, it filled every shape between the trees with inch-thick fragments of stained glass, only at arm's length out of reach. The high fronds touched my throat or caught me round the thighs. There was a powder spilled out of all living things, a spice which now made the air where I waded thick. In basements of the forest among drifts of dried leaves and crackling boughs, by boles cathedral thick, I said in the hot air what was important to me; namely the white, unseen body of Beatrice Ifor, her obedience, and for all time my protection of her; and for the pain she had caused me, her utter abjection this side death.

There must have been a very considerable battle round me that evening. Every dog has his day and at last I see that this was mine. For the spices of the forest were taken away from me, I found myself hot and sticky, coming out below the weir where the pebbles shake under water year out and the moored lilies tug and duck and sidle. So that there should be no doubt, I now see, the angel of the gate of paradise held his sword between me and the spices. He breathed like his maker on the water below the weir and it seemed to me that the water was waiting for me. I stripped off and plunged in and I experienced my skin, from head to foot firm, smooth confinement of all my treasures. Now I knew the weight and the shape of a man, his temperature, his darknesses. I knew myself to shoot the glances of my eye, to stand firm, to sow my seed from the base of the strong spine. Dressed and cooled, contained as an untouched girl I moved away from the providential waters and up the hill-side. Already there were stars, large glossy stars that had been put in one at a time with the thumb. I sat there between the earth and the sky, between cloister and street. The waters had healed me and there was the taste of potatoes in my mouth.

What is important to you?

"Beatrice Ifor."

She thinks you depraved already. She dislikes you.

"If I want something enough I can always get it provided I am willing to make the appropriate sacrifice."

What will you sacrifice?

"Everything."

Here?

"Mr. Mountjoy? An appointment? I'll just ring through."

A lion gnashed from my left hand, high up, bloodshot about the eyes, blood and rage. To my left a python writhed over a lopped and polished branch—but where was the goat for the body? I searched for him while the receptionist spoke into her telephone and he was there, African with horns of fantastication and the yellow eyes of lust. I thought to myself that I seemed not to be on the pavement but standing a little above it. This was the house of the pay-off. Here the past was not a series of icebergs aground on some personal shore. This was the grey house of factual succession. Come here to the gate-house of the stuffed lion and stuffed python and stuffed goat. Examine your own experiment.

"Mr. Mountjoy, Dr. Enticott is not quite ready but asks if you would go down to his office. Do you know the way?"

"I'm afraid I've never—that is; no."

The receptionist traced out a route on a plan. Not at all, it was a pleasure to her, professionally smooth, helpful and untouched. Accustomed to deal with too much joy, too much sorrow.

The grounds were just recognizably the same. The cedar had survived and the branches each reached up to a level of water and defined it with floating leaves. The bulk of the house was the same as before, only a little smaller. There, stretching away from my feet along the back of the house was the terrace where the man had walked ritually. Johnny and I must have hidden behind the scruffy remains of that hedge. But there were other buildings that had sprung up within the grounds, low and functional, sprung up like fungus. The wide lawn was slashed by concrete-paths and these were worn and cracked, though they had appeared since we had trespassed. I had been a prisoner so long that now, only a hundred yards from my own house and in the grounds of an English hospital I did not dare to step off the path and I zigzagged across the lawn where the concrete allowed me to walk. The gardens were as well kept as public gardens and the air was the air of the top of the hill. Yet the sense of institution lay over the whole house and gardens like the greyness of a prison camp. Two women walked arm in arm under the trees. They sauntered, but the greyness included them. There was a single figure standing in the middle of the lawn like an ungainly statue; a stolid woman who stood with arms akimbo as if time had found her like that and then stopped.

Kenneth's office was empty. There were green filing cabinets, papers, pen, blotter, ink and a couch for confidences. It was a good, airy office, workman-like and pleasant if it had been anywhere else.

He came in behind me.

"Hullo."

"Here you are."

But this was not the loud Kenneth of parties with his wonderful stories, his admiration of Taffy and his liking for me. This was no more Kenneth than I was Sam, sprawling in slacks and sweater. Here we met officially in suits and constraint.

"Won't you sit down?"

We looked at each other across the desk and I spoke first.

"I suppose this is very—irregular?"

"Why should you think that?"

"I'm not a relative."

"We are not in purdah. No."

"I can see her?"

"Of course. If she wants to see you, that is."

"Well then."

"Is Taffy coming on later?"

"She's not coming."

"But she said——"

"Why should Taffy come?"

"But she said—I mean—she wanted to meet Miss——"

"She couldn't have!"

"She said Miss what's her name was a friend of you both——"

"She said that?"

"Of course!"

"She's busy on this wine thing of hers for tonight. You'll be there, won't you?"

I saw the disappointment come into his face. He swung his pencil and bounced it on his blotter.

"Oh well."

So Taffy had been diplomatic. It looked better if we had both known Beatrice. The helping hand.

"Perhaps she can come and see Miss Ifor later on."

Kenneth adjusted his face.

"Of course, of course."

It is true then that these places are not necessarily forcing beds for humanity and understanding. You can walk a hospital and learn nothing.

Kenneth jumped up, opened a filing cabinet and took out a sheaf of papers. He thumbed through them, returning his face to what he thought was the proper face for a medical man, withdrawn and responsible. But youth will out and his mask was unmarked. He might have been my son.

"When can I see her, then, Kenneth?"

He started.

"Now, if you like."

Crestfallen a little. Yes, he has really come to see her, not me: and no, Taffy is not with him, she does not think of me.

"Well——"

He got up, abruptly.

"Come on then."

I stood up to follow. My feet were obedient but my mind was thinking strange things and behaving mutinously. There should be a pause of recollection, it thought. I will wash my hands before I. There should be deliberate thinking back, a straightening out of the time stream back to when you last saw her. Yet the spots are opening and closing in front of my eyes and Kenneth is in love with Taffy and that complex sticks a peninsula into this ocean of cause and effect that is Beatrice and me.

"This way."

She was in the main building, then, in the general's own house, the house for lucky people.

"Through here."

I remember now. It was that morning when I turned up outside the training college after walking all night, the morning when I first pretended to be half-way round the bend. I remember what she said. *You mustn't ever say such a thing, Sammy.*

But most of all I remember her terror.

"Just a moment."

Kenneth had stopped and was talking to a nurse. He did this to impress me with yes, Dr. Enticott, no, Dr. Enticott. I am not famous, Sammy, but this is my pitch.

Can't you see I am up to the neck in the ice on paradise hill?

"Here we are, Mr. Mountjoy. I'd better go first."

Formal, because on the job.

The room was huge, an old drawing-room perhaps, in which the moulded ceiling was heavily dependent, marked with dust in dull lines like the rubbing of brass or bark. The three tall windows on our left were too big for frequent cleaning so that although they let the light in they qualified it. There were no pictures or hangings, though the light-green room cried out for both. There was little enough fabric anywhere. There was only a scatter of heavy round tables, chairs, and one or two sofas arranged by the farther wall.

There was a scatter of women too, but left random as the furniture. One held a ball of string. Another stood looking out of the middle window, unnaturally still like the ungainly statue on the lawn. Nurse knew her way about this aquarium. She swam forward between the tables to the darkest corner, the right-hand one across areas of floor.

"Miss Ifor."

No.

"Miss Ifor! Your visitor's come to see you!"

There was someone sitting on a chair in front of one of the sofas. She faced the right-hand wall, hands in her lap. She was posed. Her weak, yellowish hair was cut short like a boy's so that the shape of the head was clear to see, a vertical back. I remembered then how my hand had sometimes supported her head deep in the hair at the back; and now the truth was out, in daylight, shorn. The high forehead was parallel to this vertical back, so that really there was not much room in the head, very little, I now saw when the crowning glory was away from it.

Somewhere one of the women began to make a noise. It was the same sound, over and over again, like a marsh-bird.

"Hi-yip! Hi-yip! Hi-yip!"

No one moved. Beatrice sat, looking at the wall, look-ing at nothing. Her face was in the shadow of her body; but a little light was reflected from the institutional wall and showed some of the moulding. Certainly the bones of the face were well hidden now. The flesh had hidden them in lumps—or was it the very bone that had coarsened? The knuckles of her hands seemed more prominent and under the green dress the body had thickened, was the same size from shoulder to hip.

There was a curious feeling in my hands. They seemed to be growing larger. The room was shuddering slightly as if a tunnel of the underground lay below.

I pulled my lips apart.

"Beatrice!"

She did nothing. The nurse moved briskly past my right shoulder and bent down.

"Miss Ifor dear! Your visitor's come to see you!"

"Beatrice!"

"Miss Ifor dear!"

"Hi-yip! Hi-yip! Hi-yip!"

There was a movement of sorts a kind of small lurch

of the whole body. Beatrice was turning. She was jerking round like the figure in a cathedral clock. An express was passing through the tunnel. Beatrice moved jerk by jerk through ninety degrees. Her back was to me.

Kenneth touched my arm.

"I think perhaps——"

But nurse knew this aquarium.

"Miss Ifor? Aren't you going to talk to your visitor? Come along now!"

She had the body by the shoulder and arm.

"Come along, dearie!"

Jerk jerk jerk.

"Hi-yip! Hi-yip! Hi-yip!"

The body was facing me. The entombed eyes were nittering like the hand of an old man.

"Aren't you going to say hullo, dear? Miss Ifor!"

"Beatrice!"

Beatrice was beginning to stand up. Her hands were clasped into each other. Her mouth was open and her eyes were nittering at me through my tears and sweat.

"That's a good girl!"

Beatrice pissed over her skirt and her legs and her shoes and my shoes. The pool splashed and spread.

"Miss Ifor dear, naughty—ah, naughty!"

Someone had me by the arm and shoulder and was turning me.

"I think——"

Someone was leading and helping me over acres of bare floor. Marsh-birds were sweeping and crying.

"Keep your head right down."

I could smell her still on my shoes and trousers. I struggled against a clamping hand at the back of my neck. Down, down, forced down in the fetor.

"Better?"

The words would not form. I could see them as shapes, hear them silently, could not twist them into my tongue.

"You'll feel better in a moment."

Cause and effect. The law of succession. Statistical probability. The moral order. Sin and remorse. They are all true. Both worlds exist side by side. They meet in me. We have to satisfy the examiners in both worlds at once. Down in the fetor.

"There."

The hand removed itself. Two, one on each shoulder pulled me back. I fitted a chair.

"Just sit still for a bit."

My mind wandered off into long corridors, came back, pictured Kenneth at his desk and opened my eyes. He was there. He gave me a smile of professional cheer.

"These things are a shock until you get used to them."

I made my mouth do its proper work.

"I suppose so."

I was coming back now into my body and I could hear Kenneth quacking on. But there was something I wanted from him. I felt round and found a cigarette.

"Do you mind?"

"No. Of course not. As I was saying——"

"Is there any hope?"

He was silent at last.

"What I mean is: can you cure her?"

More stuff. More quacking.

"Look, Kenneth. Can she be cured?"

244

"In the present state of our knowledge——"

"Can she be cured?"

"No."

The smell of the foul nursery rose from my shoes. Maisie, Millicent, Mary?

"Kenneth. I want to know."

"Know what?"

"What sent her——"

"Ah!"

He put his fingers together and leaned back.

"In the first place you have to remember that normality is a condition only arbitrarily definable——"

"Her life, man! What drove her mad?"

Kenneth gave a vexed laugh.

"Can't you understand? Perhaps nothing happened."

"You mean—she would have gone—like this—anyway?"

He looked at me, frowning.

"Why do you say, 'Anyway'?"

"For the love of—look. Did anything send her, send her——"

Puzzled, he looked at me, reached out for the file, opened the spring cover, looked down, flicked paper, muttered.

"Heredity. Yes. I see. Illnesses. School. Training College. Engaged to be——"

His voice faded away. I hit the desk with my fist and cried out.

"Go on, can't you?"

He was consuming himself in blood. He shut the file, looking anywhere but at me. He muttered in the corner of his office.

"Of course. It would be."

"Go on! Read it out to me."

But he was muttering still.

"Oh, my God. What a fool. I should have—now what shall I do?"

"Look——"

He swung round and down at me.

"You shouldn't have done it. How the hell was I to know? And I thought I was doing you both a favour——'

"No one can do her a favour——"

"I didn't mean—I may have done—I could be——"

"I had to see her."

He was whispering frantically now.

"No one must ever know. Do you hear? I could be struck off——"

"Paradise."

All at once his voice spat at me.

"I've always detested you—and this—that a man like you should have a woman like Taffy——"

He stopped speaking and sat down the other side of the desk. His voice was intentional.

"You and your bloody pictures. You use everyone. You used that woman. You used Taffy. And now you've used me."

"Yes. It's all my fault."

His voice ran up high.

"I'll say it's your fault!"

"Do you want it in writing?"

"That's right. Take all the blame, you think, and nothing happened. Kiss and be friends. Do anything you like and then say you're sorry."

"No. I don't believe like that. I wish I did."

Silence.

Kenneth pushed the back of his hand across his forehead. He looked at the file.

"Who can tell you anything certain? Perhaps you did. Yes. Perhaps you hurt her so badly it tipped her over. I should think so. She's been here ever since, you see."

"Seven years!"

"Your Beatrice is a foundation member."

"Seven years."

"Ever since you saw her last. In a condition which we think is rather like experiencing continual and exaggerated worry."

"Ever since."

"I hope it makes you happy."

"Do you think hurting me will help you with Taffy?"

"I'm glad we've got that straight at last. Yes. I'm in love with her."

"I know. She told me. We're both sorry."

"To hell with your sorrow. And her sorrow."

"Well there."

"And to hell with this place and life generally."

"I asked her, you see. She would have kept your secret."

Kenneth gave a high-pitched laugh.

"Oh, yes, you've got a good wife, she'll never let you down. She'll stand at your back and prop you up so that you can come across a few more suckers."

"It isn't like that, you know. Not from inside."

"Got what you came for."

"I did it then. I had a dream. Not your line of country —or is it? You could put this one in the file with the rest of the evidence. Mr. X after deserting Miss Y had a

247

dream. She was following him, stumbling, and the waters were rising round her. Exaggerated worry, you said. Cause and effect holds good. Nick was right and Miss Pringle was right——"

"I don't know what you're talking about."

"Just that I tipped her over. Nothing can be repaired or changed. The innocent cannot forgive."

I smiled wrily at Kenneth; and as I smiled I felt a sudden gust of affection for him.

"All right, Kenneth. Yes. I got what I came for. And thank you."

"For what?"

"For being so—Hippocratic."

"I?"

Suddenly the image of thick Beatrice started up behind my eyes, green, tense and nittering. I covered them with one hand.

"For telling me the truth."

Kenneth moved about uneasily between his desk and the cupboard and then settled into his chair.

"Look, Sammy. I shan't be seeing much of you both from now on."

"I'm sorry."

"For God's sake!"

"I mean it. People don't seem to be able to move without killing each other."

"So I'm telling you what the chances were as far as I can see them. Then you'll know. You probably tipped her over. But perhaps she would have tipped over anyway. Perhaps she would have tipped over a year earlier if you hadn't been there to give her something to think about. You may have given her an extra year of sanity and—

whatever you did give her. You may have taken a lifetime of happiness away from her. Now you know the chances as accurately as a specialist."

"Thank you."

"God. I could cut your throat."

"I suppose so."

"No, I couldn't. Don't go. Wait. I want to talk to you. Listen, Sam. I love Taffy. You know that."

"I can't take it in."

"And I said I hated you. But I don't. In a sort of twisted way—it's that life you both lead together, that place you've got. I want to share that. In a sense I'm in love with both of you."

"I can't take it in."

I pulled myself up and made a sort of smiling grimace, mouth dragged down, in his direction.

"Well——"

"Sammy."

I turned at the door.

"Sammy. What am I going to do?"

I adjusted myself to his face. Useless to say that a man is a whole continent, pointless to say that each consciousness is a whole world because each consciousness is a dozen worlds.

"There's too much interpenetration. Everything is mixed up. Look. You haven't hurt us. It will pass. Nothing of what you go through now will peer over your shoulder or kick you in the face."

He laughed savagely.

"Thank you for nothing!"

I went out of the door then, and as I went, I nodded him my agreement.

I had my two speeches ready, one for each of my parents not in the flesh. Now I would go to Nick Shales and do him good. I would explain gently.

"You did not choose your rationalism rationally. You chose because they showed you the wrong maker. Oh, yes, I know all about the lip-service they paid. She—Rowena Pringle—paid lip-service and I know how much lip-service is worth. The maker they mimed for you in your Victorian slum was the old male maker, totem of the conquering Hebrews, totem of our forefathers, the subjectors and quiet enslavers of half the world. I saw that totem in a German picture. He stands to attention beside the cannon. There is a Hindu tied across the muzzle and presently the male totem of the Hebrews will blow him to pieces, the mutinous dog, for his daring. The male totem is jackbooted and topee'd and ignorant and hypocritical and splendid and cruel. You rejected him as my generation rejects him. But you were innocent, you were good and innocent like Johnny Spragg, blown to pieces five miles above his own county of Kent. You and he could live in one world at a time. You were not caught in the terrible net where we guilty ones are forced to torture each other..."

But Nick was in hospital dying of a tired heart. Even then it seemed to me he had less than his share, a bed in a ward in a town he always wanted to avoid. I saw him that evening from far off down the ward. He was propped up on pillows and leaned his immense head on his hand. The light from a bulb behind him lay smoothly over his curved cranium, snowed on him like the years, hung whitely in the eaves over his eyes. Beneath their pent his face was worn away. He seemed to me then to have become the image of labouring mind: and I was awed. Whatever was happening to him in death was on a scale and level before which I felt my own nothingness. I came away, my single verse unspoken.

To her my speech was to be simple.

"We were two of a kind, that is all. You were forced to torture me. You lost your freedom somewhere and after that you had to do to me what you did. You see? The consequence was perhaps Beatrice in the looney bin, our joint work, my work, the world's work. Do you not see how our imperfections force us to torture each other? Of course you do! The innocent and the wicked live in one world—Philip Arnold is a minister of the crown and handles life as easy as breathing. But we are neither the innocent nor the wicked. We are the guilty. We fall down. We crawl on hands and knees. We weep and tear each other.

Therefore I have come back—since we are both adults and live in two worlds at once—to offer forgiveness with both hands. Somewhere the awful line of descent must be broken. You did that and I forgive it wholly, take the spears into me. As far as I can I will make your part in our story as if it had never been."

But forgiveness must not only be given but received also.

She lived in a village some miles from the school now, a bitsy village with reed thatch and wrought-iron work. She cried out delightedly when she saw me at the end of the garden path.

"Mountjoy!"

And then she took off her gardener's glove and offered me her white hand while the speech and everything I knew flew out of my head. For there are some people who paralyse us as if we were chicken, our beaks at the chalk line. I knew at once I should say nothing; but even so I was not prepared for the position and opinion of Miss Pringle; nor did our pictures of the past agree. My fame and Philip's fame, were the consolations of teaching. She liked to think that her care of me—Sammy; may I say Sammy? And I muttered of course, of course, because my beak was on the chalk line—she liked to think that her care of me had been a little bit, a teeny bit (there was a plaster rabbit sitting by the plaster bird-bath) a teeny-weeny bit responsible for the things of beauty I was able to give the world.

And so, in ten seconds, I wanted nothing but to get away. My flesh crept. She was still this being of awful power and now her approval of me was as terrible as her hatred and I knew we had nothing to say to each other. For that woman had achieved an unexpected kind of victory; she had deceived herself completely and now she was living in only one world.

All day long the trains run on rails. Eclipses are predictable. Penicillin cures pneumonia and the atom splits to order. All day long, year in, year out, the daylight explanation drives back the mystery and reveals a reality usable, understandable and detached. The scalpel and the microscope fail, the oscilloscope moves closer to behaviour. The gorgeous dance is self-contained, then; does not need the music which in my mad moments I have heard. Nick's universe is real.

All day long action is weighed in the balance and found

not opportune nor fortunate or ill-advised, but good or evil. For this mode which we must call the spirit breathes through the universe and does not touch it; touches only the dark things, held prisoner, incommunicado, touches, judges, sentences and passes on.

Her world was real, both worlds are real. There is no bridge.

The bright line became a triangle sweeping in over a suddenly visible concrete floor.

"Heraus!"

Rising from my knees, holding my trousers huddled I walked uncertainly out towards the judge. But the judge had gone.

The commandant was back.

"Captain Mountjoy. This should not be happening. I am sorry."

The noise turned me round. I could see down the passage now over the stain shaped like a brain, could see into the cell where I had received what I had received. They were putting the buckets back, piles of them, were throwing back the damp floorcloths. I could see that they had forgotten one, or perhaps left it deliberately, when they emptied the cupboard for me. It still lay damply in the centre of the floor. Then a soldier shut the buckets and the floorcloths away with an ordinary cupboard door.

"Captain Mountjoy. You have heard?"

"I heard."

The commandant indicated the door back to the camp dismissively. He spoke the inscrutable words that I should puzzle over as though they were the Sphinx's riddle.

"The Herr Doctor does not know about peoples."